An Amish Winter

OTHER NOVELS BY THE AUTHORS

AMY CLIPSTON

THE AMISH HEIRLOOM SERIES
The Forgotten Recipe

The Courtship Basket

The Cherished Quilt

The Beloved Hope Chest

THE HEARTS OF THE LANCASTER GRAND HOTEL SERIES

A Hopeful Heart

A Mother's Secret

A Dream of Home

A Simple Prayer

THE KAUFFMAN AMISH BAKERY SERIES

A Gift of Grace

A Promise of Hope

A Place of Peace

A Life of Joy

A Season of Love

YOUNG ADULT

Roadside Assistance

Reckless Heart

Destination Unknown

Miles from Nowhere

NOVELLAS

A Plain and Simple Christmas

Naomi's Gift included in *An Amish Christmas Gift*

A Spoonful of Love included in *An Amish Kitchen*

A Son for Always included in *An Amish Cradle*

Love Birds included in *An Amish Market*

Love and Buggy Rides included in *An Amish Harvest*

Summer Storms included in *An Amish Summer*

The Christmas Cat included in *An Amish Christmas Love*

NONFICTION
A Gift of Love

KELLY IRVIN

EVERY AMISH SEASON NOVELS
Upon a Spring Breeze

THE AMISH OF BEE COUNTY NOVELS

The Beekeeper's Son

The Bishop's Son

The Saddle Maker's Son

NOVELLAS BY KELLY IRVIN

Sweeter than Honey included in *An Amish Market*

One Sweet Kiss included in *An Amish Summer*

Snow Angels included in *An Amish Christmas Love*

BARBARA CAMERON

An Amish Christmas—One Child

AN AMISH WINTER

Three Novellas

Amy Clipston, Kelly Irvin,

and Barbara Cameron

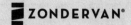

ZONDERVAN

Home Sweet Home © 2016 by Amy Clipston

A Christmas Visitor © 2015 by Kelly Irvin

When Winter Comes © 2009 by Barbara Cameron

This title is also available as a Zondervan e-book.

Requests for information should be addressed to:
Zondervan, 3900 Sparks Dr. SE, Grand Rapids, Michigan 49546

Mass Market ISBN: 978-0-7852-1722-0

Library of Congress Cataloging-in-Publication

CIP data is available upon request.

Printed in the United States of America

17 18 19 20 21 22 / QGM / 6 5 4 3 2 1

CONTENTS

HOME SWEET HOME

AMY CLIPSTON

With love and appreciation for my friends at Morning Star Lutheran Church in Matthews, North Carolina

GLOSSARY

Ach—Oh!
aenti—aunt
boppli—baby
daadi—grandpa
daadihaus—grandparents' house
dat—dad
English—non-Amish person
freind—friend
freinden—friends
gut—good
haus—house
mamm—mom
mammi—grandma
mei—my
ya—yes

CHAPTER 1

The cold air seemed to seep into the marrow of Mia O'Conner's bones, and her teeth chattered as her husband steered their pickup past a large white farmhouse. Rain splashed against the windshield and beat a steady cadence on the roof of the old Chevy truck as the tires crunched on the rock driveway beside two large barns. She held her hand over the vent and shivered. Only brisk February air whooshed through. If only they had the money to fix the heater . . .

That was the least of their worries. She glanced down at their five-month-old daughter bundled under a blanket in her car seat between them.

"Well, this is it," Chace said as the truck came to a stop. The headlights sliced through the dark and illuminated the front door of a rustic, one-story cabin. "Welcome to our new home in Bird-in-Hand."

Mia blinked twice as she studied the building. It featured a small front porch and two windows. She shivered again, hoping the tiny house was warm.

"What do you think?" Chace shifted the truck into Park. "It's not much, but it's more than reasonable. Isaac is charging us next to nothing." He paused. "Isaac Allgyer is the best boss I've ever had."

Mia turned toward her husband, and his handsome face and Caribbean-blue eyes focused on her. "Well, it's not—"

Kaitlyn's sudden screech interrupted Mia's response.

Mia unbuckled Kaitlyn and pulled the sobbing baby into her arms. "Mommy is right here, sweet pea." She snuggled Kaitlyn closer to her chest, wrapping the blanket around her little body. "I guess she'll have to sleep with us until we scrape together the money for a crib."

Chace's lips formed a thin line. "We'll figure it out."

Mia swallowed a sigh as Kaitlyn's sobs subsided.

Chace pushed his door open, and a blast of frigid air filled the cab of the truck. Mia gasped and held Kaitlyn even closer. She longed to be able to afford the warm snowsuit she'd seen at a department store after all the snowsuits had been snatched up from her favorite consignment shop. Surely her baby was cold, and the guilt that had haunted her since Kaitlyn's birth flooded her once again.

Chace pulled up the hood on his navy blue sweatshirt to cover his sandy-blond hair as he stood by the open truck door. Rain beat down on him, drenching his sweatshirt and worn jeans, and no doubt his work boots too.

"Why don't you get her inside?" he called over the rain. "It has to be warmer in there than it is in here. I'll help you, and then I'll handle emptying out the bed of the truck."

Mia nodded before Chace shut the driver side door and ran to her side of the truck.

She retrieved a blanket from the diaper bag she'd bought at Goodwill before Kaitlyn was born. After draping the extra blanket over Kaitlyn's head, Mia shouldered the diaper bag and her purse, then leapt out of the truck when Chace opened the door. She hustled through the icy rain and up the front steps of the cabin, where Chace had run ahead to hold the door open for her. It must not have been locked.

Mia stepped through the door and shivered once more as the chilly air from inside the cabin seeped through her damp jeans. She caressed Kaitlyn's head. "I think it's colder in here than in the truck."

"We just need to get the coal stove going."

Coal?

By the light of the truck's headlights shining into the cabin, Chace found a Coleman lantern that sat on a small table by the door. He flipped it on, then shut the door against the wind.

The bright yellow light allowed Mia to take in their new home. Her heart sank when she realized it was only slightly bigger than their apartment had been. She had hoped for more. A tiny kitchen with a small refrigerator, a stove, a sink, a few cabinets, and a short counter spilled into an area with a table and four chairs. Off to her right, a worn brown sofa and dark green wing chair served as a family room. Beyond the sofa were two doorways.

"How many bedrooms are there?" she asked.

"One."

"Oh." Mia adjusted Kaitlyn in her arms. Their apartment had only one bedroom. They could make do.

Chace crossed the room to a large black stove in the kitchen. He placed the lantern on top and began examining it.

Mia balanced Kaitlyn with one of her arms and ran her free hand over the wall. "Where are the light switches?"

Chace chuckled and shook his head. Normally, the warm sound of his laugh would make her smile, but tonight she frowned.

"What's so funny?" Her sense of humor waned with every passing moment.

"I've told you Isaac and his family are Amish, Mee." He leaned back on the kitchen counter behind him and held up his arms as if to gesture around the cabin. "There's no electricity."

"What?" Mia snapped, louder than she'd meant to.

Kaitlyn gasped and then began to cry again, her wails echoing throughout the cabin.

"There's no electricity?" Mia crossed the small room and stood in front of Chace. She ignored Kaitlyn's screaming as she gaped at him.

"What did you expect me to find with our income and credit?" His eyes narrowed to slits. "I'm sorry it's not the Hilton."

Mia ground her teeth as fury boiled through her veins, exacerbated by the combination of Kaitlyn's unrelenting screams and her husband's caustic remark. She opened her mouth to deliver a biting retort just as someone knocked on the front door and called out. "Chace?"

When Chace opened the door, a tall man with dark

brown hair and a matching beard that fell past his chin stood in the doorway. He was dressed in black broadfall trousers, a plain black coat, and a black hat. He looked to be in his midforties. "Chace! You made it."

"Isaac." Chace's face brightened as he greeted the man and invited him in with a nod. A woman and four children, two girls and two boys, filed into the cabin behind him. The woman and girls wore long, solid-color dresses and black coats, and their heads were covered with black bonnets. The woman, who looked to be in her early forties, had an amicable smile.

"This is my family." Isaac pointed to each one as he introduced them. "My wife, Vera, and our children, Rhoda, Susannah, Adam, and Joel." All the children had dark hair and eyes, like their parents.

Chace shook Isaac's hand and then Vera's. He gestured toward Mia and then raised his voice over Kaitlyn's howling. "This is my wife, Mia, and my daughter, Kaitlyn."

The couple both spoke, but Kaitlyn's keening drowned out their words. Mia bounced the baby in her arms as a migraine brewed behind her eyes. Could Kaitlyn sense her frustration? Mia moved Kaitlyn's fine blond hair to one side and kissed her little head. Kaitlyn continued to sob as large tears streamed from her bright blue eyes and down her pink cheeks.

"May I hold her?"

Mia looked up at who she thought must be the eldest Allgyer daughter. She had stepped closer and was smiling. Since she had already removed her black coat and bonnet, Mia could see her purple dress was plain and that a white, gauzy cap covered her hair. Her face was free of any makeup, but she had a natural beauty with flawless ivory skin.

"I'm Rhoda. I don't mean to sound prideful, but I'm *gut* with babies."

"*Ya*, she is." Her sister appeared at her side. "I'm Susannah." She was a couple of inches shorter than Rhoda, but she could nearly pass for her twin. She wore a green dress made in the same plain pattern as her sister's, and she also had a white cap over her hair.

"All right." Mia handed the baby to Rhoda, and her aching arms were grateful for the rest.

"Kaitlyn is a pretty name." Rhoda adjusted the baby in her arms.

"Thank you," Mia said.

Kaitlyn took a deep breath and then yawned before resting her cheek on Rhoda's shoulder and placing her thumb in her mouth. Her expression transformed from agitated to content in less than a minute. Mia gasped.

"I told you." Susannah grinned. "My sister is great with babies."

Rhoda pointed to the diaper bag hanging over Mia's shoulder. "Would you like me to see if she needs a change?"

"That would be wonderful. Thank you."

Rhoda and Susannah headed toward one of the doorways beyond the family room. Mia followed them to a small bedroom. Inside were a double bed, two nightstands, a lamp, and a small bureau. Mia lingered in the doorway as Susannah flipped on the lamp on one of the nightstands, and Rhoda spread the baby blanket on the bare mattress before setting Kaitlyn down on it. Kaitlyn sputtered noises at the girls, and they laughed as Rhoda checked her diaper.

"Mia," Vera said as she sidled up to her. "It's nice to meet you."

"Hi." Mia shook her hand and noted that Vera was a few inches taller than she was, possibly close to five-eight. "Thank you so much for renting us the cabin."

"You're welcome." Vera looked toward her daughters and smiled. "They enjoy taking care of babies."

"They're experts." Mia removed her damp coat and hung it on a hook by the door before coming to stand with Vera once again. "I'm thankful for the help. I wasn't sure what to do for Katie since I had breastfed just before we headed over here. I thought maybe it was the cold, but I guess she wanted to spend some time with someone else."

"Isaac checked the stove, and it should warm up soon."

"Who used to live here? Other renters?"

"No, Isaac's parents. This is what's called the *daadi-haus*, which means the grandfather's house. His parents lived here until they both passed away. My father-in-law has been gone for two years." She gestured for Mia to follow her. "Let me show you around. The bathroom is right here."

Mia followed her to the next doorway and opened it. The bathroom was small but functional, with an ordinary sink, a vanity, a commode, and a bathtub with shower. Although the fixtures showed their age, the bathroom was clean. A small window provided the only light in the room.

"Did you see the propane lamps?" Vera asked as they walked to the kitchen area.

Mia shook her head. "I saw the Coleman."

Vera stopped in the family room and turned on the lamp on the table beside the wing chair. The lamp came to life, sending a bright glow throughout the cabin. "It will get warm, so it's another way to heat the cabin. The lamp in the bedroom is propane too. Do you know how to use a coal stove?"

"No. The only heating system I've ever known how to use had a thermostat."

"Let me show you." Vera gestured for Mia to follow her.

The front door opened and closed as Chace, Isaac, and Isaac's sons lugged Chace and Mia's belongings into the house. A pile of suitcases and black trash bags already clogged the small family room. Vera's youngest son dragged in a heavy bag with his tongue sticking out of his mouth. He dropped the bag with a loud *thunk* before rushing back outside and into the rain for another.

Mia turned toward Vera. "Your sons are hard workers."

Vera shrugged. "It's our culture."

"How old are your children?" Mia leaned against the kitchen counter.

Vera nodded in the direction of the bedroom. "Rhoda is eighteen and Susannah is seventeen. Adam is twelve and Joel is ten. Are you from a large family?"

"No, I'm an only child." Mia traced her finger over the worn Formica. "I'd always longed for siblings, but my mother felt children were too much of an inconvenience. She was more interested in meeting her friends at the country club."

Vera tilted her head and frowned.

"Never mind." Mia pointed to the black potbelly stove in a corner of the kitchen. "Is that the coal stove?"

"*Ya*, it is. Isaac came over earlier today and started it." Vera pointed to a bucket full of coal beside it. "You have to check it twice every day, and you'll soon figure out how much coal you need to keep it warm overnight. If we had known you were coming yesterday, we could have started it for you then. But I understand this was a last-minute situation."

Mia's throat dried as she recalled their landlord appearing at their furnished apartment earlier that day. He had previously issued a Notice to Quit, which started the clock ticking on a ten-day deadline for Mia and Chace to pay their overdue rent before they would be evicted. Ten days, however, was not enough time for Chace to gather up the money, and the deadline arrived at lightning speed. When Mr. Newman knocked on their door that morning with an eviction notice in hand, Chace begged him for an extension. But their cantankerous landlord refused, insisting they pack their things and get out by nightfall.

Mia had never felt so distraught and humiliated. She'd dissolved in tears as Chace read the eviction notice aloud to her. He promised he would take care of them. Mia was thankful that when Chace called his boss to ask for help, Isaac offered the cabin as a quick solution.

"There's a coal bin in the mudroom back here

behind the kitchen." Vera pointed toward the doorway beside them. "That's also where the wringer washer is."

"Wringer washer?" Mia's eyes widened.

"I can show you how to use it another day." Vera gestured toward the cookstove. "The stove and refrigerator run on propane. I started the refrigerator earlier today. I can help you unpack your food."

Mia's eyes stung with threatening tears. *Hold it together, Mia. This woman probably has no interest in, or time for, your sob story. Besides, this is so humiliating.*

Then again, she might as well be honest. Isaac had probably already told his wife everything Chace told him about their problems. "We don't have much food." She paused to clear her throat against a lump swelling there. "We put most of Chace's paychecks this month toward our hospital bills from when Kaitlyn was born, which is why we couldn't get caught up on the rent. And that's why we wound up . . . homeless." Her voice quavered and she sniffed.

Vera placed her hand on Mia's arm and gave her a sympathetic smile. "It's okay. Have you eaten tonight? Do you need some supper?"

"We've eaten," Mia whispered before clearing her throat again. "Thank you."

"I'll have my sons bring over a basket of food before they go to school tomorrow morning."

Mia fought the urge to gape at Vera. Why would she offer to feed Mia and her family when she'd only just met them?

"Mia," Susannah said, walking out to the kitchen. "Do you have sheets? I'll make the bed for you."

Rhoda stood behind her with Kaitlyn happily balanced on her hip. "Do you want me to give her a bottle for you?"

Mia blinked. Were all Amish people this giving and helpful? She shook herself from her momentary stupor. "I breastfed her before we came, but thank you for offering."

"Okay." Rhoda sat down in the wing chair with Kaitlyn in her arms.

"Can I put linens out for you?" Susannah asked.

Mia nodded. "Oh. That would be great. Thank you." She pointed to a nearby suitcase. "I think the linens are in there."

"You're welcome." Susannah opened the suitcase and pulled out a set of mint-green sheets, along with a set of towels. "I'll make your bed and then put the towels in the bathroom for you." She walked back toward the bedroom.

"Do you have a crib?" Vera asked. "Isaac can help Chace set it up before we go home."

Mia frowned. "We've never had enough money to buy a crib. We only had a used portable crib I bought at a consignment shop, but we lost it during the move today. We left some of our baby things in the truck while we were packing up the apartment, and when we came back, they were gone."

Vera gasped. "Someone stole your things?"

Mia nodded. "They took our portable crib, baby seat, and baby swing."

"*Ach*, that's terrible."

The door opened and closed and they turned to see Chace with Isaac, Adam, and Joel, all dripping wet.

"That's everything." Chace shucked his soaked sweat-shirt. His damp hair was sticking up in all directions. When he pushed his hand through it, it continued to stand up, making him look younger, closer to eighteen than twenty-four. "Thank you so much for your help."

"Isaac," Vera said. "Is that *boppli* portable crib of your sister's still in our attic?"

Mia raised her eyebrows with surprise. Was Vera offering her baby supplies along with food? This family seemed too good to be true.

Isaac rubbed his bearded chin and shrugged. "It should be. She asked us to keep all her *boppli* supplies up there for her."

"Adam, Joel," Vera began, "please go up into the attic and bring down the portable crib." Then she turned to Mia. "We'll bring you the crib that's up there tomorrow."

"Vera, you don't need to do that."

"Don't be silly. It's not doing anyone any *gut* up in our attic, is it?" Vera challenged before turning back to her sons. "Hurry over there so you can get to bed. You have to be up early for school tomorrow."

Adam and Joel grabbed their lanterns and rushed out the door.

"Thank you." Mia looked over at Chace to see his reaction to Vera's generosity, but he was leaning over Kaitlyn as Rhoda held her. He whispered to her and tickled her chin, and she gurgled as she smiled up at him. Mia's heart warmed at the sight. She relished watching Chace interact with their daughter.

"I made the bed and put the towels in the bath-room," Susannah said as she reentered the family room. "Do you have a quilt or blanket? The bedroom is pretty cold." She rubbed her arms over the sleeves of her green dress.

Chace stood, breaking free from the trance of staring at his baby. "Yeah, we have a couple of blankets." He studied the sea of black trash bags. "They're in one of these."

"I'll help you find them." Mia joined him by the pile of bags and suitcases containing everything they owned in the world. She met his intense stare, and her heart pounded. Was he still angry with her for her negative comments about the cabin? Did he truly believe she would be willing to live only in a home with the luxury of the Hilton?

When a smile turned up the corner of his lips, she released the breath she hadn't realized she'd been holding. They were still a team, still a *family*, despite all the hardship they'd endured since Mia had learned she was pregnant.

"I think the blankets are in this one." Chace ripped open a bag, revealing a threadbare, blue-plaid comforter he had owned since before he and Mia met. "Here's this." He pulled it out and handed it to Mia before digging deeper in the bag. "And there's a blanket too. And here's one of Katie's blankets."

"I'll take them to the bedroom." Vera held out her hands. "Susannah and I will finish making the bed for you."

"Thank you." Mia handed off the blankets. Then she helped Chace search through a few more bags until they found two more blankets for Katie.

Soon Adam and Joel returned with the portable

crib. Chace set it up in the bedroom as Mia and Vera located sheets for it.

"Thank you for everything," Mia told the Allgyer family as they stood by the front door to leave. "I can't thank you enough for your help and generosity."

Vera squeezed Mia's hand. "We're happy to help you. I'll send my boys over early tomorrow morning with that basket of food for you."

"I'll drive you to work tomorrow," Chace told Isaac. "That way you don't have to pay for a driver. I want to do something to thank you for the affordable rent."

"I don't expect a ride for free." Isaac shook Chace's hand.

Chace grinned. "Let's argue about it in the morning, all right?"

"That sounds *gut*." Isaac turned to Mia. "*Gut* night."

"Good night, Isaac. Thank you again."

As the family filed out through the front door, Rhoda and Susannah gave Mia a little wave. Then the door shut behind them.

Chace locked the door and turned off the propane lamp by the wing chair.

"I'm going to feed Katie and put her to bed." Mia slipped into the bedroom and breastfed Katie before putting her down. Then she returned to the family room. "Katie went right to sleep when I put her in the portable crib. I put her warmest pajamas on her and covered her with a few blankets."

"That's good." Chace opened another trash bag and rifled through its contents before moving on to another. "I think my clothes are in here somewhere."

Mia took in their pile of possessions and the stark cabin. She hugged her arms to her middle, shivering once more in the cold. Would the cabin ever warm up?

Suddenly, a memory hit Mia, nearly knocking her off balance. It was last February, and Mia sat in her parents' family room, surrounded by their expensive furniture and her mother's vast collection of priceless paintings and prized figurines. A roaring fire in the brick fireplace warmed her body under the pink cashmere sweater Mom had given her for her birthday a month earlier.

Mia's hands shook and her stomach pitched. "I have something to tell you." Her voice trembled with anxiety.

"What is it, dear?" Mom's perfectly manicured, dark eyebrows careened toward her hairline.

"I'm pregnant." Mia's voice sounded strange to her—small and unsure, like a child's.

"What?" Mom's voice pitched higher than usual. "You're pregnant? How could you let this happen? I thought you were smarter than that."

"It wasn't planned, but Chace loves me, and I love him. I'm going to drop out of school and marry him."

Her parents studied her as their eyes widened. Her words seemed to hang in the air as the ticking of the antique mantel clock and the intermittent pop and hiss of the fire were the only noises echoing throughout the large room. Mia held her breath, awaiting her mother's response. Her father, she knew, would let his wife speak for both of them. He always had. She folded her shaking hands in her lap.

"Mia, you can't possibly be serious. You'll be a horrible

mother." Mom's face twisted into a deep scowl. "You're too young to even consider becoming a mother. You have no idea what it takes to raise a child."

"I'll learn." Mia sat a little taller in the chair. "I'll work hard and be the best mother I can be."

Mom clicked her tongue. "You have your entire future ahead of you. You don't need an unplanned pregnancy to ruin your life."

"Ruin my life? How can a child ruin my life? I've thought long and hard about this, and I want this baby. This child is a part of both Chace and me, and we're in love."

"You believe you're in love, but life isn't that simple. You *think* you want this baby, but you haven't truly weighed all the consequences of having a child at a young age. This doesn't just affect you, Mia. It will reflect on our entire family."

Mom's expression hardened. "Can you imagine the scandal when our friends at church and the club find out you're pregnant? It will ruin our family's name. I can't believe you let this happen. I'm very disappointed in you."

"It was an accident, but I'm going to make things right." Mia hated the quaver in her voice. She was stronger than this. "I'm going to have this baby."

"Now, wait a minute." Mom wagged her finger at Mia as if she were a petulant child. "There's only one way to make this right." She shifted on her chair and crossed one long leg over her opposite knee. "You should live with your aunt Briana in San Diego until after the baby is born. Then you can give it up for adoption. No one will ever know of your mistake. Then you can go back to college and get on with your life like it never happened, and you'll be much happier."

"You want me to just give up my child?" Mia gasped and turned to her father. Surely, he would understand.

Dad nodded. "Sweetie, your mom is right. Don't let an unplanned pregnancy ruin your good name or your future."

"All your friends from high school are getting their degrees and heading toward a bright future," Mom chimed in. "Don't you want to be like them? I'm certain they won't want to associate with you when they find out you're pregnant out of wedlock."

A surge of fury mixed with confidence bubbled up from somewhere deep inside her. "I'm going to marry Chace and have this baby with or without your blessing."

Mia didn't want to think about the rest of their conversation that day. She had stuck to her decision and marched out of her parents' house without their blessing or approval.

But now, as Mia stood in the middle of the cold cabin, her mother's hurtful words echoed through her mind. *Was Mom right? Maybe I'm not capable of being a good mother.*

Without warning, a sob escaped from Mia's throat. She covered her face with her hands as tears spilled down her cheeks.

Strong arms encircled her as Chace pulled her to his muscular chest. She inhaled the comforting scent of his spicy aftershave as she buried her face in his collarbone. She relaxed against him, pulling strength from the sound of his heartbeat.

"Everything is going to be fine, Mee," he whispered into her hair before kissing the top of her head. "I promise I'll take care of us. This is temporary. As soon as we pay off all the hospital bills and save up some money, I'll build us a house. Does that sound good?" He placed his fingertip under her chin and angled her face so she looked up into his eyes.

"Yeah."

He wiped away her tears with his fingers and then smiled before kissing her. As Chace pulled her close for another hug, Mia closed her eyes and prayed she and Chace could give Kaitlyn everything she needed.

CHAPTER 2

Anguish covered Chace like a lead blanket as he folded one arm behind his head and stared up at the bedroom ceiling through the dark. Mia's stricken expression after Isaac and his family left the cabin filled Chace's mind. Each tear that slipped down her pink cheeks had chipped away at his heart. He was grateful he was able to calm her down and convince her to go to bed since they both were exhausted after the stressful day they had endured.

All Chace wanted was to be the husband she deserved and the father Kaitlyn needed, but no matter how hard he worked, the rug had been repeatedly yanked out from under him. He had been mortified when he received the Notice to Quit, but he was certain he could find a way to get a loan to pay the past-due rent and keep their apartment. He had tried to explain their situation to the landlord and convince Mr. Newman to give them an extension, but Mr. Newman insisted he was forced to evict them. Chace had hoped to find them a place to go before today's deadline, but there weren't any decent apartments in their price range. Also, the medical bills they had incurred with

Kaitlyn's birth had destroyed their chances of finding a nice apartment in a safe neighborhood.

Mia sighed in her sleep beside him and nestled deeper under the pile of blankets. Chace touched the long, thick, dark-brown hair fanning over her pillow. He smiled as the moment he'd first seen her two years ago took over his thoughts.

Chace hadn't wanted to go to the party since he wasn't a student at the college where it was held, but his coworker at the construction company had insisted he go. He felt out of place surrounded by young people who were getting an education and would ultimately make something of themselves—unlike Chace, who had ricocheted from foster home to foster home and barely managed to graduate from high school. While his friend flirted with a sorority girl, Chace leaned against a far wall and sipped a can of soda.

But everything changed when Chace spotted Mia across the crowded room. It had been love at first sight, just like one of those sappy movies Mia loved to watch. She was breathtakingly dressed in a short black skirt and an emerald green sweater. When her milk-chocolate eyes met his gaze, he was certain she'd dismiss him with a haughty glare, but she didn't. Instead, she smiled and raised her diet soda can in a silent toast. He mustered all his confidence and crossed the room to ask her name. They spent the rest of the evening talking in a quiet corner, and she allowed him to call her the next day. They'd been inseparable ever since.

A quiet snore sounded from the portable crib next to his side of the bed. Chace leaned over and smiled.

How he adored his baby girl. Kaitlyn was the greatest blessing in his life, his greatest accomplishment. He often felt the urge to pinch himself to make certain he hadn't dreamed his family.

When his thoughts turned to Mia's parents, Chace's shoulders tightened. Why didn't they want to meet their only grandchild? How could they so easily throw away their only child and her baby? Guilt filled him as he recalled the biting remark he'd made to Mia earlier, accusing her of wanting to live at the Hilton. That was a low blow since Mia was nothing like her elitist parents, but sometimes his insecurities got the best of him. He had to work harder at curbing his temper. His job was to cherish Mia, not cut her down.

Chace moved under the blankets and shifted closer to Mia, his leg resting against hers. Closing his eyes, he listened to the soft sound of his wife's breathing until sleep found him.

* * *

Mia woke at the sound of Kaitlyn's first whimper. She glanced at the battery-operated clock on the nightstand. It was six thirty. Since Chace had fifteen minutes more to sleep, she gingerly climbed from the bed, shivering as she pulled on her pink terrycloth robe and pushed her socked feet into slippers. She tiptoed around the bed and lifted Kaitlyn from the portable crib, holding her close to her body for warmth. Did this little cabin have any insulation at all? She scooped up one of the blankets from the portable crib.

Standing in the doorway, Mia peered over at her husband, snuggled under the blankets as he snored into his pillow. Even with spittle at the corner of his mouth, Chace O'Conner remained the most handsome man she'd ever seen. She grinned as she pulled the door closed.

"Did you sleep well, sweet pea?" Mia carried her baby to the sofa.

Kaitlyn gurgled a response as Mia began to change her diaper. When she was done, she lifted her daughter into her arms.

She balanced Kaitlyn on her hip before heading to the kitchen. She glanced at the coal stove, trying in vain to remember Vera's instructions for adding more coal to increase the heat in the house. She had no business touching the stove.

Then she turned toward the cookstove and examined it, wondering how she'd ever figure it out so she could cook for Chace. She bit her lip as confusion settled over her. She'd cooked easy meals and warmed bottles with the help of a pot of water when they lived in their apartment, but the stove there had been electric. What if she made a mistake when she tried to light the burner?

Visions of an exploding stove filled her mind as Kaitlyn's whine transformed into a steady cry. Mia examined the knobs and dials on the stove for a moment longer, but her lack of confidence in her domestic skills won out over her determination. She would figure out how to work the stove later. Right now, she needed to worry about feeding her baby.

She returned to the sofa, covered Kaitlyn with the blanket for warmth, and began to breastfeed her.

A short while later Mia supported Kaitlyn on her shoulder and rubbed her back in an attempt to burp her. The bedroom door opened with a whoosh, revealing Chace clad in worn navy blue sweatpants and a faded, long-sleeved T-shirt featuring a muscle car. Clean clothes were draped over his arm, and he yawned and rubbed his eyes as he crossed the small space to the sofa.

"How are my two favorite girls this morning?" He planted a soft kiss on Mia's lips before kissing Kaitlyn's shock of blond hair.

"We're fine, Daddy," Mia simpered. "How are you, sleepyhead?"

He shrugged, but she observed dark circles under his eyes as he gave her a crooked grin. "I slept okay." He jammed a thumb toward the kitchen. "Did you see if the stove needed more coal?"

Mia continued to caress Kaitlyn's back. "I didn't feel comfortable touching it. I couldn't remember exactly what Vera told me about adding coal."

"I'll take a look." Chace touched Kaitlyn's back, and she responded with a loud belch. "That's my girl." He snickered as he walked toward the kitchen. He reappeared a few moments later, rubbing his hands together. "I added some coal. Maybe we'll finally get some heat in here. I'm going to shower."

Mia resumed feeding Kaitlyn, and just as she had finished burping her, a knock sounded on the front door. She covered Kaitlyn with the blanket again and

walked to the door. Peering out the glass, she saw
Adam and Joel standing on the steps.

Mia unlocked the door and opened it. "Good
morning."

"Hi. Our *mamm* asked us to bring these to you."
Adam held up a basket. "I can set this on the counter
for you if you'd like."

"She also said she thought you could use this." Joel
held up a baby seat. "We cleaned it up for you."

Mia beamed. A baby seat! This is just what she needed
since someone had taken their baby seat from the truck.

Adam put the basket on the counter as Joel put the
seat on the kitchen table.

"Please tell your mother I said thank you so much.
I'll try to stop by to see her later," Mia told the boys
before they left.

After securing Kaitlyn in the seat and giving her
a pacifier, Mia investigated the basket and found a
homemade coffee cake and butter tucked inside. Tears
stung her eyes.

Mia was setting two plates with coffee cake on the
table when Chace reappeared wearing jeans and a gray
Henley shirt. His hair was damp, and his chin was
clean-shaven. He was adorable.

"Wow." He approached the table. "Is that homemade?"

"Yes, it is."

"Where did you get it?"

"Joel and Adam brought it and the butter, along with
this seat." Mia touched the seat as Kaitlyn gazed up at
Chace. "I think the Allgyers are our guardian angels."

Chace nodded. "I think you're right."

As they sat down across from each other to eat, Mia smiled. *Mom was wrong. Chace, Kaitlyn, and I are going to be fine.*

* * *

Chace cast Isaac a sideways glance as he steered his pickup onto the main road. "Thank you for everything you've done for my family and me."

"You're welcome." Isaac nodded with his usual pleasant but not overly emotional expression. "Are you comfortable in the cabin?"

"Yes, we are." Chace refocused on the road ahead. "It's a little cold, but I think we'll get used to the coal stove. I added more coal before I left this morning."

"I can take a look at it later if you'd like. It does take a little getting used to." After a moment he said, "We want to lend you more of my sister's baby supplies from our attic. No one in the family needs them right now."

"We appreciate it. We don't have much." Chace stole another glance at Isaac, who was now peering out the passenger side window. He had the overwhelming urge to explain why he and Mia were in such dire straits. "I was working for a construction firm when I asked Mia to marry me. I was making a fairly good salary, and I had health insurance. But I was laid off shortly before Katie was born, and when she came she wound up in the neonatal intensive care unit for five days before we could bring her home. Katie is fine, but we found ourselves drowning in debt. We sold everything we could, but it still didn't get us caught up."

Chace slowed the truck to a stop at a red light, and when Isaac didn't say anything, he continued. "Like I told you yesterday, I never imagined I'd wind up homeless, and I'm embarrassed to admit how bad things became for Mia and me. I'm just so grateful you offered us a place to live. You've been so generous to me. You're the reason my family and I haven't wound up in a homeless shelter. You gave me a job when I had hardly any experience with cabinetry."

The light turned green, and Chace accelerated through the intersection as a horse and buggy moved along in the shoulder beside the truck.

"I didn't do much," Isaac said. "You're a fast learner, and you told me you'd learned woodworking in high school. It only made sense for me to offer you the cabin when it's sat empty since *mei dat* passed away."

In the three months Chace had worked for Isaac he'd noticed how humble and self-deprecating the man was. It was just like Isaac to not acknowledge how generous he was. He smacked the blinker as the sign for Allgyer's Custom Cabinets came into view and then steered into the lot. He parked his truck in his usual spot at the far end of the parking lot, leaving the closer spaces for the customers.

"Don't be so hard on yourself." Isaac wrenched open the passenger side door. "Vera and I struggled when we were young. Every couple endures tough times, and you and Mia will come through this stronger. Vera and I will do all we can to help you." With a quick nod, he hopped out of the truck and started toward the front door of the store.

Chace pulled his keys from the ignition and then leaned back in the seat as Isaac crossed the parking lot. He was so thankful he'd taken a chance and walked into Isaac's store the day he'd seen the Help Wanted sign. Mia was right—Isaac and Vera Allgyer were their guardian angels. Maybe, just maybe, with their help he and Mia would be okay.

* * *

Mia gritted her teeth as she paced back and forth from the small family room to the kitchen, bouncing Kaitlyn as she wailed. Kaitlyn had been screaming for nearly twenty minutes and none of Mia's usual soothing techniques had been successful. Mia had tried changing her diaper, singing to her, feeding her, and rocking her as they walked, but Kaitlyn continued her tirade.

Mia looked from the kitchen to the family room, where the sea of boxes, suitcases, and bags waited patiently to be unpacked. She had so much to do, but she couldn't accomplish any of it if Kaitlyn continued to fuss.

Mia thought she heard a knock on the door, but she ignored it, certain she had misheard the noise because of Kaitlyn's sobs. When the knock sounded again, Mia opened the door to find Rhoda and Susannah.

"Hi," Mia said, speaking loudly over Kaitlyn's moans. "How are you?"

"Our *mamm* sent us over to help you," Rhoda explained as they stepped into the cabin. She removed her coat and hung it on a peg by the door before holding out her arms to Kaitlyn. "May I hold her?"

"She's really fussy today, but you can try." Mia handed the baby over to her.

Rhoda whispered something to Kaitlyn and then held her close. When Kaitlyn continued to cry, Rhoda looked up at Mia. "Would it be all right if I took her for a walk?"

Mia grimaced. "I don't know. It's so cold out."

"My youngest brother loved to go for walks when he was little," Rhoda explained, moving her body back and forth to rock the unhappy baby. "Walks seemed to be the only thing that would calm him, even when it was cold out."

"I remember that." Susannah cupped her hand to the back of Kaitlyn's head and murmured something in her ear.

Mia hugged her arms to her chest and glanced around the cabin. She was too embarrassed to admit she didn't have a stroller either. That was something else that had been swiped from the truck while they were packing up their apartment. She just hadn't mentioned every item stolen to Vera the night before. Who leaves belongings unattended like that? But they'd been so upset and in such a rush to get out of there.

"We have a stroller," Susannah offered as if reading Mia's thoughts. "We have a snowsuit about Kaitlyn's size too. I can go get them." She still had her coat on.

Mia sighed. "You are too generous."

"It's no problem. Do you need anything else?" Susannah stepped toward the door.

Mia rubbed her arms, recalling how cold she'd been all night. Had Chace added enough coal to the stove?

"It's so cold in here. Do you have any spare blankets? I'll return them when the cabin warms up."

Susannah nodded. "I'm sure we have extra quilts. I'll be right back."

"Thank you." Mia turned toward Rhoda, who spoke softly to Kaitlyn while continuing to move her body back and forth. Kaitlyn stopped crying. "You certainly are an expert. You look so comfortable with her."

"I just have a lot of experience taking care of my siblings and my cousins." Rhoda shrugged as she lowered herself into the wing chair. "Does she take a bottle? Do you want me to feed her?"

Mia grimaced and pointed toward the cookstove. "I'm breastfeeding, and I'm getting her used to formula in a bottle too. But I can't figure out how to turn on the burner so I can warm up a bottle."

"I can show you how to do it."

While holding Kaitlyn close to her chest, Rhoda followed Mia to the kitchen area and explained how to use the stove. Mia warmed a bottle and then gave it to Rhoda to feed Kaitlyn, giving Mia the chance to unpack kitchen supplies.

Mia had the kitchen organized and was starting on the boxes in the family room when Vera and Susannah knocked, then entered the cabin. Vera held an armload of quilts and Susannah steered a stroller filled with a snowsuit, quilts, and toys.

"Thank you so much." A lump clogged Mia's throat as she took the quilts from Vera. "This is too much." She walked to the bedroom and set the quilts on the bed.

"No, it's not." Vera stood behind her. "By the way,

the changing table we have is nothing fancy, but it has room for storage." She pointed to a corner of the room. "It would fit there, and you can put the crib next to it."

"Changing table? Crib?" Mia asked.

"*Ya*, I thought I told you we have a crib you can use too. I'll have Adam and Joel bring everything over later when they get home from school." Vera placed her hands on her hips. "I think it would all fit over there nicely."

Mia blinked against threatening tears. She had the urge to laugh and cry at the same time. Why was she so emotional today? "Thank you."

"You're welcome." Vera touched her shoulder. "Susannah and I are here to help you unpack if you'd like the help. We're caught up with our morning chores."

"Thank you," Mia repeated. This woman had met Mia for the first time last night but was offering to help her unpack.

Vera chuckled. "You don't have to keep thanking me. Let's get to work."

Mia, Vera, and Susannah spent the next couple of hours unpacking all of Mia and Chace's belongings and organizing the cabin. By the time they finished, the bedroom closet and bureau were full of clothes, and some of Mia's books and photos were displayed on the small bookcase near the front door.

Rhoda put Kaitlyn down for a nap in the portable crib and soon returned to the family area. "She's already fast asleep." She eased the bedroom door shut.

"Thank you." Mia placed her favorite photo on top of the bookcase. It featured Mia, Kaitlyn, and Chace posing together in their former apartment the day Kaitlyn came home from the hospital. It was their first family photo. Mia held Kaitlyn in her arms and Chace had his arms wrapped around Mia, sporting his happy grin. They were so happy that day, so certain everything would be okay.

She scanned the small cabin and sighed. This was their home now, but why didn't it feel like a home? It just felt like a temporary place—a temporary and *cold* place—like a cheap hotel room someone would stay in overnight while on a journey to a more permanent and important location.

Vera surveyed their work. "The cabin looks *gut*."

"*Ya*." Susannah sat down on the wing chair. "It reminds me of when *Mammi* and *Daadi* lived here."

"I agree." Vera set a pile of empty boxes near the door. "It's *gut* to have someone in this *haus* again."

"How long did they live here?" Mia asked, still standing by the bookcase.

Vera was silent for a moment. "I think they were here for almost twenty years. Isaac's *mamm* passed away five years ago, and then his *dat* passed away two years ago."

"I miss them." Rhoda walked over to her mother.

"I do too," Susannah said. "I loved coming out here to visit them."

"I know you did," Vera responded. "I miss them too."

A pang of envy took Mia by surprise, and she frowned. Why didn't her parents want to be a part of their granddaughter's life like Isaac's parents had been? She dismissed the thought.

"Do you have anything to eat for supper?" Vera asked. "If not, I can bring something over for you."

Mia gnawed her lower lip while debating her response. She didn't want to lie about the meager choices she had, but they were better than nothing. "We have peanut butter, some bread, macaroni and cheese, ramen noodles, a little fruit, and a few cans of vegetables and soup. I can throw something together. We'll be fine." She was too humiliated to admit she had to save the peanut butter and bread for Chace to take to work for lunch.

Vera gave her a knowing expression. "I'll have Susannah and Rhoda bring over some food. We have plenty."

"I appreciate the offer, but you don't have to do that," Mia insisted. "I plan to go grocery shopping on Friday when Chace gets paid."

"We're happy to share our meal with you." Vera pulled on her coat. "I need to get home to finish a sewing project I started yesterday, but we will be back. Let us know if you need anything else."

Susannah and Rhoda followed suit, buttoning their coats.

"Thank you." Mia suddenly remembered a question she had. "Would you show me how to use the wringer washer sometime?"

"Oh, *ya*," Rhoda said as she stepped out to the small porch. "I can show you later when I bring over supper."

Mia waved as her new friends descended the steps and walked down the rock path leading to their large farmhouse. Then she closed the door and leaned against it. Would this tiny, dreary house ever feel like a home?

CHAPTER 3

Chace felt as if he'd been run over by his own truck. His arms, legs, and back were sore as he climbed the front steps later that evening. He'd spent all day helping Isaac build cabinets for a kitchen remodel at a huge home not far from their small cabin. Would he be able to build a similar home for Mia someday?

As he pulled open the front door, the aroma of baked chicken wafted over him and his stomach gurgled with delight. He turned toward the kitchen where Mia carried plates and utensils to the table. Her dark hair was pulled up in a messy ponytail with loose tendrils framing her face. She wore one of his old gray sweatshirts, which hung to the thighs of her jeans. Although she rarely wore makeup, she was the most beautiful woman he'd ever met.

"Hello." He hung his coat on a peg by the door. "How are my two favorite girls?"

Mia mumbled something inaudible as she placed a large bowl of noodles in the center of the small table.

He scanned the cabin. The suitcases, boxes, and trash bags were gone from the family room floor and the room was tidy. Turning to his right, he saw the small bookcase cluttered with Mia's favorite framed photos and a few books. He smiled. Mia had made the cabin a home.

"How are you?" Chace crossed to the kitchen and opened his arms in the hopes she would step into his hug. Instead, she slipped past him, her face twisted into a scowl. His stomach tightened. Something was wrong. "Where's Katie?"

"She's sleeping." Mia filled a glass with water from a pitcher. "Have a seat."

"I need to wash my hands first." Chace scrubbed his hands at the kitchen sink and then sat down across from her. A bowl of chicken and noodles and a bowl of green beans sat in the middle of the table, and his stomach growled again. He looked up to where Mia studied her plate while frowning.

"Everything looks delicious." He gave her a hesitant smile. "Thank you."

She speared him with an accusing look. "I didn't make it. Vera did."

"Oh." He paused, uncertain of how to respond to her biting tone. "Okay."

They were silent as they filled their plates and began to eat. She took small bites while studying her glass of water as if it were an intricate book she was studying for a college exam.

The reticence between them weighed heavily on Chace's shoulders. He longed to ask her about her day and share the details of his. Instead, he kept quiet, hoping Mia's fury would subside. He'd been on the receiving end of her simmering anger more than once during their two-year relationship, and he dreaded the explosion that threatened to come soon.

"This is delicious," he finally said, treading carefully. "It was nice of Vera to share their supper with us." He lifted his glass of water to take a sip.

"She insisted. She felt sorry for us when I admitted we won't have much food until you get paid on Friday."

He held the glass frozen in midair and watched his wife, trying to understand what was bothering her. "What's wrong?"

She set her fork down next to her plate and studied him. "I have never in my life been on the receiving end of handouts." She pointed toward the bowl of green beans. "This meal isn't the only thing she's given us." She began counting items off on her fingers. "She also gave us a crib, a changing table, a snowsuit, a stroller, and baby toys." Then she pointed toward the coal stove. "And she gave us quilts so we don't freeze to death. I wasn't this cold when I was living in the dorm and the windows wouldn't close all the way."

Mia lanced him with another murderous expression. "Do you have any idea how embarrassing it was to admit to her that we didn't have any food for supper other than some boxed mac and cheese and canned soup?"

Chace placed the glass on the table as his hands began to shake. He took slow, deep breaths in an attempt to calm down before he said something he'd regret.

"How can you expect us to live here? It's so cold that I'm surprised Katie isn't already sick. There's no electricity so I can't even plug in a small heater to try to warm our bedroom up for her naps. There's no phone, and I'm completely cut off from the world since we couldn't afford to keep our cell phones. What am I supposed to do if there's an emergency? Am I expected to run to the nearest hospital since I sold my car in an effort to pay some of the bills?"

"There is a phone," Chace muttered as angry heat crept up his neck.

"There is?" She fixed him with an incredulous stare. "Where?"

"By the barn. The Amish have phones. They just aren't in their houses."

"Well, you've fixed one of my four-dozen problems. How do we fix the rest of them?"

"I'm doing the best I can." He kneaded the tense muscles in his neck with his fingers. "I don't know what else I can do."

Just then Kaitlyn started to wail. With a sigh, Mia pushed back her chair and left the kitchen.

Chace stared down at his empty plate, the food souring in his stomach. Guilt and dread clawed up his sore back as Mia's hateful words echoed through his mind. He felt as if he were sixteen years old again and standing in front of Buck Richards, the most callous and critical foster father Chace had endured since his mother died and he was hurled into the foster care system when he was four.

"You'll never amount to anything, Chace, because you have no ambition. You'll just look for the easy way out. I'd bet you'll rob convenience stores, shoot the

clerks, and then wind up in jail for life, just like your worthless father."

Chace had promised himself he'd prove Buck wrong, but it seemed an impossible feat. Pressing his fingers to his eyes, Chace swallowed against the emotion lodging in his throat.

The sound of Kaitlyn's gurgle brought him back to the present as Mia returned to the kitchen with her balanced on one hip.

"Hi, baby girl." He forced a smile as Kaitlyn gnawed on her thumb and blew happy spit bubbles. "How was your day, Katie-Bug?"

"Feel her leg." She angled the baby toward him. "Feel how cold she is."

Chace pressed his lips together as he touched the leg of Kaitlyn's sleeper. It was cold.

"I don't see how this can be healthy. She's going to wind up sick one of these days." Mia lifted the baby seat with one hand and placed it on the table. She set Kaitlyn in the seat and buckled the straps. Kaitlyn responded with a happy gurgle.

"So then why don't you call your parents and ask for help?" The question leaped from Chace's lips before he could stop it. He held his breath, awaiting her eruption. The subject of her parents always sent Mia over the edge. She hadn't spoken to her parents since the day Kaitlyn was born, and from what little Mia had divulged, the conversation hadn't made any strides toward changing their decision to disown Mia.

"You know the answer to that question." She ground out the words.

He stood as renewed frustration grabbed him by the throat. "Maybe your parents would change their minds if they saw their beautiful grandchild." He pointed at Kaitlyn. "How could they possibly resist her?"

"It won't work." She gestured wildly with her hands as her brown eyes sparkled with tears. "I could send them a portfolio of professional photos of Kaitlyn and they still would refuse to help us."

"Well, I don't know what to tell you." He folded his arms over his chest. "Maybe it's time for you to let go of your pride for the sake of our child and ask your father to give us a loan until we're back on our feet."

"Let go of my pride?" Her voice quavered and her eyes narrowed to slits. "My pride has nothing to do with how my parents feel about my decisions."

A single tear trickled down her cheek, and his chest constricted. He'd done it again. He'd lost his temper and made her cry.

"Mee, I'm sorry." He reached for her, but she stepped back and out of his reach. "Why don't you sit down and finish your supper with me? I want to hear about your day."

"I have nothing else to say to you." Mia shook her head and stomped off to the bedroom, leaving Chace staring down at Kaitlyn as she kicked her feet and blew bubbles.

Chace touched Kaitlyn's toe as Buck's words reverberated in his mind again. His shoulders slumped. He wasn't worthy of Mia or this beautiful baby.

He handed Kaitlyn the pacifier that hung on a clip attached to her sleeper and then carried the dishes to the sink. As it filled with hot water, Chace peered out the small window and stared toward Isaac's house. *Will I ever be the husband Mia deserves?*

* * *

Mia sat on the edge of the bed and buried her face in her hands as angry tears splattered down her hot cheeks. She took deep, slow breaths. *Be strong, Mia! Calm down!* Soon her tears stopped, and she hugged her arms to her waist.

Her gaze moved across the room to a framed photograph sitting on top of the small bureau. In the photo, Mia and Chace stood arm in arm on the beach, their smiles wide as waves crashed behind them and the sunset bathed the sky in vivid streaks of orange, pink, and yellow. Her heart thumped as she recalled that beach trip. It was Memorial Day weekend, and she and Chace had been dating for a month. Shortly after that photo was taken, Chace told her he loved her for the first time. Back then life was simple. Mia was in college studying to become a teacher, and Chace was working for a construction company. Their future was bright with endless possibilities.

So much had changed in a matter of almost two years. Now their future was uncertain and bleak. She'd spent the day trying to convince herself she was doing the best she could as a mother, but that voice at the back of her mind kept taunting her with her mother's words: *"You'll be a horrible mother."* She had to prove her mother wrong. But how?

Her conversation with Chace replayed in her mind, and her body shuddered with a mixture of frustration and guilt. She could feel the pain in Chace's eyes when she yelled at him, listing everything wrong with the cabin and their lives. She longed for Chace to understand her parents weren't going to help them.

Mia's painful conversation with her mother after Kaitlyn's birth was still fresh in her mind. She called to tell her the baby had been born and asked her if she was ready to be the grandmother Kaitlyn needed and deserved. Her mother's response was, "I'll be ready to be her grandmother when you're ready to face the fact that Chace can't give you and your baby the life you both deserve."

When her mother refused to acknowledge Kaitlyn or accept Chace as her husband, Mia burst into tears, telling her mom she was still the cold, superficial woman she'd always been, and then Mia disconnected the call.

Squeezing her eyes shut, Mia pressed her fingers to her forehead. She was just as self-centered as her mother when she blamed Chace for their current situation. She and Chace were in this together. They were a team. More important, they were a *family*. Chace had been telling her the truth when he said he was doing the best he could. She had to apologize to him.

Shoving herself off the bed, Mia wiped her hands down her cheeks and hurried out of the bedroom. Chace was washing dishes at the kitchen sink. Without much forethought, she lunged forward and wrapped her arms around him, squeezing him and burying her face into his back.

He gasped and then his body relaxed.

"I'm sorry," she whispered, her voice wavering. "I'm so sorry."

"Hey, it's okay." He spun and gathered her in his arms as soon as he rinsed and dried his hands. "I'm sorry too, Mee."

Mia smiled at the sound of the nickname he'd given her when they first started dating. She looked up at him and her lower lip trembled. "I'm sorry for dumping on you after you worked hard all day for Katie and me. I didn't mean it." She looped her arms around his neck.

"It's all right." He trailed a fingertip down her cheek. "No more tears."

She cleared her throat. "We're in this together, right?"

"Always. And I will do everything in my power to take care of you and Katie." Dipping his chin, he brushed his lips over hers, sending shivers of electricity dancing down her spine. "I love you."

"I love you too." Closing her eyes, she hoped they would make it somehow.

* * *

Chace perched on a stool and sipped a bottle of water as the sweet smell of new wood and stain wafted over him. He'd spent all morning sanding cabinets. Although he listened to music on his ancient iPod while he worked, he couldn't stop his brain from focusing on Mia's parents. Could he talk to Mia's father man-to-man and somehow convince him to loan Chace money? He didn't want a handout from Mia's parents; he only wanted a little help getting back on his feet.

He studied the cabinet on his workbench as the idea filtered through his thoughts. It seemed a reasonable enough request, but a tiny twinge of warning rang through his head. *Mia would be furious if she found out I spoke to her father.*

Chace blew out a resigned sigh in agreement with his inner voice. Yes, she would be, but it was his responsibility to take care of his family.

My very own family.

He'd dreamt of having his own family since he was a child, and now that he had one, he would do anything in his power to preserve it. If that meant begging Mia's father for help, then he would do it.

When the other workers in the shop left for lunch, Chace approached the front office.

"Isaac." Chace leaned his shoulder against the doorframe. "I was wondering if I could use your phone book and phone for a few minutes."

"Of course." Isaac pulled a phone book out of one of the bottom drawers and set it on the desk. "Take your time. I'll be in the break room."

"Thanks," Chace said as Isaac moved past him, disappearing into the hallway. He appreciated how Isaac respected his privacy. Isaac had never pressed Chace to share why he had needed a place to live. He never accused or admonished Chace about the dire situation. Instead, he'd offered the cabin, asking how much Chace could comfortably afford to pay for rent.

Chace sat down at the desk, opened the phone book,

located the phone number for Whitfield, Price & Morgan Attorneys at Law, and dialed. His heart was in his throat when a woman answered.

"Thank you for calling Whitfield, Price and Morgan. How may I direct your call?"

"May I please speak to Walter Whitfield?" Chace hoped he sounded confident despite the anxiety threading through him.

The woman paused. "May I ask who is calling?"

"Chace O'Conner." He worried his lower lip.

"And what is the nature of your call, Mr. O'Conner?"

"I'm his son-in-law. It's an urgent family matter."

"Oh. I will transfer you right away. Just a moment, please, Mr. O'Conner."

"Thank you." Chace kneaded one temple and mentally rehearsed what he would say to Walter. He'd met Walter a few times while he and Mia dated. Walter had been polite, but he radiated a palpable air of arrogance and disapproval.

"This is Walter Whitfield." Walter's deep, no-nonsense voice rang over the line.

Chace froze, doubt stealing his courage. *Hang up now before you ruin Mia's chances of ever reconciling with her parents!*

"Chace?" Walter sighed. "Are you there?"

"Yes, I am." Chace cleared his throat. "Thank you for taking my call."

"Is something wrong with Mia?"

For a brief moment, Chace was impressed. *So Mia's father has a conscience?*

"Mia is fine, and so is our daughter." Chace ground

out the words as anger replaced his surprise. "Did you know your granddaughter's name is Kaitlyn Leanne? Leanne is after my mother. She died when I was four." When Walter didn't respond, Chace continued. "Our baby is five months old now. She has blue eyes and blond hair. I thought she'd have dark hair and eyes like Mia, but she actually has my coloring. But she definitely has Mia's smile. She's the prettiest baby I've ever seen. I suppose I'm biased since I'm her father. You should understand that."

Chace wound the phone cord around his finger. "I'd love to send photos to you and Mrs. Whitfield." He could ask one of his coworkers to take a photo and text it to Walter since Chace no longer had a cell phone. "Would you like to see photos of the granddaughter you've never met?"

"What do you want?"

"I want to talk to you man-to-man."

"Look, my wife and I feel it's best if we stay out of Mia's life."

"I know that, and I didn't expect this phone call to change that."

"So what do you want then? Is it money?"

Chace grimaced. He hated how that sounded. "Not exactly," he said, hedging. "I want to ask for a loan. I just need some help getting back on my feet, and I will repay you with interest. When Kaitlyn was born she spent five days in the NICU. The bills on top of her delivery itself have been daunting, but if I could just get—"

"Are you saying you can't support my daughter on your construction-worker salary?"

Walter's sneer radiated through the phone. Chace silently counted to ten, keeping his thoughts focused on Mia and Kaitlyn instead of allowing his anger to destroy any chance of convincing Walter to help them.

"I'm only asking you for a loan," Chace repeated, the receiver trembling in his hand.

"I'm sorry, but I can't help you. Give Mia my love."

Before Chace could respond, the line went dead. Chace slammed the receiver onto the cradle and heaved the phone book across the room. The heavy book smacked the wall before landing in a heap by the door.

He leaned over the desk, folded his arms, and rested his forehead on them as he fought back his embittered tears. He'd reached a new low. Not only had he betrayed Mia by going against her wishes, but he'd failed to help his family. No matter what Chace tried to do, he failed. How was he going to face Mia tonight? And what would she say when she learned he had called her father?

Renewed worry and frustration surged through Chace. How could things get any worse?

CHAPTER 4

Mia sucked in a deep breath and plastered a smile on her face as hope and determination coursed through her. "This is my first attempt at meat loaf." She brought a loaf pan to the table and set it on a trivet beside a bowl with leftover green beans. Chace kept his stormy blue eyes focused on his glass of water.

Since he'd arrived home nearly thirty minutes ago, Chace hadn't said anything other than his customary, "How are my favorite girls?" After kissing Kaitlyn's head, he'd washed his hands and then dropped into his seat at the table, staring at the plate and scowling. Mia tried to coax him into a conversation by asking about his day and even asking if he was upset with her. He, however, remained reticent.

Although worry had her stomach tied in knots, Mia kept smiling as she cut a piece of meat loaf and dropped it onto Chace's plate. Her smile dissolved as she examined the bottom of the loaf.

"It's burned." Her shoulders sagged. She'd gotten chop meat from Vera and planned to pay her for it when Chace received his next paycheck on Friday. She'd used a cookbook from Goodwill to mix up the meat loaf, but lost track of time taking care of the baby and left it in the oven too long.

Mia dropped a piece of meat loaf onto her own plate and bit her lower lip. Her plan to impress Chace with a nice meal had gone up in smoke. "It's probably not that good. I guess I have a lot to learn."

Chace studied the meat loaf. He cut off a piece and then moved it to the side of his plate. "That's no surprise since your mother never cooked. I guess she expected you to have a housekeeper like she did. Why learn to cook when you can pay someone to make the meals?"

Mia gaped at him. Had she heard him correctly? She started to deliver a cutting retort but then closed her mouth as worry pushed away her anger. Had something happened to Chace today? Had he lost his job? Her stomach roiled at the thought of facing Chace's unemployment for the second time in less than a year. She took a deep breath, steadying her nerves. She and Chace were married and had a baby. They had to face their problems together as a united force.

Instead of yelling at him, she had to ease him into a conversation. She had to offer support, not sardonic responses.

"Did you have a bad day at work?" Her tone was cautious.

He shrugged as he turned his attention to Kaitlyn in her baby seat on the table beside him. A swarm of emotions hurdled across his handsome face as he rubbed Kaitlyn's foot, watching her suck on her pacifier. Mia saw anger, disappointment, sadness, and regret brewing in his expression.

As the silence stretched like a great chasm between them, Mia twirled her fork in her fingers and searched for something to spark a conversation. "I've been thinking about what you said last night, and I realized you're right."

His eyebrows rose, but he kept his eyes focused on Kaitlyn. He rubbed her leg and then took her tiny hand in his. The tenderness in his touch and his love for their daughter stole Mia's words for a moment.

"I've already sold my car and most of my jewelry." She stared down at the thin gold band on her left ring finger. "I also sold my designer clothes and purses at that consignment shop, so I don't have anything left to sell."

"What's your point?"

She peeked up and found him watching her.

"I'm ready to contact my parents and ask for their help," she blurted. "I'll need to borrow the truck." She looked at Kaitlyn, and her voice trembled. "Maybe if they met her, they'd be more inclined to help us."

"Don't waste your time." Chace stood and carried his plate to the sink, his meal untouched.

"What do you mean?"

He faced her, leaning against the sink and crossing his arms over his wide chest. "I called your father today."

"You what?" Mia dropped the fork onto the plate with a clatter. "You called my father?"

Chace nodded.

"What did he say?" She stood. While she felt betrayed by Chace for going behind her back, another emotion emerged and squeezed at her chest—hope. Chace sounded like her father had said no, but maybe with time he could get through to him, make him realize he wanted to not only be a father to Mia, but, more important, be a grandfather to Kaitlyn. After all, Mia's parents were the only grandparents Kaitlyn would ever have the chance to know.

"It didn't go well."

"What did he say?" she repeated, her words slow and measured. When Chace rubbed his clean-shaven chin with hesitation, Mia's blood boiled and she clenched her jaw. "Tell me."

"At first he asked if you were okay." He rested his hands on the sink behind him. "I told him you were fine, and then I told him about Katie, offering to send photos. He said he and your mother had decided it was best to stay out of your life. He asked me if I wanted money, and when I asked for a loan, he made a crack about how I can't support you on my construction work salary."

Mia gasped.

"I even offered to pay interest. I explained how Katie was in the NICU and we're buried in debt now. He said he couldn't help me and he told me to give you his love. And then he hung up before I could say anything else." His face softened. "I'm sorry, Mee."

A single tear trickled down Mia's cheek, and she brushed it away. She couldn't allow her parents to hurt her again. She had to be strong for Kaitlyn.

"How could you?" She took a step toward him, balling her hands into tight fists as her whole body shook, the glimmer of hope gone. "How could you call my father after I told you it wouldn't work?"

He lifted one hand and shook his head. "I was desperate." He gestured around the cabin. "You and Katie deserve better than this. It's my job to take care of you, but I'm not doing a good job." He shoved both his hands through his thick hair, looking as though he either had a monster migraine or was fighting to keep from falling apart.

"I thought I could talk to your father man-to-man, and he would appreciate the situation I'm in." His tone was thin and reedy. "I got the impression he loves you, but if he loves you, then why won't he help you? Anyone who can jet off to Europe at a moment's notice and buy his daughter a luxury car can afford to loan his son-in-law money to get caught up on bills. Am I missing something here?" His lower lip trembled as he stared at Mia. He reminded her of a little boy, and the pain in his eyes sliced through her, trapping her words in her throat.

Chace took a step toward her. "I shouldn't have called him without discussing it with you first, but I'm at the end of my rope. Today I finally admitted to myself I'm in over my head and I have no idea what else to do."

Mia wiped her hands over her wet eyes. "He has the money to help us."

"So then what's the problem? Why are your parents so determined to treat us like strangers instead of their family?" As he stood over her, something inside of her crumbled.

"They wanted me to marry someone else."

"What are you talking about?"

Mia leaned against the kitchen counter. "The day I told my parents I was pregnant and going to marry you, they told me if I insisted on keeping the baby, they would help me until I found someone more 'worthy.' In fact, they hoped I could marry the son of one of my father's partners, someone they had already been thinking about, someone they thought would take me even though I was pregnant with your child. Someone willing to hide my—*their*—shame, with vested interest in keeping the firm and their standing in the community free from gossip."

Her voice was thick as Chace's eyes narrowed. "When I called my mom the day Kaitlyn was born, she said she would be a part of Katie's life, but only if I left you. She said you would never give Katie and me what we needed."

"Wait a minute." He held his hand up to stop her from speaking. "I thought your parents cut you off because you got pregnant. Are you telling me they actually disowned you because you chose to marry me?"

"Yes, that's correct. Once they accepted I was never going to make an adoption plan, that's what they offered." The words tasted bitter in Mia's mouth.

A muscle in Chace's jaw ticked. "Why didn't you tell me about this?"

"I didn't want to hurt you," Mia said, her words tumbling out of her mouth. "I don't care what my parents think of you. I love you, and I belong with you, despite what they think a marriage should be based on. I don't care what profession you choose. I just want to be with you and Kaitlyn. We're a family." When his brow furrowed, she added, "My parents have no part of this relationship. It's about you, Kaitlyn, and me. We don't need their blessing or their money."

"We promised there would be no secrets between us." He pointed between them. "You say we're in this together, but you never trusted me enough to tell me the truth. You still don't trust me, do you?"

"That's not true!" Tears clouded her vision.

He headed for the door and pulled on his coat.

"Where are you going?" Alarm gripped her.

"Out." He wrenched the door open and then stopped, facing her. "Your parents are right. I can't give you and Katie the life you deserve. You should go home to them so you won't have to worry about Kaitlyn's well-being."

"You don't mean that," Mia croaked between sobs.

Chace nodded. "Actually, I do." Then he disappeared out the door, slamming it behind him.

Mia pulled Kaitlyn into her arms, held her close, and sobbed.

* * *

Chace shivered and zipped up his coat as he descended the steps. He had no idea where he was going, but he had to get out of the cabin to process what Mia told him. Although he'd been aware of Mia's parents' disapproval of him, he never realized how deep their rejection ran. Hearing that the Whitfields had tried to convince Mia to marry someone else had nearly unraveled Chace.

What if Mia had agreed to dump me for the partner's son?

Chace gritted his teeth and stalked past his truck, continuing down the rock path toward Isaac's barns and house. His pulse pounded with resentment toward Mia's parents and also with fear that Mia would leave him. But how could he blame her if he couldn't even afford an apartment with electricity and heat?

"Chace?"

He turned toward one of the barns, where Isaac and Adam stood watching him. He nodded a greeting.

"Is everything all right?" Isaac asked.

Chace paused, torn between pouring out his heart to his friend and keeping all his swarming emotions bottled up until he finally exploded.

Isaac said something to Adam, and the boy waved to Chace before scurrying up the porch steps and into the house. Then he turned to Chace. "You look like you're carrying the weight of the world on your young shoulders. Would you like to talk?"

Chace cupped his hand to the back of his neck and squeezed at the tense muscles. "I feel like I've burdened you enough with my problems."

"You're a *freind*, not a burden." Isaac pointed toward the porch. "Let's sit."

Chace dropped his hand to his side. "That would be great." He followed Isaac up the back steps of the large porch and then sat down on a rocker as Isaac sank onto a nearby swing.

"You seemed upset this afternoon at work."

"You could tell?"

Isaac chuckled. "*Ya*, it was apparent when I saw the condition of the phone book and found the scuffs on the wall. When I saw you throw a roll of masking tape at the wall in the shop later, I was able to put it all together."

Chace winced. "I'm sorry. I try to suppress my temper, but it gets the best of me sometimes."

"We're all human. I've been known to kick a barn wall a time or two." Isaac crossed his arms over his coat. "Sometimes it helps to talk about it before it eats you up inside."

Chace rested his work boot on his opposite knee and looked out toward the cabin. "Mia and I are from different backgrounds. She grew up in a wealthy family with every privilege and opportunity available to her. I, on the other hand, grew up with nothing. My father went to prison for life when I was an infant, and my mother died in a car accident when I was four. Since I didn't have any other family members, I was swallowed up by the foster care system. I bounced from home to home until I turned eighteen."

Chace moved the rocker back and forth. "I met Mia when she was in college. Her parents didn't approve of me, but she didn't let that stop her from falling in love with me." He rubbed his chin, debating how much to share about the circumstances surrounding their quick engagement and marriage. "Mia's parents disowned her when she married me."

Isaac faced Chace, his eyebrows raised. "They disowned her?"

Chace nodded.

Isaac looked baffled. "Why?"

"They wanted her to marry someone who was successful." Then Chace explained how he'd called Mia's father, detailing the conversation as Isaac shook his head. "When I told Mia about the phone call tonight, she was upset. Then she told me more about how her parents feel about me." He shared what Mia had told him earlier, his shoulders tightening with renewed ire.

Isaac adjusted his hat on his head. "Are you angry with Mia or with her parents?"

The question was simple, but it touched something deep inside of Chace. "Now that I've cooled off, I understand why Mia kept it from me, but it still hurts knowing her parents wouldn't even give me a chance. I never had a real family, and I want to be a good husband and father. I want to show the world I'm more than just a punk who got lost in the foster care system. I want to be the father I never had." He blew out a deep sigh as tears threatened in his eyes. "Sometimes I just don't feel worthy of Mia, and I feel like I'm living a dream."

"Do you feel that way because her family had more money than you?"

Chace nodded.

Isaac frowned. "The *Englisch* put too much importance on money and worldly possessions. We're all the same in God's eyes, no matter how much money we make or how many expensive things we have collected." His expression softened. "But, aside from that, if Mia had been worried about having expensive things,

she wouldn't have married you. You need to stop pun-
ishing yourself for not being perfect in her parents'
eyes. We all make mistakes, and we have to ask God
for guidance.

"One of my favorite Scripture verses comes from
Proverbs. 'Trust in the Lord with all your heart and
lean not on your own understanding; in all your ways
submit to him, and he will make your paths straight.'"
He pointed toward the sky. "Trust in God. He is the
light of the world, and he will guide you onto the right
path if you follow his Word."

Isaac's words punched Chace right in the center of
his chest. He cleared his throat against a swelling lump.

"Mia loves you." Isaac tapped the arm of the swing.
"She's stuck by you despite her parents' attempts to
bribe her into leaving you. You need to stop worrying
about what they think and just concentrate on doing
your best. Be a *gut freind* and a *gut* husband to her. You
also need to talk to Mia. Don't run away when things
get tough. Stay and work things out." He paused for a
moment. "You don't need to beg Mia's parents for help.
If you need anything, let me know. Vera and I can help
you get back on your feet."

Chace blew out a shuddering sigh. "Thank you. I'm
grateful for your generosity."

"The Lord tells us to help our neighbors. Things
were tough for us when I started my business, so I
understand how you feel." Isaac pointed toward the
cabin. "Go home and tell Mia you love her. Before
you go to sleep tonight, pray. Ask God to guide you. If
you invite him into your heart, he will lead you down

the right path. You're a *gut* man. I'm certain you will be fine."

"Thank you." After shaking Isaac's hand, Chace hurried down the rock path toward the cabin. As he approached his truck, he suddenly remembered the two jars of baby food he'd picked up at a convenience store during his lunch break.

Chace pulled the keys from his coat pocket, unlocked the truck, and retrieved the small bag on the floorboard. He closed and locked the truck before heading into the cabin. No one was in the family room or kitchen. Panic seized him as the cruel words he'd spat at Mia before he left echoed through his mind:

"You should go home to them so you won't have to worry about Kaitlyn's well-being."

Was she packing? Was she planning to call for a cab and flee their misery?

"Mia?" His voice was tight with worry. "Mia?"

The bedroom door opened, and Mia stood in the doorway, frowning.

"I just got her to sleep." Mia pulled the door closed behind her. "She was getting cranky." Once the door clicked shut, she studied him, folding her arms over the front of her red sweater. Her dark eyes were red-rimmed, and a pang of guilt slammed through him.

He hung his coat on the peg by the door and then closed the distance between them, holding the small grocery bag out to her. "I forgot to give this to you earlier."

"What's this?" Her brow puckered.

"Take it." He gave the bag a little shake.

She pulled out the two small jars of food. She looked at them and then back up at him. "You bought baby food?"

"Yeah." Chace took the jars of baby food and put them back into the bag and set them on the chair behind him. "After I hung up with your dad, I was so furious I walked over to the nearby convenience store and picked up a sandwich and drink. I know it's wasteful to buy lunch, but I needed to blow off some steam. When I saw the display of baby food, I remembered Katie's reaction when I gave her the pears and bananas the other day." His heart twisted with contrition. "We weren't sure how she'd react to solid food since it was our first attempt at introducing them, but she'd squealed with delight. I wanted to hear that laugh again. Actually, I would do anything to make you and Katie happy." He gripped her forearms. "I'm sorry I keep hurting you. I didn't mean it when I said I wanted you to go back to your parents. If you left me, I don't know what I'd do."

Mia's lips formed a sad smile as she cupped her hand to his cheek. "I know that."

He leaned into her touch as if it were his lifeline. "Thank you for choosing me despite your parents' objections."

"My parents are so blinded by their materialism that they don't see how amazing you are. I love you. That won't change no matter what my parents say or do."

He pulled her against him and kissed her. She looped her arms around his neck, relaxing against him. When he broke the kiss, she rested her head against his chest and he breathed in the sweet scent of her shampoo.

"I'm sorry for not eating supper," he whispered.

"You don't need to apologize. It was pretty awful." She looked up at him and scrunched her nose. "I'll ask Vera for some cooking lessons."

He tucked a long strand of her soft, dark hair behind her ear. "And I'll do everything I can to take care of you and Katie." Resting his cheek on her head, he closed his eyes and recalled Isaac's advice.

Thank you, God, for bringing Mia and Kaitlyn into my life. Please show me how to be a better husband and father. Please guide my path. Amen.

CHAPTER 5

Kaitlyn blew raspberries and yanked Mia's hair as Mia knocked on the Allgyers' back door the following morning.

"Ouch." Mia laughed, trying to untangle Kaitlyn's pudgy fingers from her hair. "I should've pulled my hair up this morning."

Kaitlyn continued to spray spit bubbles and tug Mia's hair hard enough to tip Mia's head to the side.

"You have some grip for a little one," she mumbled.

The back door swung open and Rhoda grinned. "Mia! Kaitlyn!"

Kaitlyn squealed and kicked her feet into Mia's side.

"Hi, Rhoda." Mia smiled, despite her throbbing scalp. "I was wondering if I could talk to your mom."

"Of course." Rhoda held her hands out to Kaitlyn. "May I hold her?"

"That would be fantastic." As Mia handed Kaitlyn to Rhoda, Kaitlyn released the lock of Mia's hair. Mia rubbed her head and followed Rhoda through the mudroom to the kitchen. "She enjoys trying to rip my hair out."

Rhoda chuckled.

"Kaitlyn!" Smiling, Susannah rushed over from the kitchen counter to greet her, then touched Kaitlyn's hand as she gurgled. "Hi, Mia."

"*Gut* morning." Vera smiled as she finished drying a dish.

"Good morning." Mia dropped her diaper bag onto a kitchen chair. "If you're not too busy, Kaitlyn and I thought we'd come for a visit." Her cheeks heated. "I was also wondering if I could get some cooking lessons from you."

"That sounds like fun." Vera placed the clean dish on the counter. "The girls can take care of Kaitlyn, and we'll cook and chat."

Rhoda and Susannah nodded in unison.

"We have that *boppli* swing now," Rhoda said. "We can use it here and then carry it to the cabin for Mia."

Mia's eyes widened. "You have a baby swing I can borrow?"

"*Ya*, we found it in the attic this morning, and Rhoda and I cleaned it up for you," Susannah said.

"I'm certain our *aenti* would be happy you're getting some use out of it." Rhoda smiled at Kaitlyn, who gave a sweet sigh while fingering the ribbons on Rhoda's gauzy head covering.

"Thank you so much." Mia was overwhelmed. "I've missed the swing we had before."

"We're grateful you can use it," Vera said.

"Let's take Kaitlyn into the family room and see if she likes this swing." Rhoda gestured for her sister to follow her.

"So what would you like to learn how to make today?"

Vera put a large cookbook on the table and started flipping through it.

"I'm open to learning anything. My mom never cooked, so I never learned. When I was in college, I mostly ate in the dining hall or out at restaurants."

"Your *mamm* never cooked?" Vera furrowed her brow.

Mia shook her head. "We had a housekeeper. She did the cooking and the cleaning so my mom could spend her days socializing and volunteering for charities."

Vera nodded. "I see. Would you like to try a chicken casserole?" She examined the book as she spoke. "I already have enough leftover cooked chicken. We can put it together, and then you can store it in your refrigerator until you're ready to bake it. Does that sound *gut*?"

"That sounds fantastic." Mia gnawed her lower lip. "I can pay you for the ingredients when Chace gets home."

Vera peered up at her. "I'm not concerned about that. I just want to make sure you're eating well. Let's get started." She pulled out a mixing bowl and baking dish.

As she walked over to the counter, Mia scanned the large, open kitchen, taking in the plain white walls, sparsely decorated with a single shelf that held a few candles and an antique clock. The floor was a worn tan linoleum pattern, and a long wooden table with six chairs sat in the middle of the room.

The far end of the kitchen included a propane stove and refrigerator, resembling the appliances in the cabin. This kitchen, however, had ample counter and cabinet space. A small window over the sink looked out over a yard with large, thick trees decorated with birdhouses. The kitchen was warm and homey, despite the absence of her mother's ornate decorating.

"How was the meat loaf last night?" Vera asked.

Mia groaned and rolled her eyes. "Terrible. That's why I need cooking lessons. I burned it. I put it in the oven and then Katie woke up from her nap. I changed her diaper and spent time with her, and I lost track of time. I didn't realize it had burned until I served it to Chace, but obviously the meat loaf had been in too long."

"Don't be so hard on yourself. I've done that too." Vera explained the recipe to Mia and soon they were gathering the ingredients and supplies.

"How did you meet Isaac?" Mia asked while dicing chicken.

"We met at a singing."

"What's a singing?"

"That's when the youth get together to play games and sing hymns. Isaac grew up in a neighboring church district, so we went to different schools. Our youth groups were combined that night, and we became friends." She looked over at Mia. "How about you and Chace?"

Mia wiped her hands on a paper towel. "It was sort of the same situation. I was in college and we met at a party. I didn't want to go, but my roommate insisted I studied too much and needed some fun. Chace and I saw each other across the room. He smiled, and I smiled back at him. He was the most handsome man there." She laughed. "He introduced himself to me, and we spent the rest of the night talking. He asked me for my number, and that was it. That was almost two years ago."

"What did you study in college?"

"I wanted to be a teacher, but I didn't get to finish." Mia frowned, waiting for Vera to ask why. She was too embarrassed to admit she'd gotten pregnant, but Vera didn't question her. Vera never questioned or judged her, and Mia was grateful. Besides, once she mentioned how recently they had married, Vera would know the truth.

"We met when I was nineteen and only in my second year of college," Mia continued. "When we decided to get married last March, I quit school. I hope someday I can finish up my degree. I've always wanted to be a teacher, even though my mother didn't approve."

"Why didn't your *mamm* want you to be a teacher?" Vera sliced more chicken.

"Teachers don't make enough money. My mother only cares about status. She always told me to marry well so I could enjoy a nice lifestyle. That's why she never approved of Chace either."

"Have you asked them for help? I'm sure they would want to help you."

"They disowned me."

"How can that be? You're family! Kaitlyn is their grandchild."

Mia shared what her father said when Chace called him yesterday.

Vera shook her head. "I'm so sorry for everything

you've been through. I hope someday your parents will realize how wrong they've been to reject you—and your family."

"I do too." Mia's voice was thick. "I can't thank you enough for everything you've done for us. We would probably be in a shelter right now if it weren't for you and Isaac."

"I meant it when I said we know how hard times can be. Isaac's *dat* had a dairy farm, but Isaac wanted to become a cabinetmaker. We struggled when we first started his business. Our parents tried to help us, but they had fallen on hard times too. We made it through, but there were days when I wondered if we had enough food to last until Isaac finished a job. When he told me Chace needed a place to live, I wanted to help you."

Mia sniffed as tears flooded her eyes. "You are a blessing to us."

"We're happy to see a family in the little cabin." Vera turned back toward the recipe. "Now let's finish this casserole so we can figure out what we want for lunch."

"Okay." Mia smiled, grateful for her new friend.

* * *

"I can't believe how big Katie has grown during the past month." Susannah looked down at Kaitlyn, who sat on her lap and sucked on her pacifier.

Mia nodded as rain pounded on the cabin roof above them. "She's outgrowing her clothes. I need to go by the consignment shop after Chace gets paid next week." She carried four mugs to the table and then gathered tea bags and creamer. As she turned toward the table, she stepped in a puddle. She looked up at the ceiling to see water dripping. "Is the roof leaking?"

Vera turned in her chair and frowned. "*Ya*, I think it is. I'll tell Isaac."

"Chace can help him fix it." Mia brought the tea bags and cream to the table. "He has plenty of experience with roofs."

Rhoda stood. "I'll finish the tea, and you can find a pot to catch the water."

"Thanks." Mia dried the floor and then set out a large pot. They could hear water splash into it as Mia sat down at the table.

"The past month has gone by so quickly." Vera lifted her mug. "It feels like you just moved in."

"I know," Mia agreed. "Our first wedding anniversary is next week."

"Oh, that's so exciting." Susannah held Kaitlyn up to her shoulder.

"Do you want me to take her?" Mia asked.

"No, she's fine." Susannah caressed Kaitlyn's head.

Kaitlyn nuzzled closer against Susannah. Would Mia's mother be affectionate and cuddle with Kaitlyn the way Susannah and Rhoda did? Mia pressed her lips together.

"We can help you plant a garden in the spring," Rhoda said, yanking Mia from her thoughts. "My grandmother had a garden right outside the back door." She pointed toward the mudroom. "If you want, we can plant one there."

"That's a great idea," Vera chimed in. "Your *mammi* had the most beautiful vegetables."

"That sounds great." Mia cupped her mug in her hands. Would they still live in the cabin by the time the vegetables were ripe? Her heart tugged at the thought of leaving her new friends. But was it fair to raise Kaitlyn in the cold, rustic cabin with a leaky roof and no electricity? Would Mia be a terrible mother if she chose to raise her child here?

* * *

Chace rolled over in bed and yawned. His back and neck were sore from sanding and painting cabinets all day yesterday. He reached his arm to the left and expected to feel Mia beside him, but he found cold sheets instead. He rubbed his eyes and then focused his attention on the bright green numbers on the clock next to the bed. It was almost nine. He'd overslept.

Groaning, Chace rolled onto his back and stared up at the ceiling. It was Saturday, and he felt like a train had hit him. He'd worked hard all week, hoping to help Isaac get ahead on projects and also increase his paycheck. Now he had to fling himself out of bed and complete the honey-do list Mia had prepared for him all week. First on the list, he'd promised Mia he'd fix the leaky roof today after she'd complained about it last night. Now he just had to find the energy to do it.

With a moan and a grunt, he shoved himself out of bed and shuffled out to the kitchen, where Mia stood at the counter, beating an egg in a bowl. She glanced over her shoulder at him, her pink lips turning up in a breathtaking smile. She was so beautiful with her thick, dark hair falling to her lower back. What possessed Mia to pick him when she could've had any man she wanted?

"Good morning, sleepyhead." She nodded toward the bowl. "Do eggs and toast sound all right?"

"Sounds great. Thank you." He smiled down at his daughter, kicking her feet in her baby seat. "Hey, princess. How are you this morning?" He clicked open her safety belts and lifted her into his arms. He breathed in her familiar scent, baby lotion and diaper cream. "Are you going to help me fix the roof today?"

Kaitlyn babbled a response, latching a hand to his T-shirt.

"I'll take that as a yes." He leaned against the table and faced Mia. "I didn't mean to oversleep. I'm just exhausted."

"It's all right." She scraped the egg into the pan. "I suppose you deserve it after working all week."

Kaitlyn coughed, and Chace's eyes widened. "How long has she been coughing?"

"She started yesterday. I have some medicine left from her last cold." Mia adjusted the flame under the frying pan. "Hopefully that will take care of it since we can't afford to take her to a doctor."

Frowning, Chace rubbed Kaitlyn's golden hair. Someday soon he'd find a way to give his daughter everything she needed.

* * *

Mia wiped a cloth over the pane of one of Vera's kitchen windows later that afternoon. She hummed to herself while enjoying the simplicity of the work.

"You really don't need to help us clean," Vera said as she scrubbed the counter.

"I'm happy to help you. You've done so much for us." Mia peered out the window to where Chace helped Isaac and two other men carry benches into the barn. After Isaac and Chace finished fixing the roof on the cabin, Chace had offered to help Isaac prepare for the church service they would host in their barn tomorrow.

Vera chuckled a little. "You can't possibly want to clean my windows. One of the girls can do it if you'd rather do something in the cabin."

"It's no trouble at all. I'm glad to help you prepare for the service." Mia moved the cloth over another pane as she again looked out toward the barn. Chace laughed as he and Isaac stood with another Amish man. Mia admired how the sun brought out the golden hue of Chace's sandy-blond hair. He was so handsome dressed in jeans and a blue, long-sleeved T-shirt, with mirrored sunglasses shielding his eyes. He chuckled again before he and Isaac unloaded another bench from the long buggy that had delivered the benches yesterday.

Vera sidled up to Mia. "It seems as if Isaac and Chace have known each other for years. He thinks very highly of Chace. That's why Isaac sometimes slips into speaking Pennsylvania Dutch with him. He just feels that comfortable with Chace, and now we all feel comfortable with both of you. And also, your husband is a talented carpenter."

"Thank you." Mia began working on another window-pane. "He is talented, but he often doesn't acknowledge how good he is."

Kaitlyn squealed, and Mia turned to where Rhoda sat at the table feeding Kaitlyn a jar of pears.

"Let me know if you get tired of holding her," Mia said.

"It's fine. We're having a *gut* time, right, Katie?" Rhoda smiled. "She's a *gut boppli*. She's much happier than Joel was."

"That's true," Susannah called from the family room, where she was mopping the floor. "Joel cried all the time."

"Do you two go to youth group?" Mia asked the girls as she continued to work.

"*Ya*, we do," Rhoda said. "We like seeing our friends."

"Do you have a boyfriend, Rhoda?" Mia asked.

Rhoda's cheeks turned bright red as she focused her eyes on Kaitlyn.

"Rhoda has a crush on Sam Swarey," Susannah sang.

"Be quiet," Rhoda warned through gritted teeth.

"Sam?" Vera asked. "Lydia's son?"

Rhoda nodded, her cheeks as bright red as an apple.

"I had no idea," Vera said.

"I'm sorry." Mia frowned. "I didn't mean to embarrass you."

"It's not your fault." Rhoda rested Kaitlyn on her shoulder and caressed her cheek. "Sam is nice to me. We enjoy talking to each other at youth gatherings."

"It's *gut* to start out as friends." Vera wiped down the refrigerator with a rag. "Your *dat* and I were friends before we started dating."

"We're just friends," Rhoda said.

"He likes you," Susannah insisted.

"You think so?"

Susannah nodded. "It's pretty obvious with the way he looks at you."

Rhoda sighed, and Mia and Vera exchanged knowing smiles.

"How did you know you were in love with *Dat*?" Rhoda asked Vera.

Vera smiled. "He was my best friend, and we could talk about anything. I always felt comfortable with him."

"What about you, Mia?" Rhoda asked.

Mia looked out toward the barn, where Chace helped carry another bench inside. "Chace and I clicked the first time we met. He was easy to talk to, and he treated me with respect. I just knew he was the one." She turned toward Rhoda, who grinned. "Make sure Sam treats you well. If he makes you feel bad about yourself, then he's not the one."

"Mia is right," Vera added. "Take your time and get to know him. Marriage is for life."

Rhoda nodded. "I plan to take my time and get to know him. There's no rush."

"That's right," Vera chimed in.

"We should plan a big meal together." Susannah had moved to the doorway where they could see her. "Mia, Chace, and Katie can eat at our *haus*. Maybe we can do that one night next week. What do you think, *Mamm*?"

Vera nodded. "That sounds like a great idea. What do you think, Mia?"

She smiled at Susannah. "We would love to come. What can I make that's easy? I don't want to mess it up."

"You won't mess it up," Vera said.

As Rhoda began discussing the menu for their supper, Mia glanced over at Rhoda and Susannah and smiled. What would it have been like to grow up in a warm, loving family like the Allgyers'?

Then Kaitlyn coughed in Rhoda's arms and Mia frowned.

* * *

Mia held Kaitlyn to her chest as she looked out the window Sunday morning. "Look at all those buggies. Probably two hundred people are sitting in Isaac and Vera's barn for church this morning." The rock driveway and the nearby field were clogged with buggies while horses filled the nearby pasture.

Chace came up behind her and rested his hand on her shoulder. "That's a sea of buggies."

"It is." Mia smiled up at him. "It was nice of you to help Isaac set up the benches yesterday. I heard him tell Vera you were a tremendous help."

He shrugged as he kneaded the knots in her shoulders. "I heard you were helpful inside the house too."

"It was the least I could do." Mia looked out the window again. "I think it's neat how they have church in their barns. It's a lot of work for the family that's hosting the service, but it's also special to share church in your home."

"Yeah, that would be special." Kaitlyn coughed, and

he rubbed the baby's arm. "I told Isaac I would help him load up the benches tomorrow. They aren't permitted to do it today since they don't do even that much work on Sundays."

"That sounds like a great idea." Mia turned toward the sofa. "Why don't you get comfortable and I'll make us hot chocolate. Let's just relax today."

He grinned. "That sounds amazing." He held out his hands and took Kaitlyn. "Let's snuggle, baby girl."

Mia smiled as she walked to the kitchen. She couldn't wait to spend the day with her family.

* * *

Mia sat between Rhoda and Susannah at the Allgyers' kitchen table Tuesday night. Just as Susannah had suggested, they had planned a family dinner, surprising the men when they arrived home from work. Mia smiled across the table at Chace as Joel and Adam shared stories about their day at school.

"How was work today?" Vera asked Isaac when the boys were done talking.

"It was *gut*." Isaac nodded. "Chace is doing fantastic work, and we got a contract for another new *haus*."

"That's great." Mia grinned at Chace.

"Thanks." He shrugged.

"Chace," Mia said, and he looked up at her. "I'm proud of you." Something unreadable flashed across his face.

Katie coughed from the swing they'd brought with them behind Mia, and Mia spun to face her. When

Katie coughed again, Mia pulled her from the swing and held her close to her shoulder.

"Is she okay?" Vera asked.

"I think her cough has gotten worse since the weekend." Kaitlyn coughed again, and Mia stroked her back.

"Do you want me to hold her?" Chace offered.

"No, it's fine. I'll hold her." Mia balanced Kaitlyn with one arm and ate with her free arm.

When supper was over, Chace followed Isaac, Joel, and Adam outside to take care of the animals. Mia strapped Kaitlyn into the swing and helped take the dishes, glasses, and utensils to the counter.

When Kaitlyn became fussy, Susannah rushed over to the swing. "May I change her and give her a bottle?"

"That would be wonderful," Mia said. "Her diaper bag is in the corner."

"Do you need help?" Rhoda offered.

"No." Susannah lifted Kaitlyn into her arms. "You always get to take care of Katie. Now it's my turn."

As Susannah carried Kaitlyn into the family room, Mia placed the platter of leftover chicken and dumplings on the counter and began scooping them into a large container. When she heard Kaitlyn coughing in the family room, Mia stilled, listening to the sound of the cough. Could she possibly have pneumonia?

The coughing stopped, and Mia continued to scoop the food into the container. The worry that had taken hold of her last night resurfaced as she thought about her baby's health. She needed to get Kaitlyn to a doctor. But how would they pay for it? All their credit cards were still maxed and their savings account was bare.

She had applied for medical insurance, but the deductibles were enormous. She was able to get formula and a little bit of food through government assistance, but it didn't cover much—not even diapers. She might be forced to find some cloth diapers and give the wringer washer some extra use.

Mia could ask her parents for help, but she couldn't propose the idea again without hurting Chace. Now he knew the truth about the extent of their rejection. *Still, Mom might be apt to help me if she had a chance to meet Kaitlyn.* She grimaced. She didn't want to hurt Chace, but she had to put her child's needs before hers or her husband's.

"I'm concerned about Kaitlyn. Would you like to try a couple of home remedies I've used for my children?"

Mia looked up at Vera, who was drying a dish as Rhoda washed. "Yes, that would be great."

"After we finish the dishes, I'll give you a few things that should help."

"Thank you." Mia hoped the home remedies would work as she turned her attention back to the leftovers, snapping the lid onto the container. What if the remedies didn't work? Knowing how hurt she'd been when Chace contacted her father without consulting her, she hoped she would never deliberately betray him the same way. But her concern for her child settled onto her shoulders and squeezed at her muscles.

Was Mia denying Kaitlyn the medical attention she needed by not asking her parents for help? The question rocked Mia to the core.

CHAPTER 6

Chace's shoulders slumped, and the weight of his anxiety pressed down on him as he followed Isaac out to the barn later that evening.

"Thank you for your help with the chores," Isaac said.

"You're welcome." Chace shivered and hugged his coat tighter to his chest. "I can't believe it's March already. Our first wedding anniversary is Friday."

Isaac grinned. "That's a special day."

"It is." Chace frowned.

"You have the same expression on your face you had the day you spoke to Mia's *dat*." Isaac leaned against the barn wall. "What's on your mind?"

Chace pursed his lips and glanced toward the house. Peering through the window, he saw Mia sitting at the kitchen table talking with Vera and the girls. "I didn't expect my life to turn out this way."

"What do you mean?"

Chace took a deep breath, preparing to tell Isaac the whole truth about his marriage to Mia. "When I asked Mia to marry me, she was pregnant with our child." He paused, awaiting Isaac's criticism, but instead, Isaac simply nodded. "It wasn't the best situation, but I was already deeply in love with Mia and had planned to ask her to marry me after she graduated from college. Unfortunately, she didn't get to finish. She quit her junior year, and we got married."

Chace leaned against the barn wall beside Isaac and folded his arms over the front of his coat. "I've already told you about Mia's parents. I knew we would have a rough start, but I thought I could provide for Mia and Kaitlyn. I'd hoped we'd have a house by now. At lunch today, I went by the bank to ask for a loan to consolidate all our medical bills and credit card debt, but they turned me down, saying my credit wasn't good enough." He looked up at Isaac. "I don't know how long we're going to be here. I'm just grateful we have a safe place to live."

Isaac patted Chace's shoulder. "You take all the time you need. Vera, the children, and I are enjoying having you all here. You've become like family to us. You just do your best to take care of your family, and it will all come together in God's time. You can't rush God's plan for your life."

Chace nodded as Isaac's words rolled through his mind. He understood Isaac's words—he needed to be patient. He just hoped Mia would be patient too.

* * *

Chace stared down at Kaitlyn in the crib. He reached in and touched her head before tucking the pink quilt around her little body. As he studied his precious baby,

Isaac's words echoed through his mind. He could wait for God's time. He'd found himself praying while he stained a cabinet at work, and he realized Isaac was right. Praying was the best solution. He'd attended church with one of the foster families that had hosted him during his tumultuous childhood, and church had helped him find peace during those tough times. Unfortunately, his time with that family was cut short, and he hadn't attended church since. Would Mia attend church with him? The thought of sitting in church beside her warmed his heart.

The bedroom door opened, and Mia padded into the bedroom, dressed in pink flannel pajamas with matching slipper socks. With a frown twisting her face, she placed the lantern she was holding on the nightstand by her side of the bed and then raised her eyebrows. Half of her attractive face was in shadow and the other half was lit by the soft yellow glow.

She's asleep, he mouthed.

Mia nodded and then climbed into bed, sinking under the mountain of quilts.

Chace kissed the tips of two of his fingers and placed them on Kaitlyn's head before climbing into bed beside Mia. She leaned over and flipped off the lantern. After she was settled, he circled his arms around her small waist and towed her to him in hopes of stealing a kiss. But she kept her back to him, facing the wall. His eyes adjusted to the dark room with only a dim light spilling in between the edge of the green shade and the window casing.

Why had Mia suddenly turned cold toward him?

She'd kissed his cheek when he arrived home from work, and she'd smiled at him from across the table during supper at the Allgyers' house. Her demeanor had changed, however, when they arrived home. She only gave him one-word answers to his questions, and her pretty face was fixed with a permanent frown.

"Is everything all right?" he whispered.

"Yeah." Her voice was muffled by the quilt pulled up to her chin.

Chace longed for Mia to turn toward him and kiss him, but she didn't move. His earlier thoughts about attending church as a family returned, and he opened his mouth to discuss it with her. Before he could share his idea, Kaitlyn coughed, and Mia sat up ramrod straight, worry radiating off her.

When the coughing subsided, Mia lay back down, facing the ceiling. "I'm almost out of the cold medicine I had, but it hasn't helped much anyway." She turned toward him. "I don't want to take the chance that Vera's home remedies won't work. Our baby needs to see a doctor."

Chace's shoulders tightened as frustration washed over him. So this was the source of her aloofness. "Work is getting busier, and my paychecks should improve soon." He reached for her hand, but she pulled it back, the rejection lancing through him. He bit his lower lip in an effort to assuage his temper. "Things are going to get better. It's just going to take some time. We may be here longer than I'd hoped, but you have to trust me. We'll have our own house someday."

"I understand that, but that doesn't help me right now when Kaitlyn needs medical care."

Kaitlyn coughed again, and Mia moved to the crib. Chace scooted to the edge of the bed as Mia leaned in and stroked Kaitlyn's back until the coughing ceased. Then she returned to bed, again facing the wall, and Chace crawled over to her.

"Mee." He touched her arm. "I have a couple of dollars to spare, so I'll pick up cold medicine on my way home from work tomorrow. Just tell me what you want me to get, okay? I don't know what else I can do. Let's try the cold medicine one more time."

"Fine." She pulled the quilt over her shoulder.

Chace rolled onto his back and hoped once again that Mia would have patience with him. And that more of the cold medicine and Vera's home remedies would take care of Kaitlyn's cough.

* * *

Mia kneaded her temple where a headache throbbed as she held a screaming Kaitlyn against her shoulder. Kaitlyn moaned and coughed again, the sound deep and wet in her little chest. The home remedies Vera recommended hadn't helped, and the bottle of cold medicine was empty. Mia touched Kaitlyn's head, now burning with fever. The Tylenol she'd given her had worn off and that bottle was empty too. Panic seized her stomach as she paced back and forth in the tiny kitchen. Kaitlyn had become progressively worse throughout the afternoon and needed a doctor *now*. Mia glanced at the clock on the counter and gritted her teeth. Chace should've been home an hour ago.

Where is he?

Above her, rain pounded on the roof of the cabin and droplets of water sprinkled down through the ceiling, peppering the linoleum floor with small puddles. When a drop of water splashed on her shoulder, Mia shivered, and anger shoved away her panic. She was tired of this cold cabin, tired of running out of food, and tired of not having the money to take care of her daughter the way a mother should.

Mia longed for their tiny apartment, but then a vision of the large house that had protected her during her childhood filled her mind. Didn't Kaitlyn deserve to grow up in a warm, safe home similar to Mia's childhood home? Tears stung Mia's eyes as the pain behind them flared.

Kaitlyn moaned and coughed again, and Mia patted her back.

"It's okay, sweet pea," she whispered, her voice wobbly. "Just hang in there. Mommy will take care of you."

They needed help, but could she risk destroying her relationship with Chace for the sake of their child?

Headlights bathed the family room in a soft yellow glow, and trepidation trickled down Mia's spine. She had to make Chace understand that Kaitlyn was their top priority, even it if meant living on ramen noodles for a few weeks. She couldn't let their baby suffer any longer. Chace was going to take Kaitlyn to the emergency room now or Mia was going to take Kaitlyn to her parents.

Mia's eyes widened and she swallowed a gasp. Was

she going to actually do that? Was she ready to give up on Chace, leave him? Was she going to abandon him the way his father and foster parents had?

Her mouth dried and her hand trembled as she cupped the back of Kaitlyn's head. She closed her eyes and took a deep breath. *Chace, please support my decision to take our baby to a medical facility.*

If Chace didn't agree, Mia hoped she had the courage to do what she needed to do for Kaitlyn.

* * *

Chace sat alone in his truck and studied the tiny cabin in front of him. He blew out a frustrated sigh and tried to muster the emotional strength to thrust himself out of the truck and into his home. Still, he sat glued to the worn and cracked vinyl bench seat.

The old truck's engine rumbled as it idled, a fitting melody to accompany his defeated mood. He'd picked up a few essential groceries along with the new bottle of cold medicine at lunchtime and walked to find one of the truck's rear tires flat. He took the tire to a nearby shop hoping to get it plugged, but it was too far gone for an easy fix. Instead, he had to use the rest of the money in his wallet to buy a tire.

Tomorrow was their first wedding anniversary, and thanks to the new tire, Chace didn't have enough money to buy Mia flowers or even a card. And he wouldn't be able to afford anything from tomorrow's paycheck either. Mia would be crushed, convinced he'd forgotten their special day.

Chace was a failure, just as his foster father Buck had predicted.

Leaning forward, he folded his arms over the steering wheel and rested his forehead against them. The engine continued to rumble, causing the steering wheel to vibrate. After a few moments, his inner voice came to life, elbowing its way through his self-pity.

Get it together, Chace. Be a man. Be a father. Be a husband. Go inside and tell Mia what happened.

After a few moments, he sat up straight, shut off the truck, and gathered up the bags of groceries he'd purchased, the cold medicine inside. Chace stepped into the cabin and came face-to-face with Mia, glaring at him with venom in her dark eyes. Kaitlyn was tucked into Mia's shoulder, moaning and crying between coughs. Chace opened his mouth to ask how Kaitlyn was feeling, but Mia cut him off.

"Where have you been?" She pointed to the clock on the kitchen counter. "It's after seven!"

Whoa. He blinked and clenched his teeth in an attempt to bite back the bitter, defensive words threatening to explode from his lips.

"Were you planning on sitting outside all night?" She nodded toward the front door. "Why did you have to hide in your truck instead of coming in to check on your baby? Did you forget she's been sick?"

Chace pinned his lips together as anger roared through his veins. Unable to trust his mouth with a retort, he marched over to the counter and slammed down the bags of groceries and his truck keys.

Startled, Kaitlyn jumped, and a howl escaped from

her small mouth. Mia hugged her close, whispering something in her ear. Guilt washed over him for a brief moment, but then evaporated when Mia glowered at him.

"Good job," she snapped. "Now she's crying." She walked over to the kitchen area and peered down at the groceries on the counter. "What did you buy? How did we have the money for all this?"

"I only bought the things you mentioned we needed and the cold medicine." He ground out the words as he put a half gallon of milk in the refrigerator. When he turned to face her again, his foot slipped on a small puddle, and he grabbed the edge of the counter, righting himself. He looked up at the ceiling and groaned. "The roof is leaking again?"

"Again?" She gave a harsh laugh. "It never stopped leaking. And it's still cold in here." She lanced him with a furious stare. "I need to take Kaitlyn to a doctor. She's running a fever now, and her cough is worse. She needs medical attention. Did you spend all our money today?"

Chace leaned against the counter and scrubbed his hands down his face. Heat radiated from his cheeks as he scowled at Mia.

"You did!" Mia's voice rose as Kaitlyn screamed, her face as red as a cherry. "You spent all our money without discussing it with me first?"

"Please give me a second to explain," he said, holding his hands up in an effort to calm her. "When I came out of the grocery store, my truck had a flat tire. I tried to get it repaired, but it couldn't be fixed. I had to buy a tire."

"You had to buy a tire?" She waved her free hand in the air. "So our baby needs medical attention and you spend the rest of our money on a tire. That's just fantastic." She spat the words at him and then marched toward the bedroom.

"Mia!" he called, but she kept walking away. "Mia!" He shouted her name louder, and she stopped and spun toward him, her eyes shooting daggers at him. His body shook with raw fury. "I'm sorry I don't work hard enough for you. I'm sorry I don't make enough money to give you the life of privilege you were used to before you got tangled up with me."

She shook her head. "That's not what I—"

"Wait." He held his hand up to silence her, and to his surprise, she complied. "I can't work any harder than I already do. I didn't plan the flat tire, but I convinced Isaac to stay late to finish up a few things so I can make up the tire money in next week's paycheck." He pointed toward the door. "The last thing I wanted to do was spend money on that old truck, but I have to get to work every day so I can bring home money for you and Kaitlyn." He drew in a shaky breath. "I had hoped I could surprise you by getting groceries and still have enough money to buy you flowers and a card for our anniversary tomorrow. But now I can't get you anything."

"You think I'm worried about getting flowers and a card on our anniversary?" Her eyes widened. "If that's what you think, then you don't know me at all. I don't care about anniversary gifts. I just want to take my baby, *our* baby, to a doctor. She's getting sicker, and I'm terrified she has bronchitis or worse." Her eyes shimmered with tears. "I'll eat ramen noodles for a month if that's what it takes to get her to a doctor. You can keep your flowers and card. I care about our child's health."

Chace's eyes narrowed. "So you think I don't care about Katie?"

Mia lifted her chin, her expression obstinate.

Something inside of him broke apart, and Buck's words rang loud and clear in his mind for the second time this evening. The room closed in on him, and he couldn't breathe. He had to get out of that cabin and clear his head before he said something hateful to Mia that he could never take back. He stalked toward the door.

"Where are you going?"

"I need to cool off." As he wrenched the door open, he glanced over his shoulder to Mia holding Kaitlyn against her chest.

Tears streamed down Mia's face. "You're going to just walk away from us?"

"Yeah, I am," he said, his answer seething with sarcasm. "Isn't that what you and your parents expect from me? After all, I'm nothing but a piece of trash from the foster care system. I have no ambition or potential, and I could never measure up to your high-class parents or their friends. You'd have been better off if you'd married the man your parents suggested. He could've bought you a mansion in that swanky Philly neighborhood where your parents live. It would have been an improvement over this life, where you're shackled to me and a life of poverty."

Mia gaped at him as Kaitlyn cried out and then coughed.

With his pulse pounding in his ears, Chace marched out the front door, then slammed it behind him. He shivered in the cold rain and pulled up the hood on his coat as he strode past Isaac's barns toward the large pasture.

Leaning against the wooden fence, he took a deep breath in an effort to placate his shuddering body. He hated himself for spewing those cruel words at Mia before rushing outside. Why couldn't he keep his temper in check? Why did he always have to hurt her?

Chace stared across the dark pasture as ice-cold rain dripped down his face and soaked through his coat. He needed time alone to sort through his confusing emotions. After he calmed down, Chace would have a civil conversation with Mia and work things out with her. He just needed time to figure out how to fix this before it was too late.

* * *

Mia stared at the door, the slam echoing through her mind. She stood frozen in place, waiting for Chace to reappear with an apology and a warm hug, but the door remained closed. Kaitlyn whined and coughed, and the sound propelled Mia into action.

She rushed into the bedroom and changed Kaitlyn's diaper before packing a bag for Kaitlyn and one for herself. After they were bundled up in warm coats, Mia snatched the truck keys from the counter and dashed outside.

She hoped Chace would be waiting for her on the steps, ready to apologize before offering to drive Kaitlyn to the hospital, ready to beg for medical attention even though they had no way to pay for it. But the front steps were empty. Balancing Kaitlyn on her hip and their bags on her opposite shoulder, Mia scanned the area in a desperate search for Chace's tall silhouette in the dark, rainy evening.

When she didn't find him, Mia loaded Kaitlyn into her car seat and set the bags on the truck's passenger side floor. Then she started the engine and steered toward the main road, heading toward Philadelphia and her childhood home.

Mia's stomach roiled as she imagined begging her parents for help. Would Chace ever forgive her? Kaitlyn coughed again, and Mia dismissed her concerns about Chace's feelings. All that mattered right now was Kaitlyn. She just hoped Chace would someday understand her decision to put Kaitlyn before their marriage.

* * *

Chace heard the rumble of his pickup and panic rocked him to his core. *Mia is leaving me! I have to stop her!*

He took off running toward the driveway. Sliding through the mud, he came to a stop at the bottom of the driveway just as the truck bounced onto the main road, accelerating out of his sight.

Reality slammed into him, knocking him to his knees in the muddy, rocky driveway. Chace had finally pushed Mia too far, and now she and Kaitlyn were gone.

What did you expect? You couldn't support them! Mia had no choice but to leave you. She's better off without you!

Tears burned his eyes as he tried in vain to swallow against the messy lump of despair and regret clogging his throat. His world crashed down around him. It was over. He'd lost everything he loved most in this world. He pressed at an ache in the center of his chest and tried to breathe.

Chace buried his face in his hands. He wasn't worthy of Mia or Kaitlyn, and they were better off without him.

But how could he let them go? Mia and Kaitlyn were his reason for living. He was nothing without them by his side.

As he slammed his eyes shut, Isaac's words filtered through his mind like a salve to his tortured heart: *"Trust in God. He is the light of the world, and he will guide you onto the right path if you follow his Word."*

Kneeling on the muddy driveway, Chace opened his heart. *Please, God, bring Mia and Kaitlyn back to me. Please help me be worthy of them. In Jesus' name, amen.*

Then Chace sobbed.

* * *

Mia steered the pickup into her parents' horseshoe-shaped driveway ninety minutes later. Her pulse pounded as she wiped her hands across her cheeks. She'd spent most of the trip crying and whispering to Kaitlyn, promising her they would be okay. But Mia would never be okay without Chace by her side.

She turned the key and the loud engine died, leaving

the cab of the truck silent except for the tapping of the raindrops peppering the windshield. She stared up at the brick mansion, taking in the lighted, manicured landscaping and dozen large windows staring back at her. The oppression that had haunted her when she lived in that house weighed heavily on her, pressing down on her chest.

Mia looked down at Kaitlyn. She resembled a tiny angel as she slept with her pacifier plugging her mouth. Mia couldn't stomach the idea of Kaitlyn living in that same cold, contemptuous house with Mia's mother dictating to Kaitlyn what to wear, whom to choose as friends, and, ultimately, who was worthy of her love. Kaitlyn deserved a home full of love and acceptance, not judgment and price tags.

"What am I doing here?" Mia's heartbeat galloped with anxiety. She had to find help elsewhere. She couldn't run the risk of her mother manipulating her in exchange for monetary assistance.

Kaitlyn coughed, her chest rattling, and Mia turned the key. She pulled out of the driveway and drove down the street, her parents' home fading in the rearview mirror.

When she slowed at a stoplight, Mia's childhood church came into view. She slapped on the blinker and steered into the parking lot, which was half-full with cars for Wednesday night services and committee meetings. Mia parked near the front of the lot and lifted Kaitlyn into her arms, folding a blanket around her. Then she slipped in through the front door of the church, careful not to draw attention to herself.

When she entered the sanctuary, a peace settled over Mia. She glanced around, taking in the large, colorful stained glass cross and the familiar wooden altar. Memories of Easters and Christmases spent sitting between her parents in this holy house filled her mind. She sank into a pew in the back row and held Kaitlyn to her chest as renewed tears threatened to spill. Mia closed her eyes.

God, I'm lost and have no idea where to turn. I'm terrified Kaitlyn's illness is progressing, but I don't know how to find her help. I'm also terrified of losing Chace. The last thing I want to do is break his heart. Everyone he's ever loved has abandoned him. How can I find help for my baby without losing my husband? Please help me, God. Please guide me. Send me a sign. Amen.

Mia hugged Kaitlyn as tears rolled down her cheeks. She kissed the top of her head as silent pleas continued to pour from her heart. Mia's mind was suddenly flooded with images of Chace and Kaitlyn—Chace holding Kaitlyn, hugging her, whispering to her, and watching her with love in his eyes. Kaitlyn needed and deserved both of her parents, but how could they take care of her if they were living in poverty?

"Mia Whitfield? Is that you?"

Stunned, Mia craned her neck over her shoulder to see the church's pastor standing at the back of the sanctuary. "Pastor Deborah?"

Pastor Deborah Morgan approached. "I didn't mean to startle you. I was walking past the sanctuary, and I saw you sitting here alone. May I join you?"

"Yes, of course." Mia scooted over and wiped her tears.

Pastor Deborah was in her midforties and had dark hair and warm brown eyes. She sat beside Mia and peered down at Kaitlyn. "Who is this little cherub?"

"This is Kaitlyn Leanne." She angled the baby toward her. "She just turned six months."

"She's beautiful. May I hold her?"

"Of course." Mia handed Kaitlyn to Pastor Deborah. When Kaitlyn coughed, Pastor Deborah frowned. "Has she been seen for that cough?"

Mia shook her head and sniffed. "My husband and I don't have any health insurance or any money. I live in Bird-in-Hand now, but I came here to ask my parents for help. When I got to their house, I couldn't face them because my mother told me I had to leave my husband before she'd help me." She took a trembling breath in an attempt to calm her frayed nerves. "I didn't tell my husband I was going to see my parents, and he's going to be so upset when he realizes I left. I didn't even think to leave a note. I'm so confused. I don't want to hurt Chace. I just want to be a good mom."

"Slow down." Pastor Deborah touched Mia's shoulder. "Someone here can help. She's in a committee meeting right now. Come with me, and I'll get her for you."

Mia followed Pastor Deborah out to the hallway. Deborah disappeared inside a classroom and then reappeared with someone Mia knew, Dr. Renee Simpson. She was tall with graying brown hair and bright hazel eyes. She wore a fashionable red coat and designer shoes with an expensive designer purse and matching messenger bag slung over her shoulder.

"Mia!" Dr. Simpson hugged her and then looked down at the baby in Pastor Deborah's arms. "Is this your baby?"

Mia nodded. "Yes, she is."

"May I hold her?" Dr. Simpson asked.

Pastor Deborah handed off the baby and then nodded toward an empty classroom. "You can go in there and talk. I need to check on another meeting before I head home."

"Thank you so much, Pastor Deborah." Mia hugged her.

"I'm happy I could help you." Pastor Deborah smiled and then headed down the hallway.

After they sat down at a table in the classroom, Dr. Simpson held Kaitlyn while Mia told her about her situation. Kaitlyn coughed a few times, and Dr. Simpson's brow furrowed.

When Mia finished, Dr. Simpson shook her head. "Why didn't you call me? You know I would see Kaitlyn without charging you."

Mia blinked. That was a valid question. Dr. Simpson had been Mia's pediatrician when she was growing up, but it had never occurred to Mia to ask her to see Kaitlyn.

"I'll listen to her chest right now," Dr. Simpson said. "You can bring her to see me for a follow-up next week."

"Thank you," Mia whispered.

"But first, I want you to tell me what's going on with your parents." Dr. Simpson touched Kaitlyn's arm. "I had no idea you had a baby."

Mia shared everything, beginning when she told her

parents she was pregnant and ending with her trip to their house this evening.

"I've seen your parents occasionally in church during the past several months, but your mother never mentioned your marriage or baby." Dr. Simpson clicked her tongue. "When I ask about you, she gives me a tight smile and says you're fine."

Mia leaned her arm on the table. "I'm not surprised since I'm her biggest disappointment."

Dr. Simpson frowned. "Don't say that. You're doing the best you can." Her expression softened. "Gary and I were broke when we were in medical school at the same time, but we got by. It may seem like the end of the world now, but you and Chace will be fine." She smiled. "Is Chace the handsome man who was with you at your parents' Christmas party two years ago?"

"Yes." The time of that party seemed like a decade ago.

"Gary and I talked to Chace, and we liked him." She looked down at Kaitlyn. "You have two good parents, little girl. You will be just fine." Then she peered up at Mia. "I'm sorry your parents can't see the good in Chace. They're making a huge mistake by not accepting your choices. Your mother has a darling granddaughter right here. I will have to tell her all about her." She nodded toward the messenger bag on the floor. "Would you please open that and hand me my stethoscope? We can do the exam right here."

"Thank you." Mia opened the bag.

Nearly an hour later, Mia stood outside the truck with Dr. Simpson as Kaitlyn lay asleep in her car seat.

"You get the prescription filled right away." Dr. Simpson explained where the closest all-night pharmacy was located. "Do you have money for the prescription?"

Mia shook her head. "No, I don't, but Chace will be paid tomorrow."

"That's not soon enough." Dr. Simpson pulled out her wallet and gave Mia a handful of bills. "I would have given you free samples if we were in my office, but it's late and Kaitlyn needs this medication now. Use what's left for diapers and gas."

Mia stared at the money in her hand. "Dr. Simpson, I can't accept this—"

"Don't be silly." Dr. Simpson waved her off. "Consider it a wedding and baby gift since I wasn't able to celebrate with you. And call me Renee. You're a grown woman now." She wagged a finger at her. "I know it's a long drive, but I want to see Kaitlyn in my office early next week. Call my office and tell the scheduler I'm expecting you, all right?"

"Yes." Mia hugged her. "Thank you so much."

"You're welcome, sweetheart. You'll get through this. Don't give up on Chace. He's a good man. I could tell the minute I met him." She frowned. "And I will talk to your mother when I see her at church." She tapped her pocket where she'd stowed her cell phone. "I'll show her the photos I took of her adorable granddaughter and she'll see how wrong she's been about you and Chace."

Mia held her breath as an unexpected pang of hope filled her. Could Renee be the one to convince her parents to become the loving grandparents Kaitlyn needed and deserved?

Mia tucked that hope deep inside her heart. Then she thanked Renee again before climbing into the truck and heading home to Bird-in-Hand.

* * *

Mia glanced at the clock on the dashboard as she parked the truck in front of the cabin. It was twelve fifteen in the morning—the day of their first wedding anniversary. Her stomach fluttered as she looked up at the cabin. A light glowed in the front windows. Had Chace waited up for her? Would he ever forgive her and understand why she'd driven off without an explanation?

She got out of the truck and went around to the passenger side, then gathered up the bag from the pharmacy on the seat and began working on unhooking Kaitlyn's safety belts.

"Mia?"

She jumped, dropping the bag onto the floorboard of the truck. She spun around and faced her husband. "Chace!" She wrapped her arms around him. "I'm so sorry for not telling you where I went."

"We can talk about it after we get Katie inside." He patted her back. "It's cold out here. Let me pick her up."

"Okay." Mia gathered the bag, jogged up the steps, and held the door open for Chace as he carried Kaitlyn into the cabin. Her eyes widened as she stepped inside. It was warm, toasty warm. She dropped the bag on a kitchen chair and scanned the room. Two quilts were draped over the sofa and lighted candles flickered throughout the family room, giving it a romantic glow.

She crossed to the bedroom doorway as Chace pulled off Kaitlyn's snowsuit. Mia's heart swelled with love and admiration as he kissed Kaitlyn's head before gently tucking her under the blanket in her crib. He was the daddy Kaitlyn needed.

Chace motioned for Mia to walk out to the family room. He closed the door behind him and then raked his fingers through his hair, causing it to stand up in all directions. He was so handsome her breath caught in her throat for a moment.

Mia crossed her arms over her middle as her heart pounded. "Are you ready to talk?"

"Yeah." He pointed toward the sofa. "Let's sit."

She sank onto the sofa and he sat down beside her, draping a large quilt over their laps. "I'm sorry. I shouldn't have run off, but I was afraid Kaitlyn had pneumonia and I panicked. I found out she has bronchitis, and I got her medicine. I have a follow-up appointment next week, and she's going to be just—"

"Mee, wait." He held up his hand. "Start from the beginning." He paused, frowning. "What did your parents say? Are you leaving me to move in with them?"

"My parents?" Mia shook her head. "I didn't see them."

"You didn't?" His frown softened. "But if you didn't see them, how did you see a doctor and pay for the medication?"

Mia explained what happened.

"So you didn't see your parents?"

Mia shook her head, moving closer to him. "No."

"Why not?"

She reached up and touched his face, enjoying the feel of his whiskers. "Because this is my home. This is where my heart is, and this is where Kaitlyn and I belong."

He pulled her into his arms. "I'm so grateful to hear you say that."

"I could never stay away from you," she whispered into his shoulder as she circled her arms around his neck. "Kaitlyn and I need you. I'm so sorry. I had no right to be so cruel to you earlier."

"I'm sorry too." He rested his cheek on the top of her head. "I was so worried when you left. Isaac found me in the driveway and told me to have faith in you. He helped me get the stove working properly. I wanted the place to be inviting when you got home, so I found the candles. This is the best I can do for an anniversary gift this year."

"It's perfect." She smiled up at him. "Everything is perfect if I'm with you."

"I feel the same way." He trailed a finger down her cheek. "What do you think about finding a church to attend as a family?"

"I love that idea." She smiled. "And I love you."

His eyes sparkled in the flicker of the candlelight. "I love you, Mee."

She tilted her head. "How did you know I'd be back?"

"I told you. Isaac told me to have faith in you, and I

do have faith in you. Because I know you. Happy anniversary, babe."

Chace leaned down and brushed his lips against hers. Closing her eyes, Mia lost herself in his kiss and enjoyed the feel of their home sweet home.

DISCUSSION QUESTIONS

1. Mia went against her parents' wishes when she chose to marry Chace. Have you ever felt compelled to go against your family to do something you believed in?

2. The Allgyer family members were like guardian angels to the O'Conner family. Not only did they offer Chace, Mia, and Kaitlyn a safe home, but they also showered them with friendship, food, and baby supplies. Why do you think Isaac and Vera decided to help Chace and his family?

3. Chace suffered with a verbally abusive foster father. Were you ever betrayed by a close friend or loved one? How did you come to grips with that betrayal? Were you able to forgive that person and move on? If so, where did you find the strength to forgive?

4. Mia realized by the end of the story that her home is wherever she, Chace, and Kaitlyn are. What do you think was the catalyst for Mia's change of heart?

5. Which character can you identify with the most? Which character seemed to carry the most emotional stake in the story? Was it Mia or Chace?

6. Mia and Chace were down on their luck when they moved into the *daadihaus* on the Allgyers' farm. Think of a time when you felt lost and alone. Where did you find your strength? What Bible verses would help with this?

7. What do you think inspired Dr. Simpson to help Mia and Kaitlyn? Have you ever helped someone in need? If so, how did you feel after you helped that person?

8. By the end of the story, both Chace and Mia found solace through prayer and they decided to find a church to attend. Think of a time when you found strength through prayer. Share this with the group.

9. What did you know about the Amish before reading this book? What did you learn?

A Christmas Visitor

Kelly Irvin

*To my husband, Tim. I consider every day with
you in my life a gift from God. Love always.*

Glossary of Pennsylvania Dutch Words Used in Bee County, Texas

aenti—aunt
Ausbund—hymnal
boplin—baby
bruder—brother
daed—dad
danki—thank you
Deutsch—Pennsylvania Dutch
dochder—daughter
Englisch—English
Englischer—a non-Amish person
fraa—wife
galluses—suspenders
Gelassenheit—yielding to God's will and forsaking
  selfishness
Gott—God
groossmammi—grandmother
jah—yes

kaffi—coffee
kapp—white head covering
kinner—children
mann—man
mudder—mother
nee—no
onkel—uncle
Ordnung—the written and unwritten rules that guide
the Amish way of life
rumspringa—the running-around period
schtinkich—stink

CHAPTER 1

They meant well. All of them. Frannie Mast ladled another spoonful of steaming okra gumbo into her bowl. The spicy aroma tickling her nose did nothing to calm the willies in her stomach. She couldn't help herself, her gaze wandered down the crowded table past *Aenti* Abigail and her self-satisfied smile to Joseph Glick sitting on the other side with Caleb and her cousins. A giggle burbled in her throat. *Stop it. Be kind.* Did Joseph know he had a smear of butter on his upper lip? Did he know her aunt and uncle were doing a little matchmaking? Not that they would admit it. Plain boys and girls were to find their own mates during their *rumspringas* with no interference from their elders.

Apparently her situation had been deemed an exception to the rule.

Joseph flashed Frannie a smile. A chunk of venison had found a home in a gap between his lower front teeth. She suppressed a sigh and forced a smile. None of this could be construed as his fault. She remembered Joseph from school. He had been a so-so student, but a good softball player and a hard worker. He was easy to look at, with toast-colored hair, green eyes, and tanned skin. He was also the third single man *Aenti* Abigail and *Onkel* Mordecai had invited to supper since her return to Bee County, Texas, three weeks earlier.

It seemed more like two years had passed since her arrival in her childhood community after three years in Missouri.

They meant well, but what were they thinking? Joseph was Leroy Glick's son. Leroy, the bishop. Did they think Joseph would keep an eye on her, too, and report back to his father and to Mordecai, the district's deacon? Would he keep her from going astray?

She wouldn't do that. If they'd give her half a chance, she'd show them.

A fierce burning sensation assailed Frannie's fingers. She glanced down. Gumbo dripped on her hand. The burning blush scurrying across her face had nothing to do with the soup's heat. She dropped the ladle and grabbed her napkin, attempting to wipe the hot liquid from her fingers.

"Ouch!" She stood. Her pine chair rocked on spindly legs, then tumbled back. "Sorry. I'm sorry."

"Child, you're always spilling something." *Aenti* Abigail's fierce blue eyes matched the frown lurking below her high cheekbones and long, thin nose. "Get it cleaned up."

"It's fine. No harm done." Deborah King leaned over and wiped up the soup with her own napkin. Something in her tone reminded Frannie of the way her favorite cousin talked to her two-year-old son, Timothy. "Stick it in some water."

"Rub some butter on it. It stops the sting and helps it heal." Joseph held out the saucer with the puddle of half-melted butter that remained, still unaware it seemed of the smear on his own lip. He grinned. The venison hadn't dislodged from his teeth. "That's what my *groossmammi* used to say."

"Old wives' tale." *Onkel* Mordecai shook his head. His shaggy black beard, streaked with silver, bobbed. Mordecai mostly knew everything. "Water is best since we have no ice. Go on to the kitchen then."

Relief washed over Frannie. Escape. She whirled, stumbled over a chair leg, righted herself, and rushed into the kitchen. A tub of water sat on the counter in anticipation of the dirty dishes. She shoved her hand into it, barely aware of the stinging skin on her fingers. Gumbo stained her apron. Tomato juice from the canning frolic earlier in the day provided background color. Without looking, she knew sweat stains adorned the neck of her gray dress, like jewelry she would never wear. She was a mess as usual.

Why did *Aenti* Abigail insist on having gumbo in this weather? Something about soup cooling a person off because it caused him to sweat. This had to be an *Onkel* Mordecai theory. He had tons of them, each stranger or funnier or more interesting than the last. At least life with him would not be boring. Which was good, because Frannie likely would spend the rest of her life in his house if she behaved like that in front of every man in the district. She wanted to marry and have babies like her cousins and her friends. Like every Plain woman.

Why did that seem so hard for her?

She swished both hands in the lukewarm water and stared out the window at the brown grass, wiry mesquite, live oak trees, and a huge cluster of nopals. No breeze flapped the frayed white curtains. September weather in Bee County hadn't changed, just as nothing else had. No one who grew up here minded hot weather. They embraced it. Still, Frannie would savor her memories of evenings in Missouri this time of year. The air steamed with heat and humidity, but huge elm, oak, hickory, and red mulberry trees populated the countryside. A breeze often kicked up the leaves in the evening hours, making it a perfect time to sit in the lawn chairs and watch the sun dip below the horizon.

Nee, she wouldn't think of that. Thinking of those long summer nights made her think of him.

Rocky.

She swallowed hard against tears that surprised her. Rocky was only a friend. He couldn't be any more than that. Not for a faithful Plain woman such as herself. She understood what that meant even if her parents didn't trust her to make the right choices.

Gott, help me be good.

"Frannie, come out here."

Clear notes of disapproval danced with surprise in *Onkel* Mordecai's gruff voice. What had she done now? Drying her hands on a dish towel, Frannie trudged from the kitchen to the front room where her family sat, scrunched together like peas in long pods at two rough-hewn pine tables shoved together. No one looked at her when she entered the room. They all sat, not moving, staring toward the door as if mesmerized by a hideous rattlesnake coiled and ready to strike a venomous blow.

She plowed to a stop.

Nee. It couldn't be.

CHAPTER 2

Frannie managed to clamp her mouth shut without biting her tongue. All six foot two, two hundred pounds of muscle known as Richard "Rocky" Sanders towered in the doorway. He waved his St. Louis Cardinals ball cap at her with a hand the size of a feed bucket. Acutely aware of the gazes of a dozen pairs of eyes drilling her in the back, Frannie waved a tiny half wave. Her burned fingers complained.

Rocky cleared his throat and shuffled work boots in the size-fourteen range. "Hey, Frannie."

"Hey." Her voice came out in an unfamiliar squeak that reminded her of the stray cat out by the shed when she fed him table scraps and accidentally stepped on his tail. A drop of sweat ran down her nose and dripped onto her upper lip. She fought the urge to scratch the spot. "Rocky."

No one spoke for several long seconds. Rocky shifted his feet again. His dark brown almost black curls hung damp around his ears. His blue eyes, so like the color of Missouri sky in summer, implored her. She took another step forward.

"Introduce your guest, Frannie." *Onkel* Mordecai's

disapproval had been displaced by the politeness they all were taught from childhood to show guests. "Invite him in."

"This here's Rocky Sanders from Jamesport. I . . . knew him up yonder." Frannie couldn't help herself. She glanced at Joseph. He studied his bowl as if gumbo were the most interesting food he'd ever tasted. "He used to come into the restaurant where I was a waitress."

She kept to herself the longer version, how Rocky began to make an appearance at Callie's Restaurant and Bakery two or three times a week. How he left big tips on small meals and complimented the food as if she'd cooked it herself. How he showed up at the school fund-raiser on July Fourth and spent too much on a treadle sewing machine he said his mother wanted to use as a "conversation piece" in their living room. Her throat tightened at the memories. *Breathe.*

Mordecai nodded. "We're having gumbo if you want to pull up a seat."

"No, no, I can see you're having dinner. I don't want to barge in on you." Rocky edged toward the door, but his gaze remained on Frannie. "I'm sorry to drop in without letting you know I was coming. Being you don't have a phone—not that there's anything wrong with that. No calls from those pesky salespeople at dinnertime. I was . . . in the neighborhood."

After that preposterous statement, he tugged a red bandanna from the back pocket of his faded blue jeans and swiped the sweat dampening his face. "Begging your pardon, but could I have a quick word with your niece . . . on the porch? I won't keep her long."

Frannie's breathing did that same strange disappearing act it did when she jumped into the cold water at Choke Canyon Lake. She dared to hazard a glance at *Aenti* Abigail. Her lips were drawn down so far it was a wonder they didn't fall from her face onto the planks of the wood floor. The blue-green of *Onkel* Mordecai's eyes had turned frosty. "Go on, but make it quick. There's dishes to wash and chores to do."

Frannie whipped past Rocky, catching the familiar, inviting scent of his woodsy aftershave and Irish Spring soap—what she'd come to think of as Rocky smell—as she opened the screen door and led the way outside. To her relief he followed without another word. On the porch, she drank in the sight of him, now that they had no audience. Same tanned face, same little scar on his chin where he fell from a swing in the second grade, same little twist to his nose where he took a punch in a boxing match. "What are you doing here?"

The words sounded inhospitable. She wanted them back as soon as they fell on the early-evening air. Rocky's smile faded. His Adam's apple bobbed. He ducked his head and smoothed the cap in his hands. "Like I told you before, I have a bit of a wanderlust. You talked about this place so much, I figured I'd come see it for myself."

A wisp of disappointment curled itself around the relief that rolled over her. He simply wanted to travel. He knew her so he stopped by. Like stopping by Bee County in the far reaches of south Texas was an easy feat. Most folks couldn't find it with a map. "Are you staying long in the area—*where* are you staying?"

"I just got here." An emotion Frannie recognized—disappointment—soaked the words. "You want me to leave?"

Nee. *Not at all. Stay. Please stay.* She swallowed the words before they could spring forward and betray her. "It's just . . . surprising."

"My Uncle Richard passed."

"Oh, Rocky." With no thought for appearances, Frannie touched his hand. Richard had been the only true father Rocky had ever known. His eyes blazed with sudden emotion as his long fingers turned and wrapped around hers. His strong grip seemed to embrace her. A slow heat warmed her from head to toe. "I'm so sorry. What happened?"

"Heart attack. Sudden. He left me a small nest egg."

She itched to give this bear of a man the hug he deserved. That he needed. She kept her gaze on their entwined hands. "That was nice of him."

"He was a nice man. He was a good man." Rocky's voice had a sandpaper roughness about it she'd never heard before. "Anyway, he gave me the chance to have a fresh start if I want."

The last sentence seemed more of a question than a statement. A fresh start. Was Bee County his fresh start? Was Frannie his fresh start?

The screen door slammed. Frannie tugged her hand back, fingers burning worse than when she'd spilled the gumbo. Joseph clomped past them, a painful smile plastered across his face. "Mordecai said to tell you there's plenty of leftovers if your friend has a hankering." He tossed the words over his shoulder without looking back. "I'm headed home. Chores won't wait. I imagine those dishes won't either."

"Be safe." Now what a thing to say. Like Joseph couldn't take care of himself. Like he hadn't grown up with the javelinas, the bobcats, the rattlesnakes, and the occasional escapee from the prison outside Beeville. "Bye."

"You too." This time Joseph looked back. His gaze skittered from Frannie to Rocky. "You never know where danger lurks."

CHAPTER 3

Rocky smoothed the folds in the tattered road map. He'd found the King farm once, he could do it again. Even though it had been by sheer beginner's luck the first time. He would find it and he would take Frannie for a ride, like he'd done in Jamesport. He liked the idea of shining a flashlight in her window. It was sweet, like Frannie. Her uncle might be stern-looking, but he was a pacifist. All the Amish were. Frannie had assured him of that the first time he picked her up for a ride after her parents went to bed that momentous evening six months earlier. The night he'd fallen in love.

Best get to it or she'd be asleep. He studied the map. His scribbles on the margins had been gathered from a convenience-store clerk, a guy at the Dairy Queen, and the librarian in Beeville. Did the Bee County Amish District go out of its way not to be found? Surely not, considering their store, the honey sales, horse training, and saddle-making businesses. They needed outsiders to survive. What Rocky needed was a GPS. He patted the steering wheel as if the old Dodge Ram with a hundred-fifty thousand miles on its odometer had heard the traitorous thought and taken umbrage.

"We made it this far, we're doing fine," he muttered. To himself, not the truck. He'd replaced the battery in Oklahoma City and the water pump outside Dallas. Blown a tire in Killeen. What else could go wrong? "We should hold off a day or two anyway, let them get used to the idea."

Let Frannie get used to the idea. She'd looked as surprised and horrified as her family at his sudden appearance. Her relief had been abundantly clear when he'd taken his leave of the porch shortly after the surly-looking man named Joseph the previous evening. Somehow he'd seen their reunion going differently than that. Her face would light up with that trademark Frannie Mast grin that spread across her face so wide her freckles nearly popped off her nose and cheeks. She'd run to meet him like those cheesy commercials on TV.

They'd kiss.

As if they'd done that before. He respected the line Frannie had drawn, even if he longed for so much more. He'd settle for a handshake at this point.

Frannie wasn't a beauty by most standards. Rocky's friends went so far as to call her scrawny when he announced his plans to follow her to Texas. They pointed out he'd never seen her legs, what with the long skirt, or her hair, hidden under that cap, even on the hottest day of the year. He liked her modesty and the thought that she guarded those secrets for the one she would love for the rest of her life. In his eyes, her beauty was unquestionable. The south Texas drawl with the strange German—*Deutsch* words, as she called them—sprinkled in. From the prayer *kapp* setting askew on hair the color of carrots to the sea of freckles to the black sneakers she wore everywhere, even to church, she captivated him. Even with tomato stains on her apron and sweat on her dress.

And she had feelings for him. He had no doubt of that. No matter what lines she drew or how she'd acted the evening before. No waiting. Time to put up or shut up. He shoved his hat back on his head, turned the key in the ignition, and pulled out from the motel where, in a moment of eternal optimism, he'd plopped down a month's worth of rent up front. It took a chunk from his nest egg. He'd have to find a job soon or stick to eating ramen noodles like he had during his college days.

Thirty minutes later he saw the SUPPORT BEEVILLE BEES, BUY LOCAL HONEY sign on Tynan Road. *Score.* Three minutes later, the Combination Store, a long, dirty white building with rusted siding and a tin roof, came into sight with its adjacent junk graveyard of buggy parts and farm equipment. They weren't much for sprucing up around here.

Close. He was very close. The King farm was a few miles from here. The sun had begun its descent in the western sky. That would make it harder to find the turnoff. Maybe someone at the store could point him in the right direction for one last turn.

Likely the store was closed. Still, a wagon with a weary-looking Morgan hitched to it stood near the door alongside a shabby black buggy that sported an orange triangle dangling from the back along with a FOR SALE sign. It couldn't hurt to try.

Rocky hopped from the truck and strode to the door. To his relief it opened. After a few seconds his eyes adjusted to the dusky interior. Jars of honey, baskets of fresh produce, stacks of straw hats, candles, cookbooks, a quilt, dusty saddles, a couple of handmade rocking chairs, even lip balm made from beeswax. A veritable collection of unrelated stuff. No customers perused the aisles. Nor a salesman.

Someone had to be here. "Hello?" His voice sounded weak in his own ears. "Hello, anyone here?"

A man nearly Rocky's height, beginning to stoop with age in his broad shoulders, strode through a door behind a streaked glass counter. His long beard was snow white. That and the round, wire-rimmed glasses made him a Santa Claus look-alike, or it would have if the beard hadn't lacked a mustache. "Hello yourself. I'm closed. Just doing some recordkeeping. What can I do you for?"

"I was wanting some directions to the King farm. I found it yesterday, but I think it was beginner's luck. I think I've gotten turned around or something."

"Mordecai or Phineas?"

"Pardon me?"

"We have father and son Kings in these parts."

Of course. When Frannie spoke of her favorite cousin, Deborah, she'd also mentioned her husband, Phineas, the younger part of the beekeeping father-and-son duo who tended an apiary of more than three hundred hives in this small patch of south Texas. "Mordecai."

The man's genial smile disappeared. His wrinkled

hands dotted with brown age spots grasped at suspenders as his steely-blue eyes did a once-over that left Rocky feeling as if he'd just been thoroughly frisked. "You must be Frannie's Rocky."

Frannie's Rocky. The words had a sweet ring to them. He'd like to be Frannie's Rocky. He swallowed. "So to speak, sir."

"No need to 'sir' me. The name's Leroy."

Leroy. Rocky did a quick check on his mental Rolodex. *Leroy. Leroy Glick.* Frannie had mentioned him during her rambling explanation of the Amish faith and how their communities were structured.

The bishop.

Lord, have mercy or shoot me now and put me out of misery.

"It's good to meet you, sir, I mean Leroy. You're the bishop."

"I am. Among other things. I reckon Frannie explained what that means."

Rocky slipped his ball cap from his head and fanned his face. Sweat slid between his shoulder blades and dampened the back of his best checkered, western-style shirt with its pearl-covered snaps. So much for looking fresh when he visited with Frannie. *God, don't let my deodorant fail.* His mama's preacher said a person could take everything to the good Lord in prayer. Surely he knew what he was talking about. "You make the rules."

Leroy shook his head, causing his beard to sway ever so slightly. "The district makes the rules. The *Ordnung.* We all meet twice a year and decide on them, whether they need changing. I help make sure folks follow the rules."

"Right."

"Frannie's on her *rumspringa*. You know what that is?"

"Yes, sir—I mean, yes, she explained the running-around thing."

"She explain how she has this time to find a proper husband, then she has to decide if she wants to join the church and be Plain for the rest of her life?"

She did. When she told Rocky she could never yoke herself to an English man. That's what she called him. An English man. Now it didn't seem so funny. "I know that."

"Then you know coming here isn't helping her. If you care for her, you'll go on home."

Rocky thought about moving closer to the counter. His feet seemed stuck to the rug in front of the door. "I didn't come just for Frannie."

Leroy's expression could only be described as skeptical. He leaned forward and planted his elbows on the counter. "We have a phone there in the back. The only one in the district. It's for business and emergencies." He cocked his head toward the door through which he had appeared. "Frannie's *mudder* and *daed* call me every day to see how their *dochder* is. They think this is an emergency. They sent her here to get her away from you. You know that. Yet, here you are."

"I know that's how it looks."

"Then most likely that's how it is."

How could he explain? Yes, all he could think of every night when he laid his head on his pillow was

Frannie. Her image danced in his mind's eye, and he fell asleep imagining what their life could be like if it weren't for this one thing that separated them. This one big thing.

He went to church every Sunday morning. He slapped a twenty in the basket when it came down his row. All the while wondering how they could talk about this God as the Father, *Abba*. His own experience with fathers hadn't amounted to much. The man left his mama—and his ten-year-old son—for the daughter of the feed-store owner. So Rocky bowed to Mama's demands that he attend church. Then he went home and inhaled her fried chicken, mashed potatoes, gravy, and biscuits, determined not to give the Father thing another thought. His emptiness had been filled by college, coaching, and by helping his uncle. Now Uncle Richard was gone too. "I came to see what all the fuss is about."

"Fuss?" Leroy straightened, his white caterpillar eyebrows doing a quick push-up. "If you don't know what the fuss is about, you truly don't belong here. You'll only cause her heartache."

"I want to know. Isn't that worth something? I came all this way to find out . . ." He didn't know Leroy well enough to explain his reservations, so he stopped. Forcing himself to move, he trudged to the first aisle and picked up a large jar of honey the color of amber. It had a bit of honeycomb in it. "The honey looks good. I'll take a jar of it."

He turned and strode to the counter, jar in one hand, the other reaching for the billfold in his back pocket.

"It's on the house." Leroy waved one hand, his expression dismissive. "Consider it a going-away gift."

Rocky was not a quitter. "How do I get to Mordecai's farm?"

Leroy walked around the counter, his work boots making a *thump-thump* sound. He tapped the glass in the door. "Head east and make a right turn at the first four-way stop. Follow the dirt road." He let his hand drop and turned to face Rocky. "What kind of name is Rocky?"

"I'm named for my Uncle Richard. He was a professional boxer." He let his voice trail away. Leroy would never understand. Not having a father who stuck around, Rocky had treasured his relationship with his uncle. "He went by Rocky in the ring. So did I."

"You hit people for money?"

"No, I was an amateur." The words caused a fiery burn to engulf Rocky's face. He shuffled his feet, working to keep emotion from his voice. "But my uncle did. That's how he helped my mom out and raised me, so I don't turn up my nose at what he did for his family. After he retired, he went back to farming. I helped him—until recently."

"Reckon you got a point there." Leroy's tone was a tad more conciliatory. "So you're a farmer."

"I'm a high school coach now. My mom sold our acreage after my dad left us." At least Rocky would've been if he'd signed the new contract offered by the school district instead of coming to Texas. Somehow the idea of coaching his own basketball and baseball teams at a small Missouri high school didn't light a fire under him the way it had all through college. "I liked helping my uncle whenever I could. It felt good to be outside working the land."

The older man pursed his thin lips, his expression grim. The silence held for a good ninety seconds. "You want to know what the fuss is about? Come see for yourself. Church is at my place Sunday morning in two weeks. Three hours. In German. You'll see and then you'll go. In the meantime, give Frannie a wide berth."

Leroy Glick did not know Rocky. He only needed a foot in the door. After a quick thanks, Rocky shut the store door behind him, pumped his fist, and whispered, "Yes." He almost ran to the truck, whistling under his breath.

All he needed was a foot in the door.

CHAPTER 4

Frannie stared at the bedroom ceiling. As it had so many nights since her return to Bee County, sleep eluded her. The sweltering heat, *Aenti* Abigail's constant vigilance, the curious side glances of her cousins, the feeling that something was about to happen over which she had no control—all these things conspired to keep her eyes open and her stomach swirling with a mixture of excitement and dread that seemed to be trying to outdo each other. Sweat trickled from her temple into her hair and tickled her ear. Desperate for a breath of air, she eased from the bed, careful not to rock the thin mattress laid over a box spring that squeaked worse than a herd of mice. Hazel muttered in her sleep, turned over, and smacked Rebekah with her chubby hand. Rebekah shushed her sister without opening her eyes.

Holding her breath, Frannie waited for her cousins to settle, then tiptoed to the room's only window. No breeze stirred the tattered white curtains. Sounds were muted and distant. The sad coo of a mourning dove carried in the still night air. A barn owl hooted. A dog barked. An eighteen-wheeler changed gears on the highway. A multitude of stars lit the cloudless sky. *Gott, what is the plan? Why do I feel this way? Like I have a hole in my heart the size of Texas only Rocky can fill? I know it's wrong. I want to do the right thing. Help me do the right thing. Send Rocky home. Thy will be done.*

Tears formed. She forced them back. To never see Rocky again. The ache where her heart should be took her breath. God's plan surely did not include an *Englisch* man. Doing the right thing wasn't always easy. *Daed* taught her that. The memory of her parents' anxious faces as *Daed* handed the ticket to the Greyhound bus driver kept her company every day. *Daed* had clapped his arms around her in a rib-crushing hug. She couldn't remember him hugging her since she was old enough to sit on his roomy lap and braid his beard. *I'm trying,* Daed. *I'm trying not to disappoint you.*

How Rocky must've hurt when his *onkel* passed. He would've been so heartbroken. The little boy who needed a father would still be heartbroken. She peered up at the stars, seeking the constellations her *daed* had pointed out to her on the long evenings under the Missouri sky. *Let Rocky find peace and comfort even if it doesn't come from me. Give me the strength to do Your will.*

The unmistakable *clip-clop* of horse's hooves thudding against sun-hardened dirt rang in the distance. Who would arrive at the King house at this late hour? Everyone slept. Except her. A suitor for Rebekah? It seemed unlikely. Abigail employed the same vigilance over her third daughter as she did Frannie, given cousin Leila's decision to leave the district to marry outside her faith.

The buggy came into sight. The darkness hid the driver. The buggy stopped and a shadowy figure hopped out. Butch barked once, twice, then stopped. The dog always welcomed folks he knew. A minute later the flashlight's beam bounced and found her second-story window. She shaded her eyes and forced herself to keep her voice down. "Who is it?"

"Who were you expecting?"

Joseph.

Frannie drew back from the window, suddenly aware of her thin nightgown. "It's late. Why are you here?"

"I reckon that's obvious." His hoarse whisper mingled with the night sounds. "Come down. We'll take a ride."

Gott's answer to her prayer? The tightness in her throat told Frannie it wasn't the answer for which she'd hoped. A person didn't always get the answer she wanted. *Gott's* plan was bigger than her. She swallowed the lump. So be it. She dressed quickly in the dark, comforted by the steady breathing of her two cousins. Sneakers in her hand, she padded barefoot from the bedroom, down the stairs, and out to the porch where Joseph sat on the steps, one hand scratching Butch's bony back, staring at the sky as she had done only minutes earlier. Butch, with his black patch of fur around one eye that made him look like a pirate, scrambled to greet her, tail wagging. "No barking, Butch. You'll wake *Onkel* Mordecai and he needs his rest."

"He's a good watchdog." Joseph waited while she tugged on her shoes and then stood. "It'll be cooler in the buggy. We'll whip up a breeze."

Something about his clear assumption that she would

go with him irked her. *Aenti* Abigail's stern face loomed in her mind's eye followed by *Mudder's* worried one. "Sounds good."

She lifted her chin and offered him her hand to help her up. His fingers were warm and damp. When he trotted around to the other side, she wiped her hand on her dress. She couldn't blame him. Hers was surely damp too.

"Here we go." Joseph clucked and snapped the reins. The buggy jolted forward. "So, I reckon you were expecting your *Englisch* man."

"Rocky doesn't drive a buggy." Nor was he her *Englisch* man.

"True."

How so much could be said with one word amazed Frannie. "Is that what you came out here to talk to me about? If it is, you should get on home because I get plenty of that from *Aenti* Abigail."

"*Nee.*" He paused. The pause grew and grew. Joseph snapped the reins again. The buggy picked up speed. "I heard you might help out at the school, now that you're back."

As good a topic as any. She wouldn't think of the silly jokes and funny stories with which Rocky regaled her about his childhood with a boxing farmer uncle. He knew how to laugh despite the sadness that lurked behind those enormous blue eyes. "My aunt's idea. Susan has been doing it for years. She doesn't need help. And if she does, Rebekah fills in." *Aenti* Abigail didn't need Frannie's help either. She had Hazel to help with cooking and cleaning. Frannie's role remained to be seen in this tiny district with only a handful of young single men, most of whom had already set their sights on their future *fraas*. "I worked as a waitress in Jamesport. The money helped out a lot. I liked it."

"Ain't likely *Daed* will allow that, after what happened with my brother and Leila. No one is working in town anymore."

His tone was matter of fact, but losing a *bruder* to the outside world surely caused Joseph pain. Leila and Jesse had left the district so Jesse could be a minister and they could practice a different form of faith. Frannie often caught sadness settling on her aunt's face in the midst of baking a pie or canning or washing clothes. She never wanted to cause such pain for her own *mudder*. Surely Joseph, having lost a *bruder*, felt the same about his *mudder* and *daed*. "That's understandable. What about you? Working in your *daed's* store then?"

"*Nee*. My cousin Will does most of that. I'm helping *Daed* break horses and build buggies. I like being outdoors more. I don't abide with spending time with the *Englisch* folks who come into the store itching to take pictures and wanting to know why we don't have more quilts for sale."

The disdain in his voice made Frannie squirm. She'd enjoyed working as a waitress. Maybe too much. Rocky's visits became the highlight of her days even as she knew they could lead nowhere. The other *Englisch* folks might have been curious, but they tipped generously, and their questions were born of a desire to know and understand. Most showed the courtesy of waiting until she turned away to snap a photo. "It will all work out for the best, I reckon."

"There's been lots of talking. Working at the school would shut the grapevine down."

Undoubtedly. "Folks should mind their own p's and q's."

"That's for certain."

"I came back to Bee County to honor my parents' wishes."

"*Jah*, but the look on your face yesterday when that *Englischer* showed up said it all."

"You're wrong." *Nee*, he surely wasn't. "Then why did you come to fetch me tonight?"

A molted red crept across his whiskerless cheeks. "Your *aenti* Abigail . . . she made it sound like you might have an interest. I realize now that was her way of steering you from your *Englisch* man. "

Heat burned Frannie's face. She hadn't known until right this moment of Joseph's feelings. "Rocky's not my *Englisch* man."

Joseph cleared his throat. "Remember school? You learned *Englisch* faster than any of the rest of us, and you were the best at kickball and volleyball—for a girl."

"I was okay. No better or worse than the rest." Surely he thought of how *Englisch* would be helpful if she courted an *Englisch* man. "Anyway, not skills likely to help me be a good *fraa* and *mudder* now."

"Maybe, maybe not."

Nothing to say to that. Silence again.

Twin bright lights lightened the darkness on the road ahead, blinding Frannie. The deep rumble of an engine filled the air. A truck engine. The horse whinnied, an uneasy sound that matched the feeling in the pit of Frannie's stomach. She recognized that rumble. She'd spent more than her share of evenings in that truck, rambling on about her family and her faith and trying to make a man understand why Amish didn't mix with *Englisch*.

A man trying to rebuild a faith shattered by circumstances beyond a young boy's control. Could Leroy understand such a situation? Surely *Onkel* Mordecai could after losing his first wife in a van accident that scarred his son for life. Frannie understood it, and the worst thing that had ever happened to her was the loss of their house and everything down to their last bit of clothing in a fire caused by a lightning strike. Life was hard. People like Rocky deserved a chance.

She shouldn't be sitting next to Joseph and thinking about Rocky.

Illuminated in the buggy's battery-operated lights, the black-and-silver truck drew even with them. The driver's-side window was down. The AC must be out again. His expression hidden in the shadows, Rocky waved and gunned the engine. The truck rocketed past them. Exhaust fumes filled the night air, a *schtinkich* that reminded Frannie of the enormous chasm that existed between her buggy-paced world and the man driving the truck.

As if she didn't already know. *No need to rub it in,* Gott.

Joseph jerked on the reins as if to stop the buggy.

"*Nee, nee,* keep going." Frannie stuck her hand on the reins. He couldn't stop. Nothing good would come of it. "Don't stop."

Joseph pushed her hand away, a gentle, warning motion. "Are you sure?"

Nee.

"*Jah.* Very sure." She took a deep breath and focused on the road ahead. Joseph had come for her. She owed him the courtesy of paying attention to his conversation. "Breaking horses must get exciting. Ever had one throw you?"

* * *

Murphy's Law. Rocky glanced at the dashboard and groaned. The CHECK ENGINE light shone brilliantly in the dark, like a big stop sign. A headache gathered strength behind his temples. He should turn the truck around and head to Beeville now. That way he'd be close to an auto repair store and mechanic's shop come daylight. The engine temperature continued to climb. No sense driving on to Mordecai's house.

Rocky knew all this, but he couldn't help himself. If he turned around now, he would simply overtake the buggy and then have to pass them again. To see Frannie in there with that Amish man, snug as a bug. He knew all about the courting rituals. He'd shared them with Frannie while her parents—her *mudder* and *daed*—had slept blissfully unaware. The *mudder* and *daed*. She laughed at how he pronounced the *Deutsch* words.

No one laughed now. Rocky rolled in to the Kings' front yard with its withered grass and weeds trying valiantly to survive in a sea of brown dirt. He switched off the lights and the truck. His hands gripped the wheel until his fingers hurt. He forced himself to ease his grip. *No. No.* He smacked his fist on the wheel. "Ouch."

He needed to do a hundred push-ups, fifty sit-ups, then run ten miles. Maybe then the ache in his chest would ease enough to allow him to turn around and drive home. All the way to Missouri.

The silence pressed on him. He'd driven nearly a thousand miles and almost twenty hours with stops for repairs to get to Bee County. And for what? Thinking that for once God would answer his prayers. He hadn't brought Rocky's dad back. He hadn't saved Uncle Richard. What made him think God would see fit to give him this happiness?

"Who's out there?" A light blinded Rocky, then danced away. A flashlight. "I said, who's there?"

Had to be Mordecai. Rocky took a breath and pushed his door open. "Me. Rocky. Rocky Sanders."

Mordecai lowered the flashlight. As his eyes adjusted to the dark, Rocky could see that the tall, muscle-bound man seemingly unfazed by middle age stood on the porch, his shirttail out, no suspenders, head and feet bare. His hair, usually covered by a straw hat, looked like he'd stuck his finger into an electric socket. If he had one. Most days, Rocky could say the same about his own. "Figured as much."

"Sorry. I didn't mean to wake you."

"I keep telling my *fraa*—my wife—that it's none of our business." He moved down the steps, his bare feet slapping on the wood. "*Rumspringa* and all."

"Nothing to worry about. Your wife—your *fraa*—will

be pleased to know I just saw Frannie on the road in a buggy with that Amish man who was eating dinner with you last night."

"That would be Joseph." Mordecai sniffed. "That was Abigail's idea. We don't abide much by matchmaking."

Rocky leaned against the truck's bumper. His legs waffled under him. An exhaustion the likes of which he'd never experienced before invaded his muscles, head to toe. The hood steamed against the back of his shirt. A faint burned smell wafted around him. "Why not?"

"Because *Gott* knows what's best for each one of us. He'll provide. He has a plan. We need only obey and try to stay out of His way."

"You really believe that?"

"I do."

"Your bishop is allowing me to come to church next service. He thinks once I see how you worship, I'll get the picture and leave."

If this news surprised Mordecai, Rocky couldn't tell in the darkness. The man plopped down on the step and leaned back on his elbows as if it weren't the strangest thing in the world to be having this conversation with an *Englisch* man—a virtual stranger—in the dark of night. "Leroy has been bishop for many years. He's a wise man."

"You think I don't know there's a mountain separating Frannie and me right now." Rocky did know, but couldn't every mountain be climbed with the right amount of persistence, perseverance, and dedication? Olympic athletes knew it. Folks who climbed Mount

Everest knew it. Triathlon athletes knew it. "It's not in me to be a quitter."

"I wouldn't be so prideful as to claim I know what *Gott's* plan is for Frannie or for you." Mordecai rolled the flashlight from one hand to the other and back. "But it's my job to hold her close and pray that she makes choices that are pleasing and obedient to Him."

Choices that couldn't include an outsider named Rocky Sanders. "I best get home and let you get back to sleep." Rocky trudged to the truck door and slid onto the ragged cloth seat. It seemed he'd spent the better part of the last year in this truck that looked as weather-beaten as its owner. "Sorry to have bothered you."

"No bother. I hope you find what you're looking for."

He had. Or so he thought. No sense in trying to make sense of it. "Thanks."

He turned the key. The engine cranked, coughed, then fell silent. He tried again. More coughing. Smoke seeped from the front end and dissipated in the late-night breeze. Rocky bowed his head, fighting the urge to smash his fist against the wheel again. "Come on, don't do this to me. Not now."

He cranked again. Nothing except more smoke.

"Looks like you're having some trouble there." Mordecai stood outside the truck passenger window. His big hand rested on the frame. "You know about fixing these things?"

"A little." Rocky dug his flashlight from the glove compartment and slid from the truck. "Thing is I don't have the tools or the parts I'll surely need."

Mordecai rounded the front end and stood there as if offering silent commiseration.

Rocky shoved open the hood. Smoke billowed out. He staggered back, doing his own coughing. "Great. Perfect."

Mordecai crossed his arms over his chest. "Something you can fix?"

An oil leak, most likely. It had expensive written all over it. "No."

"I reckon you have one of those cell phones to call for help?"

"I do." He only kept it for his mother's sake. He wasn't much for talking on the phone or for electronics in general, though they came in handy for emergencies. Like this. Rocky glanced at his watch. "It's late, and I don't know if they'll be able to find us out here in the dark."

"It's not like the auto fix-it folks have to come to our place much." Mordecai's dry chuckle eased Rocky's discomfort. "I have a stall in the barn with your name on it. You'd be surprised how comfy a bed of straw can be. I reckon we have a few horse blankets out there as well."

"I don't know. What about your wife?" Not to mention Frannie. She would come back with her date to find his truck parked in front of the house. "I don't want to upset anyone."

Mordecai cocked his head toward the house. "My *fraa* puts out a good spread for breakfast. Stop in and eat while you're waiting for the tow truck."

A strange sense of unreality settled on Rocky. He was too tired to do anything else but wait for Mordecai to show the way. He slipped into the house and returned a few seconds later with a lit kerosene lamp. He led the way to the barn where he dropped a pile of blankets in a stall next to three others occupied by some decent-looking horses. "Don't be surprised if a mama cat joins you. I think she's about to have a litter, and she's already staked out her territory."

"There's plenty of room." Rocky squatted and smoothed the blankets, folding one at the top to serve as a pillow. "Thanks for the hospitality. I hope it doesn't get you into trouble."

"Kindness and hospitality don't count as trouble in our book." Mordecai shoved the stall gate closed. "I don't know what you're looking for, but it don't seem likely you'll find it here. Frannie is a good girl with a good heart. Pursuing her can only cause her misery. Yourself too."

"I'm getting that." Rocky turned his back and re-arranged the blankets. Heat burned behind his eyes. He heaved a breath and turned to face Mordecai again. "I don't know what I was thinking when I got in my truck and drove down here. It seemed like the only thing I could do. Nothing else made sense. Haven't you ever felt that way?"

"Yep, I have, but we don't know each other well enough for that story. In my case, a girl's life with her family and her community—her church—wasn't at stake."

"But what about that plan you were talking about. God's plan. You claim to know what that is?"

"*Nee*. I am *Gott's* humble, obedient servant." Mordecai's

expression was kind, but his tone stern. "I would never be so arrogant as to say or think such a thing. We believe in what's called *Gelassenheit.*"

Rocky shook his head. "Gela-what?"

"*Gelassenheit.* Yielding to God's will and forsaking selfishness. Thy will be done."

"So you think me coming here for Frannie is selfishness?"

"That's something only you can know. Ask yourself, whose will is being done here?"

Could love and selfishness come in the same prettily wrapped gift? "Then maybe we should just see how it plays out."

Mordecai's head bobbed. He strode to the barn door, tugged it open, and looked back. "We also value the virtue of patience. We wait on God's plan instead of rushing to judgment or conclusion."

"Exactly."

"Godspeed, son, and sweet dreams." He shoved the door shut. The barn went dark and sweet silence like a soft blanket fell over Rocky.

Son. He closed his eyes against the pain of that one word. No one had called him 'son' in a long time. He inhaled the scent of hay and manure and dust, familiar smells that had grounded him his entire life. Working on the land, sowing and reaping. God's work. That's what his uncle always said. He never understood Rocky's desire to leave home and teach sports to kids. "You want to play games for a living? That's almost as bad as hitting guys for money." He'd shove back his white, sweat-stained cowboy hat and shake his head. "Putting food on people's tables, now there's an honorable living."

Hard work, honest work. Close to the land. Close to God. That was Uncle Richard's life. Could it be Rocky's too? *God, if You're really there, help me. I'm too stupid to figure this out. I need a hint.*

The answer was as clear as the night sky. A broken-down truck sitting in front of Frannie Mast's uncle's house despite every attempt to drive him away. What more direction did he need?

He closed his eyes and slept.

CHAPTER 5

Frannie's hands shook. She smoothed her apron. Ridiculous. Her stomach roiled at the mingled aromas of *kaffi* and baking bread, normally two of her favorite smells. She hadn't done anything wrong. She wavered at the end of the hallway that led to the stairs that would take her to the front room. No point in procrastinating. A quick peek from the window had confirmed the worst. Rocky's battered two-tone black-and-silver pickup truck still took up space in the front yard, just as it had when she returned from her ride with Joseph. No way Joseph had missed it. He simply doffed his hat and snapped the reins, his disapproval apparent in the rigid set of his broad shoulders.

She didn't invite Rocky to come. Yet she could think of nothing else now but seeing him.

What would *Onkel* Mordecai think? And *Aenti* Abigail? She must be having a cow or even two.

Frannie closed her eyes, breathed a quick prayer, and opened them. Squaring her shoulders, she marched into the front room. She plowed to a stop. There he sat. Eating a pancake slathered in butter and dripping with syrup. Across the table from her uncle, who sipped *kaffi* from his usual chipped blue mug. He smiled at something Rocky said.

Not so with her aunt. She plopped a pan of corn mush on the table and turned. From the expression on her face, she'd apparently eaten an entire jalapeño, seeds and all. "It's about time you got out of bed. I've already made breakfast. I reckon you can clean up."

With that, she flounced from the room.

Rocky turned to stare. He had bits of hay in his ruffled hair. His khaki pants and gray checkered western shirt were wrinkled. Lines around his eyes spoke of a restless night. He smiled. "Hey."

How dare he "hey" her? Any minute the women would start showing up for the sewing frolic. Their tongues would wag until they fell off over that pickup truck sitting in the yard at the crack of dawn. *Had it been there all night? How could her uncle allow it? What would Leroy say?* They'd be gobbling like a rafter of turkey hens. "What are you doing here?"

"He had some trouble with his truck last night." *Onkel* Mordecai set the cup on the table and burped gently. "He's already called for a tow truck."

"I'll be out of your way soon as they get here." Rocky rose and dropped his napkin by his plate, his smile gone. "Thank you for the hospitality, Mordecai."

"I'll expect you back tomorrow then." *Onkel* Mordecai stood as well. He settled his straw hat on his head. "We'll get that cement poured for the honey house in no time. I reckon we can finish up Albert's milk barn and milk house combo at the same time.

We've got cabbage, broccoli, and onions to plant. Lots of work for willing hands and a strong back."

"You're working here?" How was she supposed to move on if he kept showing up? "Why?"

"Rocky here says he did construction work to put himself through college. He's handy with tools and such." Her uncle seemed unperturbed by her distress. "And he's a farmer. Not a combination you find all the time. He offered to help, and we can use all the help we can get."

Frannie didn't ask permission this time. "On the porch."

Rocky led the way, holding the screen door for her in such a polite way she wanted to kick someone in the shins, something she'd never done in her entire life. "Why are you here?"

His gaze bounced from her to Caleb, who kicked a half-deflated, gray soccer ball as he made his way out of the yard, headed to school. "Has he ever played basketball?"

"What?"

"You know, not everything is about you."

It took Frannie a second to realize her mouth had dropped open. She shut it. *Breathe.* "What is that supposed to mean?"

"Sure, I came down here because of you, but the more I see, the more I realize something else brought me to Bee County."

"Like what?"

"I'm not sure, but I aim to find out." He slapped his ball cap on his tousled hair. "I see a line of dirt blowing on the road out there. I imagine it's the tow truck. I better go wave them down or they'll miss the turn in."

He stalked down the steps without looking back.

"Rocky."

"Don't worry about it."

"I'm sorry about last night." Even in wrinkled clothes, hair a mess, sleepers around his eyes, he looked like the best, most wonderful specimen of a man she'd ever seen. "I didn't mean to cause you hurt. I don't want to ever cause you hurt."

He turned and lifted his huge hand to shade his eyes from the morning sun. "I know you're between a rock and a hard place here. I'm sorry I'm making it harder for you. But I'm not giving up on us. I have to figure some things out first, but in the meantime, I'm asking you, don't make any rash promises to someone else. Please."

He spun around and marched away, leaving Frannie standing on the porch, her mouth open once again. "I don't make rash promises," she sputtered. "I only make promises I can keep."

"Promise me you'll wait, then." He kept walking. "First I need to fix my truck. Then I need to get me a job. Then I need to see a man about a horse. Then we'll talk."

"Or we could talk now."

"*Nee.*" *Aenti* Abigail let the screen door slam behind her. "You can't."

Frannie faced her aunt. "I know. I know, but I just—"

"You can't help but think with your heart instead of your head? Don't do it. You'll only be hurt or hurt others."

"Doesn't love come from the heart?"

"It does, but that doesn't mean you rule out all reason when you make your decisions." *Aenti* Abigail smoothed an errant blond hair back under her *kapp*, her blue eyes pensive. "I know how hard it can be. I moved to Bee County thinking I would marry one man and ended up marrying Mordecai. I hurt a good man in the process. I'll always regret that."

"But you married for love."

"The difference is my faith wasn't at stake. I didn't stand to lose my family and my church if I made the wrong decision."

"I would never marry outside the church." As much as the words pained her, Frannie knew they were true. She might never marry as a result, but her faith would stand the test. Gott, *is this some kind of test? If it is, it stinks.* "I plan to be baptized in the spring."

"I'm glad to hear that." Her aunt's hand rubbed Frannie's shoulder for a brief second. "I'll get the sewing supplies out while you finish the dishes. I see the women coming down the road."

Indeed they were. Frannie lingered on the porch, watching the two wagons that carried almost a dozen women, girls, and babies pull in next to Rocky's truck.

They hopped out in a melee of laughter and high voices that carried on the soft breeze that spoke of autumn just around the corner. Every one of them gave a second look at the truck. Even the little girls.

"Nice truck." Deborah padded up the steps first, little Timothy toddling behind her. "That the same one that was here the other night?"

Frannie breathed and lifted her chin. "It is indeed a nice truck. It's a classic. Needs a little work, though."

Nodding as if she didn't know what else to do, Deborah moved on. Leroy's wife, Naomi, was next. She said nothing, but her expression conveyed a passel of disapproval. Leroy would get an earful at the supper table.

The others didn't ask Frannie directly, but their faces were full of curiosity and concern as they chattered among themselves. The words *Englischer* and *truck* and *early* floated on the air as they bustled into the house, their bags of sewing supplies hoisted on their shoulders, their bare feet slapping against the wood. A few looked as if they might burst before they could tell someone. Frannie's *Englischer* had his truck parked at the King house at the crack of dawn.

Tongues would wag until they fell off. Let them. It would be hard to eat beans without tongues.

CHAPTER 6

Frannie inhaled the sweet, fresh smell of fall weather. October had brought with it cooler temperatures and the promise of rain soon. She wiggled, trying to get comfortable on the bench between Rebekah and Hazel. Her gaze wandered to the windows beyond the men's side. Leroy's house had more windows than *Onkel* Mordecai's. More opportunity for a breeze. She liked that. Everything in the front room looked scrubbed and freshly cleaned. The Glicks knew how to prepare for service. The last sermon was drawing to a close. She could tell by the way Leroy had ceased to pace and his thunderous voice had lost volume. As if he'd worn himself out. Soon they would sing, pray, and then eat.

A bang resonated through the room, causing more than one young girl to gasp as if jolted awake. Clutching her *Ausbund* hymnal to her chest, Frannie pivoted and craned her neck. The screen door stood open. And there, like the proverbial prodigal son, stood Rocky. Once again towering in the doorway.

"Sorry, sorry!" Off came the ball cap once again, revealing damp ringlets of hair. "I still don't have the hang of how long it takes to get around in a buggy." He laughed, a low, embarrassed laugh, not like the ones she remembered from their drives. "I'll just grab a seat."

He plopped down in an empty space on the last bench, right next to the young boys, who, by age, sat in the back.

Grab a seat? Buggy? She turned to Deborah, who shrugged, her eyebrows popped up so high they might touch her hairline. "Did he say 'buggy'?"

Deborah put a finger to her lips. "Hush!" She tugged Frannie's arm and they both sank to their knees for prayer. Frannie couldn't help herself. She looked back. Even on his knees Rocky towered over the boys. He looked as if he needed his handy-dandy playbook from his basketball-playing days to know what was going on.

How could she possibly concentrate knowing his eyes gazed on her back? She hadn't seen hide nor hair of him in the two weeks since he'd helped *Onkel* Mordecai and the other men build the honey storage shack and put up the milk house. They'd planted the winter vegetables and then he'd left without staying for supper or saying a proper good-bye.

Nothing. It was as if he'd picked up and gone home. That thought had made it nearly impossible for her to sleep most nights since.

Now he sat in her church in his Sunday-best black pants and white long-sleeved shirt with a button-down collar, the most agreeable-looking man she'd ever seen. Her throat went dry at the thought. Heat crept up her neck and scurried across her cheeks. *You're in church, Frannie Mast, in church.* Gott, *help me.*

They stood for the benediction. She breathed a sigh

of relief. *Almost done. Almost.* The closing hymn, slow and steady, calmed her. At the tail end of the last endless note, she skirted Deborah and the others on her row, intent on getting to the kitchen. A safe haven. Much as every fiber of her being ached to rush back and ask Rocky what all this meant, she would do the right thing. She would serve the fellowship meal, keep her mind and her hands busy. She would not give the women who stared at her, expressions ranging from curious to disapproving, more to talk about. No one could fault her for this.

"Frannie."

Rocky blocked her path. He smiled from ear to ear as if he had no clue as to the predicament he represented for her. He knew. He was no fool. He had a college education and a good head on his shoulders. "Rocky."

"We need to talk."

Talking would only lead to other things. She inhaled his scent. If only she could bottle it and hold it close. "I have to help with the meal."

"After, then."

"It's not done."

"Only for a minute. I want to show you something."

"I have to go home after."

"I have something for the *kinner*. I'll bring it by then."

He did *not* just use a *Deutsch* word in a sentence as if it were the most natural thing in the world.

"That's between you and *Onkel* Mordecai, then."

He grinned like a boy who'd just caught his first fish. "See you in a bit."

Frannie couldn't help it. Her smile escaped like a

kitten from a cardboard box. She would see him again, even if only for a few minutes. She would inhale his scent and memorize his smile. "See you."

It sounded like a promise. She scurried into the kitchen, not at all sure it was one she could or should keep.

*　*　*

Rocky tied the reins to the hitching post near the Kings' barn. The spot above the long sliding doors would be perfect. He sauntered to the back of the buggy, at peace for the moment. For once, he was doing something he knew how to do. After pushing back the basketballs rolling around, he slid out the basketball hoop. He hoisted it to his shoulder, grabbed his tool bag with his other hand, and headed to the barn. Caleb, Mordecai's youngest stepchild, who looked to be about eleven or twelve, sped across the yard toward him, gangly legs flailing. "Hey, Rocky, what's that you got?"

The boy knew his name and who he was. That made Rocky feel good. Acceptance came easier to the younger folks. Now if he could get Frannie to understand his intentions. "It's a basketball hoop."

Caleb double-stepped to keep up. "Whatcha gonna do with it?"

"You got a ladder?"

"Sure we do."

"Haul it out here."

Caleb grinned and disappeared into the barn. He

reemerged a few minutes later with the ladder on his back, dragging the end behind him. Together they positioned it against the barn. Rocky started up, Caleb holding on at the bottom, just for good measure. Seconds later, Rocky stood on the top rung, his tool belt slung over his shoulder. He'd hung plenty of hoops in his day. Pickup basketball games kept boys—and girls—out of trouble. Even if it was a freestanding hoop in a paved cul-de-sac, it was an invitation to play, to work off excess energy, to stay out of trouble, to get away from computers and video games and TV programming that turned young brains to mush.

Not that these kiddos—a half dozen had gathered around since he started screwing in the bolts—had access to any of those things. The curiosity and wide grins on their faces told him they were like other kids in more ways than one. They liked to play games and have fun.

"You know, you might have asked *Onkel* Mordecai before you started hanging things on his barn." Frannie's voice wafted over the chatter of the *kinner*, as he had learned from Leroy to call them in the two meetings he'd had with the bishop and Mordecai in his role as deacon. Leroy was concerned about the influence Rocky's presence might have, especially on the boys. He would show the bishop the good he could do, for all of them. "You're banging on someone else's property, you know."

Funny thing was, she didn't sound all that upset.

He clopped down the ladder and gathered up his tools. "You can put it away." He nodded to Caleb and a boy about the same size who stood next to him. "I'll be right back."

He strode past Frannie, with her tantalizing scent of vanilla and soap, without giving her a look. He knew what he'd see. Hands on her hips, her cheeks pink, her mouth open to scold him some more. She would look so pretty he'd forget what he planned to do next. "Help me get the balls from my buggy."

"Your buggy?"

He'd set the trap and she'd fallen right in. "Yep."

She strode after him. "What are you doing here?"

"Seems like you ask me that every time I come around." He opened the back door on the buggy and tossed her a clean, fresh orange ball. He loved new basketballs. The smell of rubber. "By the way, I did talk to Mordecai. He graciously accepted my gift. Surely, you can do the same. Or hush up. One or the other."

Her mouth closed, but he could see her brain turning, *clickity-clack*, a hundred miles an hour. That was his Frannie.

His Frannie. Gott, *please*.

Gott. Another word he'd picked up in his visits with Leroy and Mordecai. Not just God the Father, as he had once thought. But God of all. He spent most of his daily morning runs contemplating this concept. One of the Hostetler boys nearly hit him with a buggy when, deep in thought, he meandered into the road. This God with a plan so big, no man or woman could understand it with their little pea brains. He certainly couldn't. Neither man approved of his intentions with Frannie, and neither would give an inch, but their tradition gave them no choice but to hear him out. If he truly had an interest in their faith, they had to see it through. Bless both of them for being so honorable.

For giving him a chance when disapproval oozed from their pores.

Frannie sauntered to the front of the buggy and began to stroke the Morgan's thick mane. "He's a beaut. Where'd you get him?"

How did he afford the horse? That's what she really meant.

"Belongs to Seth Cotter. I took a job with him. He has that big farm right there where you turn off the highway. He's getting up there in years, and there's a lot of work he can't do himself anymore, even in fall and winter. I'm staying in his bunkhouse now."

Contemplating how she'd react to this news, Rocky motioned with the first basketball. She held out her hands. He tossed it to her. Grinning like he'd just given her the keys to his old truck, she caught it. The ball smacked against her long, thin fingers. Giggling, she tossed it up and down. Another thing among the multitude of attributes he liked about Frannie. She had a natural-born aptitude for sports. Not only that, she liked them. Under different circumstances, she would've been an athlete.

She shook her head so hard her *kapp* slid a little more cockeyed than usual. "You're thinking of buying a horse to go with the buggy. When you have the money. I don't understand. I truly don't."

"When I said it wasn't just about you, I meant it." He snagged two more balls. "I've been doing a lot of reading and thinking. I visited with Leroy and Mordecai a couple of times."

Her full lips were shaped in an *O*, but no sound came out.

"I got rid of my cell phone and iPad. I never turn on the radio or the TV in the bunkhouse. I heat my ramen noodles on the woodstove."

"How will you stay in touch with your mother?"

That's what she chose to latch onto? "I write her letters." He gave her his best grin. "Isn't that how you stay in touch? And if there's an emergency, she has Seth's number."

Frannie nodded, but she didn't meet his gaze, instead studying the lines on the basketball as if memorizing them.

"I sold my truck. That's where I got the money for the buggy."

"You sold your truck?" The words came out in a squeak. She stared up at him. "You loved that truck. It's a classic."

"I'll love this buggy too." He started toward the barn. She trailed after him, still tossing the ball from one hand to the other. "Leastways I will once I get used to driving it on the highway with all those eighteen-wheelers whizzing past me."

"It's five to eight miles an hour."

Rocky glanced back at her. "What?"

"Horse-drawn buggies travel about five to eight miles an hour. That's what *Onkel* Mordecai says and he knows everything." She smiled. His heart catapulted to a spot by his collarbone in a spectacular jump shot, then plummeted back to its normal resting spot. "Keep that in mind. Leroy doesn't like folks to be late to church."

She was warming up to the idea. Leastways, Rocky could hope. He tossed a ball to Caleb and another to a boy half his size. "Hold these, while I mark the out-of-bounds lines."

"Out-of-bounds?"

Frannie let her ball sail. It smacked against the backboard and slid around the hoop's rim before falling through the net for a neat two points. The kids dived for the ball and tussled over it, laughing and cheering.

All was right in the world when a pickup basketball game took off.

"Beginner's luck." Rocky took the ball from Caleb, raced toward the basket, jumped, and jammed the ball through it. "Wahoo, nothing but net!"

Frannie wrestled Caleb for the rebound, but her cousin had more strength. In a flash, he made another basket. "That's two points, right? Are we having teams?"

"Teams. It's more fun if you keep score. I'll be on one team, Frannie on the other, since we're the grown-ups." Grown-ups, of a sort. Rocky grabbed a stick and began marking the out-of-bounds lines and the free-throw line in the hard-packed dirt that passed for a yard. "We'll do a half-court game. I reckon you don't know what that means."

Frannie snorted, a very unladylike sound that only served to endear her more to Rocky. "Sure I do. They had games on the TV in the restaurant."

"And you watched? Shame on you."

"*Nee*, I heard. Who could help, the way they yell and scream over a game?" Frannie snatched the ball from Caleb. She scampered past Rocky, her long dress flapping behind her. "Hurry up. We're playing basketball."

Indeed, they were.

* * *

"What is wrong with you?"

Frannie whirled. She hadn't heard *Aenti* Abigail enter the room she shared with Rebekah and Hazel. She smoothed her straggling hair with both hands. Her *kapp* hung by a hairpin. Dirt and sweat marred her apron from top to bottom. "What do you mean?"

"Don't act all innocent with me." Her aunt crossed her arms over her chest. "Everyone saw you out there playing games with him."

"Him" had a name. Rocky. "Having fun. There's no rule in the *Ordnung* that says we can't have fun."

"Don't make me the bad person here. There's fun and then there's *fun* and you know it."

Frannie did know it. She'd had more fun playing basketball with Rocky and the *kinner* than she'd had in all the days since she returned to Bee County. Running and shooting and scuffling over the ball. Rocky towered over her and the other players, making it easy for him to block shots. Sometimes he took pity and let her make a shot here and there. Two-pointers, as he called them. She'd learned to defend the basket and what a foul was. Her specialty seemed to be free throws. With no one defending the basket, she couldn't miss. Her arms ached and her legs shuffled like wet noodles, but she felt . . . happy.

"It's just a game."

"A game everyone saw you playing with a full-grown man."

"There were a bunch of us."

"You were the only woman."

Frannie sank onto the bed. *Aenti* Abigail joined her. She patted Frannie's dirty hands. "I don't want you to think I don't understand what you're going through, but you told me you would never marry outside the church. I took you at your word."

"I meant it."

"That's not what it looked like today."

"We had fun, that's all."

"Joseph is coming for supper tonight."

"Joseph isn't interested in me. He just likes your casserole." Frannie went to the window. Dark clouds hung close to the earth, heavy and damp. Rain had finally begun to fall, heralding the end of a long, hot summer. For everyone. She breathed in the scent of moist dirt, fighting the urge to bawl. Plain women didn't bawl. Inhaling, she faced her aunt. "You didn't marry Stephen because you knew you didn't love him."

"I gave him a chance before I made that decision." Aunt Abigail plucked at a thread on her apron, her expression distant, remembering. "I told your *mudder* I would watch out for you and I am."

"My *mudder* would like a good game of basketball."

"She wouldn't like it if her child left the district and she couldn't see her anymore, ever. That's what's at stake here." Her aunt's voice trembled. Surely she thought of her own daughter, Leila. "You know that. Do you want to give up everything and everyone you love for a man?"

"I'm not Leila. I will never do that. I'm Plain through and through."

"So was Leila. Or so I thought."

"If you believe in *Gott's* will, wasn't leaving here *Gott's* plan for Leila and Jesse?"

"I'm not smart enough or prideful enough to think I know what *Gott's* plan is. It will unfold on *Gott's* time, not ours." Aunt Abigail sounded so sure of herself. Even the loss of her daughter didn't shake her faith. "*Gott* is good. What we see today or tomorrow is not the end. We have to have patience and wait on the Lord."

Patience had never been one of Frannie's strong suits. "I'm sorry. I have trouble seeing my life without Rocky in it."

There, she'd said it. Her aunt's arms came out and Frannie found herself embraced in a warm, sure hug. Surprise overcame her. Tears formed. She sniffed. *Aenti* Abigail did the same and sat back.

"Did you know I have a new granddaughter whom I haven't seen? Deborah received a letter from Leila." She wiped at her face with her sleeve. "Her name is Grace. You'd be surprised at what you can get through. I know I am."

"There have been times when people have joined our faith and become members of the district, haven't there?"

Aenti Abigail sighed. "Wishful thinking, child."

"Why? He bought a buggy."

"He's thinking with his heart too. A buggy doesn't a Plain man make."

"Doesn't it count for something?"

"It's true that it's happened in other districts. I've heard." Aunt Abigail smoothed her apron, leaving the loose thread to its own devices. "Different districts do it differently, but usually the person who joins spends at least a year getting used to the idea of giving up all those luxuries like electricity and cars and such. The bishop interviews the person to see if his heart is really in it. Sometimes the whole church votes. I don't know how Leroy would do it."

"So it is possible?"

"But not likely." Her aunt stood. "Get cleaned up. I need to warm up the enchilada casserole. You can set the table. Put out the pickled jalapeños. You know how Mordecai likes those with his enchiladas. And don't forget to set a place for Joseph."

Her aunt disappeared through the door.

A pain pierced Frannie's chest so sharp she doubled over. The happiness of only a few minutes earlier dissipated like dew in the rising sun on an August morning. She closed her eyes and rocked, willing the pain to subside. *Gott? Gott!*

Nothing.

She jerked off her apron, wadded it up, and slung it across the room. "Thy will be done?" She spoke the words aloud in the still silence of her room. She'd heard them a million times it seemed, and she still couldn't understand how a person knew. How did she know?

Gott?

Silence. Heart as heavy as a year's supply of firewood, she trudged across the room to pick up the apron.

Thy will be done, but please let it include Rocky. Somehow. Some way.

Some kind of prayer that was. Trying to say, "Lord, have it Your way, but first, Lord, have it my way."

Lord, have mercy on my rebellious soul.

Worn to a frazzle, she combed her hair, replaced her *kapp*, and slipped on a clean apron.

Time to set a place for Joseph.

CHAPTER 7

The horsey smell mixed with the rank odor of manure should be considered for a man's cologne. Rocky smiled to himself. Women might not think so, but any cowboy worth his salt would wear it. The rhythm of his strokes across Chocolate's wide back and flanks was almost as calming to him as it was to the horse. He leaned his head against Chocolate's long neck for a second and heaved a sigh. Take away everything going on in his life right now, capture the soft evening glow of sunset, a mourning dove cooing in the distance, two calico kittens chasing each other in a rough-and-tumble race across the yard outside the corral, and this moment could be almost perfect.

Almost.

The distant *clip-clop* of horse's hooves and the *squeak-squeak* of wheels traversing the rough terrain of the dirt road that led to the Cotters' homestead forced him to raise his head and squint into the setting sun. A buggy. Too soon to say whose. Chocolate raised his head and nickered.

"You and me both, sweet thing, you and me both." Rocky gathered the harness and led the horse toward the fence. "Well, I'll be a monkey's uncle. That there is the bishop, Chocolate. What do you think he wants?"

To tell Rocky to get out of Dodge and leave a certain young Amish woman in peace? Surely not. Rocky ducked his head. His jeans, so worn they were a pale blue with skin peeking through thick threads at the knees, were dirty. His jacket had bloodstains on it from where he'd cut his hand chopping firewood, and he probably smelled a lot like Chocolate.

Leroy parked near the gate and descended from the buggy. Once both boots were on the ground, one hand went to his back. He was slow to straighten. "Evening."

"Evening."

Rocky waited. He'd learned in his dealings with the bishop to let the man do the talking. He got in a lot less trouble that way.

"Tomorrow is the annual auction." Leroy wiped his face with a bandanna that might have once been white but now looked a dingy gray. "It's our annual fundraiser for the school and our emergency medical fund."

Rocky shoved through the gate and latched it behind him. "I might have heard something about that."

Leroy propped both arms on the top plank of the wooden fence and leaned against it. "Have you finished your readings?"

The older man's shift in topics from the auction to a barely legible translation of the Dordrecht Articles of Faith and its eighteen articles had meaning, but Rocky couldn't say what it was. "I'm working on it."

"Those articles are very important to a Plain man of faith."

"Yes, sir."

"Don't 'sir' me."

"Yes, sir—Leroy." Why had the man made this trip out here to repeat a conversation they'd already had? More than once. "I know that."

"You talk to your mother lately?"

Now that was indeed a new topic. "I gave up my phone."

"You don't know how to come to the store and use the community phone?"

Surely that was a privilege meant only for the members of the district. "Well, yes, I mean, I didn't know, I didn't think—"

"Never underestimate how much a parent misses a child who's left the nest." Leroy cleared his throat. His gaze drifted over Rocky's shoulder. Surely he thought of his own son, whom he refused to see and with whom he would never break bread again. "Mother or father. It's as God intends when a grown child strikes out on his own—for the most part—but that doesn't mean it doesn't hurt a parent's heart."

"Understood."

He'd talked to his mother every night from his hotel room on the trip down, regaling her with stories of the people he'd visited within the diners along the way, describing parks where he'd stopped to eat a sack lunch and take a quick snooze. She thought he would pick up Frannie and bring her home. If things didn't work out, he wouldn't have to tell her how close he'd come to assuming a Texan citizenship. Texas had been its own country more than once, and some still thought it was or should be.

Writing letters was a lost art in the English world,

but one he had given due diligence since coming to Bee County. His mother deserved to know what was going on with her only son.

"Tell me something about your mother."

Leroy's abrupt command blew away Rocky's reverie. "Beg your pardon."

"Your mother raised you to be a decent human being, best I can tell." Leroy stared at Rocky over streaked wire-rimmed glasses that rested halfway down his long nose. "Tell me something about her."

Food always came to Rocky's mind first when he thought of his mother. That and the way she used to put vapor rub on a cloth diaper, warm it on the gas register in the living room, and then pin it around his neck when he had a bad cold. Her hands were always cool on his hot forehead. She always hummed a George Strait song under her breath when she made chicken noodle soup from scratch. "She makes the best fried chicken in the state of Missouri."

"And your father? What do you remember about him?"

"What does this have to do with me joining the church?"

"You are who you are because of your parents. They taught you what's right and what's wrong. They taught you what to value."

"My dad mostly taught me what not to do." Rocky let the rough wood of the fence absorb an anger that never really went away. It bubbled under the surface and reared its ugly head at inopportune times. "He wasn't a real dad. My Uncle Richard, he was my dad."

"The boxer who became a farmer."

"Yes."

"He raised a good man."

Rocky ducked his head, his throat tight at the unexpected, matter-of-fact assessment from a man he'd come to respect. "He used to take me to auctions up in Jamesport. I loved the auctioneers. I used to practice all the way home, in the backyard, at the kitchen table, until my mama finally told me to hush."

"Any good at it?"

"Uncle Richard said I could always become an auctioneer if the NFL thing didn't work out."

Leroy sniffed and straightened. He turned and ambled toward the buggy, his limp more pronounced than it had been earlier. At the buggy he turned. "I reckon I could use some help tomorrow."

"Help?"

"Are you deaf? *Jah*, help. At the auction. It's a long day and my legs aren't what they used to be. Throat gets mighty parched too."

A chance to be at one of the most important events in the life of this district and he was invited, by the bishop, no less. Rocky squashed the urge to pump his fist and whoop. As an added and particularly sweet bonus, Frannie would be there. "I'll be there with bells on."

"No bells needed. Show up before dawn."

"I'll be there."

"Don't be late."

"I won't."

Leroy touched the brim of his hat, hauled himself into the buggy, and drove away.

When his visitor was well down the road, Rocky succumbed. He pumped his fist, did his best Snoopy dance, and whooped until Mrs. Cotter came to the window and looked out, a perturbed expression on her face. Chocolate simply nickered.

CHAPTER 8

Englisch folks sure worked up an appetite at auctions. Still pleased that *Aenti* Abigail had trusted her with taking money and making change, Frannie recounted the bills in the shoe box. More than two hundred dollars just from the food shack since the beginning of the auction. More money than she'd ever seen in one place. From the number of cars and trucks parked in front of the Combination Store, the crowd would equal or surpass those she remembered from previous years. From her vantage point seated by the tables laden with pans of hamburgers, meat loaf, green beans, potato salad, and coleslaw, along with bread and pie, she couldn't see much. All the same, the stream of *Englischers* and the steady singsong sound of the two auctioneers said all went well.

Her mouth watered as she batted away flies buzzing the table. The women wouldn't eat until the flow of customers became a trickle and then disappeared. This event, held the first Friday every November, was about raising money for the school, their medical fund, repairs, stocking up for winter, and preparing for emergencies that might occur during the year. Everyone understood that.

"I'll have the meat loaf plate."

She'd been so sure Rocky would know better than to seek her out here, in front of Aunt Abigail and the other women. She'd been so careful to avoid him since the impromptu basketball game. She'd taken her *aenti's* words to heart and accepted a handful of invitations to go riding with Joseph. He asked almost nothing of her, and he'd never brought up the topic of Rocky again. He was a nice man. Smart. Funny. A hard worker. Easy on the eyes, if that counted for anything, which it didn't. Not much, anyway.

She counted off his attributes on her fingers at night in bed. She told them to Rebekah in the dark as they both tried to sleep. Rebekah cheered her on every time, and every time Frannie found sleep eluded her for hours.

She patted damp sweat from her cheeks with a paper napkin. Even in November, she felt warm. Or maybe it was his presence. "Good choice. Five dollars." She glanced up at Rocky for a split second. Blue shirt, black pants, boots. All he needed was a straw hat and suspenders to look the part. That's all it was—a part. "It includes your choice of wheat or white bread, apple, cherry, or lemon pie."

"White and apple, of course. You should raise your prices. You could get a lot more for good grub like this." He tugged a worn leather wallet from his back pocket and handed her a crumpled twenty. "Can I take something to Leroy? He must be getting hungry. He's been up there auctioneering for hours."

She fumbled with the box lid. It took her two tries

with trembling fingers to count out the three fives for his change. "He'll eat when it's over."

"You could at least look at me. I'm just trying to help."

"If you want to help, take your plate and have a seat at one of the tables." *Aenti* Abigail slipped into the space next to Frannie. Her tone was polite, but her expression stern. "What kind of pie would you like?"

"Apple, but I can't sit. I have to get back. I'm helping spot the bidders. Leroy invited me to help out when I met with him last night." Rocky's tone had a *so-there* quality to it. He'd met with the bishop. He'd been invited. Would wonders never cease? "I may spell him after a bit as auctioneer. He looks pretty tuckered out."

Frannie held out his change, trying to ignore her aunt's surprised stare. Leroy had invited Rocky. That was a good thing. Besides, a man had to eat. She hadn't done anything to encourage him. Not one thing. "You know how to call an auction?"

"Uncle Richard used to take me to the livestock auctions up in Jamesport all the time." Rocky waved away his change and picked up his plate instead. "I loved going and I used to imitate the auctioneers in our backyard. Uncle Richard said I got to be pretty good."

"You forgot your change."

"*Nee*, this is a fund-raiser, isn't it? Consider it my donation."

There he went using a *Deutsch* word again. Frannie eyed her aunt, whose eyebrows knotted in a fierce line across her forehead. "We appreciate it."

Humming a soft tune that sounded like a Christmas

hymn, he sauntered away, already picking at the meat loaf with his plastic fork.

"He is quite the talker, isn't he?"

"*Jah*." Frannie counted the bills again. And again. Sitting here in the food shack far from the auction had become unbearable for no apparent reason. The first time she met Rocky outside the restaurant had been at a Jamesport school fund-raiser auction. The memory of his smile and the way he asked her if he could call on her sometime—that's the way he put it—was so sweet it hurt to think of it. "Maybe I should take food to the boys at the water table."

"I don't think so." Aunt Abigail pursed her lips, her eyes narrowed. "But you could take a plate to Joseph. He's partial to hamburgers. And lemon meringue pie, it's his favorite."

"There's nothing between Joseph and me." And there never would be. Both of them knew it.

Smiling, her aunt whipped from one end of the table, wrapping a burger with all the trimmings in a paper napkin and placing it on a Styrofoam plate, along with a baked potato steaming in its tinfoil and a thick wedge of pie. "Sometimes you have to work at it a little. Give things time to grow. Get it to him while it's hot."

Frannie sighed. She needed a breath of fresh air. She needed to be someplace else. Anyplace. Skirting folks who stopped in the middle of the road to chat and sip sodas or bottled water covered in condensation, she trudged past the Combination Store intent on her errand. At least Joseph would get a decent meal out of it. He would appreciate that.

"Where're you headed?"

Frannie stumbled. Rocky grabbed her arm. She tugged away. "Are you following me? You're supposed to be eating your meat loaf."

"I lost my appetite after you gave me the cold shoulder. We have to talk."

"I know." Frannie glanced around. A crowd of *Englischers* pressed them, no one she knew, but that could change any second. "Not here."

"I was thinking of buying some chickens. The Cotters don't have any." He pointed toward the livestock area. "Maybe you can help me pick them out."

Joseph's plate clutched in her hands, Frannie veered to her right. Her mind said, Nee, nee, nee, but her heart seemed to be in control of her body. She slipped between the sheds to the pens that held chickens, pigs, goats, and sheep. The stench nearly knocked her back a step.

"Remember the auction in Jamesport?" The smell of manure didn't seem to bother Rocky. He leaned on a fence post with one elbow and surveyed a mama hen and her chicks.

"I do."

"You looked so cute with your sunburned nose. Your freckles tripled in one day."

His teeth had been white against his tan, and his eyes, always so vivid blue, were made even more vibrant by his blue shirt.

"It was so hot that day, at least a hundred and two."

"You drank three cups of lemonade and ate two helpings of homemade ice cream."

"You kept track?"

"I didn't want to get you in trouble. So I gazed upon you from afar until I realized I wouldn't get another chance like that to ask you out."

She giggled. "From afar?"

"Yeah, haven't you ever read a romance? Mr. Shakespeare or something." His hand came up and his fingers brushed at her cheek. They were so warm. "I keep telling myself to follow the rules, to wait, to be patient, but when I see you, all I can think about is . . ."

He leaned so close she caught a whiff of peppermint on his breath. She found herself stretching on her tip-toes to meet him. "Think about what?"

He pulled back. She felt as if she'd been dropped into a deep well of cold water. "Rocky!"

His face flushed, he straightened. "Sorry, I'm sorry."

"I feel the same way." The words came out in a stammer. "I'm trying so hard to do the right thing."

"But sometimes it's hard to know what the right thing is."

"Exactly."

Rocky returned to the fence post, his hands gripping the wood as if determined to stay put. "Remember the sewing machine?"

"The Singer treadle?" It was a nice machine. They had one just like it in their front room. Most Plain folks did. "Of course I do."

"My mom embroidered a tablecloth and draped it on top." He shook his head, his expression sheepish. "She set her begonias on it. Looks very pretty."

Frannie chuckled. "Not much of a sewer, I guess."

"Nope. She likes the way it looks in her living room, but if she wants to fix a hem or something, she drags out her Sears electric and lets it rip."

The chuckle they shared had a homey feeling, as if they'd known each other years and years.

"My parents bought a used wringer wash machine." Frannie rubbed her hands across the slats of the fence, the wood rough under her fingers. "Can you ever imagine them filling it with dirt and planting begonias in it?"

"Or using the canning jars you bought for them as planters?" Rocky shook his head. "They're practical people who live in a practical world."

"Our worlds *are* different." For one thing, her parents couldn't afford to buy something for looks. "Besides, when you work the land, you have a lot of dirty clothes."

His sigh had a strange, sad echo in it. "That doesn't mean never the two shall meet."

"You are in a funny mood today."

"Very literary."

His college education sometimes bled through, making Frannie feel worlds apart. As if she didn't already. "I don't know what that means."

"I know. Do you understand why I'm meeting with Leroy?"

"To talk to him about . . . being Amish."

"Exactly."

"What does he say?"

"He says it's a very big change, not one most *Englischers* can make. They try, but they fail."

"What do you say?"

"I'm not big on failing or losing. I'm not doing this

because I want a simpler way of living. I don't have any illusions about how hard your life is."

"Then why are you doing it?"

He shook his head without meeting her gaze. "There's something in me that needs filling up, I guess."

Not for her. That was good. Very good. "Because of your dad and your uncle?"

"Because of my life." His gaze leveled with hers. "Who's the burger for?"

Frannie glanced down at the plate in her hands. She'd forgotten about it. Grease had begun to congeal on the bun. "Oh, that."

Rocky took only one step back, but the gap between them widened to a chasm. "Joseph?"

As much as she wanted to deny it, she wouldn't. She could never lie to Rocky. "Yes."

"These chickens look a little small." He took another step back. "I should spell the boys in the auction barn. It might not be a hundred and two, but it's warm and muggy. They might need a swig of water."

"Taking a plate to someone doesn't mean anything." Only to her aunt. Even Joseph knew where he stood, and he didn't seem all that upset about it. "He's a friend of the family."

Rocky's face twisted with pain. "I love you."

He whirled and strode away.

The words floated in the air around her. She wanted to collect them and hold them close to her heart where she could hear them over and over again in the middle of the night or in broad daylight, morning and afternoon. "*Ach*, Rocky!"

He kept walking. Soon he disappeared into the steady stream of folks moving between the auction barn and the food shed and the buggies for sale in front of the Combination Store.

She closed her eyes. *Love you too.*

In her world, love might not be enough. Faith and community also counted. Rocky knew that.

They both did.

A chicken squawked and the goats bleated in response. The smell choked her. She glanced at the plate in her hand. The offending hamburger needed to be delivered. She plodded toward the honey table, glad only the animals could see the misery and pain riding piggyback on her shoulders.

Joseph leaned over the table, sacking an array of jars ranging from honey to wild mustang grape jelly to strawberry jam for an elderly lady leaning on a walker that tilted unsteadily on the uneven ground. He smiled at Frannie and went back to his chore. She set the plate on the table and touched the woman's arm. "Can I help you carry that?"

"Thank you, young lady, but my grandson is around here somewhere. He'll be back any second to help me to the car. Sweet of you, though."

Indeed, the young man in overly tight blue jeans and a fluorescent orange T-shirt that matched his orange-and-green sneakers returned just as Joseph handed the lady her change. "Enjoy, ma'am."

"I plan to. Deacon here loves strawberry jam on English muffins. Don't you, Deacon?"

The teenager's big ears turned a deep shade of

purplish red. She leaned on her walker and tottered away, Deacon's arm around her bowed shoulders in a surprising—to Frannie, anyway—show of affection.

"That was sweet of you to offer to help her." Still smiling, Joseph snapped the plastic lid onto the battered coffee can that served as his cash box. "You do have a sweet disposition under all that sassiness."

"Sassiness?"

"*Jah.* You give a lot of lip, but I see more to you."

None of this was his fault. It was her Aunt Abigail's fault. "I'm so sorry."

"Sorry for what? For being lippy and not the best housekeeper? Don't be." He rearranged the jars on the table, from four in a row to five, still smiling. "You may not be the most ordinary Plain woman, but I like you just the way you are. Life with you would be interesting."

More likely irritating and annoying in the long run. The shiny would wear off. Most Plain men would wish for a *fraa* who could make gumbo without burning it and bread that wasn't hard as a rock. Men like Joseph would want a *fraa* who knew her place and also knew how to sew a tear in his pants so that it held. "You will find your special friend one of these days."

"And you don't think she'll be lippy?"

"I think you know what you like, and you're too nice to tell my aunt to leave well enough alone." She slid the plate toward him. "I brought you your favorite pie. *Aenti* Abigail said you'd rather have a hamburger than meat loaf, but I can always take it back and trade it."

"It's too bad Abigail is already taken. She does make a fine pie."

He grinned at her despite the *Englisch* girl in a pink T-shirt—why did young *Englischers* wear their clothes a size too small—who flashed a five-dollar bill at him and said her mother wanted to know if she could get two jars of honey with that. The answer was no, but Joseph ignored her for the moment. "Your *aenti* is only trying to save you from a world of hurt."

"You have a customer."

He tended to the girl, who seemed happy with her one jar. Whether the mother would be was another question. She traipsed away and he turned back. "Abigail is a wise woman."

"Sometimes the heart doesn't listen to wise words."

"For your sake and the sake of your parents, you should try harder." He plopped onto an overturned bushel basket, unwrapping the hamburger. "Don't worry. I won't tell anyone your secret. I can even keep coming around to take you on rides if you want."

"That's okay. You shouldn't waste your time on the likes of me."

"It wasn't a waste. Abigail is a good cook." He grinned. "And Rebekah is a firecracker."

"She is indeed." Frannie grinned back. "See you around."

"Not if I see you first."

As she walked away, the sound of the auctioneer floated from the big shed. "I've got two, who'll give me three, there's three, how about four, anybody give me four . . ."

Rocky's voice, deep and sure and full of delight. Leroy had let him take over.

Wonders would never cease.

Frannie could use unceasing wonders about now.

CHAPTER 9

Rocky snapped the reins again. Chocolate picked up his pace. Such a good piece of horseflesh. Rocky felt guilty monopolizing Seth's horse all the time, but the elderly farmer assured him it was no imposition. Seth paid Rocky well, and he squirreled away every penny he could in savings. Even with his nest egg, it would be awhile before he could afford to buy his own horse and some property for settling down. If he was here that long. *Gott* willing. The soupy gray sky hung so low it felt as if it weighed on his shoulders. He wouldn't miss the south Texas weather, that was for sure. November in Missouri meant crisp fall weather with leaves turning brilliant oranges, reds, and golds. Frost sparkled on the grass in the mornings. "Downright dreary" described Bee County this time of year. Dreary matched his disposition this morning.

On the bright side, warmer weather meant winter strawberries could be planted, along with cabbage, broccoli, onions, and English peas. Which gave him an excuse to head to the district to help out. Maybe Mordecai would extend an invitation for Thanksgiving.

Stop it.

He hadn't seen Frannie since the auction. Frannie with her plate for another man. Leroy said Rocky must leave her out of the equation. Regardless. Make a decision based on a desire to live out his faith according to the Bee County district's *Ordnung*. Could he do it? Did he want to do it? Did God call him to do it?

Leroy asked all the hard questions. Rocky turned the buggy onto the farm-to-market road, contemplating his answers. The sun broke through clouds that began to scud across the sky in a chilly breeze that hadn't been there a few minutes earlier. The sudden brightness blinded him for a second. Chocolate snorted, whinnied, and began to pick up speed. "Whoa, whoa, what's gotten into you?" He tightened the reins with one hand and pushed down the bill of his cap with the other. If he planned to stay, he really should get a straw hat. More of a visor. Chocolate whinnied again, the sound high and nervous.

Rocky saw what had the horse worried. A buggy capsized in the ditch just beyond the turnoff that led to the highway and Beeville. A horse, still tethered to it, bucked and tried to free itself. Mordecai's Morgan. A vise tightened around Rocky's chest. Fear choked the flow of blood to his heart. "Come on, Chocolate, let's go."

He gave the horse free rein for several hundred yards and then pulled him in as they approached the overturned buggy. "Easy, easy does it."

Don't let it be Frannie.

He hopped into the ditch and shot across the muddy terrain, slipping and sliding despite the tread on his work boots. "Hello? Are you okay?"

A moan greeted the response. The orange SLOW triangle dangled to one side on the rear of the buggy. He squatted and shoved it back. Abigail lay on her back, her right side under the buggy. Mud covered her face. Blood streaked her forehead.

"There you are. Can you move?"

"Help me out of here." Abigail's voice was soft, but determined. "I'm stuck."

"Are you sure you can move? Is anything broken?"

"I'm fine."

He took the hand she held out and gently pulled. She groaned and jerked away. "My wrist. Something's wrong with my wrist."

"Okay, we'll do this a different way." Rocky slid his hands under her arms. She stiffened but didn't protest. "I'm going to lift you out now. If anything hurts, tell me and I'll stop."

Seconds later he had her out from under the buggy. Mud, bits of dead grass, straw, and weeds covered her apron and dress. One of her shoes was missing. Her *kapp*, normally so perfectly situated, had slipped down her back. Her hair, now tousled and falling from its bun, was a deep blond highlighted with a few strands of silver. He wanted to push the *kapp* back into its rightful place, but he didn't dare. "Where does it hurt?"

"I'm fine. A little headache and some pain in this arm." She clutched her wrist against her muddied apron. "It's nothing. I need to get home, that's all."

"*Nee*, you need a doctor."

"No doctor."

Finances were tight. If anyone understood that, he

did. "Then let me take you up to the Cotters. It's closer than home. Mrs. Cotter will have first-aid supplies. You can get cleaned up, and we can decide if that will do it, or if you need more medical attention."

She touched a finger to her forehead, winced, and drew it away. The sight of the blood seemed to give her the answer she needed. "Home. We have first-aid supplies too."

"The Cotters are right down there at the end of the road. It's much faster. You're bleeding."

She shook her head. "I'm fine."

"You're not fine."

Their gazes locked. She looked away. "Fine. The Cotters."

A lifetime of letting men take the lead couldn't be overcome in a day. Rocky would never take advantage of her upbringing, but in this instance, he felt relief. She needed his help. "Let me help you up."

"I can do it."

Stubbornness definitely ran in the family.

Abigail scrambled to her feet, slipping in the mud, then managing to hoist herself upright. Her knees buckled. Rocky caught her before she went down again. "There's no shame in letting a person help you."

"I know. It's good of you to stop."

Something about the emphasis on *you* puzzled Rocky. Was it because he was an Englisher or because he was Rocky Sanders, the man trying to steal her niece away from her family?

"Of course I stopped. Who wouldn't?" He lifted her into his buggy—surprised to find she weighed not much more than a child—and settled her on the seat. "Tuck this blanket around you. You're shivering. I'll take a quick look at your horse."

Even though her expression could only be described as dubious, she pulled the scratchy, stinky wool blanket up to her chin without a word.

He took two minutes to unhitch the Morgan and tie him to a nearby tree. It wouldn't do to have him take off and get hit by a semi on the highway. Adding another expense to the repair of the buggy. If it could be repaired.

"All set." He climbed into the buggy and picked up the reins. "What happened?"

She clutched the blanket tighter. Her teeth chattered. Shock. "A deer ran across the road and spooked Brownie. I couldn't get him under control."

"That would do it."

"I should've been able to handle it. I don't know if the buggy can be repaired."

And they couldn't afford to replace it. "It would've happened to anyone. Especially when it takes you by surprise like that. Leroy and his boys are excellent at buggy repair. I have no doubt they'll give it their best shot."

"*Jah.*"

"What were you up to?" Maybe conversation would take her mind off her predicament. "Going into town?"

Women didn't usually go alone.

"Mordecai had to fix the shed. The wind blew off some of the roof overnight." She swiped at her face. Her sleeve came back with a trail of blood. The distinct sound of her teeth chattering filled the pause. "He'd promised a box of jams and jellies to Belle Lawson—the one who has the This and That antique store. I told him I was quite capable of taking a box of jellies into town."

A hint of tears tinged her attempt at a laugh.

"It could've happened to anyone," Rocky repeated.

After that his dogged attempts at small talk were met with monosyllabic responses. She allowed him to help her from the buggy when they arrived at the Cotters' farmhouse, but she moved away when he attempted to put an arm around her to hold her up on the walk to the front door.

A book in one hand, Mrs. Cotter answered the doorbell on the second ring. She took one look at the two of them through thick dark-rimmed glasses that made her look like a horned owl and shooed them in.

"Goodness gracious, whatever happened to you?" She drew Abigail into the living room made cheery by a fire in the fireplace and pretty Tiffany lamps on either side of two recliners that faced the pine bookshelves that filled one entire wall. The room smelled of coffee and mesquite. "Sit, sit. It's Abigail King, isn't it? I'm Lorraine. Lorraine Cotter. You probably don't remember me. I stop by the store for honey and jam all the time now that I'm too lazy to make my own homemade jams."

At seventy-five the woman didn't have a lazy bone in her body, as evidenced by the pristine cleanliness of her house.

"*Jah*—yes, I remember you." Abigail still clutched the blanket, which stank a bit of wet horse, with one hand as she edged toward the fire. The other hand stayed limp at her side. "I'm sorry to barge in like this. Rocky said—"

"She's had a buggy accident. I thought we might use your first-aid kit."

"Absolutely. Of course." Mrs. Cotter dragged an oak rocking chair across the thick, evergreen carpet toward the fireplace. "You sit here and we'll be right back. You need a good cup of coffee to warm you up or would you rather have hot chocolate? I'm a bit partial to hot chocolate, as Richard will tell you."

Mrs. Cotter always called him Richard. She said Rocky reminded her too much of an aging action-film star.

"Don't trouble yourself. I'm fine."

Again with the fine. Rocky shook his head. One stubborn woman. "Have some hot chocolate. You know you want to."

"Fine, hot chocolate would be fine."

He followed Mrs. Cotter down the long hallway to the kitchen and watched as she bustled about, filling a basket with medical supplies and a warm washcloth. "Are you sure she doesn't need a doctor?"

"No, but she wouldn't let me take her."

"No money?"

"I reckon."

"You know what to do?"

"Yes, ma'am. Part of my recreation training. Sports injuries and such."

"Good, skedaddle in there and figure out if it's something we can deal with. I'll bring the hot chocolate. After we get her warmed up, we'll let her fix herself up in the bathroom. She'll feel better once she gets cleaned up."

He felt better already. "Thanks, Mrs. Cotter, you're a peach."

"I keep telling you, call me Lorraine."

He'd like to call her Grandma. He'd never had one of those. His mama's mother had been gone by the time he was old enough to remember. His father's mother had never been in the picture, as far as he could tell. "She's not going to want me to touch her."

"I'll be right behind you with her hot chocolate. I understand their need for propriety, but it's no different than having a doctor tend to her wounds with a nurse present. Go on."

He scooped up the basket of medical supplies and headed to the door.

"Rocky."

"Yes, ma'am."

"She's the aunt of your Frannie?"

He'd spilled the beans about his reason for coming to south Texas over the very first supper of ham, mashed potatoes, gravy, green beans, and coconut cream pie what seemed like years earlier. "Yes."

"Things have a way of happening for a reason, don't they?"

"God caused that deer to run across the road in front of Abigail's buggy?"

Mrs. Cotter chuckled and shook a long, bony finger at him. "I wouldn't go that far, but it's possible He placed the right person there to help her out when she needed it."

Fortified by that thought, Rocky settled the basket on an end table and tugged it closer to Abigail. She'd smoothed her hair. The *kapp* was exactly where it should be now. She looked almost asleep with her blanket tucked around her and the wood crackling and popping in the fireplace. Shock did that to a person. He hated to bother her. "Abigail?"

Her eyes opened and she peered up at him. She sat up straighter. "*Jah.*"

He pulled up Mr. Cotter's fancy cushioned footstool and plopped down in front of her. "Can I see your arm, please?"

She drew back. "It's fine."

"Don't start with the 'fine' again." His tone was sharper than he intended. "I mean—"

"It's okay. I'm being silly." She extended her right arm and took a sharp breath. "Is it broken?"

With as tender a touch as he could muster, Rocky pushed up her long gray sleeve and began to probe and bend. She pressed her lips together but didn't cry out. He smiled at her in what he hoped was his best reassuring manner. "I think it's just a sprain. No broken bones. What I'm going to do is wrap it in an Ace bandage. If you were anybody else I'd suggest ice, but in this case, you'll rest it for a couple of days, swallow some ibuprofen, and let the girls take care of business around the house until it heals."

"I don't think so."

That was Abigail. "You'll be there to oversee their work."

"True." She sounded less snappy.

He slipped the stretchy beige bandage around her wrist and began to wrap toward her elbow. "It could've been so much worse. When I rode up on that buggy tumbled by the side of the road, I . . . I don't know. I didn't know what to think."

"You were afraid it was Frannie and relieved it was only me. That's human."

"That's harsh. And not true." He picked up the washcloth and dabbed at her forehead. She jerked back. "Try to relax, I need to clean it. Yes, I was relieved it wasn't Frannie, but I wasn't relieved to see it was you."

"Sorry. Clean it." A pulse throbbed in her jaw. "Don't fib. It would only be human, especially considering I haven't been very nice to you."

"I'm not fibbing." He picked through the bandages in the basket until he found one that would cover the gash on her forehead. Better dab on some antiseptic ointment first. "I understand your concerns, but you have to believe me when I say I never want to do anything to hurt Frannie or take her away from her family. If I'm not accepted into your community, I will leave here without her. That's a promise."

Tears welled in the woman's eyes, whether from pain or emotion, he couldn't say. "I only want to do what's right for her. I promised her parents that. After what happened with my Leila, I know what pain the wrong choice will cause them. Not seeing my daughter is a hard cross to bear, but it's worse knowing she might not have eternal salvation, which is even more important."

"I understand." Rocky smoothed the bandage over

her cut and leaned back to survey his work. Leila still worshipped, she still had her deep faith, from what Frannie had told him, but he wouldn't argue with a mother's fear. "I don't want Frannie to spend her life apart from her family or from God. But being with me doesn't have to mean either of those things . . . if everything goes as planned. Nothing is more important to me than Frannie's eternal salvation, as you put it."

She ran her fingers across the bandage. From her high cheekbones to her neck, her skin was stained red. Rocky figured his was the same color, what with having such a personal conversation with a woman so important to his future. "Staying with her family, being baptized, living her faith, marrying a Plain man, and being a mother, that's what is best for her."

"Agreed, but love's also important. You married for love, didn't you?" He held up his hand. "Sorry, I don't mean to be so personal. It's none of my business."

The red deepened to scarlet. "She told you . . . about me?"

"It's obvious whenever you and Mordecai are in the same room." They had a look about them, like newlyweds, that he tried hard not to covet. "You still get that glow I imagine you had on your face the day you married the man."

"In this case, there's more to be considered. Even if you stay, if you are accepted into the faith, how do we know it will work out?" Her voice quivered, but her gaze stayed on his. "It almost never does. It's too hard for your kind to give up all the things that make your life easier."

"Easier or more cluttered and difficult to navigate?"

"If anyone can do it, Richard can." Mrs. Cotter carried a tray filled with three huge mugs of hot chocolate topped with dollops of whipped cream. "I've never seen anyone more determined. He never turns on the TV or the DVD player or even the radio in the bunkhouse. He's showered us with gifts of his cell phone, his laptop, an iPad. He's turned the place into a workout room instead, with barbells and such. Of course, we don't know what to do with most of that electronic stuff. We just turn it over to the grandkids, being fairly simple folks ourselves."

She couldn't have done better if she were writing him a job recommendation. Rocky shot her a quick look of thanks. "Besides keeping in shape, I've been reading books in the evenings instead of watching TV." He pointed at the Cotters' extensive library on the nearby shelves. "Being a jock through high school and college, I missed out on a lot of good books while I was on the road playing whatever sport was in season."

Abigail looked at him as if he spoke Greek. To her, he probably did. She nodded slowly. "Mordecai reads."

Which was how he knew so much about so many things. "We have that in common then."

Among other things. Like concern for Frannie's well-being.

The silence held for a full thirty seconds.

Mrs. Cotter placed the tray on the other end table with a soft thud. "Now, let's get some hot chocolate in you and get you warmed up. There's nothing that chocolate doesn't help, is there?"

"Will it fix the buggy?" Abigail's tone was tart, but she smiled at the older lady as she accepted the mug. "Your kindness is appreciated."

Her gaze moved to Rocky. "Yours too."

CHAPTER 10

Nothing like a good game of softball to get the blood circulating. Frannie hoped it would give her brain a jump start. Susan managed a blooper into center field over second baseman Hazel's head. The six-year-old was so short it wouldn't take much. Frannie hitched up her dress and raced for third. The *kinner* screamed for her to head for home. *Why not?* Her legs were strong and her lungs stronger. Sally Glick hurled the ball with a much better arm than most boys. It smacked into catcher Jacob King's mitt seconds after Frannie crossed the plate, letting her momentum carry her toward the school porch.

"Woo-hoo! We win, we win!" she shouted in glee, even though she knew no one was keeping score. A fact that would've made Rocky crazy. She shooed the thought away. She hadn't seen him since the auction. Aunt Abigail's story of his rescue after the buggy accident had warmed Frannie's heart, but she saw nothing in her aunt's face to indicate she'd changed her mind about the man. Her aunt continued to try to invite Joseph to supper, even though he'd found a variety of excuses to turn her down. "Good hit, Teacher, good hit."

Susan laughed and two-stepped away from the old rug that served as first base. "Too bad it's time for recess to be over."

"*Nee, nee.*"

The chorus of scholars' voices couldn't have been more in unison.

"One more batter, Teacher, one more," Caleb called from his shortstop position. "Let Frannie hit again. She hits good."

"She hits well or she's a good hitter." Ever the teacher, Susan corrected with firmness. She made the *kinner* practice their English at recess when she played games with them. They seemed to find it a good trade-off. Everyone wanted her on their team. "One more hitter, then it's time for *Englisch*. We need to practice our grammar."

"Let Sally hit. I'm old and tired." Not old, but tired. Frannie hadn't been sleeping much, and when she did, her dreams were filled with an aching sadness over unborn babies and people who were invariably lost to her. Her parents roamed the fields looking for her. Her little sister Hannah cried at the supper table, her hand patting the empty chair next to her. "Go on, it's not fair. You know I'll get a hit."

Sally picked up the scarred wooden bat, leaving Frannie to slip down the makeshift first-base line to where Susan hopped on and off the base as spry as a kindergartner. Uncle Mordecai's sister was a shorter, rounder version of her brother with the same dark-brown eyes and unruly black hair trying its best to escape from her *kapp*. Give her a beard and they'd be twins. The thought made Frannie giggle. She hadn't giggled much lately.

"So what are you doing here?"

"Huh?" Frannie kept her gaze on pitcher Luke Hostetler, who kept peeking over his shoulder as if he expected thirty-something Susan to steal second base. "*Aenti* Abigail made an extra big batch of fry pies. She thought it would be a nice treat for the *kinner* so I offered to bring them over. I thought it would be fun to visit, and it gets me out of *Aenti* Abigail's hair for a while."

Her aunt had been unusually quiet since the buggy accident. She didn't wear the bandage on her wrist anymore, but the wound on her head seemed to be taking its time healing. She had bruises up and down her right side from shoulder to ankle. Most were now an ugly yellow and green color. Frannie had been on her way for a cup of *kaffi* this morning when the sight of *Onkel* Mordecai kissing his *fraa's* forehead in the kitchen had caused her to slip back to the front room. Her uncle's love for her aunt was written on his face every day. Theirs was a second chance at love, yet it seemed as strong and as sweet as any Frannie had ever seen. She longed for a tenth of what they had.

Which brought her back to the school yard and her reason for wanting to escape such a lovely scene.

"I know better. You couldn't wait to get out of the schoolhouse a few years ago." Susan edged from the base, her skirt hitched up around her shins. "The only time you come around is for the Christmas pageant. And then it's for the cookies."

"Not true. I love the hymns and the scholars' performances." She studied her sneakers. "I was thinking maybe you'd need a helper now that Esther is married."

"Get a hit, get a hit, Sally! I have essays to read!" Susan clapped her hands. Her high voice carried over the *batter-batter-swing* chant of the infield. "I can always use help, but I'm having a hard time imagining you here, inside, every day. At recess, *jah*, but doing reading with the little ones, *nee*."

"I have to do something." Frannie fought the urge to stamp her feet. "I can't stay at *Aenti* Abigail's all day long, doing laundry and washing dishes."

"That's what she does. That's what *fraas* do."

"I didn't mean it that way. She does it for her *mann* and her *kinner*."

"You don't think you'll have your own *mann* and *boplin* one day?"

"It's not looking that way."

"Oh, ye of little faith."

"Susan!"

Susan stomped on the base with both sneakers. "You don't know what *Gott's* plan for you is. You don't. So right now, the best thing to do is wait upon the Lord. Wait and be patient."

"Is that what you did?"

"What do you mean?"

"You never married. You never had your own *boplin*."

"*Nee*." Susan clapped and shouted encouragement to Sally, who took a big swing and missed. Strike two. "Things might not have turned out exactly as I planned, but they turned out as *Gott* planned. In that I am certain and I'm content. When Mordecai's first *fraa* was killed in the van wreck and Phineas nearly died, Mordecai needed me. They needed me. I was there and ready and able to step in when I was needed. I thank *Gott* for that. I know Mordecai does too."

Feeling thoroughly small and chastised, Frannie crossed her arms over her chest. "You're right."

"*Jah*, I'm right. And *Gott's* plan for me is not at an end yet. Who knows what the future will bring? Only *Gott*. The same is true for you. Be patient. Wait to see what He has in store for you. It'll be greater than anything you can imagine for yourself." Susan grinned at her, unaware that Frannie had heard all this before from Aunt Abigail. It bore repeating, no doubt. "Besides, as a teacher, I get to play games every day at recess. Who could ask for more?"

The crack of bat against ball filled the air. Susan took off, arms and legs pumping. "See you at home plate."

Stop being so self-centered. That's what Susan meant to say, only she was too kind to use those words. Stop thinking of only herself.

* * *

Frannie climbed into the wagon and picked up the reins, still picturing Susan's cheerful face. *Sorry,* Gott. *Thy will be done. If that means Leroy sends Rocky home and I end up an unmarried aunt to a boatload of nieces and nephews like Susan, so be it.*

"Hey, Frannie."

She looked back. Susan scampered across the yard, her hand on her side as if running had given her a stitch. "Come back tomorrow. I'll talk with Leroy."

"You mean it?"

"If nothing else, you can be my recess monitor."

"I'll do more than that."

"No eating their lunches."

"Just their cookies."

"It's not forever, Frannie."

Maybe not. "*Danki.*"

Susan laughed. "You'll be sorry when I make you practice their times tables with them."

"Two times four is nine, right?"

Susan's laugh followed her as she drove the buggy from the yard and out onto the dirt road that led to Mordecai's. It wasn't forever. *Nee*, maybe not. But this was her show of faith. She had a job. She would move on with her life if that was what *Gott* required.

Thy will be done.

She repeated the words over and over on the ride home until they sounded like a hymn sung to the *clickety-clack* of the wagon wheels on the dirt road and the *clippity clop-clop* of the horse's hooves.

Finally, she began to say them aloud, sure she could learn to mean them.

CHAPTER 11

Some folks might think hunting was about camaraderie among men more than the sport itself. It might be, but Rocky could see that Mordecai and Caleb were serious about bagging a wild turkey or two. Otherwise, most likely they'd be eating chicken for Thanksgiving. Not that anything was wrong with chicken when a person had an empty belly, but Thanksgiving by all rights should include turkey. Being asked to come along on this hunting trip was an honor. He had to remind himself of that. In the dusk before dawn, the air was soupy with rain that misted on their faces and dampened their coats. His boots made a squelching sound in thick mud that made it difficult to pick up his feet. If only he could help them put a big bird on the table. Today was their last chance. So far they'd seen not a feather nor heard the *kerr-kerr* of a hen.

"This land has been picked clean." Caleb shoved his hat down on his head with one hand and nestled his shotgun against his chest with the other. He sounded like a grown man, not an eleven-year-old. He'd likely been hunting for years. "We might as well head home."

Mordecai put a finger to his lips and smiled. "It's early. They're still roosting. You know turkeys don't like getting wet in the rain any more than we do. When it's raining they can't hear predators approaching. They'll head out to the fields to look for insects for breakfast any minute now."

As always, Mordecai was a fountain of information delivered in a soft, gruff voice. "Until then, I could use a spot of hot *kaffi*." He tugged a thermos from a knapsack on his shoulder. "How about you, *Englisch* man?"

Something about the way he said *"Englisch* man" made it a term of endearment, which surprised Rocky to no end. He accepted the offering, popped the cup from the top of the thermos, and unscrewed the lid. "I was surprised when you asked me to come along."

Mordecai eased onto a fallen tree trunk, seemingly unaware or uncaring that it was damp from end to end. "Would you be surprised if I invited you to Thanksgiving tomorrow?"

"Yes." Might as well be honest. If a man couldn't be honest on a hunting trip, then there wasn't much left to do on this earth. "Why would you put me in close proximity to—"

"To my family." Mordecai shook his finger at him, his gaze on Caleb, who squatted nearby drinking hot chocolate from his own small thermos. "First, it's a way of thanking you again for the kindness you showed my *fraa*. When I think of her alone there on the side of the road, hurt, well, I . . ."

His voice had grown hoarse, as it had the first time he thanked Rocky for stopping to help Abigail when the buggy overturned. Who wouldn't have stopped? Anyone with a heart surely would help a woman on the side of the road. "No need to thank me for being a decent human being—"

"I also have been following your progress with Leroy and in general," Mordecai interrupted, also surprising as it wasn't something Plain folks generally did. The man had something to say, it seemed. "You've worked hard and walked quietly among us, following the lead of the other men. You seem earnest in your endeavor."

"I am earnest."

"It's a hard row."

"It is."

"Are you prepared to learn German?"

"I am."

"Not just *Deutsch*, but High German as you've heard in the services?"

"I am."

"Is your heart prepared?"

Rocky contemplated the question, trying to follow Mordecai's thinking. "If you mean do I understand the calling to faith and how it's practiced in this community, yes, my heart is prepared. More than prepared. I feel as if I've waited my whole life for this."

"No more competitive sports. No more boxing matches."

"I wouldn't be here now if those were more important to me than my walk in faith."

Rocky paused, the images from his past life painting a montage in his mind. Parent-pitch and T-ball with his dad, Pony league with his uncle, flag football, tackle football, YMCA basketball, competitive basketball, tryouts, making the teams in multiple sports in junior high, high school, college. Championships and trophies. Cheerleaders, bonfires, and pep rallies. His life had revolved around something Mordecai would never understand. But if Rocky knew anything, it was that sports were simply games. Games that taught children leadership, teamwork, loyalty, and social skills, but still games. They didn't make a life, but they helped hone character. Sports crafted leaders, but they did nothing to fill the void in his chest where his faith should reside.

"Don't get me wrong. I don't apologize for my previous life choices," he said finally. "I believe in sports. As a teaching tool for good values, but also for health and physical fitness. For helping kids blow off steam at recess so they can sit still and learn in class. I'm sure you've seen this at your school and with your *kinner*, so you know what I'm saying is true."

"I don't question your past choices. I'm only trying to understand your current choices." Mordecai took a swallow of coffee that steamed in the chill of the early morning. "And to make sure you won't regret them."

"*Nee*, I won't." Rocky elbowed Caleb, who grunted and nearly spilled his hot chocolate. "I fully expect to play a lot more basketball and softball in these parts, given the chance. I'll even play volleyball if nothing else presents itself."

Caleb stood. "Yeah, after we eat tomorrow we can play ball."

"Sure. We'll work off all those carbs."

"Carbs?"

"Wait." Mordecai held up a hand. "Hear that?"

His voice had dropped to a whisper. A sound like yelps and then the *kerr-kerr* sound of hens talking to one another. "Kerr-kerr. Yamp, yamp, kerr, yamp," Mordecai called back, mimicking the sounds perfectly. "Kerr, kerr, yamp, kerr, yamp."

Rocky reached for the thermos. Caleb tucked his in the knapsack and stood, his Winchester at the ready. With luck the calls would bring the birds their direction. Time to hunt.

A *crack* broke the silence. Like a firecracker or . . . a gunshot.

Something whizzed over Rocky's head, so close he felt the cool breeze. A pinging sound echoed from behind him.

A shot.

A second bullet *thunked* as it dug into the trunk of a mesquite tree behind them.

His cup hit the mud near his boot.

Feeling as if he moved in slow motion, Rocky hurled himself at Caleb. The boy let out a *humpft* as they hit the ground face-first in the mud.

Another shot pinged over their heads.

"Cease fire!" he hollered, aware of Mordecai flat on his stomach next to them. "Cease fire."

Mordecai yelled something in *Deutsch*.

Adrenaline pumping through him like an out-of-control geyser, Rocky inched up his head and waved his cap. "Stop shooting now!"

Voices clamored. A few seconds later two *Englisch* men in drab brown-and-gray camo tramped toward them, their shotguns pointed at the ground. Both looked stricken. "Hey, are you guys okay?" The shorter man with a full Duck Dynasty beard and thick glasses had a cigarette-roughened voice. "So sorry, man, I thought I saw a tom fly out of the trees in this direction."

Rocky scrambled to his feet. Mordecai and Caleb did the same. For a few seconds, the only sound was their heavy breathing.

"This is private property." Rocky spoke first. Mordecai was busy inspecting every inch of Caleb as if he couldn't believe his stepson hadn't been hit. "You must've wandered through a gate without realizing."

The taller man shoved back a hat with GUARD YOUR SECOND AMENDMENT RIGHTS embroidered on it. "Sorry, man, we might have gotten a little off track, what with following the droppings and the molting." Curiosity etched across his face, his gaze fluttered to Mordecai and Caleb. "You're Amish folks? I didn't know you hunted. I thought you were pacifists."

The shaking in his legs made it hard for Rocky to stand. He eased onto the tree trunk Mordecai had vacated. "We only hunt what we eat." The *we* came out like the most natural thing in the world. "You'll find the road off this property up there to your left. Follow the path."

"Sorry about that. We'd didn't see y'all."

"Like I said, no harm done."

He watched them trudge away until they were out of sight, somehow not convinced they would actually leave if he didn't.

"We're fine." Mordecai squatted next to him. Caleb

flopped down on his knees, seemingly oblivious to the mud, bits of weeds, and grass that covered his clothes. "Like you said, no harm done."

"Way too close for comfort."

"It's one of the risks of hunting season. Too many folks, too little territory. Some of them are weekend warriors who don't give a hoot about safety or don't know any better." The pallor on his usually brown face reflected more concern than Mordecai seemed to want to admit. "You handled it right."

"How so?"

"You thought quickly and moved quickly under fire, however shaken. Then you were firm but calm with those fellows." Mordecai brushed leaves and dirt from his black jacket and pants. "Just as you should have been. Oftentimes a scare like that will cause a person to react with anger."

Rocky examined the last few minutes in his mind's eye. Anger had been there, but also the understanding that it was an accident. They didn't seek out fellow hunters at whom they could shoot. It could have been tragic. Thanks be to God, it wasn't. "I think the time I spent over the years coaching kids has a lot to do with the way I react to things. Usually calm works best."

"Agreed. It's good to know you're not one to fly off the handle under duress. Plain folks don't abide by that much." Mordecai gave Caleb's shoulder another squeeze. The boy's face still looked pasty. "You good?"

Caleb nodded. "We're still hunting, aren't we?"

"*Jah*." Mordecai clapped Rocky on the back. "My

fraa will be very disappointed if we come home without a bird for the table tomorrow."

Rocky blew out air. One thing was for certain. He couldn't afford to disappoint Abigail.

CHAPTER 12

The once heady aroma of Thanksgiving turkey now made Frannie want to open a window. The food had been wonderful. She'd eaten too much of it, in fact. Like the others, she wasn't used to such a bounty of rich foods. That second piece of pecan pie had been the breaking point. Or maybe it was the second yeast roll slathered with fresh butter. Wishing she could loosen her dress somehow, she placed the last of the clean plates on the shelf above her head. Since she'd chosen to dry, she was the last one in the kitchen. Rebekah had dragged Hazel off for a much-needed nap. Frannie could use one herself. Hours to prepare, minutes to eat, hours to clean up afterward. That's what her *mudder* always said with a certain air of satisfaction. Men might bring home the turkey, but womenfolk did the lion's share of the work when it came to this holiday and most others.

A wave of sadness swept over her. This was her first Thanksgiving away from her parents and silly little Hannah and baby Rachel, who wasn't a baby anymore. Her brother Obadiah would be there with his *fraa* and *kinner*, as would Rufus. Joshua was courting, according to Hannah, but they weren't sure with whom. If Frannie were there, she'd figure it out. She had a way of doing that.

Someone else was spending the holiday away from his family. Rocky. It hadn't hurt his appetite. He'd put away two helpings of turkey, exclaiming over how much better the darker meat was than a store-bought bird, cornbread stuffing, mashed potatoes, sweet potatoes, gravy, cranberries, and two pieces of pie—one pumpkin, one pecan. Not that she was watching or counting.

They hadn't spoken since the auction. Since his declaration. He hadn't shone his flashlight in her window. Or sent her a note. Nothing. Right now he was out in the front room by the fireplace playing card games with Caleb and her other cousins.

Which was why she would head out the kitchen door for a nice, long walk far from temptation. She needed to work off the food anyway. Grabbing her shawl from the hook by the back door, she bundled up and put her hand on the doorknob.

"Where are you going?"

She bowed her head. Almost made it. Her heart began to thump like Butch's tail against the porch railing when she petted him. "You have to stop doing that."

"What?"

"Popping up everywhere."

"I didn't pop up. I came for another glass of lemonade. Is that a crime?"

Crime? So often he talked nonsense. Still, Frannie wanted to smile. "What kind of question is that?"

"Are you going for a walk?"

What was his first hint? "*Jah*."

"Can I go with you?"

"*Nee*."

"Don't be that way."

"My *aenti* is out there."

"She went to her room for a nap. *Onkel* Mordecai is passed out in the rocking chair. The boys are going to play kick the can or some such game I've never heard of."

"I thought you promised Caleb a game of basketball."

"I did as soon as the food settles. I ate so much I might vomit . . ." Rocky's grin spread. "Not the most romantic thing I've ever said to a girl."

The potential existed that she might do the same, but it wouldn't be from playing games. Frannie tightened her shawl around her shoulders and opened the door. "And there's been a lot of them, I'm sure."

With his long legs he caught up with her all too quickly, zipping up his black leather bomber jacket as he went. "A few, I won't deny it. But none like you."

Frannie had no doubt of that. She pounded down the back porch steps and lengthened her own stride, picking her way around rain puddles and dodging droopy nopals that didn't care for the winter weather's penchant for hiding the sun. They walked in silence, Rocky's last statement ping-ponging between them. She truly didn't know what to say so she said nothing.

At the stand of mesquite and live oak that separated Mordecai's property from the Hostetlers', Rocky caught her hand. His fingers slipped between hers and tightened. He stopped walking, forcing her to do the same. "About what I said the other day at the auction."

"The other day? That was three weeks ago." She tugged at her hand, but he wouldn't give it up. "A person doesn't say that and then let three weeks go by."

"I had no choice."

She swiped at her face with her other hand. "I know." She did know. That was the trouble.

"I meant it."

"I know."

"I'm trying to do the right thing."

"Me too." She gazed at his face, memorizing the way his curls sprang up around his ball cap, damp and wiry. "I took a job as Susan's helper at the school."

"You did?" Uncertainty washed over his face. "I thought—"

"Single girls take that job, that's what you thought?"

"Sort of. I mean, it was kind of understood."

"It is."

"So you're thinking you'll remain single."

"That's what I'm thinking." Her knees shook, but she forced one foot to move, then the other, until she stood in his space. "I love you too."

"And what does that have to do with you working at the school?" He took a step toward her, enveloping her in that tantalizing Rocky scent. "Exactly?"

"It means that if Leroy decides you should go back to Missouri and never see me again, I'll abide by his decision." His fingers tightened, the white knuckles matching her own smaller ones. "I'll ask you to do the same."

"I will." The words sounded raw, his voice husky. "I promised myself I wouldn't keep you from your faith or your family."

"Joseph isn't coming around anymore. He was more interested in *Aenti* Abigail's cooking than in me anyway. Says I'm too lippy."

"You are lippy." The muscles in Rocky's jaw contracted. His breathing quickened. "You'll not court another? That's what you're saying?"

"I love you. That's that."

His free hand touched her face. He shook his head. "I never thought loving someone would make me so crazy."

"You know how to pick them, I guess."

He laughed, more pain than mirth in the sound. "Don't I, though?"

"Look at it this way. You'll be home for the holidays with your family, instead of missing them on days like today."

"Missing you instead."

She acknowledged the truth of that statement with a quick, hard hug, stepping back before he could respond. "We shouldn't make it harder."

His arms came out, then dropped to his sides. "What do you mean?"

"Don't come around anymore."

"I may only have a few weeks left and you want me to waste the chance to spend time with you?"

"We can't court unless Leroy decides you'll stay. It's best that we not see each other until he makes a decision."

"I'll get to say good-bye?"

Mourning already soaked his words. *Don't make it worse.* "We'll see."

"I have two more sessions with Leroy and then the interview."

"I know. Mordecai mentioned it." To Aunt Abigail. But in front of Frannie, giving her the gift of knowing what was going on. "That means you'll be here through Christmas."

"Yes."

"A sweet time of year to be with family."

"My family's here." He wrapped his long arms around her in a bear hug against his chest. His heart beat in her ear. His breath touched her forehead, warming her. "You're my family."

"Rocky."

His arms dropped, leaving her cold and bereft in a gray, sunless day. "We better get back to the house."

They walked side by side, not touching, but Frannie savored the lovely sensation that he still held her hand. All the way home.

CHAPTER 13

Rocky paused on the school porch to remove his ball cap. Balancing the pan of pumpkin bars Mrs. Cotter had made against his chest, he used one trembling hand to slick back his unruly hair. Leroy would make a decision in the next few days. The interview had taken only an hour after all those long, frustrating days of study and discussion. Depending on Leroy's decision, the Christmas pageant might be Rocky's last gathering with folks he'd come to like, admire, even love.

Including Frannie. If he were anyone else, he would rue the day he'd trotted into Callie's Bakery and Restaurant in Jamesport, Missouri, to see this skinny girl with hair the color of carrots and more freckles than a guy could count hefting a rubber bin of dirty dishes almost as big as she was. He would never regret meeting Frannie Mast. Everything that followed had made him a better man—a better person—with greater faith, new friends, a passing knowledge of south Texas and all that region encompassed. It had brought him love, bittersweet though it might be in the end.

If Leroy decided against allowing him to join the

church, Rocky would have to go back to Missouri, whether he liked it or not. He'd agreed to that provision. He must've been out of his mind. The pan of pumpkin bars weighed heavy in his hands. Laughter and chatter wafted from the building. Another buggy pulled in next to his. Time to get in there and get it over with.

Enjoy it while he could, better yet.

The door opened and Caleb grinned up at him. "Whatcha doing standing out there? It's cold. We're getting ready to start."

"Cold for south Texas. This would be balmy weather up north." Rocky took a breath and summoned a smile. "Merry Christmas."

Inside, a wood-burning stove created a warm glow that matched the happy faces that filled the room. It might not seem cold to him, but these folks wore coats. A chorus of Merry Christmas's greeted him. Mordecai, Deborah, Phineas, Abigail, even Naomi Glick seemed to have put aside differences for the moment. After setting the pumpkin bars on a table already loaded with sweets, Rocky took his time, made the rounds, greeted each one, memorizing faces and making memories to carry home.

Frannie offered a tiny half wave from across the room. She wore her Sunday gray dress and had managed to arrive without a single stain on her apron. Her hair behaved itself behind a clean, neat *kapp*. He nodded. No sense in getting her in any more trouble than he already had. They'd agreed not to see each other, and they'd kept their word over the past few weeks. A simple hello wouldn't be too much, would it? He side-stepped little Timothy King and angled his way past the second row of benches.

"You should have a brownie. They're really good." Joseph stepped in front of him. "I heard Hazel say Frannie made them, but I'll believe that when I see her mixing the batter."

Rocky looked over the shorter man's shoulder. Frannie sank onto a bench between Rebekah and Abigail. "I was just going to—"

"Say hello?" Joseph inched closer. His voice dropped. "Don't spoil the night for her. Half of courting is knowing when and where."

"I'm not courting."

"I know." Joseph chucked him on the back. "That's what she says."

"Really, I—"

Susan clapped her hands twice. Silence fell as her scholars trotted to the front of the room and disappeared behind sheets that had been tacked up across one corner for a makeshift backstage. Much giggling and whispering ensued. Rocky swallowed his retort. Truth be told, the man was right. This was the crux of the matter. He couldn't choose the Plain life for Frannie's sake. It had to be for the sake of his own faith. He inhaled and lowered his head. Gott, *Thy will be done.*

The children sauntered from behind the sheet in their costumes. Caleb made a fine Joseph. Leroy and Naomi's Sally struggled to straighten her head covering while nestling a baby doll against her skinny chest. Mary and the infant Jesus. Sweet.

Their enactment of the "no room at the inn" scene brought smiles to the faces in the audience. Singing of Christmas songs followed. What they lacked in musical talent, these youngsters made up for with their enthusiasm. Rocky found himself watching the faces in the audience. The Amish didn't have a speck of pride in them, but he could pick out the parents, the way they watched their children, the way they smiled with pleasure to see them celebrate the birth of Christ. God incarnate sent to earth to die for each one of them.

Such goodness. Such sweetness. He bowed his head and swiped at his face. *Good Lord, Father, Abba, give me strength. Whatever Leroy decides, I know it will be the right thing. If I need to go home, so be it. I'll go because I know You'll be with me wherever I am.*

Abigail and Mordecai's little Hazel rounded out the show with a cute poem she'd written with the help of her classmates. One hand on her cheek as if to hide her face, she managed to make it all the way through with only one prompting from Susan. Then she ran from the impromptu stage right into her mother's arms. Cheering and clapping rocked the room with choruses of Merry Christmas and blessings for the New Year.

Rocky swallowed hard, stood, and slapped his hat on his head. No matter what happened, this would be the best Christmas of his life.

* * *

Frannie's hands hurt from clapping. Her throat hurt from holding back tears. Christmas would always be her favorite time of year. Nothing could be allowed to change that. This was not about her. Exactly as Rocky had said on Thanksgiving Day. So eloquently and then he left. She hadn't seen him since that day a month ago. She'd heard of how he helped bale the last of the hay and chopped wood for the school and helped load the horse trailer with the Kropfs' furniture when they decided to move back to Carrollton in Missouri after only a year in Bee County. He had to do what God called him to do, as did Leroy. If only Leroy would make a decision, ending her suffering and Rocky's.

Aunt Abigail turned and leaned close. "Patience is a virtue."

Indeed. That didn't make it any easier. Frannie gave Hazel a big hug and a quick shove. "Go get a brownie before they're all gone. Bring me a cutout cookie with lots of frosting."

Hazel frowned. "But I want that one too."

"If there's enough, you can have one of each."

Grinning from ear to ear, the little girl took off. To be so young and innocent that a cookie could make her day. Frannie allowed herself to do what she hadn't done all evening. She sneaked a glance across the room. Rocky stood near the dessert table, a gingersnap the size of his palm in one hand and a cup of hot chocolate in the other. He looked content.

As he should.

"Don't even think about it." Deborah offset the sternness of her words with a pat on the shoulder. "You've been doing so well, don't give in now."

Frannie studied her sneakers. "He looks like a doofus chewing on that big cookie."

Deborah giggled, sounding like Hazel. "Don't be mean."

"I'm trying to put myself in the right frame of mind."

"You don't have to say good-bye just yet."

"You think Leroy will say no?"

"I think Leroy is praying and heeding *Gott's* word. He'll do what is right and wise."

The ache in Frannie's throat threatened to choke her. "That's what I'm hoping."

Rocky tucked the last bite of cookie in his mouth. He picked up a napkin and handed it to Hazel. They seemed to be having a conversation. He rubbed his bare chin, looking serious. After a minute or two, he placed a cookie, and then another, on the napkin. He patted Hazel's head and gave her a little shove before turning back to the table without looking in Frannie's direction.

The girl trotted back to Frannie. She held the napkin with both hands as if conveying a precious gift. "Rocky says to give you the star. He says it reminds him of you because you shine so bright."

Frannie closed her eyes. *Don't cry. Don't cry. Don't cry.*

"Are you going to eat it? If you're not, I will."

Frannie opened her eyes and took the cookie from her cousin. "Of course I'll eat it."

She lifted the cookie to her mouth and glanced across the room, hoping Rocky would be watching.

He wasn't.

Leroy stood between her and Rocky. They were talking; rather, Leroy talked, and Rocky simply nodded. The older man's hand came out. They shook.

Then Rocky shrugged on his coat without looking at a single soul.

And he left.

Leroy trudged across the room. For the first time, Frannie realized he was limping a bit. He looked old and tired. He tipped his hat to her and smiled. "Merry Christmas."

Joy dawned in those words. No matter what happened, God still reigned in heaven and on earth. "Merry Christmas."

Leroy limped on, this time stopping to talk to Uncle Mordecai, who nodded. Her uncle began to circle the room, speaking to the older folks, the married ones. After a moment Frannie realized he was speaking to all those who'd been baptized. The members of the church. She sidled up next to Abigail. "What's going on?"

Abigail settled onto the bench, a paper plate filled with Christmas goodies in her hands. "Leroy has called a meeting."

"For when?"

"Now. Everyone's here. He's putting it to a vote."

"Everyone will decide?"

"He says that's the proper way. Take Rebekah and Hazel on home. We'll get a ride from Phineas."

Pinpricks of purple and light flickered in Frannie's eyes. She tried to breathe and found she couldn't.

"Go on, child." *Aenti* Abigail smiled up at her. "Go home. Say your prayers and remember, *Gott's* will be done."

She wanted to ask how her *aenti* would vote, but Frannie didn't. That, too, was between Aunt Abigail and *Gott*.

She tried to form her own prayer as she helped Hazel bundle up and slipped into her own shawl. The only word that came was *Please*.

CHAPTER 14

Chores first, of course. Rocky didn't mind. He dumped feed into the horses' trough and inhaled the crisp morning air. He'd awakened with such a sense of peace. Even though Leroy hadn't said he could stay, he hadn't sent him away. His handshake had been firm, his words of farewell kind. Either way, Mordecai's last-minute invitation to join his family for Christmas Day had been the frosting on the cake. Christmas with Frannie. Truly a gift all its own. His gifts for them were small, a new faceless doll for Hazel, a baseball mitt for Caleb, basketballs for the rest of the boys, orange spice tea for Abigail, a book of crossword puzzles for Mordecai. He had nothing for Frannie because he simply couldn't decide yet what that gift should be. He would give her something special before he left for Missouri.

If this was to be their only Christmas together, it had to be a special gift. Memorable. Lasting. He would figure it out. Just not today. She would understand.

"Come on, it's time for breakfast," Caleb hollered from the barn door. "Hurry up. We get presents now. Maybe we can play some basketball later."

Rocky had to laugh at the boy's exuberance. Kids were all alike when it came to gifts. Even Plain *kinner*.

He went to the kitchen first to wash his hands. The water was icy. He ducked his face and splashed it, trying to wash off the sensation that this would be the last time he did each one of these tasks with these people. A tiny piece of tissue floated in the water. He'd forgotten the wound along his jawline. Learning to shave with a razor had taken a daily toll on his face. Maybe that particular struggle had ended. He straightened and grabbed a threadbare dish towel from the counter, taking his time memorizing the warm kitchen. A stack of pancakes as tall as a toddler sat warming on the stove next to a huge pan of scrambled eggs. The house smelled of maple syrup and fresh baked biscuits and bacon. His mouth watered.

"Come on, come into the front room." Hazel tugged on his hand. "Your seat is next to Caleb's."

Rocky followed. He sank into his chair, glad to sit. He'd never felt so blessed or so welcome or so sad.

"Presents first?" Hazel danced around Mordecai, keeping him from making much progress from the kitchen to the table. "Presents are first, aren't they?"

"Not if I stumble over you and break my neck." Mordecai scooped her up and carried her on his hip like a sack of potatoes. She shrieked, her giggles contagious. His low rumble of laughter mingled with the girl's. "Patience is virtue, my child."

Even though he'd heard that phrase a hundred times, it had never meant more to Rocky.

Frannie set a basket loaded with biscuits on the

table. At the sight of him, she smiled, a broad, happy smile the likes of which he hadn't seen in a month of Sundays.

"Morning."

"Morning."

"Presents?" Hazel touched a small stack next to her plate, but she didn't pick anything up. "Now?"

"Prayers first." Mordecai bowed his head. Everyone followed suit.

Silence swept over the room, bringing with it a sense of peace and a kind of prosperity that had nothing to do with material goods. Rocky prayed for each person in the room and for his own salvation.

"Since we have a guest this bright and beautiful morning, I think we should start with his gifts." Mordecai broke the silence. "What do y'all think?"

"There's no need to give me gifts." Rocky squirmed in his seat. These folks had no extra of anything. They worked hard to feed and clothe themselves. There was nothing left after that. "Honestly, I wouldn't feel right."

"A person should never reject a gift given from the heart." Mordecai shook one long and calloused finger at Rocky. "Accept and be blessed by these offerings."

Nothing could be said to that, especially with the tightness in his throat and the heat behind his eyes, so Rocky opted for a simple nod.

"Me first, me first!" Hazel scooted from her chair and ran around the table, a small brown bag in her chubby hands. "Open it, open it."

Rocky obliged. The bag held two apples and three

long carrots. Uncertain, he smiled at her. "Thank you. I love apples and carrots."

"For your horse. For Chocolate." Hazel held up her hands as if amazed she had to explain this. "Horses like Christmas too."

Silly Rocky. "Of course they do."

Caleb went next. A hunting knife wrapped in newspaper funnies. A nice one. "Are you sure, Caleb? This was expensive."

"*Jah.*" The boy shrugged, his grin philosophical. "I had two."

"Perfect."

"We have to go deer hunting soon."

"Absolutely." If he was still here. "It will come in very handy."

Deborah handed him a box across the table. Phineas sat next to her, his arm thrown across the chair behind his *fraa*. The word came naturally. *Mann* and *fraa*. Something Rocky might never have. He focused on the box, afraid they would all see the emotion that threatened to overwhelm him. No fancy paper or bows. A simple box with the flaps entwined to keep the lid shut.

"Y'all shouldn't have done this."

The *y'all* made everyone laugh. He would take a bit of Texas home with him, no doubt about it. He tugged open the flaps. A beautiful, pristine straw hat. He lifted it with gentle hands. "You shouldn't have." It was the nicest hat he'd ever owned. "I mean, I—"

"I hope it's not too big." Deborah slapped a hand on her husband's broad chest. "Phineas insisted you have a big head."

"To match my big feet." Rocky managed a laugh. It sounded strangled in his ears. He set the hat on his head. It fit just as it should, a little snug so the first south Texas wind wouldn't send it sailing. If he were to look in a mirror right now—if there was a mirror in this house, which there likely wouldn't be—he'd see a man the spitting image of an Amish person. He had no doubt of that. "He's right. It's perfect."

Abigail went next. "From Mordecai and me."

A small package wrapped in white tissue paper. Suspenders. This time he had to take a long breath. What were they saying? Did they know something he didn't? A straw hat, suspenders, a hunting knife, food for his horse. It seemed to add up to an enormous gift he hadn't expected to receive.

"*Galluses*, right? That's the word for suspenders?"

Abigail nodded and smiled. "*Galluses*."

"Thank you." He cleared his throat. "I know you don't stand on ceremony, and you're not much for flowery sentiment, but I have to say it. Thank you for making me feel so welcome and so a part of this family today. It's the best Christmas ever."

"That's not all."

Frannie slipped from her chair and picked up a box nestled on the floor next to the fireplace. When she turned, tears shone in her eyes. He'd never seen her cry. Not that she would admit to crying now. The box was heavy. He unfolded the flaps. An enormous English–German translation of the Holy Bible sat on his lap. He lifted it from tissue paper that protected it. Leather bound. Substantial in his shaking hands.

He lifted his gaze from the book and let it travel to Frannie. Her smile trembled. "Nothing is more important than your path with God. Our journey through this world is short. You'll need that to navigate."

She plopped into her chair, her hand over her mouth as if to keep from saying more.

He cleared his throat again. "I'm not sure I understand what this means."

"You already have the most important tool." Mordecai leaned back in his chair, his expression expansive. "You have faith, despite or because of the travails you've experienced. You've shown Leroy and me and the rest of our community your commitment, your willingness to set aside the trappings of the world, to keep yourself apart."

Rocky heard the words, but they still didn't compute. "Leroy made a decision?"

"We all did. The district voted after the pageant."

"All y'all said yes."

Mordecai's laugh rumbled deep in his chest. "We all did."

"*Jah, jah*!" Hazel crowed. "Merry Christmas."

"I'm in?"

"You have to take the baptism classes in the spring and be baptized."

"Hence, the Bible." He touched the black leather cover. His jaw ached with the effort to corral his emotions. He wouldn't start out by bawling like a baby in front of members of his new community. "I'm speechless."

Caleb smacked his fork against his plate in a beat

reminiscent of a Christmas song. "Enough talk. Let's open our presents so we can eat pancakes."

Indeed. All the important words had been spoken. Almost.

* * *

Frannie scraped the last of her scrambled eggs and bacon into Butch's dish on the back porch. The dog's snout turned up in an obvious smile under one eye with the "pirate patch." If the *schtinkich* of his doggy breath was any indication, he'd already bagged a rabbit or some such critter for breakfast. Regardless, his behind wagged a stubby tail. Tightening her shawl around her in the chilly December breeze, she glanced back, feeling only slightly guilty. *Aenti* Abigail didn't like for her to feed table scraps to Butch, but even the dog deserved a Christmas treat. After the gift exchange, she'd found herself with little appetite. She wanted to run after Rocky when he left the table with *Onkel* Mordecai. Ask him, What now? What does this mean for us? A woman didn't do that. Especially in these circumstances. It wasn't about her or her feelings for Rocky. This was about Rocky's path on this earth. Nothing was bigger than that, no matter how she felt.

All the same, it wasn't fair, making women wait until men grew enough smarts to know what they wanted out of life. Women always got down that road first, it seemed. Always.

"There you are."

A shiver swept through her that had nothing to

do with the damp winter weather. She turned. Rocky loomed over her. The Rocky scent engulfed her. He wore his new straw hat. He looked so Plain. Appearances meant nothing, Frannie knew that, but the sight of him made her want to sit down right where she stood. Her feet were lumps of wood. If she tried to walk, she'd keel over. "Here I am."

Rocky scratched Butch behind floppy ears. The dog panted in sheer delight and went back to eating. "Does Abigail know you're feeding Butch bacon? That has to be some form of sacrilege."

"Hush. He's a good dog. He deserves a treat."

He shrugged those massive shoulders. "I reckon you're right."

His hand came up and his thumb brushed against Frannie's cheek. Suddenly she didn't need her shawl after all. "What are you doing?"

"At least you're not still asking me what I'm doing *here*." The humor in the words didn't match his serious expression. "You had a smudge of syrup on your face."

The plate clattered against the wood beneath her feet. She bent to pick it up. Her head collided with his. "Ouch. Ouch!"

"Yikes, ouch, sorry!" They both straightened. Rocky held the plate, by some miracle, unbroken in his hand. "Sorry. That's what happens when I try to be helpful."

Would it always be this hard for them? Frannie wanted to find out. She couldn't wait to find out. She snatched the dirty plate, tempted to press it against her apron for fear it would fall again. "Was there . . . something else?"

"Yep. I mean, *jah*."

"What is it?"

"I'm so happy about being allowed to stay. I was wondering . . . are you happy too?"

"Of course I am. It's what I wanted. For you. And for me. If it's what you want."

"It is. It truly is. I'm looking forward to spring and the baptism classes."

A question not asked echoed through his words.

"Me too."

"You'll be baptized with me, then?"

With or without him, of course, but Frannie knew what he meant. "I'll be baptized."

Rocky shuffled his big feet, his smile almost shy. "I feel bad. I don't have a Christmas gift yet for you. I couldn't decide."

She'd already received the gift of his continued presence in her life. A chance that they could be together. "You don't have to get me anything. It doesn't work that way—leastways not around here."

He would learn that now. It would be a pleasure to watch him embrace this new season in his life. If he planned to share it with her. Surely, he did. Still, a girl didn't like to take these things for granted.

"There are so many things I thought of getting you." He stared over her shoulder. "I just thought . . . well, now that we know I'm staying, well . . ."

Come on, Rocky. "Well, what?"

"I wondered what that means for us."

"What do you think it means?"

"I know what I hope it means."

The man was seriously addled. Frannie set the plate on the porch banister. She grabbed his hand and entwined her fingers in his. "Do I have to do all the work here?"

"No. You don't." His Adam's apple bobbed as his gaze fastened on their hands. "I hope it means you'll take a buggy ride with me—a lot of buggy rides. That I'll need lots of batteries for my flashlight, and neither of us will get enough sleep anytime soon because we'll be driving around the countryside talking all hours of the night."

"That's all you've got?" Frannie tugged her hand from his and crossed her arms. "You can do better, Rocky Sanders, I know you can."

He snorted and shook his head. "You make me crazy, Amish woman."

"You make me crazy, *Englisch* man."

His belly laugh mingled with her higher, softer giggle. Frannie loved that sound almost as much as she loved Rocky.

He sighed and wiped at his eyes with the back of his sleeve. "I keep thinking about how patient God is with us. It takes us so long to figure everything out. We moan and carry on about His will and His plan, trying to figure it out."

She certainly had done her share of moaning and carrying on in the last year. "We do."

"We need to be patient."

"We do?"

"I love you. I want to marry you. But I have things I need to do first. A lot of learning. A lot of changing to do. Can you understand that?"

Love you. Marry you. Frannie's brain was stuck on the first two sentences. *Fraa. Mann. Boplin.* The life for which she'd prayed and hoped. "*Jah.*"

"Do you understand?" He looked so worried, so uncertain. "Will you wait?"

"Of course I'll wait." Frannie inhaled. Finally. A breath. "I love you too."

He sighed as if he'd been holding his breath. "What will your parents think of all this?"

"Leroy called and left a message at the phone shack last night. They left their own message this morning at the store."

"No argument?"

"They trust folks here. They trust Leroy."

"What would you think about going home then?"

"Back to Jamesport?" Sweet relief ran through her. No more holidays without cheeky Hannah and baby Rachel, who surely wasn't a baby anymore. Obadiah and his brood. Rufus. Joshua and his mystery special person. "Back to my family and yours? I'd like that, but truth be told, I only want to live wherever you live."

"We'll go home, then, when the time is right."

His gaze, full of emotion, full of love, wandered across her face. His expression held her there, unable to look away. *Aenti* Abigail could storm onto the porch at this very moment, *Onkel* Mordecai bringing up the rear, and Frannie wouldn't be able to move.

His hands came up, both of them this time. They cupped her face. His expression gave her a hint of what was to come, but she didn't have time to brace herself. He leaned down. His lips touched hers. She closed her eyes, wondering at the softness of his skin on hers. She reached for something to hold on to before she fell into the whirling vortex of emotion. Her hands found and gripped his solid biceps. He would always be the rock to which she could cling.

Her heart quivered and opened like a sunflower seeking the warmth and brilliance of the sun. Rocky filled up every nook and cranny that had been waiting for him to simply come home to her. He tasted of *kaffi*, maple syrup, dreams, and hopes. The kiss deepened and lingered with a sweet promise of many more such kisses.

After a time, he raised his head a scant few inches. His arms dropped. For an instant, Frannie felt cold. Then he wrapped them around her waist, lifted her off her feet, and pressed her against his chest. "How about that?" he murmured. "What do you think of that?"

Frannie felt as if she were flying, wings spread for the first time in her life. She rested her forehead on Rocky's shoulder. "You found the perfect gift."

"I reckon it's the first of many such gifts."

He proceeded to make good on that promise.

DISCUSSION QUESTIONS

1. Rocky follows Frannie from Missouri to south Texas, knowing her family disapproves. Do you think he is right to pursue her, knowing she'll have to give up her faith and family to be with him if he doesn't join her faith? Do you think love is more important than approval?

2. Frannie and Rocky both say they will abide by Leroy's decision. Rocky will go home and Frannie will become a teacher's aide, knowing she'll never marry. Do you believe in a love so strong, you'd be willing to forego all other chances for marriage and family because of it?

3. Rocky has never felt close to God because he identifies him as "abba" or "father." His father abandoned him and left his mother for another woman. Do you have trouble relating to God the Father because of problems in your own life? How do you overcome those feelings?

4. Rocky is willing to give up electricity, computers, his phone, even his beloved Dodge Ram pickup in order to put distance between himself and the world so he can be closer to God. What are

you willing to give up in order to have a closer relationship with God?

5. Abigail tells Frannie that English people are rarely successful when they join the Amish faith. They're unable to adapt to such a plain, austere lifestyle. What can you do to lead a simpler, more Godly life without going so far as to give up electricity, cars, computers, and phones?

WHEN WINTER COMES

BARBARA CAMERON

GLOSSARY

ab im kopp—off in the head
aenti—aunt
allrecht—all right
bensel—silly child
boppli—baby
brechdich—magnificent
bruder—brother
bu, buwe—boy, boys
budder—butter
budderhaffe—butter dish
daadi—grandfather
daed—dad
danki—thank you
Deitsch—Pennsylvania Dutch language
demut—humility
dochder—daughter
dumm—dumb
elder—parents
Englisch—English
Englischer—a non-Amish person
fiever—fever
fraa—wife
frack—dress
Gebottsdaag—birthday

geh—go

groossmammi—grandmother

guder mariye—good morning

gut—good

gut nacht—good night

haus—house

hochmut—pride

hungerich—hungry

kaffi—coffee

kapp—prayer covering or cap

kich—kitchen

kind, kinder, kinner—children or grandchildren

liebschen—dearest

mead—girls

mamm, mammi—mom

mann—man

mauseschtill—mouse

mei—my

minutt—minute

mudder—mother

nachtess—supper

nau—now

nee—no

onkel—uncle

Ordnung—the written and unwritten rules that guide the Amish way of life

redd-up—clean up

rumschpringe—the running-around period that starts when a teenager turns sixteen years old

schpass—fun

sehr—very

sohn—son
snitz pie—dried apple pie
vatter—father
wasser—water
wie geht—how are things?
wunderbaar—wonderful
ya—yes

CHAPTER 1

Rebecca wrapped her arms around herself as she stood at the edge of the frozen pond. She felt drawn to it in spite of herself. It was here, one bitter cold day five years ago, that her life had changed so much.

She used to love rushing here after school and her chores. She'd quickly exchange her boots for skates and fly across the ice. No one understood her fascination with skating, not even her twin. Her parents thought it was a passing interest, but when it didn't fade as she got older, they bought her bigger skates as she needed them.

She wasn't trying to be special or stand out. That would be against everything she and her community believed in. *Demut*—humility—was valued above all among the Plain people.

It had been years now since she'd skated. The accident had changed everything. It had been her fault, and she'd had to pay for it. But as bad as she felt about losing a sister, she knew that it had to be worse for her parents, who had lost a daughter. Even if it appeared that they had been able to forgive her, Rebecca didn't believe it. She blamed herself so much . . . how could they not blame her too?

If she'd been a good daughter, Lizzie wouldn't be gone.

So she became the best daughter she could be, to make up for the missing one. She enjoyed cooking and helping out around the house when she wasn't working at the gift shop in town. And she watched and worried over her siblings like a mother hen, concerned that bad things might happen if she didn't.

It was so quiet here now she could hear the icicles tinkling like glass wind chimes as the chill breeze rustled the bare tree branches. The fields lay dormant beneath the blanket of snow that also covered the nearby farmhouses and barns. Farmers who'd worked so hard harvesting their crops now studied seed catalogs and planned their spring plowing and planting. They repaired farm equipment, and even with the winter's shorter days, some of them enjoyed having a few hours to do some carpentry.

Families gathered indoors in front of the fireplace and played games. When friends came to visit, there was plenty of time for holding quilting circles and catching up on the latest news over cups of tea and cookies warm from the oven.

In quiet Paradise, Pennsylvania, things became even more peaceful in winter.

But Rebecca felt anything but peaceful. She'd come home from her job and found herself restless. So she donned her coat and bonnet again and went out for a walk in spite of the cold.

Stop being afraid!

Startled, Rebecca whipped her head around and

scanned the field behind her. There was no one in sight. Hers were the only footsteps in the vast expanse of snow-covered fields that led to where she stood.

The voice was so familiar. She hadn't heard it for a while, but she'd never forget it.

Stop being afraid. It's time to stop being afraid.

"I'm not afraid!" she cried out.

But her words vanished in the wind that swept across the icy white surface of the frozen pond. She shivered and wrapped her arms around herself as the chill seeped into her feet, then her legs, then her body, and finally her heart. Still she stood and stared out at the pond.

She thought she saw something, there, at the far edge of the pond. Something—someone? Blinking, she looked again, but there was nothing. Her eyes were just watering a little in the cold, that was all. She should get home, help her *mamm* with *nachtesse*. On these cold winter evenings, it was so nice to sit at the big carved wooden table with her family and share a meal and try not to think about how she felt each year when winter came.

Her mind wandered. She felt herself moving, light as air, gracefully skimming across the icy surface of the pond, the wind a cold caress on her face. Flinging her arms out, she soared like a bird, her cape and long skirt rippling in the wind, the only sound her skates as they barely touched the ice. She leaped and spun and felt her heart lift and warm and beat harder and harder, faster and faster as the old excitement burst through her as she circled the pond.

Surely this was what it felt like in heaven, she thought, smiling.

Lost in her dreams, she didn't hear the crunch of steps on the snow behind her.

"I knew I'd find you here."

Startled, her eyes flew open, and she spun around at the sound of the deep male voice behind her. "Ben! What are you doing here?"

Her feet slipped on the snowy bank, and she started to fall. He reached out and caught her, but then his feet slid out from under him too. As he fell, he held tighter and tried to shield her from the worst of it, pulling her over as they landed on the snow.

Winded, Rebecca found herself staring down into the face of Ben Weaver. His brown eyes were full of concern. "Are you all right?"

"I asked you what you're doing here."

"You were skating."

"Skating?" She stared at him incredulously. "Look at my feet, Ben Weaver. Do they look like they have skates on them?"

"Skating," he repeated. "Flying across the ice like you used to."

"You're *ab im kopp,*" she muttered. Shaking her head, she struggled to get to her feet.

But her long, dark blue *frack* had a mind of its own. It was tangled with Ben's trousers, and he didn't help her extricate herself. Instead, he just chuckled and watched her struggle. Finally, she yanked the material away and stood, her hands on her hips.

"What are you doing here?" she demanded again as she brushed at the snow on her skirt and coat.

"Your *mamm* sent me," he told her.

"Is something wrong?"

He held out his hand, seeking to reassure her. "Nothing's wrong."

"Then why would she send you?"

Ben got to his feet without effort, picked up his black felt hat, and brushed at the snow on his jacket and trousers. "She was worried about you," he said.

* * *

The moment the words left his mouth, Ben regretted them.

Rebecca went still, and it was like a shutter came down over her face. "She has no reason to worry," she said. Turning, she started to climb the slope, slipping and sliding as she went.

Ben followed her, but even with his long strides it wasn't easy to keep up. "Rebecca, let me give you a ride home."

"I walked here. I can walk home." Then she bit her lip. "But thank you," she said.

"Stop it!"

She halted and stared at him. "Stop what?"

"You're just too polite."

"Too polite?" Her eyebrows rose higher, if that were possible.

"You don't have to pretend with me, Rebecca. I know you're upset."

"I'm fine. I need to get home."

"I thought we were friends."

His quiet words stopped her.

She turned. "We are. But no one needs to worry about me. I'm fine."

"No, you're still sad sometimes, especially this time of year." His eyes searched hers. "You're freezing, and I'm cold. Just get in the buggy and let me drive you home. Please."

Turning, he began walking to the buggy, not sure if she'd follow. He knew how stubborn she could be. But surely she wouldn't insist on walking home, as cold as she must be.

He heard her sigh of exasperation behind him and the stomp of her feet in the snow, and he couldn't hold back a chuckle.

"You think it's funny?" She hurried to catch up with him. Her breath huffed out in the cold wind.

"No, Rebecca."

As they walked, he cast her a worried glance. She was shivering even harder. "Here, let me give you my coat."

"You can't do that. You'll catch your death of cold without it."

"Better me than you."

She put out her hand to stop him. "I'll be fine. We're almost to your buggy. It'll be warmer there."

Something inside him relaxed. So at least she was going to let him drive her home.

What was it about her that attracted him so? There were other girls he could have pursued, but no . . . five years ago he'd realized how much he cared for Rebecca, and no one else would do.

He'd decided to ask if they could date, but before he could, her life had been forever changed. Nothing before the accident seemed to matter now. But it had been five years. Wasn't that long enough for her to heal?

And did she—could she—forgive him for what had happened to Lizzie?

Rebecca's steps were awkward by the time they were at the buggy, and getting in seemed to be an effort. He lifted her in his arms, startling her so that she whipped around and stared at him, her eyes wide.

"I can get in by myself."

His heart did a funny little flip in his chest as he realized how close their faces were. He settled her on the seat and reached for the blanket to tuck it around her.

"Really, there's no need to fuss—," she began, then sneezed.

He pulled out a handkerchief and handed it to her. "Do you want to worry your *eldre* if you get sick?" he asked quietly.

As what little color she had faded from her cheeks, he knew his words had hit home. He finished tucking the blanket around her legs, then walked around to his side of the vehicle and climbed inside.

She stared straight ahead as the buggy began moving, her black bonnet hiding her expression. "I thought you were at the Brownfield home today."

"I stopped by to see your father."

Ben worked for Amos, so Rebecca didn't question

that. But business hadn't been the topic of their conversation today.

They passed their old schoolhouse, and he stopped the buggy for a moment. "We had some good times here, didn't we?"

"When you weren't annoying me, you mean?"

He grinned, unrepentant. "I was a young boy then. Besides, I was just teasing you."

"I looked it up in the dictionary. The word *tease*. It means 'to annoy in fun,'" she told him dryly.

He'd had fun, he reflected. Rebecca had always been so quiet, so composed, that he'd enjoyed getting a rise out of her. Then her cheeks would turn pink, her hazel eyes would flash, and she'd tell him in no uncertain terms to leave her alone.

From the time he was sixteen, he'd decided he wanted no other woman for his *fraa*. He told himself that all he had to do was wait until they were older. Then he'd ask if they could date.

That was before what he'd come to think of as *that day*.

She sneezed again, jerking him from his thoughts.

"Are you still cold?"

"I'm fine," she told him, using a tissue to blow her nose. "I'm sure it's allergies."

"To what? Snow?"

She rolled her eyes. "People can have allergies in the winter."

"You don't."

"Since when do you know everything about me?"

He opened his mouth and then shut it. How could he answer that question? They'd grown up together in the same small community and attended the same school. Everyone knew everyone else's business here in Paradise.

But sometimes her father confided his concern about his eldest daughter to Ben as they worked on a joint project. And her mother looked on him like another son and did the same.

He'd bided his time until he thought his suit would be successful with Rebecca.

And waited some more.

He glanced at her again and caught her looking at him. She quickly glanced away, but not before he caught the expression on her face. *Curiosity*, he mused. *Hmm*. Well, if she didn't yet look at him the way he wished, at least she was looking.

He'd take it.

* * *

Rebecca felt herself blush when she realized Ben had caught her staring at him.

She looked away quickly, but not quickly enough. He'd been looking at her so seriously. Did he feel more for her than friendship? No, it was just that she wanted it to be so. But time couldn't be turned back, as much as she wished it possible.

Sometimes she felt he was about to say something, then he'd stop. She wished she had the courage to ask him about it.

Risking another glance, she saw that his attention was on the road now. She wondered why he hadn't yet gotten engaged or married as many of their classmates had. Girls had always liked him. She'd stood with them at recess and listened to them talk about how sweet, how sensitive he was. He might not say much, the girls said, but they saw that as a good thing. He wasn't trying to impress them or chase after them the way some boys did.

And then there was his appearance. He was tall, with impressive muscles from helping his father on the farm. He was square-jawed, his hair a dark russet, and his eyes were such a handsome brown color. According to the other girls.

"Like dark chocolate," one girl said with a sigh.

"And he's always making me laugh," another reported.

He didn't make Rebecca laugh. All he did was tease her and look at her with eyes that promised mischief. He didn't do that with other girls who flirted with him at singings. Mary Anne even confided that he'd kissed her once. Yes, Ben Weaver could have had—still could have—his pick of young women in the community.

So why wasn't he married?

"My mother didn't tell you where I was, did she?"

He glanced at her. "No."

"I wouldn't want her to think—well, you know, to . . . ," she trailed off, not knowing how to put it into words.

"To think that you were brooding by the pond?"

Rebecca frowned. "I wouldn't call it brooding."

"What would you call it, then?"

Her eyes flew to his, and in them she saw compassion.

She looked away. "I can't help but think of Lizzie when winter comes."

"I know. Me too."

"Really?"

"Life changed for both of us the day Lizzie died, Rebecca."

The simple words struck at her heart. She nodded. "What made you look for me at the pond?"

He looked back at the road. "I've seen you there sometimes when I drive by."

She thought about that. It was the one place she'd thought she had privacy. How many others had driven past and wondered if she was—what was the word he'd used? *Brooding.* She sighed. Oh well. There were, after all, no secrets here in Paradise.

With a jerk of the reins, Ben let Ike know that he wanted to turn down the drive to Rebecca's house.

"Why did you say I was skating?" she asked suddenly.

He glanced at her. "You were moving and swaying, lifting your arms."

She studied him, looking into his eyes to see if he was teasing. But his expression was serious, his eyes kind. "Ben Weaver, I think you need to have your eyes examined," she said at last.

"I'm not crazy," he told her. "Weren't you wanting to be out on the ice, skating like you used to do?"

It felt like all the air in her left her body. "How can you ask me such a thing after what happened?" Her voice sounded strangled.

Ben stopped the buggy and reached out a hand to her. "I'm sorry. I didn't mean to upset you."

"How could I do it again?" she asked him, feeling tears rush into her eyes. "I got Lizzie to go with me that day. If I hadn't, if I'd been watching better, she wouldn't have died."

Rebecca saw a look of pain cross Ben's face. He reached out and took her hand, squeezing it so hard that it hurt.

"If you're going to blame anyone, blame me."

CHAPTER 2

The front door opened, and her mother appeared. "You found her!"

Rebecca pulled her hand from Ben's, feeling faintly guilty. "Thank you," she said, then quickly shoved aside the blanket that covered her legs and climbed out.

"I'm sorry I worried you," she told her mother. "I just went for a walk. I'll be down as soon as I change."

Mamm nodded as Rebecca rushed through the kitchen and up the stairs. In her room, Rebecca shed her damp things and put on another *frack*. Then she searched in her drawer for a fresh *kapp*.

She stood before a small mirror and stared at her reflection. Her cheeks were pale. She brushed her hair until it crackled with static electricity, parted it in the center, rebound it at the back of her head, and donned the *kapp*.

Her gaze returned to her reflection for just a moment. She didn't spend much time looking at herself in mirrors. Her looks were just average: hazel eyes, brown hair. Slender figure with barely any curves.

Her twin had gotten those.

And more. *Mamm* had always said the two were as

different as night and day. From the time they were born, she always said that one chased after life and the other followed, worrying about the adventurer.

Everyone knew that while Rebecca was the oldest by six minutes, she was the follower, the worrier—never the dreamer or the adventurer.

She sighed. No, she'd never envied Lizzie. But sometimes she'd felt like she came in a pale second. Lizzie had been like a comet streaking across the sky. Rebecca was the homebody, lovingly taking care of the other *kinner*, helping her *mamm* with the house.

Except for when she was out on the ice, skating. There, everything was different. She felt like a bird— free, graceful, daring.

Sinking down on the bed, she thought about what Ben had said about her skating: that she was moving as she stood there in the snow, as if she were skating in her imagination. How ridiculous.

She missed skating so much, but she just couldn't face doing it again.

When she went downstairs, she found Ben leaning against a kitchen counter, laughing and talking with her *mamm*.

"I talked Ben into staying to eat," *Mamm* said. "After all, he went to find you for me."

Ben sneaked a cookie from the jar on the counter. Rebecca waited for her mother to chide him since it was so close to suppertime. But Naomi merely smiled fondly at him.

Rebecca moved to the counter and began slicing the loaves of homemade bread that sat on a wooden board.

"It smells wonderful," Ben said. "Nothing better than a good stew on a cold night."

"There's deep-dish apple pie too."

"My favorite."

Rebecca stopped slicing and looked over at him. "Everything's your favorite."

"Yes," he agreed, grinning. "I love everything your *mamm* makes."

"Everything's ready. Call the *kinner*," *Mamm* said.

Rebecca did as she was asked, hollering up the stairs. They came clattering down and seated themselves around the table. Rebecca frowned when she saw where Ben was sitting. Lizzie had always sat there . . .

He looked up at her, and she saw the light fade from his eyes. He started to move to a different chair.

"Sit, sit," Rebecca's father, Amos, said as he came into the room. "Glad you could join us, Ben."

Glancing uneasily at Rebecca, Ben nodded. "Me too."

Amos bent his head and the family followed, joining in prayer. Then noisy chatter filled the room as bowls and platters were passed and plates were filled.

Looking around the big carved wooden table that was the heart of a Plain kitchen, Rebecca felt a sense of quiet satisfaction. She was needed here. Her *mamm* often told her she didn't know what she'd do without her help. When her mother's last two pregnancies had been difficult, Rebecca had taken over running the house. She was good at it; she enjoyed cooking and baking and even cleaning, because that meant putting things back where they belonged, getting a sense of order.

And when she was going about taking care of their

home, she didn't hear that voice in her head urging her to do something, to stop being afraid.

She'd been like other girls her age, thinking about boys, about dating, about getting married, before the accident. Now the boy she'd been interested in sat next to her as a friend and not as a husband.

She'd thought she'd be married, have her own *kinner* by now. This wasn't the life she'd imagined she'd lead by the age of twenty-two. But she could put aside her dreams, her desires, for the sake of her family . . .

Ben was saying something. Jerking to attention, Rebecca accepted the bowl of stew he passed her, then the basket of bread. Taking a slice, she passed the basket on and reached for the *budderhaffe*. Her hand collided with Ben's, and she pulled it back.

"Ladies first," he said, pushing the dish toward her.

With a slight smile, she nodded, scooped up some of the *budder* with her knife and spread it on the bread, then pushed the *budderhaffe* toward him.

"Rebecca, guess what I did at school today!"

Rebecca turned with a smile, but before she could respond to Esther, six-year-old Annie launched into a monologue about her day. Bright and eager to learn, she was thriving at her lessons, especially math.

Looking up, Rebecca caught Ben watching her, his expression thoughtful. What had he meant when he said if she was going to blame anyone, she should blame him? What did she have to blame him for? He'd been such a good friend, listening to her whenever she needed to talk about Lizzie. She didn't know what she'd have done without him since Lizzie died.

She wondered again why he hadn't yet married. He came from a large, happy family, just as she did. From what she'd observed, his parents had a happy marriage.

After leaving school he'd worked with her father, learning the carpentry trade, building and installing custom kitchen cabinets, built-ins, and bookcases in area homes, sometimes Amish, sometimes *Englisch*. He'd often been invited to stay for the evening meal at the Miller home—or charmingly found a way to invite himself, Rebecca noted—so he'd become a fixture in her home.

"So, Ben, I'm thinking that we're going to finish the White kitchen on Wednesday," *Daed* said, leaning back in his chair as he watched Naomi cut and serve slices of deep-dish apple pie.

"We can't go to the Anthony house early," Ben told him. "Remember, Mr. Anthony wants to take his wife off to a hotel while we work on the kitchen, get her away from all the noise and dust. They made arrangements to be out of their house for a week starting Friday, not Thursday."

"Don't you two spend enough time talking business during the day?" Naomi asked, but she smiled.

Amos nodded. "*Ya.* We'll figure it out tomorrow."

Mamm was passing slices of pie down the table and handed a plate to Marian. "This is for Rebecca."

"No, thanks."

"No dessert? You love apple pie."

Rebecca shrugged. "I'll have some later. I'm just not all that hungry right now." A headache was forming behind her eyes, and the stew was lying like a lump in her stomach.

She got up and collected stew bowls and put them into the sink. It had been a long day. She was looking forward to bed already, even though it was early. Her father smiled at her as she refilled his coffee cup, then her mother's.

"This is your piece, Ben," said Marian, the second oldest. She handed him the plate with a smile. Their fingers brushed, and a faint blush crept up her cheeks.

Rebecca stopped beside Ben and stared. Her sister was flirting with Ben!

* * *

Ben realized that Rebecca was standing beside him, coffeepot in hand. Her expression was as cold as the ice cream topping the pie he'd just been handed. "More coffee?" she asked.

"*Danki*," he said and frowned as he watched her pour the hot liquid. Why did she look upset with him?

"Cream?" Marian asked. "I know you like it in your coffee."

"Yes, thanks," he told her, tearing his gaze from Rebecca, who seemed focused on her sister.

Confused, he glanced over at Marian as he accepted the pitcher of cream from her. She was looking at him from beneath her lashes, shy . . . flirty? No, it couldn't be, he told himself. She was what—sixteen? He searched his memory. Seventeen? Whatever she was, she was too young for him. And besides, he wanted her older sister.

He looked at Naomi. She was also watching Marian. Then her gaze moved to him.

"Ben, how is your pie?" she asked.

He took a bite. "Wonderful," he pronounced. He glanced at Rebecca, who had returned the coffeepot to the stove and sat back down. She was rubbing her forehead and looking down at her untouched cup of tea.

When Rebecca sneezed, her mother gazed at her daughter in concern. "Are you catching cold?"

"I'm fine, thanks."

"Maybe it's allergies," Ben said slyly.

If looks could hurt, he'd have been bleeding. He glanced around, but no one else noticed.

"Yes, I think it is," Rebecca responded, and she took a sip of her tea.

Ben sat back. He was pleasantly full from the meal and pleasantly tired from the day's work. Just plain pleasant, sitting here in the warm kitchen at the big kitchen table next to Rebecca. He wouldn't trade it for anything. Well, yes, he would. He'd trade it for a kitchen of their own, a family of their own. But he didn't think she was ready for that conversation.

"What kind of kitchen cabinets did you build for the Delaney family?" Marian asked Ben.

There was nothing Ben loved to talk about more than working with wood. With farmland becoming more expensive in Lancaster County, more men were turning to trades like carpentry. He'd worked with Amos for several years learning the trade, and while he could build just about anything, he found the most satisfaction helping to create kitchens. Maybe that was because he'd always considered it the heart of the home, the place where a family gathered to share God's abundance of food and talk about the events of the day.

He loved working with wood, all the varieties from maple to oak to birch—and, for some of the fancy *Englisch* kitchens, woods that came from faraway places like Brazil and Costa Rica.

But the more he talked, the more he realized that Rebecca was quiet. She looked even paler than before.

"Ben? Another slice of pie?" Naomi asked.

"No, thanks. I should be going. I'll see you in the morning, Amos."

Rebecca pulled out a handkerchief and wiped her nose. He started to say something, but she shook her head and glanced at her mother, who was supervising the clearing of the table. He got the message and nodded.

His going to find her this afternoon hadn't kept her from catching a chill. And it had only complicated things for him. He was going to remember for a long time how it felt to hold her and have her face so close to his. And he already regretted blurting out what he'd said about blaming him. He knew she'd be asking him about it the next time they were alone.

He pulled on his coat and watched as Naomi walked over to Rebecca and put the back of her hand against her daughter's forehead. Rebecca shook her head and said something too low for Ben to pick up, but Naomi put her hands on her hips and gave her the look, the one only mothers know how to give.

So, he thought, *Rebecca hasn't been able to hide her*

not feeling well from her mother. It didn't surprise him. Parents could always sense such things. Especially mothers.

* * *

"Rebecca, you go on to bed. I think you're coming down with a cold."

She turned and shook her head. "I'm fine." Taking several bowls from Annie, she put them into the hot soapy water in the sink.

"Annie, why don't you go ask Marian to read you a story before bed? I'll help Rebecca with the dishes."

Rebecca watched Annie, always a good helper, hesitate. Then she scampered off. Trying not to sigh, Rebecca turned back to the dishes. She sensed that her *mamm* wanted to talk, and she wasn't in the mood for it. All she wanted was to finish the chores and go to bed.

Picking up a clean dishcloth, Naomi came to stand next to the sink. "Is everything okay?"

Rebecca nodded. She handed her mother a bowl to dry.

"You were gone a long time."

"I just went for a walk."

"It was awfully cold for a walk."

Rebecca handed another bowl to her mother. "I know."

"Are things okay with you and Ben?"

She nodded. "Why do you ask?"

"I don't know. You were frowning at him when he went to sit down."

"He was going to sit in Lizzie's seat." She stared at the soapy water.

"It's not Lizzie's anymore," her *mamm* said gently.

"I know that!"

Naomi blinked at the sharpness in Rebecca's voice.

Rebecca bit her lip. "I'm sorry," she said stiffly.

"*Nee*, it's all right. You're not feeling well."

It wasn't all right to talk to her *mamm* that way no matter how she felt. Rebecca was ashamed. She cast about in her mind for something to say. "I thought I'd ask Anita for a morning off later this week so I can help take Abram and Annie for their checkups."

Naomi stopped drying a dish. "I'd rather you took some time for yourself, Rebecca. All you do is work here or at the shop."

"You need the help."

Setting down the dish, Naomi placed her hand on Rebecca's shoulder. "What I need more is to see you looking happier, *Dochder*."

"A daughter should—"

"You are a most dutiful daughter, but we want you to have your own life too. You don't go out enough with your friends, do the things a young woman does."

"I was just out with Ben," Rebecca told her with a slight smile.

"A ride home isn't out with a friend."

Rebecca took the dishcloth from her mother and began wiping down the counters. "I'm fine."

"Rebecca, I noticed that Marian—"

Amos walked into the kitchen. "There you are," he said to Naomi. "Would you look over a proposal for me?"

"Rebecca and I were—"

"It's all right," Rebecca said quickly. "I want to get to bed. I'll see you in the morning. *Gut nacht.*"

Looking away from the expression of disappointment on her mother's face, she kissed her cheek, then her *daed*'s, and walked quickly to the stairs.

* * *

Rebecca woke in the night, feverish, her head clogged and her body aching. Wrapping herself in a bathrobe, she went downstairs, found aspirin, and took two with a glass of water. When she climbed into her bed this time, she was warm—too warm—so she lay atop the covers. Several hours later she woke again, cold, and pulled the quilt back up to her chin.

When she woke next, Marian was shaking her shoulder. "Time to get up."

Muttering, Rebecca nodded. "*Minutt.*" She fell back asleep.

Her shoulder was being shaken again, this time by her mother. "Rebecca?" A hand touched her forehead. "Marian, Rebecca has a *fiewer*! Go get her some aspirin and some *wasser.*"

"Some *wasser* would be good," Rebecca agreed as she sat up. "But I'm getting up. I have to go to work."

"No, you cannot go to work today," *Mamm* said firmly.

"It's just a cold," Rebecca said, hoping to convince herself. She was seldom ill, but this felt like the flu. She stood, and the room whirled about her. She sank back down on the bed. "Maybe in a minute."

Her mother shook her head. "Maybe tomorrow. I'll get Amos to go by the gift shop and let Anita know you won't be in today."

Marian returned with the aspirin and water.

Rebecca washed the pills down with the water, drinking every drop. "I'll lie down for a little while and see how I feel. I'm really not that sick. It's just a cold."

"I'll bring you breakfast after I get the *kinner* off to school."

"No, I'll come down," Rebecca muttered as she sank down onto the bed. "Don't want you to go to any trouble."

Her mother stroked her hot forehead. "It's no trouble, *liebschen*. You're no trouble. Ever. Rest, dear one. Let someone take care of you."

Rebecca watched her mother leave the room and felt guilty. How, she wondered, could *Mamm* still show her such love? She was supposed to watch out for her sister. She was supposed to keep her from harm.

The Bible talked about being your brother's keeper. She'd tried to be her sister's. She'd failed.

CHAPTER 3

Rebecca heard the whispering as she slowly came awake, her head throbbing and her throat tight and hot.

"Shh, be quiet!"

"*Ya, mauseschtill!*"

"Why do people say that? Are mice quiet?"

"I don't know. I don't like mice."

"Shh, if we wake her, *Mamm* will be mad at us!"

"She looks pretty sick."

"She's okay. She gets sick every winter. It's because she goes out there looking for Lizzie."

"No, she doesn't! She's not crazy!"

"Didn't say she was. But she stands out there in the snow looking at the pond. Marian says—"

Rebecca opened her eyes. "What does Marian say?"

Her brother Jonas, ten years old, slapped a hand to his chest. "You scared me to death!"

"You woke me up."

"I tolded him not to," said Abram, five years old.

"Told," Jonas corrected.

"Yeah, I tolded you."

Jonas sighed. "Anyway, are you feeling any better, Rebecca?"

She nodded and sat up. The room didn't whirl around her. "A little."

"Are you hungry? *Mamm* made you some chicken soup for supper."

Rebecca glanced at the window. Had she slept through the entire day?

Her mother walked into the room carrying a tray. "I wondered why it was so quiet up here. I should have figured someone was waking up Rebecca."

A chorus of "I didn't!" and finger pointing ensued.

Clutching her head, Rebecca shushed them. "*Ach, mei bruders*, not so loud! My head hurts!"

Immediately they were contrite. "Sorry," they chimed quietly. His eyes huge, Eli patted her hand.

"Jonas, maybe you could get your sister a wet washcloth for her hands."

He went for the cloth and returned with it dripping. Gingerly, Rebecca used it to wash her hands, trying not to get her quilt wet.

"I'll go help Marian set the table," he told their mother. "Come, *kinner*."

"*Mamm*, tell him to stop treating me like a *boppli*," complained Annie.

"You shouldn't be waiting on me," Rebecca said as her mother set a tray on her lap. She knew how hard her mother worked, and here she was waiting on her grown daughter.

"It's no trouble." Naomi put the back of her hand on her daughter's forehead. "Still warm. If you're not better tomorrow, maybe we should take you to the doctor."

"It's just a cold," Rebecca insisted. "I'm feeling

better." But her voice came out sounding like a croak. She spooned up some of the chicken soup. "Mmm, this is good."

Looking up, she saw her mother frowning at her. "I'm better, *Mamm*, really. The nap helped. If you call sleeping all day a nap."

Her mother pursed her lips. "Are you sure? You've just been . . . delicate since you had pneumonia."

"That was five years ago."

"We nearly lost you too."

Rebecca saw that her mother was blinking back tears. "I'm sorry. *Mamm*, I'm sorry. You didn't need to have that happen after we lost Lizzie."

"It wasn't your fault you got sick."

But it was my fault that I stayed sick, thought Rebecca. "I got better. And I'm not going to get that sick again."

"A pneumonia shot," her mother said, nodding. "I feel better when I remember that you had the pneumonia shot. It seems there's a shot for everything these days. What will the *Englisch* come up with next?"

Both of them fell silent. Rebecca wondered if her mother was thinking, as she was, that no one had come up with a way to keep Lizzie from falling through the ice.

She set her spoon down on the tray. "Thank you for bringing me the soup. I'm sorry I'm so much trouble."

Mamm moved the tray to the dresser and returned to stroke her daughter's hair. "You are never any trouble. Drink your juice and try to get some more rest."

Rebecca nodded. "I'll be all better in the morning."

Bending, her mother kissed her on her forehead. "We'll see. For now, no worrying about your job and your chores, *allrecht*? Your father stopped by the gift shop, and Anita said to tell you to get well and come in when you're better."

Her energy gone, Rebecca lay back against her pillow. Before she could pull the covers up, her mother was tucking her in. It brought back memories of being tucked in when she was a child, and she smiled.

"Sleep now, *liebschen*. Things will be better in the morning."

* * *

Ben pulled his buggy up to the familiar figure walking beside the road.

"So you're feeling better," he called out.

Rebecca stopped and looked up as the buggy pulled abreast of her. Ben leaned forward, the reins loose in his hands. His eyes were serious as he stared down at her.

"*Ya*, I'm well."

Her cheeks were pale, and she was breathing heavily. Each exhale produced a white puff in the cold air.

"Get in, I'll give you a ride home."

"I can walk. It isn't far."

"Your *daed* said your *mamm* was worried about you going into work."

Rebecca climbed into the buggy. "I'm fine. She worries too much."

"She worries because this time of the year you get sick a lot."

"I'm stronger than I look," she told him firmly.

Ben handed her the lap blanket, and she tucked it

around her legs. They traveled without speaking for a few minutes, the only sound the *clip-clop* of the horse's hooves on the recently cleared road. There were few cars this time of year, so it was easy to imagine that only the Amish lived here. Tourists who clogged the roads and sometimes came dangerously near the buggies on the road were few and far between as winter lengthened.

The pond came into view. Children of varying ages, bundled up against the cold, skated on the icy surface. Ben noticed that, after an initial glance, Rebecca looked away.

"Rebecca, I've been meaning to talk to you . . ." He broke off as she began coughing. "Rebecca? Are you all right?"

She nodded but couldn't stop coughing. Ben pulled on the reins and stopped the buggy, tried patting her on the back. She pressed one hand to her mouth, the other to her chest, and spasms racked her. He stared at her. What if she stopped breathing? He focused on her mouth, trying to remember what he'd read about CPR. With his luck, he'd just do more damage, he decided. Or make Rebecca think that he was making improper advances.

Desperately, he looked around. What should he do? Then it came to him—there was a volunteer fire station just down the road. He turned the buggy in a U-turn and urged Ike into a run.

"What—what are you doing?" she gasped, grabbing at his arm to hold on. "Are you trying to kill us?"

She'd stopped coughing, although her face was still red and her breath was rasping in her chest.

"Are you okay?"

"I will be if you'll slow down!"

Ben brought the buggy to a halt and took a good look at her. Her color was returning to normal—well, at least her face was no longer bright red. And the coughing that had scared him to death had indeed stopped.

"You're sure?"

She nodded. "I'll be fine, really."

Leaning back in his seat, Ben hesitated as he studied her. What was it about this wisp of a woman that had made him want her as his *fraa* for so long? That made him wait for her and feel so protective of her?

"Where were you going?"

He made another U-turn and started for home. "To the volunteer fire station."

"Where's the fire?" she teased.

His eyes widened. She was always so serious. And after the past few minutes, he was surprised she could joke on the heels of such a coughing fit.

"I'm sorry if I scared you," she told him quietly. "I'm fine now."

"You shouldn't have worked today."

She bent her head and sighed. "Probably not. But if I'd stayed home, my *mamm* would have fussed over me like I was a *kind*." Her head snapped up then, as if she'd just thought of something.

"What?"

She shook her head. "Nothing."

In a few minutes they pulled up in front of her house. Jumping out of the buggy, Ben walked around to Rebecca's side and held out his hands to help her down. Judging from the surprise on her face, she hadn't expected such courtesy from him.

And why should she? he asked himself. He tried to keep their relationship strictly friendly. He didn't want to scare her off; he'd always felt that if he didn't approach her about a change in their relationship in just the right way, at just the right time, she might reject him.

Before she could say she could get down by herself, he clasped her around the waist and lifted her out of the buggy. They stared at each other for a long moment.

Ben set her on the ground.

She caught her breath. "Are you coming in for supper?"

He shook his head. "Not tonight. I told my family I'd be home."

Her hands fell to her sides. She nodded and started inside, turning at the door to look at him. "Thank you for giving me a ride."

He watched her as she went inside, then he turned to get into the buggy. He wished he hadn't promised he'd have supper at home tonight. Somehow, it felt as if their relationship was changing lately.

He hoped he wasn't imagining it.

* * *

Rebecca's head was whirling as she climbed the steps to her room.

Ben turning the buggy around to get help wasn't so remarkable. Probably anyone would have done it. But the way he'd helped her from the buggy, like a gentleman, that's what had surprised her.

There was a different mood between them. And then, when he'd lifted her down, well, she didn't know what to think.

She walked to her dresser to brush her hair before going back downstairs and saw how wan she looked. *That was it,* she thought as she removed her *kapp* to redo her hair. He'd felt sorry for her because she still looked so ill.

She bound up her hair again, replaced her *kapp*, and, exhausted by her day, sank down onto her bed for a few minutes to get a second wind.

The bed on the other side of the room had been Lizzie's. But Marian, just thirteen then, began sleeping there to keep Rebecca company the first weeks after their sister died and Rebecca came home from the hospital. And then she'd just stayed instead of returning to the room she had shared with Esther.

Tired. Rebecca was so, so tired. She thought about what she'd said to Ben . . . If she'd stayed home, her *mamm* would have fussed over her like she was a *kind*.

Was it possible that this was why she'd stayed? Why she hadn't ventured outside the safe, loving circle of her family to create one of her own? Because here she could stay a *kind* her parents worried over, and she didn't need to assume responsibility for herself?

Stunned by the revelation, she didn't hear Marian calling her name until her sister came into the room.

CHAPTER 4

Rebecca! Supper's ready." Marian stood at her bedside. "Do you want to come down and eat, or shall I bring you up a tray?"

"I'm coming down." She yawned. "I should have helped *Mamm*—"

"It's okay. I did."

"You are such a sweet sister," Rebecca told her, touching her arm. "Thank you."

Marian peered at her. "Are you feeling better? I heard you coughing last night."

"I'm sorry I woke you."

She smiled. "I'm sure I've woken you up sometimes."

"Yes. When you snore."

"Snore?" Her sister stared at her, aghast. "I don't snore!"

"Like a grizzly bear in hibernation," Rebecca said.

"I don't snore!"

Rebecca couldn't stop her lips from twitching.

"Oh, you!" Marian said. "You had me going there for a minute!"

The sisters walked downstairs to the kitchen, their arms entwined.

Naomi glanced up from where she stood at the stove and smiled. "I heard the two of you laughing. Did the nap help, Rebecca?"

Rebecca gave her mother a hug. "*Ya*, but you should have woken me up. I wanted to help you."

"It's better that you get well," her mother said. "And look, everything is almost done."

Abram was putting the silverware on the table, Esther was pouring glasses of water, and even little Annie was helping by putting a napkin on each plate. Rebecca washed her hands and set to work slicing the bread while Marian helped their mother set dishes of hot food on the table.

Daed entered the room and greeted Rebecca. "Feeling better?"

"*Ya*," she said. "It was good to get back to work today."

He nodded. "Where's Jonas?" he asked as he took his seat at the table.

Naomi turned, frowning. "I thought he was out in the barn with you."

"I thought he was in here helping you."

Rebecca paused in the act of slicing the bread. She frowned as she caught the furtive glance two of her brothers exchanged.

"Abram? Where's Jonas?"

He hesitated.

"Abram?"

Naomi set down her spoon and crossed the room. "Tell us where Jonas is."

"He went sledding by the pond."

Rebecca heard *pond*, and her knife clattered to the

counter. Fear clutched her heart, and for a moment she couldn't breathe. She rushed to grab her coat and bonnet from the peg by the door.

"I'll go," her father said, taking the outdoor things from her and hanging them back on the peg. He reached for his own coat and black felt hat. "I don't want you out in the cold."

The door opened at that moment, and Jonas walked in.

"Jonas, you did *not* have permission to go sledding," *Daed* told him sternly. "You know the rules. Your *mamm* here was worried, and you worried Rebecca as well."

"Me too," said Abram. "I was wordied too!"

Jonas hung his head. "I'm sorry."

"Go put on dry clothes and get your hands washed," Amos said sternly. "We'll talk about it after supper." He looked at Naomi, then at his oldest son. "My own *daed* would have sent me to bed without supper," he told him. "But your *mamm* here won't send a child to bed hungry."

"*Danki, Mamm,*" Jonas said fervently. "I'm so very *hungerich.*"

"Getting into mischief makes a youngster hungry, eh, Naomi?"

She nodded. "*Ya,* sometimes they return home because their stomach is helping them remember where they're supposed to be."

Jonas reddened and ran to change. When he returned and slipped into his chair, he wore a chastened expression. But Rebecca saw the sly look he sent Eli.

Sometimes Jonas reminded Rebecca of Lizzie. He was the Miller child who was always looking for adventure and not afraid to get into trouble to find it. The abraded skin on his cheek told Rebecca he'd taken a spill on the sled and encountered something harder than snow. She'd clean it and put some medicine on it before he had to face their father for his transgressions, she decided.

"Where's Ben tonight?" Marian wanted to know.

"He promised his family he'd eat at home tonight," Rebecca told her.

"Did he give you a ride home?" *Daed* asked.

"*Ya.*"

He gave her a satisfied nod. "Ben always does what he says he will."

* * *

Dinner at Ben's home was quieter than at Rebecca's. He was the youngest of the Weaver children, and all his brothers and sisters had their own families now.

Ben's mother, Emma, smiled at him. She was a tall, thin woman who had worked beside her husband in the fields. Years of being outside in the sun, years of smiling through joy and adversity, had etched lines around her eyes.

"It's good to have you home for supper, *Sohn.*"

"Boy found out you made pot roast," his father muttered before putting a big forkful in his own mouth.

"You've never missed her pot roast either," Ben reminded him equably. "I remember the time you were lying in the emergency room having your broken arm set, and all you could talk about was how *Mamm* was making pot roast for supper and you were worried it would be all gone before you got home."

His father slapped him on the back, a little harder than affection usually merited. "You're right there." He shoveled in a forkful of oven-roasted potatoes and carrots. "Been spending a lot of time over at the Miller place. How long are you going to wait for her?"

"Samuel! It's not our way to pry into our children's lives in that area!"

"A man knows when he's found his *fraa*," he went on blithely. "You've been a little bit slow, haven't you, *Sohn*?"

Ben just looked at his father. "It's taking a little longer than I expected," he admitted.

"You sure she's not a lost cause?" Samuel Weaver asked bluntly.

"That's what he'd like best," his *mamm* said before Ben could answer. "He's never been one to do things the easy way."

Samuel nodded. "True. Aren't you worried that another man could come along and catch her eye, move faster?"

"Samuel!"

"It could happen," he asserted as he dragged a piece of bread through the gravy on his plate and put it into his mouth. "You know it, too, don't you?"

Ben nodded. "One day she could stop looking inward, blaming herself for her sister's death. She could look out and see someone else. Date him. But I can't rush her. It wouldn't be right."

"It's hard to know sometimes when to wait and when to press the issue," Emma said carefully.

His father thought about it and sighed. "Listen to your *mamm*," he told Ben. "Wisest woman I ever met."

His parents' eyes met, and Ben saw the love they shared. He wanted that kind of relationship, that warm glow of love after so many years of marriage. His *eldre* had weathered many challenging times together.

It was worth it to wait for the one you loved, wasn't it? Marriage was supposed to be forever.

"She's a lovely girl," his mother was saying. "I'm not saying this to sway you one way or the other. You've been a good friend to her."

Ben looked up and waited for her to gently say that perhaps he should move on, find someone else to marry him and give him children, and her, grandchildren. But she simply smiled.

"I know she took the death of her twin very hard," she went on. "There's no accounting for how long it takes for someone to accept the death of someone they love, to accept God's will."

"She still blames herself," Ben said, setting down his fork. "She hasn't said it in so many words, but . . ."

"But you know because you care."

He nodded. She understood him so well.

She touched his hand. "And I know that you blamed yourself for not being able to save Lizzie. The two of you have had much to deal with. Things will work out if they're meant to. In God's time."

"Sometimes it's hard for a man to accept God's

time," his father said. "Maybe you should—Is that my favorite?"

Emma set the pan of baked apples fragrant with cinnamon in front of him on the table. "There's ice cream for on top if you want it."

Samuel jumped up to get it.

Emma winked at Ben as she handed him his own dessert. By the time his father returned to the table, Emma was talking about the upcoming quilting at the Millers'.

* * *

Rebecca walked into the barn a few days later and was startled to hear her father asking Ben to drive her to the doctor.

"Is she still sick?"

She stopped. Ben sounded concerned.

"No, no, she's fine," her father assured him quickly. "It's an appointment with one of those head docs, that's all."

Closing her eyes, Rebecca shook her head. *Great, just great,* she thought. *Now Ben's going to think I'm crazy.*

"It'll be on the clock," Amos said. "I need to stay here and work up a bid for the Brown kitchen."

"*Ya,* I'll be happy to do it."

"*Guder mariye, Daed,* Ben," Rebecca said as she strode forward.

"Rebecca. I was just asking Ben here to drive you to the appointment."

"I can drive myself."

"*Ya*, I know," her father said, handing Ben a list. "But I want Ben to pick up some supplies at the hardware store, so this will kill two birds, if you'll pardon the expression."

Rebecca rolled her eyes.

Her father grinned. "Ask your *mamm* if she needs anything in town."

"So we can kill three birds?" Rebecca shot back over her shoulder as she walked out of the barn.

"Smart mouth, that one," she heard her father say with a laugh.

She was still smiling when she entered the kitchen.

"You're in a good mood this morning," *Mamm* remarked as she looked up from her seat at the kitchen table. A steaming cup of tea sat before her.

"*Daed* said to see if you need anything in town. Ben's driving me and picking up some supplies from the hardware store."

"Is that why you were smiling?"

"I don't get excited about picking up supplies."

Her mother looked at her. "You know what I mean."

"Because Ben will be driving me? No."

But the last two times she'd seen him, it felt as if things were changing between them. There had been an awareness between them that couldn't be missed.

Her mother went to the refrigerator and pulled a list from under a magnet. "I'd appreciate it if you can pick up these things from Nellie's store. I'll need them for the quilting."

"Sure."

"Rebecca?"

"*Ya?*"

"Why do you think Ben stays for supper so often?"

"Because you're such a good cook?"

Naomi laughed and shook her head. "No. His mother is a better cook than me. Maybe if you think about it, you could come up with a reason."

Rebecca stood there for a moment. "Now why would I want to do that?"

Then she looked up and saw Ben striding toward the house. "I have to go." She kissed her mother's cheek. "See you later."

* * *

The drive into town was silent.

Ben looked over several times and saw that Rebecca looked lost in thought.

"You okay?"

"Hmm? Yes, why?"

"You're being quiet."

"I'm not a chatterbox. You know that."

"There's quite a distance between quiet and a chatterbox."

"You're not exactly talking much yourself."

He nodded. "Feels strange not to be on the job on a weekday. Not that I mind, you understand. It's good to have a change."

Turning, she raised her eyebrows.

"What?"

"That's more than I've heard you say in a long time."

"I think you're teasing me."

She laughed. "I guess I am. Imagine that."

Ben wondered why she was going to the doctor. She didn't appear ill. There was no way that it was to see a "head doc" the way her father had teased. He knew of no one more levelheaded than Rebecca. Not that there was any shame in seeing a counselor if a person had emotional or psychological problems.

But the only thing Rebecca had, in his opinion, was a mantle of grief that was finally lifting.

Then it struck him: she could be going to see a doctor about a woman thing. The thought made the tips of his ears burn with embarrassment. He forced the thought aside and looked out at the passing scenery. "Nice day. You warm enough?"

"I'm fine. Thank you."

"Are you going to the singing on Sunday?"

"Thought I would."

"Shall I pick you up?"

She nodded. "That would be nice."

They talked about the last singing, the friends who'd attended, what couples were pairing up, Leah Petersheim and Aaron Lantz's recent marriage, an editor showing interest in publishing Leah's first story. They speculated on how the Petersheims had felt when three of their four daughters became engaged in such a short time.

A car came up behind them very quickly. Ben pulled over to the shoulder and it went speeding past, startling Ike. He reared, and Ben fought to steady him, to keep control.

His heart pounding, Ben turned to Rebecca and found her looking pale and shaken, clutching at the dash of the buggy.

"Someone should do something about drivers like that!" she muttered.

Nodding, Ben pulled the buggy back onto the road. Sharing the road with modern day horsepower could be dangerous. It was easy to get lulled into a false sense of security, listening to the *clip-clop* of the horse's hooves, talking and gazing at the scenery. When there were accidents, it was the buggy occupants who were hurt the worst.

Thank goodness nothing had happened. He couldn't stand it if something happened to Rebecca and he wasn't any more able to save her than he had been Lizzie.

Amos and Naomi didn't need another tragedy in their family.

CHAPTER 5

D r. Prato held out her arms. "Rebecca! It's so good to see you."

Rebecca hugged the woman who'd listened to her tears and fears after Lizzie died. She took a seat, and the older woman sat opposite her. The office was a comfortable place, filled with books and photos of Dr. Prato's children.

"So tell me how you've been," Dr. Prato invited. "I haven't seen you for, let's see here"—she consulted her file—"three years."

Her eyes were warm as she gazed at Rebecca over the rims of her poppy-red reading glasses. She'd once confessed that she was in her sixties, but she looked much younger with her streaky blonde hair and trendy *Englisch* outfits.

Bringing her up to date took a few minutes. Then Rebecca fell silent.

"So tell me why you wanted to come in today."

Rebecca stared at her hands.

"You don't need to choose the right words. Just say what's on your mind."

Looking up, Rebecca met her calm gaze. "I noticed my family sometimes still acts worried about me."

"They're responsible for their own behavior. You can't control that."

"I know." She twisted her hands in her lap.

"There's something else, isn't there?"

"I'm hearing voices. *A* voice," she corrected.

To her amazement, the other woman didn't blink. "And whose voice is it? When we first started our sessions, I recall you thought you heard your sister's. I told you at the time that that wasn't unusual. Twins have quite a close bond."

"*Ya.* I remember."

"And your sister was quite—well, how would you describe her?"

"Dominant," Rebecca confessed. "Stronger, more outgoing. Definitely more adventurous."

"A risk taker."

Rebecca nodded.

"Which is why it wasn't surprising that she died that day."

"But I should have—" She stopped. "I know, you've been telling me for a long time that it wasn't my fault."

Dr. Prato smiled. "And one day you'll believe me. One day you'll forgive yourself. But you haven't yet, have you?"

Rebecca shook her head. "Not entirely. I'm supposed to believe it's God's will. That's what we learn from the time we're children, that everything is in order. That God is in charge. That it's His will—"

"If people live or die." Dr. Prato looked at Rebecca over her glasses. "From the way you're talking, I wonder if it isn't only yourself that you haven't forgiven. Maybe you haven't forgiven God?"

Rebecca bit her lip. "No, I don't think I have," she whispered. "I stopped being angry at Him. But how long is it supposed to take to stop missing her? To not feel bad that she's gone? To not remember the way that she died?"

"I wish I could tell you. Everyone's experience with grief is different."

"Some people tell me that it's time to be over Lizzie's death—not lately, you understand, but they've said so. Not *Mamm* and *Daed*. They never have. Or Marian."

Or Ben. He was around constantly, and though he'd seen her at her worst moments, he'd never suggested that she should be setting aside her grief. He just listened. And listened and listened.

"Something you want to say?"

Rebecca shook her head. She wanted to think about it for a while.

"So let's return to this voice you're hearing," Dr. Prato prompted.

"I heard it the other day when I stood by the pond."

"What did it say?"

"*Don't be afraid.*"

"Are you afraid, Rebecca?"

Rebecca started to shake her head, then stopped. "I could say that I'm not afraid, that it's simply that I haven't wanted to put on my skates since the accident. But that wouldn't be truthful."

"And you're always truthful."

There was no need to look at Dr. Prato to see if she was questioning or implying anything. She was simply stating the truth.

"You don't—you don't think I'm crazy?"

"Absolutely not."

"You don't think there's something wrong with someone hearing a voice?"

Dr. Prato smiled. "Do you?"

"Now you're answering a question with a question." Rebecca smiled in spite of herself. "No one else I know talks about hearing voices, so I have to think it's a little strange."

"Since I moved to this community, I've gotten to know a number of Plain people. I've never heard any of them having such experiences, no," Dr. Prato admitted. "But that doesn't mean that they don't." She leaned forward. "Sometimes, when others don't talk about deeply personal things, you can start to wonder if you're different, if something might even be wrong with you. Now, think about what the voice is saying."

"*Don't be afraid.*"

"Could it be you, talking to yourself? Is it possible that it's your inner voice? Maybe you didn't hear it a lot before, since you were around such a strong sibling. Maybe you're hearing your inner voice urging you to stop being afraid to live? To do things you haven't done since Lizzie died? You said you heard it when you were looking at the pond. That's where you loved to skate, where you did something that made you feel happy and free."

"And it's where Lizzie died."

"Yes. That voice could even be you telling yourself not to be afraid of going on without her, couldn't it? To not feel guilty any longer for not being able to save her?"

Rebecca stared at the doctor, her eyes wide. "I—I hadn't thought of that."

"Think about it. See if it makes sense to you." She sat back.

"I will."

"And maybe . . ." She hesitated.

"What?"

"Maybe it's God talking to you?"

Rebecca frowned. "I don't know. I doubt it. He knows I was so angry with Him for so long for taking Lizzie home."

"Was there anything else on your mind?" the older woman asked after a long moment.

"I was thinking on the way here that I'll always be grateful that you talked to my parents about me," Rebecca said quietly. "You really persisted."

"You were worth fighting for," Dr. Prato told her. "I can't tell you how gratifying it's been to see your community being more accepting of seeing a mental health professional when they need to." She smiled. "You've come a long way from the first time I met you."

Rebecca was ashamed to remember how she hadn't wanted to live after Lizzie died. She'd developed pneumonia and had been hospitalized for two weeks when Dr. Prato had stopped by her room at the request of the attending doctor.

Her parents were dubious at first about her talking with Rebecca. Medical care was one thing, but Rebecca's *daed* had felt his daughter didn't need to speak to a psychologist. But something Dr. Prato had said convinced them. After Rebecca left the hospital, she visited Dr. Prato in her office in town a number of times.

"I know it was difficult for them to consider at first." Then she frowned. "That reminds me. I overheard my father calling you a 'head doc' today."

"It sounds like that bothered you."

Rebecca stared at her hands. "He was telling Ben, a friend of the family. Someone who works for him. I went to school with him; he's my friend. But I never told him that I've seen you. I'm not ashamed of it, but I live in a small community. I don't need people talking about me."

"Would Ben do that?"

"No," Rebecca said at last. "He's such a good friend to me."

Was it her imagination that the doctor was sitting up a little straighter, looking a little more attentive?

"Tell me about this Ben."

Rebecca shrugged. "He's just a friend." She picked at a thread on her skirt. "Well, he's just always . . . around, you know? People have asked me if he's a friend or more."

Dr. Prato's brows lifted. "And how do you feel about that?"

* * *

Ben glanced at the clock in the hardware store. He'd dropped Rebecca off almost an hour and a half ago. She'd said she'd meet him here. But maybe she'd started feeling worse. Maybe she was waiting there for him to come get her.

He returned to the building where she'd asked him to drop her off and walked inside. He examined the building directory. Dr. Seaton, gerontologist. Hmm. No, that was a doctor for old people. An obesity clinic. No. Rebecca was slim.

There was a listing for a cancer specialist. His heart stopped for a moment, then beat again when he saw a little note attached that said they'd recently moved to a different location. Ben scanned the small list remaining. A pediatrician and a urologist specializing in male patients.

Then he saw the listing for a Dr. Hannah Prato, psychologist. Maybe Amos hadn't been joking about Rebecca seeing a "head doc." Maybe the thoughts Rebecca thought were dark, not insightful. Grief often did strange things to people. Sometimes they couldn't function anymore. Sometimes they even tried to hurt themselves.

Although . . . Amos hadn't been expressing worry about his daughter. He'd been almost jovial. And Rebecca had responded lightly, teasing him in return.

"Do you need some help, young man?"

Ben turned and took off his black felt hat in deference to the *Englisch* woman beside him. Her appearance was so different from that of the Amish women he knew: her hair was short, light brown with streaks of blonde that he didn't think came from being outside in the sun. She wore a very short dress that matched the bright red glasses perched on her nose. Instead of minding the way he stared at her, she gave him a direct and inquisitive smile as she waited for him to speak.

"No, I—uh—" He felt like a dolt standing there, unable to frame a reply. "I'm looking for a friend."

"Perhaps she's waiting outside."

He hadn't said *she*. He shook his head. "No, she wasn't outside."

Her eyes narrowed just a bit, as if she were sizing him up. "I see. Do you know which doctor she was seeing?"

Again he shook his head. "I don't think it was any of them."

The woman scanned the list. "No? Well, let's see if we can figure this out." She ran over the same list of specialists he had, and he shook his head at each one. "That leaves just Dr. Prato?"

He must have looked appalled, for she reached out and touched his arm. "It's okay, you know. Sometimes we all need someone to talk to."

"I don't know anyone who sees a head doctor," Ben told her. "Well, that's not exactly true. A friend of mine was diagnosed as bipolar last year, and he's been see-ing one."

A man entered the building just then. The woman waited until he'd gotten into the elevator and the doors closed. "Sometimes a person needs to talk to someone other than their people or their God. It's okay, really. I've counseled Plain people." She stuck out her hand. "I'm Hannah Prato."

Ben took her small, smooth hand in his larger, work-roughened hand, feeling like a big, clumsy bear. "The head doctor."

She laughed. "Yes."

"I'm Ben Weaver." Was it his imagination, or did he see the faintest flicker of expression? "I think you know who I am," he said slowly.

Her smile never faltered. "I do?"

Ben tilted his head to look at her and nodded.

"Well, you know, whoever saw your friend wouldn't be able to tell you so," she said. "Doctors must maintain patient confidentiality."

"I know that. But I'm worried about her. She was supposed to meet me at the hardware store, and she didn't come. I started thinking—"

Dr. Prato's smile faded, and her eyes were sympathetic. "You're concerned that it could be something far worse than you imagined. I understand." She studied him. "This person you're worried about—she's very lucky to have a friend such as you. I can tell that you care about her very much. And what I can tell you is what I said before, that sometimes people see me because they need to talk to someone other than their people and their God. They need to say things and not feel judged. They need to feel that they can explore topics that are outside of the way they usually think." She paused. "You know what I mean, don't you?"

"Ye-es," he said slowly.

"I thought you might." She gave him a nod of approval. Shifting her big shoulder purse and the files she carried, she fished in her pocket and then held out a business card. "If you'd ever like to talk to me, just let me know. When Plain people feel they need to see a doctor, they should feel they can see whatever kind of doctor they need."

"I'm glad my friend came to see you," he told her.

"I didn't say—"

"I know. And I'm glad I met you too."

Frowning, she searched his face. "Thanks. But I'm not sure I'd mention our conversation to your friend. I'm not saying to lie; that would be wrong."

"I agree. I wouldn't want her to think I tried to find out her business, even if it was because I cared. But I doubt the subject will ever come up."

The doctor's face cleared. "Let's hope not. Unless you ever find a good time to tell her, one when you know your looking for her will be understood and appreciated."

He let out a gusty sigh. "*I'm* not appreciated by her," he said, then his eyes widened at what he'd blurted out.

"Do you really think so?" she asked, and as she turned and walked away, he thought he heard her chuckle.

Tucking the card into his pocket, he began walking back to where he'd parked the buggy.

He was waiting there when Rebecca rushed up, carrying a bag from a popular sewing and craft shop. "Sorry I took so long. There was a line in the shop."

"Ready to go?"

"*Ya.*" She walked to her side of the buggy and looked surprised when he quickly appeared at her elbow to help her into it.

He frowned. He was always polite. Then he thought, *Maybe she's nervous since we got so physically close the last time I helped her into the buggy.* His face flaming, he rounded the buggy and got inside. With a jerk of the reins, he got the buggy moving. They traveled a few miles in silence, then Rebecca startled him by speaking.

"You're doing it again."

"Doing what?"

"Staring at me." She turned to him. "Are you wondering if I'm going to do something crazy?"

"I—why would I wonder that?"

"Because my father said I was going to a 'head doc.'"

Ben didn't know what to say. "I don't know much about them."

"Then ask. If I don't want to answer, I won't."

"*Allrecht.* Why did you go to one? Is something wrong with your head?"

"I met Dr. Prato in the hospital, when I had pneumonia. She helped me through the grief process."

"Then why see her today?"

She looked at him and hesitated. Shrugging, she looked out at the passing scenery. "I just wanted to talk with her." She smiled at him. "I'm glad I did. She thinks I'm doing really well."

"*Ya?*" He looked at her. There was a lightness to her mood that had been absent earlier that morning.

She nodded. "She says that grief's different for everyone, and there's no set time for people to come to terms with it."

Ben remembered how his mother had said something similar. "Sounds wise."

"And since Lizzie was my twin, there was more of a bond than I might have had with another sister."

"The two of you were always together," he recalled. "I hardly ever saw you apart." But he'd only been interested in her, not Lizzie.

She looked at him again. "You know, I thought

about my *mamm* and *daed* and how they've never been impatient with me, never chided me about grieving for Lizzie for so long. It occurred to me that you hadn't either. I've never thanked you for it."

"You look surprised."

"I am." She stared straight ahead again. "Well, you don't make it easy to talk to you, you know."

"I—don't?"

Shaking her head, she turned to him again. "I mean, we've talked a lot about important things, like Lizzie dying. But then . . ."

When she closed her eyes and bent her head, he touched her hand. Her eyes flew open in surprise.

"Talk to me."

She lifted her shoulders, let them fall. "We've been friends for such a long time." She stopped, hesitated. "But something's felt different the last few days." Her eyes widened at what she'd said. It had never been in her to be so . . . bold.

He let that sink in. Maybe it was time to do some real talking. Ben pulled the buggy to the side of the road and turned to face her. "I don't always have the right words like some men." Now it was his turn to hesitate.

"I know. But when I was trying to say something to Dr. Prato earlier and I was searching for the right word, she said for me to just say what was on my mind."

He looked away, not sure what to say. While he'd waited until he felt she was over the death of her sister, while he worried that she blamed him for not being able to save Lizzie, he hadn't planned on what he'd say, what he'd do.

Looking back at her, he nodded. "Good advice." He hesitated, wary of blurting out his feelings and being rejected. "Five years ago I had started thinking about whether we could be more than friends," he said carefully. "Then Lizzie died."

"And everything changed," she whispered. "But why didn't you say something before this?"

"When? How? I felt it would be selfish of me. And you weren't ready."

"No," she said, sighing. "I wasn't. Still might not be. Oh, Ben. So many years you wasted. You waited when you should have been looking at someone who could be there for you."

He touched her hand. "I wanted to be there for you, Rebecca."

"This is a lot to think about," she told him, pressing the tips of her fingers to her temples. "When I was talking to Dr. Prato, she kept asking me questions about you."

"About me? Why? She doesn't know me."

Rebecca smiled. "I was telling her how patient *Mamm* and *Daed* had been with me about grieving for Lizzie. And my sisters and brothers, of course, especially Marian. Then I said you had been, too, and suddenly Dr. Prato was asking all these questions about you, asking me why I thought you were hanging around so much. She said that was a lot of effort on your part, even for *mei mamm*'s meals. Told me maybe I needed to take another look at you and think about things."

Ben let out the breath he hadn't realized he'd been

holding. "Well, I guess I'm glad your father asked me to drive you to your appointment today."

"Me too."

A car drove by, and a passenger looked out to gawk at them. Ben glanced at the darkening sky and picked up the reins to urge Ike back onto the road and toward home.

"So where does this leave us?" he asked as silence stretched between them.

Rebecca turned to him and took a deep breath. She didn't think he was going to like her answer, but she needed to say it.

CHAPTER 6

Rebecca made tiny stitches in the section of quilt before her. Outside it was cold, and snow was predicted for later in the day. But inside the Miller home there was a roaring fire in the fireplace, and it was time for talking and sewing. They drank cup after cup of tea and coffee and ate cookies while discussing everything from speculation about who was dating whom to when spring would arrive.

Quilting was such good therapy, Rebecca thought, feeling content. There was something so reassuring about sitting around talking with friends and family, sewing patterns that had been passed down for generations, here in a home that had been in her family for more than a hundred years.

She looked around the circle at her friends and family. Marian was helping her and *Mamm* to host the quilting frolic. The three of them had worked hard at *redding-up* the house and putting chairs in place. Little Annie wasn't happy about having to go to school today instead of being here, but one day she'd be old enough to sit with the womenfolk in the circle.

The Petersheim sisters were here today—well, they'd

been Petersheims before three of them had gotten married this past fall. Rebecca couldn't help thinking that they all glowed with happiness. New *fraa* Edna, expert seamstress, had laid out the design of the quilt they were working on today. Mary Carol had brought thumbprint cookies filled with the jam made from mouthwatering strawberries she'd grown in her garden and Kathleen had preserved.

And Leah. Rebecca smiled as she watched Leah struggle with making tiny stitches and then laughingly give up and retreat to a corner to write in the notebook she carried as a constant companion. Leah wasn't talented in the typical skills of an Amish woman—she'd nearly set the *kich* on fire more than once when she tried to cook. But Aaron, Leah's new *mann*, insisted that she was the only *fraa* for him. Those who loved saw with different eyes than others, Rebecca thought.

Amanda Graber was chatting with Leah. Amanda reminded Rebecca of Lizzie with her exuberance. But Amanda bustled around taking care of others, not worrying them with her risk taking.

Sisters Lydia King and Miriam Fisher worked well together cutting pieces of fabric for the quilt. Rebecca watched them and reflected on how they both had married men they'd known years before. Circumstances had separated the couples, but God's will had drawn them together again for great happiness.

As she sewed, Rebecca thought about her conversation with Ben on the drive home from her appointment with Dr. Prato. Now she knew how he felt about her. Had felt about her for years. But after she'd admitted she had feelings for him as well, she'd told him that she needed a little more time.

"I know it's a lot to ask, considering how long you've been waiting. But this is the first time I've had a chance to really think about it. The part of me that dreamed about the future, about how I felt about you, has been in cold storage," Rebecca told Ben.

When he glanced over, she took a deep breath and smiled at him.

"Okay. I understand." Ben had returned her smile, and the mood had been lighter, happier on the drive home.

She pricked her finger and quickly glanced about to see if anyone had noticed her daydreaming.

How could she have missed seeing how Ben felt about her? Even as lost in grief as she'd been at first, she should have known that his frequent appearance at the Miller kitchen table wasn't due only to her mother's cooking.

Sometimes she'd wondered if Ben hung around so much because he felt guilty. He hadn't been able to save Lizzie when she fell through the ice. No one had, not the other boys who'd tried to help, not the paramedics who'd arrived so quickly and tried to make her breathe. Not the doctors at the hospital.

She still had to ask him what he'd meant when he said if she was going to blame anyone for Lizzie's death, she should blame him. Even if she had trouble accepting Lizzie's death as God's will, it was time to stop reliving what she couldn't change. It was time for Ben to stop blaming himself, too, if he was doing that.

The door opened, and her father came in, stamping his feet on the mat. He took off his black felt hat and shook the snow from it before hanging it and his coat on a peg. *Mamm* rose and walked to the stove to pour him a cup of coffee. They spoke quietly for a moment and then he looked over and caught Rebecca's eye. With a tilt of the head, he silently asked to speak to her.

She got up and followed him into the hallway, wondering what was going on. When she stopped before him and he wouldn't meet her eyes, her breath caught. Visions of tools running amuck, saws biting into flesh, blood spurting from arteries flashed before her eyes.

"Ben? Did something happen to Ben?"

"Whoa, nothing's happened to Ben," he said quickly. He glanced over at Naomi. "Rebecca, your mother told me I need to apologize to you."

"Apologize? For what?"

"For telling Ben that you needed to go to your 'head doc,'" he said. "It's a family matter, and I shouldn't have said that."

"I'm not ashamed of seeing Dr. Prato."

"No, I know you're not. And your mother and I will always be indebted to her for helping you so much."

She looked up at him, at this man who had been such a rock for her, and she nodded. "I knew you were just teasing. I know you don't think I'm crazy."

He hugged her. "Of course you're not. You're the most levelheaded young woman I know."

Rebecca hugged him back. "I don't know about that. But I love you, and I'm not upset."

"Well, I guess I'd better be getting back to work. Now that we've talked."

"Amos? Is everything all right?" Naomi came to stand next to him.

"It's fine," Rebecca assured her. "*Daed* apologized like he said you wanted him to."

"I didn't mean you had to do it right now, while we're having the quilting!"

Amos shrugged. "Best to apologize as soon as you know you've done wrong," he said. "Besides, I think I was doing a little . . . interfering."

"Interfering?"

Amos cleared his throat. "I—uh, well, I think I was trying to find out how Ben felt about Rebecca. If it bothered him that she was seeing Dr. Prato, he wasn't the kind of *mann* that I wanted around our daughter."

"Amos!" Naomi stared at him, shocked. "I don't think we should interfere—"

"*Ya.*" He looked at Rebecca. "Sorry."

These things were supposed to take place in privacy. Some couples only told their parents of their engagement after they'd arranged for the banns to be read in church.

But Rebecca could tell they were concerned, and she wanted to reassure them. "Ben just told me how he felt on the way home after I saw Dr. Prato," she told them carefully.

"What about you? How do you feel?" her mother wanted to know.

"What, is Rebecca sick again?" Marian asked as she

stepped into the hallway. She peered at her sister. "You didn't say you weren't feeling well."

Rebecca threw up her hands. "Enough!" she said, laughing. "This has gotten completely out of hand."

Standing on tiptoe, she kissed her father's cheek, then her mother's and her sister's. "I love you all, and I'm going back to the quilting. Everyone must be wondering what kind of hosts we are!"

When she returned to the living room, Rebecca found needles poised in midair and everyone looking curiously at her.

"*Daed* needed something," she told them.

Rebecca picked up her needle and began making small, meticulous stitches. There was silence for a long moment, then the other women went back to stitching. Sarah Fisher began talking about Katie Ann, her toddler, and asking advice about teething problems, and suddenly there was chattering around the quilt frame as the mothers in the group gave advice.

Rebecca glanced over and gave Sarah a grateful smile. Sarah smiled back. *She knows what it's like to be the object of concern because of a loss.*

Yes, Rebecca thought, it was good to sit here sewing on familiar patterns while she thought about the change that had suddenly presented itself in the pattern of her own life. She had much to think about, but nothing had to be decided in a day. She'd take things slowly and carefully to make sure that Ben was as right for her as he thought she was for him.

* * *

"Something wrong?"

Amos looked over. "What?"

Ben planted his hands on his hips and looked at his boss. "You've been watching me all morning."

Shaking his head, Rebecca's father ran his measuring tape along a wall in the Greenstein kitchen. "You must be imagining it."

Ben watched Amos jot some numbers down on a pad of paper. "No, I'm not. Is there something you don't like about the way I'm doing the job today?"

"'Course not."

"Then it's about Rebecca and me."

Amos looked up. "*Is* there a Rebecca and you?"

"That should be between us at this point, don't you think?" Ben said it respectfully, but he felt his heart beating hard in his chest while Amos regarded him, his bushy black eyebrows drawn together in a frown.

"You're right," the other man conceded after a long moment.

When he muttered something beneath his breath as he turned back to his measuring tape, Ben's ears perked up. "What did you say?"

"You'd think you'd be grateful to me," Amos told him, sounding a little irritable. He let the metal measuring tape snap back into its container. "After all I've done to put the two of you together."

Ben leaned against the counter behind him. "Are you saying you've been playing matchmaker?"

"Why do you think you get invited for supper so often? I do have enough mouths to feed."

But although he sounded like he was growling, Ben

saw the corners of the other man's mouth quirk up into a grin. "Why, you're as bad as my *daed*, trying to push us together," he said at last.

"Even sent you to town with her that day when she could have driven herself. Girl knows how to drive a buggy better than you."

Letting the joking insult slide—at least, he thought Amos was joking; he didn't think anyone knew he'd had that little accident with the chicken last year—Ben thought about what he'd said. "So you didn't really need those supplies at the hardware store?"

Amos shrugged. "They could have delivered them."

"Why, you—I don't know what to say."

"Well, I shouldn't have said what I did that day. About Rebecca seeing a 'head doc.' Naomi made me apologize to Rebecca for that. But I knew it'd get your curiosity up. Thought you'd either stick with her, or it'd finally make you run."

Ben stood straighter. "I don't run," he said quietly. "If I did, I'd have decided not to wait like I have."

"And now?"

"I don't know what's going to happen, but she knows how I feel now. I'm giving her a little time to think things over."

"Don't let her take too long," Amos said gruffly. "Enough water under the bridge."

"She's not the kind of person who'd treat my feelings lightly."

Amos gave Ben a long, measuring look and nodded, then he turned back to his work.

Ben didn't need reminding. He knew how long

he'd been waiting. Even this space they were standing in was a reminder. It had gone on the market just last year, and Ben had thought about buying it. He knew he would get married eventually, even if Rebecca didn't want him, and the place had been a good price because it needed a lot of repair—just the kind he and his friends and family could do in the evenings and on Saturdays.

But he'd waited, and the house had sold. Well, there'd be another. And if things went the way he hoped with Rebecca, they'd find it—or build it—together.

He and Amos worked together companionably, talking little for the rest of the afternoon. When quitting time came, they loaded their tools in the buggy and climbed inside.

"Staying for supper?" Amos asked casually.

"Not tonight," Ben told him. "I'm giving Rebecca a little time to think. A *little* time," he repeated before the other man could speak. "And, Amos, you'll have one less mouth to feed tonight."

Amos chuckled as he lifted the reins and got the buggy moving.

* , *

Rebecca was about to enter the kitchen when she heard her parents talking. Thinking it might be a private conversation, she hesitated.

"Ben's not staying for supper? You didn't scare him away, did you?" Naomi asked.

"Of course not. He says he's giving Rebecca a little time to think." He caught her look. "I told him not to give her too long."

Rebecca's eyebrows went up. *Well, that's interesting,* she thought. She knew her parents liked Ben, that he was the kind of person *Daed* wanted working for him. But interfering in Ben's relationship with her?

She stepped into the room. "Are you taking sides?"

"Eavesdropping?" her mother asked mildly.

"No, I was just walking in and I heard my name."

Her father reddened. He glanced at his wife, then back at Rebecca. "What I meant was, your mother and I know that Ben has been interested in you for a long time. If he sees you're not feeling the same way, he shouldn't keep waiting."

"But I didn't know that he was interested until now. I thought he just looked at me as a friend."

"She took Lizzie's death hard, Amos," Naomi reminded him. "She wasn't thinking about boys. Unlike another young woman in the house," she muttered.

Rebecca tried not to smile. She'd noticed Marian was already showing interest in the opposite sex—and not just Ben. She walked over to the stove and looked into the simmering pot. "Mmm, tomato soup. Perfect on a cold night. How can I help?"

"Amos, here's your coffee," Naomi said, handing him the mug she'd just poured.

"I've got some paperwork to do. Call me when supper's ready," he said and left the room.

Rebecca could have sworn she saw the two of them

exchange a look. In her opinion, there was suddenly too much interest in what was going on—or not going on—between her and Ben.

"Why don't you slice some bread so we can make grilled cheese sandwiches to go with the soup? I baked brownies for dessert. That should be plenty."

Nodding, Rebecca began slicing bread, then turned to slicing cheese. Her mother spread butter on the bread, stacked slices with cheese, and set several sandwiches sizzling on the grill pan on the gas stove.

Naomi gave the sandwiches her attention. "I don't want you to feel pressured by what your father said," she offered, breaking the silence and looking up at Rebecca. "Ben chose not to reveal his feelings to you before this, but that doesn't mean you're obliged to suddenly conform to his plans for a life together."

"He's not pressuring me."

"Good. *I've* seen how he feels about you, but the fact that you haven't tells me that you weren't ready . . . or that you don't see him as the man you want to marry someday."

"I think marrying him would make *Daed* happy."

"And that should be the least of your concerns," her mother told her tartly. "You're the one who'll live with him for a very long time." She glanced in the direction of the den where Amos had retreated to do his paperwork. "I want you to be as happy with your marriage as I've been."

Rebecca hugged her mother, and they stood there for a long moment. "I love you, *Mamm*."

"I love you, too, *liebchen*."

"What's burning?" Marian asked as she walked into the kitchen.

Naomi spun around. Tsk-tsking, she used a spatula to lift the sandwiches from the grill onto a plate.

"The pigs will have these for breakfast," she said with a rueful laugh. "Rebecca, cut some more bread and cheese, please."

Marian sidled up to her sister at the counter. "So, Rebecca," she said, "is Ben joining us tonight?"

CHAPTER 7

No one expected Rebecca to attend any funerals in the community for several years after Lizzie's death. But the Lantzes' flamboyant Auntie Ruth had died last summer, and a few days ago, a beloved *onkel* had died, so Rebecca went to the services. She was grateful that both had been elderly and lived good, long lives. But she couldn't help it; going to *Onkel* John's funeral made her think about Lizzie's.

Now she wanted a connection with her sister, a more cheerful one. She pulled Lizzie's journal from under her pillow and climbed onto her bed. Somehow, reading her words almost made her feel as if Lizzie were in the room with her—even in the same bed. She smiled as she remembered how, when they were little girls, her parents would find them sleeping together, as if they still wanted the closeness of the womb.

After Lizzie died, Rebecca felt she was invading Lizzie's privacy when she read her journal. But she justified it by telling herself that she missed her sister so much, she just wanted the closeness. Besides, she and Lizzie had always shared everything.

Well, she'd thought they shared everything. The

first time she opened the journal and read an entry, she'd been shocked. She turned to that page again.

I've known my twin sister, Rebecca, all my life, Lizzie had written in the journal, in the quick, careless scrawl that would have made their teacher wince. *It still surprises me that we're so different. She's almost timid compared to me. And she's always watching me and worrying over what I do, almost like she's my mother, not my sister. I love her, but I wish she'd stop that. She tells me that she's the oldest and it's her job to look out for all of us. She was born six minutes before me. Six minutes! Should that really mean she's the oldest? Maybe she crowded me when it came time to be born. No, I don't really mean that. Rebecca would never put herself first. She never does.*

Rebecca winced. Lizzie sounded . . . annoyed that she'd simply cared enough to look out for her. Imagine!

She heard footsteps on the wooden stairs and quickly thrust the journal behind her. Marian walked into the room. "You okay?"

"Sure, why?"

Marian shrugged. "I just thought maybe you were upset after going to the funeral."

Rebecca studied her sister. Marian's forehead was drawn in concern. It was an expression she saw often on her sister's face.

Marian was becoming her! She was worrying over Rebecca the way Rebecca had worried over Lizzie. Guilt swamped her. "I'm fine. Really. I was just reading. It was a long morning."

Her sister nodded. "I'm going to have some hot chocolate with *Mamm*. Want some?"

"No, thanks."

Marian walked out and Rebecca stared after her. When she heard her sister's footsteps descend the stairs, she got up and walked over to her chest of drawers. Reaching back behind a stack of underwear, she pulled out a leather-bound journal and took it to her bed. She leafed through the pages and frowned. The last entry was a year to the date from Lizzie's death.

The handwriting was large and dark, slashing across the page, not her usual neat writing. Here and there the words were marked by patches where her tears had fallen.

It's not fair! she'd written. *God, why did You take my sister from us?* It was written over and over again, a litany of anger. She glanced heavenward. Thank goodness her God wasn't an angry God, or He'd have struck her down.

She leafed through the pages and found more of the same, until she reached the page where she'd written about the awful day at the pond. Taking a deep breath, she moved on and found the entries before that.

I wonder what will happen one day when one of us finds that special man, the one we want to spend the rest of our lives with. I'll be happy, of course, to be with him. But it will be strange to be so completely separate from this sister I've lived so close to from the moment our hearts started beating in the womb. We share thoughts without speaking, have shared memories. Mamm always talks about how we had our own language no one else understood until we started talking with others in the family.

My husband will have to understand that Lizzie will be a frequent visitor, of course. We'll visit often. Maybe we'll get married at the same time . . . find our special men and have a double wedding? And wouldn't it be so wunderbaar *to have our* kinner *play together and grow up close cousins?*

Maybe one of us will even have twins. I know God determines these things, but I think Lizzie should have them. I know she thinks of me as a little mudder, *always watching over her. But she has a sense of adventure I admire.* Kinner *need that, not just the mothering.*

I wonder if it'll be Ben I marry. He's so cute. And he's been paying attention to me, not the other girls. Well, teasing me, but he doesn't do it with them. I think he likes me, and I know I like him. A lot.

Rebecca smiled as she closed the book and slid the two journals under her pillow. That's where Lizzie had kept hers—under her pillow. She hadn't made any secret of it to Rebecca, pulling it out and writing in it each night before bed. But no one else had known about it. Rebecca felt a little guilty that she hadn't shared it with her mother, but the time had never been right. Maybe one day. There were entries in there about *Mamm* and *Daed.* Some of the things that Lizzie had written would make them smile, even when she complained about their being too strict. There were lots of those entries because Lizzie frequently wanted to do things that she shouldn't. But she had written just as often of her love for her parents and for her sisters and brothers.

Her entries about Rebecca had made her smile and made her frown. But Rebecca didn't want to think about those now. So what did *she* want to do now? Rebecca found herself thinking about Ben, how he'd looked at her that day. How it had felt to be held in his strong arms when he picked her up to put her in the buggy. How they'd looked at each other, breath held, their faces inches apart. How it had felt when his hand touched hers.

She wanted to see him again. Be with him.

So what was she waiting for?

She jumped up, freshened up, and then went clattering down the stairs. Her *mamm* and Marian looked up in surprise.

"Are *Daed* and Ben still out in the barn?"

Naomi nodded.

Rebecca threw on her coat and slipped out the door. As she went to shut it, she heard Marian saying, "Bet it's Ben she wants to see, not *Daed*," then her mother's answering laugh.

* * *

Ben and Amos looked up in surprise when Rebecca entered the barn.

"*Daed*, could I talk to Ben for a minute?"

Amos put down the sandpaper he'd been using on a cabinet and nodded. "I think I'll get a cup of coffee," he said as he strolled out.

As he passed Ben, out of sight of Rebecca, he turned and winked at him.

"*Guder mariye.*"

Ben nodded as he searched her face. "*Guder mariye.*"

He hesitated and then plunged ahead. "I'm glad you went to your *onkel*'s funeral. It meant a lot to your *Aenti* Esther. I wasn't sure you'd go."

"I'm fine." She smiled. "People don't need to baby me, Ben. Not anymore."

He found himself smiling back. Weak sunlight came filtering in through the half-open barn door, bringing out the golden flecks in her hazel eyes. He could stand and look into them for hours. Then he realized she was talking to him. "What?"

"I wondered if you'd like to go on a picnic tomorrow?"

"Tomorrow?"

"*Ya*, it's Saturday, remember? I have this Saturday off."

"I was just thinking it's cold out."

She laughed and shook her head at him, and he thought how he loved her laugh. He hadn't heard it much these past few years.

"I know. So we'll wear coats and sit in the buggy if it's too cold to sit at a picnic table somewhere. I thought I'd pack us a basket lunch, and we could go for a ride."

Ben swallowed. This was more than he'd expected when he'd first tentatively talked with her about their seeing each other.

"That'd be great."

"Good. I'll make some of your favorites." She started for the door, then turned and glanced over her shoulder. "That would be food and food and food, right?"

Laughing, he nodded. "Right. Noon?"

"Noon." She looked back at him for a long moment. "Bye."

Ben stood there for a long time after she left. What a surprise.

He didn't know how long he might have stood there thinking about what had happened. The barn door opened, and he quickly picked up a hammer just in case it was Amos.

"Did I give you enough time?" Amos asked politely.

"Yes." Ben gave him a level stare, then followed the older man's gaze to the hammer in his hand.

Before Rebecca came, he'd been sanding the wooden cabinet in front of him. Setting down the hammer, he picked up the sandpaper and began running it over the wood.

Amos just chuckled.

* * *

Rebecca shut the barn doors and grinned. Well, that had been easier than she'd thought it would be.

And Ben had looked surprised. Well, it wasn't something she'd ever thought she'd do—ask a *mann* out. But Ben wasn't just any *mann*. He was—Ben, her best friend.

She was humming when she walked back into the house. Taking off her coat, she turned around and found her mother and Marian staring at her.

"What?"

"Something in the barn make you happy?" *Mamm* asked.

"More likely some*one*," Marian said.

Rebecca clapped a hand to her mouth. She'd meant

to talk to her sister about how she felt about Ben. "Oh, Marian, I hope—"

"*Nee*, it's all right!" Marian said, laughing. "I'm not interested in Ben. I was just practicing."

"Practicing?" Rebecca and *Mamm* said at the same time.

She batted her eyelashes at them. "Yes, practicing." Then she giggled and jumped up to hug Rebecca. "It's always been you and Ben. Always."

Rebecca smiled. "*Ya*."

* * *

"I should have taken you somewhere." Ben gestured at the spot beside the road where he'd pulled the buggy. "A restaurant or something. We haven't been anyplace like that for a long time. Remember when we went to a movie?"

"That was a long time ago. During our *rum-schpringe*." She looked around, enjoying the quiet. "You never ran with the boys who wanted to see more of the *Englisch* world."

He shrugged. "I had everything I wanted here. Family. Church." He paused. "You."

A blush crept up her cheeks. She'd felt the same. This was her world, so aptly named Paradise, full of friends and family. And a man who had waited for her.

"You warm enough?"

Nodding, Rebecca poured hot chocolate into a cup and handed it to Ben. "*Ya*. You?"

"That chili you made for us should be melting the

snow from the roof of the buggy," he told her with a laugh. "I can't believe I ate two bowls."

As they'd expected, it had been too cold to sit outside, so Ben had taken them for a drive and found a place where they could pull the buggy off the road and park for a quiet picnic.

"It wasn't so hot it kept you from eating it."

"I'm stronger than I look."

"Guess you had to be, to be around me the past five years," she said with a rueful smile.

He touched her hand. "Don't say that. I cared about you. I care about you."

Rebecca looked down at his hand and turned hers over so that she could clasp it. A gust of wind shook the buggy, and cold crept in with icy fingers. She shivered.

"We should go."

"Not yet." She stared out at the landscape. "I'm ready for winter to be over."

"Rebecca?"

Turning, she saw that he was watching her with those serious eyes of his. "Does this mean you want us to be more than friends?"

"Yes," she said simply and was warmed by the look in his eyes.

* * *

They went for drives and to singings. Ben often stayed for dinner with her family. On the surface, nothing appeared different to the casual observer.

But the way they looked at each other was different.

Rebecca had the sense that Ben was being careful, that he knew this was important and wanted to take the time for them both to be comfortable with their changing relationship.

They held hands under the table as they ate dinner at her parents' table and when she walked outside to talk to him privately, quietly, before he left for home.

And one night, when Rebecca went to bed, she pulled out her journal again. Instead of the angry, slashing words demanding to know why God had taken her sister, she wrote: *Forgive me, God, for being angry with You. I still don't understand why You took Lizzie home. But I trust You.*

Then, as if the pen had a mind of its own, she wrote: *God, is this the man You have set aside for me?*

CHAPTER 8

Rebecca looked startled to see him walk into the gift shop in the middle of the day. She hurried to his side.

"Ben! What are you doing here? Is something wrong with *Daed* or *Mamm*?"

"No, nothing's wrong," he reassured her. "I came into town for supplies and such. I thought I'd stop in and see if you'd like to have lunch."

She glanced at the clock. "I'm not due for lunch break for another fifteen minutes."

"That's fine." He glanced around and saw a woman he assumed was her boss looking over curiously. "I'll wait outside."

Even on a cold day—maybe because it *was* a cold day—there were some people out shopping, walking briskly along the sidewalks, going in and out of shops, eager for after-Christmas bargains.

Ben felt odd being in town in the middle of the day during the workweek. Even odder was thinking about having his midday meal at a restaurant instead of eating at home or with Amos and Naomi and sometimes Rebecca, if she were home. Or, if they were on a job site, sometimes he and Amos ate a packed lunch to save time.

A female tourist walked past, eyeing Ben's Plain clothing. Her hand moved to the camera that hung by a strap around her neck. He frowned, and she apparently thought better of it. She smiled apologetically and hurried on.

Ben sat down on a nearby bench and idly watched people passing. Now that he'd decided to move forward, he wondered why he was feeling a little anxious. Maybe it was because it was unaccustomed territory. Once a man decided he wanted a woman for his *fraa* and he was assured that she was indeed interested in a serious relationship, there was no uncertainty. They got to know each other better in the months before their marriage and that was that. Occasionally a couple might decide not to proceed to marriage, but it didn't happen often.

He didn't know why things had to be so complicated with him and Rebecca. He knew how he felt about her, and he knew she was attracted to him. They'd been friends for years, and that was the best foundation for a marriage, wasn't it? Long after that initial passion for each other faded to a warm glow, the love they'd shared, the friendship they'd nurtured, their strong faith in God guiding them . . . well, that would be what kept them together. He'd seen this in the many enduring marriages around him in the community.

As a practical man, he didn't rush into things. But from the way his parents and his friends, even Rebecca's *daed*, talked, he'd been dragging his feet. While he wasn't going to allow someone else to influence him, he was tired of watching other men he knew marrying and starting families.

He knew family was important to Rebecca. But did she want a *mann* of her own? *Kinner* of her own? Or was she content to stay with her parents and her siblings?

What if he'd hung around all this time only to find out she didn't want what he wanted? What if his steadfast belief that it was God's will that they be together was just his own stubborn determination to get what he wanted? He wiped suddenly damp palms on his pants. *Enough of this.* He didn't need to feel nervous. This was Rebecca.

Then she walked up to him. He saw the anxiety in her eyes even though she smiled.

"My boss let me go a little early. I think she was surprised that someone came in for me."

"I haven't been to town to eat in a long time. Why don't you show me where the food is good and the service is fast. You have just a half hour, *ya*?"

"She said that I could take an hour today if I wanted to. It gets slow this time of day when people stop to eat." She gestured toward a small restaurant down the block. "They have good food, and the prices are reasonable. This time of year there won't be a lot of tourists."

They walked down the sidewalk, and when another couple approached, Ben reached out and took Rebecca's hand to draw her closer, to keep her from getting bumped. She glanced at him, and he saw surprise but also shy pleasure in her eyes. After the need passed for them to touch, she didn't pull away and he didn't let go.

He was sorry when they reached the restaurant and he had to take back his hand to open the door and remove his hat.

The restaurant was quaint, decorated to look like a big, comfortable Amish kitchen, and the food was good, familiar country fare. A waitress came and took their orders, then they were left alone.

Rebecca fiddled with the silverware. He watched her take a deep breath and then look up at him.

"So, Ben, why are you here?"

Ben started to talk, but the waitress interrupted to set their drinks on the table. "Your order will be right out," she told him with a bright smile.

His throat was suddenly dry. He took a sip of iced tea, then set the glass down. *Don't rush things,* he told himself. *This is too important. And what were you thinking, doing this at a meal? If you ask now and she says no, how are you going to sit here and force your sandwich down?* So he made small talk, asked her about her job, got her talking. Their food came, and he found himself eating quickly.

Rebecca ate more slowly, as she usually did. Both of them declined dessert—Ben because the sandwich he'd eaten lay like lead in the pit of his stomach. Their plates were removed, and they were left to finish their drinks.

Ben cleared the frog from his throat and wished he'd spent more time hanging out with young men he knew who were smoother with the ladies. He'd been too serious, too focused on apprenticing with Rebecca's father, and then too focused on Rebecca.

"I wanted to talk to you about something," he began.

She smiled slightly. "*Ya*, I figured you did. You've never asked me to have a meal out."

"We've known each other for a long time. Been friends for a long time."

"I couldn't have gotten through these past years without you."

He sat back, a little surprised. "You've never said that before."

She dropped her gaze to her silverware again. "I'm coming to realize that for some time now I've been a little . . . self-centered."

Ben reached to touch her hand. "That's not true."

She stared at his hand covering hers, then raised her eyes to look at him.

His hand curled around hers. "Rebecca, I want us to be married."

It was a good thing she was sitting down, he realized. She paled, then blushed, and her eyes widened.

"I—this is sudden—" she began.

"I think we'd suit," he said, and the minute the words were out, he knew he'd made a mistake.

She straightened, and her expression became blank. "Suit?"

"We get along so well, enjoy the same things. That's more important than being madly in love, isn't it?"

She pulled her hand back and placed it in her lap. "I suppose so, for some people." She took a deep breath, then her eyes met his. "I'm sorry, but I don't think we want the same things, Ben."

"Well, we haven't talked about having *kinner*, but you want to, don't you?"

"Yes, but that wasn't what I was talking about," she said softly.

"I don't understand."

"I'm sorry," she said again. She pushed back her chair, and it scraped the floor and jarred his nerves. "I have to get back to the shop."

She fled before he could even get to his feet.

Stunned, Ben sat there staring after her. "Nice job, Ben Weaver," he muttered. "Real smooth."

* * *

Rebecca found herself out on the sidewalk, in the midst of people who parted and moved around her like water around a stone in its path. She blinked at the tears that threatened. *Don't cry*, she told herself firmly. There was no way she could go back to the shop all upset. A quick glance at a clock hanging outside a shop showed that she still had some time, since her boss had been so generous about a longer lunch break.

Glancing back, she saw Ben emerging from the restaurant. He looked to his left. Before he could look in her direction, she ducked into a shop. She couldn't endure talking to him right now. He walked past the shop a few minutes later, and when she drew closer to the front window, she saw that he stood outside the one where she worked. His hand went to the doorknob, then it fell to his side. Shaking his head, he walked away.

Rebecca bit her lip. Wasn't it bad enough that she'd started to feel like an old maid without having the least romantic proposal in history? And she wasn't even the kind of woman who harbored silly, girlish dreams of a man sweeping her off her feet. She'd been raised to be a practical woman, concerned with what was really important—faith, work, dedication to family.

But was it so wrong to want a man to want her because he *loved* her, because he felt something so powerful that he could envision spending the rest of his life with her? Did he have to say they'd "suit"?

"Can I help you with anything?" a salesclerk asked.

The voice sounded familiar. Rebecca's heart sank. With a sigh, she turned.

"Oh, Rebecca, hi. I didn't realize it was you."

"Hi, Mary Anne." The woman was several years younger than her, small and sharp-featured. Rebecca gestured at the rack of embroidery thread. "I had a few minutes left of my break. I thought I'd pick up a few things for my *mamm*."

Mary Anne's eyes narrowed. "Are you okay?"

"*Ya.*"

"Your eyes look red, like you've been crying."

"The cold wind made my eyes burn."

The other young woman glanced outside, then back at Rebecca. "Did I see you go past with Ben Weaver a little while ago?"

"Yes. He was in town picking up supplies."

"You didn't come in with him?"

Rebecca busied herself picking out colors of thread. None would be wasted, and it was a good way to stay casual and not give Mary Anne something to gossip about.

"No, I'm working today. He just decided since he

was here we could have lunch. He has meals at our house a lot, since he works with *Daed*."

"So you think he wouldn't want to do it if he didn't have to," Mary Anne said, her small eyes scanning Rebecca for a reaction.

"Yes, wouldn't you?" Rebecca responded with a nonchalance she didn't feel.

"I always wondered if the two of you would get married."

"Really? We're just friends." She moved away, and Mary Anne moved with her, standing too close. "I think I'll get *Mamm* a new thimble too. The one she has is so old and worn, you can nearly see through the metal."

"Not to discourage you from buying it," Mary Anne said, "but sometimes a woman gets attached to such things and won't use a new one."

Rebecca nodded and put the thimble down. "You're right. Lizzie bought her that thimble that last Christmas."

Glancing at the clock, she moved to the counter with the cash register. "Can you ring these up for me? I need to get back to work."

Her package in hand, Rebecca left the shop. She didn't want to go back to work, but she had no choice. There was no way she'd let her employer down, even if Anita had said things were slow today. Fortunately, when she returned, the other woman looked up in relief.

"Thank goodness you're back," she exclaimed. "It started getting busy a few minutes ago."

The distraction was just what Rebecca needed. She put the package away and turned to help a customer choose some stationery with photographs of Paradise printed on it. The hours passed quickly, and when it was time to turn the Open sign around and lock the door, Rebecca realized she'd gotten through the afternoon without thinking about Ben and his disappointing proposal.

"We were so busy I forgot to ask how your lunch with your young man went."

"He's not my young man," Rebecca told her politely. "He's just a good friend."

"Really?" Anita glanced up from counting money. "Hmm..." She stopped and shrugged. "Well, I probably shouldn't be so nosy. After living here in Lancaster County for twenty years, I've learned that Plain people don't talk about such things, especially to the *Englisch*."

"It's all right," Rebecca assured her. "I meant to tell you that I did appreciate your letting me have the extra time. Ben doesn't come to town often."

Anita nodded and slipped the money into a bank deposit bag, then filled out a deposit slip. She looked at Rebecca and sighed. "You're such a sweet girl, and I know you've had some real tragedy in your young life. I'd just like to see you find a young man, get married, and be happy. Even if it meant that one day I'd lose the best employee I've had since I opened the shop."

"That's really sweet," Rebecca managed. "But I don't have to be married to be happy."

"No, of course not. Blame my romantic heart." She retrieved her purse from a locked drawer under the cash register. "I had thirty-four wonderful years with my Phil."

She gave the shop a quick look over, nodded, then turned to Rebecca. "Ready to go home? I'm looking forward to having a nice supper and putting my feet up."

Rebecca was too. Then her eyes widened. What if Ben came to supper at her house? What would she do if she had to sit next to him and pretend nothing was different? Because everything was different now. Everything about her relationship with Ben had changed in just a few minutes. And she didn't know what she was going to do about it.

With the workday finally over, Rebecca was glad to be home. That is, until she shed her coat and bonnet and walked into the kitchen.

Ben was sitting in his usual place at the table, having a cup of coffee. He looked up, then away as she stopped and stared at him.

Her mother smiled. "Did you have a good day?"

"It was fine. Hello, Ben."

"Hello."

"Ben's staying for supper." *Mamm* opened the oven door and peered inside.

What's new? Rebecca wondered, trying not to look at him as she went to wash her hands.

But what was he thinking? He wasn't going to act like nothing had happened today, go on the same way he had for years, was he?

"Your mother insisted I stay because it's Abram's *Gebottsdaag*," he told Rebecca quietly as Naomi pulled a big casserole from the oven.

As was family tradition, the meal consisted of the birthday child's favorites. The chicken and noodle casserole was one of Rebecca's favorites, too, but her stomach was in knots. She took just a small portion and pushed it around on her plate.

"Ben, you're not eating much," Naomi said.

"Sorry, I had a big lunch in town today while I was picking up supplies."

Rebecca casually placed her napkin over part of her plate and jumped up to collect them so dessert could be served.

"Well, you must have a slice of birthday cake, right, Abram?"

"He doesn't have to. I could eat his piece for him." But Abram, just turned five, grinned to show he was joking.

Ben accepted a plate with cake and ice cream and passed it to Rebecca. There was a look in his eyes, she thought, a silent accusation, as if he wondered how she could eat. Why should he care when he'd been so casual and unemotional with his proposal?

She knew she wasn't as attractive as her twin sister, and she didn't have as interesting a personality. But even if she'd been looking at him with different eyes lately, that didn't mean that she was willing to give up the right to a life with a man who loved her. She'd lost enough in her life. Did she have to lose the dream most young girls dreamed too?

Rebecca stabbed at a bite of cake with her fork and shoved it into her mouth. It tasted too sweet, and the frosting stuck to the roof of her mouth. Food just wasn't agreeing with her tonight.

And it didn't appear Ben was doing much better. He shoveled in a couple of mouthfuls and then, quietly taking her cue, covered the rest with his napkin. When she glanced over and saw what he'd done, he gave her a look that was a silent challenge. She shrugged, not interested in making him look bad to her family.

She just wanted him gone.

Finally the meal was over and she could turn her back—politely—on Ben. Get the dishes done and escape to her room.

Six-year-old Annie got up on a step stool and held out her hands for a dish towel. She smiled as Rebecca handed her a dish to dry and worked on the task with great concentration.

She looked up. "Becca?"

"Yes?"

"Are there birthdays in heaven?"

Rebecca nearly dropped the dish she was washing. "I don't know. I guess so. I mean, birthdays are good and heaven's good, right?"

"So Lizzie gets to have birthdays?"

Tears threatened. Rebecca nodded. "With lots of cake and ice cream."

"And Jesus sings the 'Happy Birthday' song to her?"

"Yes, *liebschdi*." Wiping her hands on a towel, Rebecca turned and bent to hug her little sister.

"I think she's having a wonderful time in heaven," Ben said.

Startled, Rebecca turned at the deep timbre of his voice. She hadn't realized he'd come up behind them with an empty coffee mug.

"You do?" Annie asked him, staring up at him with big eyes.

"I do," he told her, stroking her hair with his big, work-roughened hand.

"We're all done. Why don't you go ask *Mamm* if she needs any help?" Rebecca suggested.

"Okay. Bye, Ben."

"Bye." He turned to Rebecca. "I'll wash this since you're already done."

"Don't be silly. You're a guest." She tried to take it, but he resisted for a moment, then released it. She turned back to the sink.

"I'm sorry. I tried not to stay," he said in a low voice.

"I'm sure you did."

"What's that supposed to mean?"

Glancing over her shoulder to make sure no one was in hearing range, Rebecca met his eyes. She sighed. "I'm sorry. That was rude. I don't want to fight with you."

"I don't understand what happened today."

He stopped as Amos came into the room to get himself a cup of coffee, then left.

"You acted like I did something wrong. What did I do?"

Quivering with emotion, Rebecca put the last dried mug in the cabinet and slammed the door. "If you don't know, Ben Weaver, I'm not going to tell you." And she turned and left the room.

CHAPTER 9

Rebecca nearly ran into her mother in her rush out of the kitchen.

"I heard raised voices. What's going on?" When Rebecca didn't answer, *Mamm* looked past her. "Ben? What's the matter?"

"Ask her," he said shortly and started to walk past her. Then he stopped. "I'm sorry, Naomi. I don't know. You'll have to ask Rebecca. Tell Amos I'll see him in the morning."

Then he left.

"Did the two of you have an argument?"

Rebecca avoided looking at her mother. "Not exactly."

Naomi touched her daughter's cheek and frowned. "It's obvious you're upset about something. Tell me what's wrong."

"It's—personal."

Naomi took her daughter's hand and drew her down to sit. "You would tell me if Ben . . . touched you or said anything inappropriate."

"Ben would never do that."

"But you're angry at him. Can't you tell me why?"

"It's complicated," Rebecca said finally. She was tired, so tired of holding in how hurt she felt. How could she tell her mother that Ben had asked to marry her in just about the most passionless way that a man could?

He'd been a good friend to her, knew her better than anybody except her family. But even when she'd been grieving, when she'd been depressed, when she'd been in emotional deep freeze, she was still a person who wanted someone to think she was pretty, to want her for a better reason than that they would "suit"—whatever that meant.

It sounded like they'd be like two passionless people walking together through decades.

She couldn't tell her mother that. She could barely wrap her mind around it herself.

Naomi squeezed her hand. "Love doesn't always run smoothly." Her voice was gentle, her eyes warm and compassionate.

If only she could have heard Ben, Rebecca thought.

"It's a mother's wish that you find a *mann* who'll love you and who you'll love," Naomi said gently. "If it's God's will, you'll find him and experience the joy of married love, grow together spiritually as a couple, as parents."

Annie came running in. "*Mamm*, Abram says his tummy hurts."

"Tell him I'll be right there." She turned back to Rebecca with a smile. "I shouldn't have let him have that second slice of cake."

"Do you want me to go?"

Naomi got to her feet and bent down to kiss Rebecca on the cheek. "No, you've had a long day."

Rebecca looked around the kitchen, found it spotless, and then went into the den to say *gut nacht* to her father. It took a few minutes to look in on each of her brothers and sisters and wish them sweet dreams.

Then, dressed in her nightgown, snug in her bed, she pulled out her journal and wrote about her day, pouring out her disappointment in the pages. When she thought she'd written all that she could, she started to slide it back under her pillow. Her fingers touched Lizzie's journal, and she brought it out to stare at it for a moment. Sweet Annie had asked if Lizzie got to have birthdays in heaven. When she thought of her twin, Rebecca thought of Lizzie at the age of seventeen when she'd left the earth.

She'd been feeling sorry for herself earlier, when she'd let what Ben had asked make her unhappy. But Lizzie wasn't going to have the chance to marry a man she loved or have children with him or grow old with him. Guilt swamped her for a moment. Then she shook her head. She needed to make peace with God's will.

Ben had been there for her so many times when she'd been grieving for Lizzie. Maybe their friendship was all that they were supposed to have, maybe he just wanted someone safe—something safe. When he'd approached her at the sink in the kitchen, he'd sounded like he truly didn't know what he'd done wrong.

Maybe Ben was as lonely as she was sometimes. After all, it was written in the Scriptures that a man should not be alone. Perhaps he was simply trying to find someone to walk down life's path with. She had to find it in her heart to forgive him, to give up this hurt and anger she was feeling. Otherwise it was going to be too hard to bump into him at church services, at frolics, at so many events and in so many places in their community.

Even though she felt tears of hurt well up in her eyes again, she blinked them away. A verse from the Psalms came to her: *"Tears may endure for a night, but joy comes in the morning."* Tomorrow would be better.

* * *

Even though it was cold in the barn, Ben was grateful that he was able to work here this morning instead of within the close confines of someone's kitchen. It felt good to be doing manual labor, pounding out his frustrations with his hammer.

Why had he thought that the only answer that he could get from Rebecca would be yes? Why had he been so assured that Rebecca was the one God planned for him that he hadn't considered that he would be going home with his heart discouraged and colder and lonelier than ever?

All these years he'd waited for her, and now he wondered if he'd wasted his time. Had he stubbornly been insisting on what God's will was for his life instead of listening for God to tell him?

He rubbed at his chest, feeling as if his heart hurt, physically hurt, this morning as the monotony of his work gave him the time to reflect.

How did he go within hours from being someone's friend and confidant to a person to be avoided, even treated with hurt and anger?

His eyes filmed, and his sight wavered. When he swung his hammer, he missed the nail and hit his thumb instead. With a cry of pain he jumped back, stuck his injured finger in his mouth, and sucked on it to relieve the pain.

"Ben? You okay? *Sohn?*"

He felt a hand on his shoulder and turned to stare into the face of Amos. Nodding, he pulled his hand from his mouth. "Just hit my thumb."

"Looks like you really hurt yourself there. Your eyes are watering something fierce." Amos pulled a bandanna out of his back pocket and handed it to Ben.

Ben nodded his thanks, too miserable to speak.

"Let's go inside, get some ice on this."

"No need. It'll be okay."

But Amos shepherded him inside the house and nudged him into a chair in the kitchen. Naomi was working there, preparing the noon meal. Two-year-old Ruth was coloring at the table.

"Naomi, we need some ice. Ben hit his thumb."

She rushed to get the ice. Ruth crowded closer to Ben and investigated his hand with wide eyes. "Ben got boo-boo?"

He laughed. "Yes."

"Kiss it make it better," she said, and she pressed her lips to his thumb.

Ben stroked her hair with his other hand. "Thank you, Ruth."

"Here, this should help," Naomi said as she handed him a kitchen towel filled with ice.

"Thanks." He watched her fill a plastic cup with juice and give it to Ruth. Although he knew she was in her late forties and the mother of eight *kinner*, Naomi didn't look much older than Rebecca. This was what Rebecca would look like when she was older: an attractive woman who was strong and capable, a woman who was the heart of her home.

He swallowed hard.

"Want some coffee?"

"I can get it; you're busy."

She pressed a hand to his shoulder. "It's no trouble. I'm going to get you some aspirin too. You're in pain."

His heart hurt more than his finger. Then he shook his head. He was being melodramatic. Two years ago, a childhood friend of his had asked a young woman if he could see her, and she'd turned him down. His friend had been disappointed and moped around for a few months, then met someone else, fallen in love, and married her. They'd just had their first child last month. Life had moved on.

Naomi went to get some supplies from the pantry, and Ben drank his coffee. When she returned, she placed a pan with two roasting chickens in the oven.

"Will you stay for supper?" she asked as she did every day.

"*Danki*, but not tonight. I'll be eating with my parents."

He glanced at the kitchen clock. It was nearly time to stop work for the day. He wanted to be gone by the time Rebecca came home.

Just then he heard the door open, then close, and she walked into the room.

"Rebecca! You're home already?" Naomi exclaimed.

"Anita decided to close a little early." Taking off her bonnet and coat, Rebecca hung them on pegs. "We're doing inventory later in the week. Hello, Ben." She walked over and looked down at his hand wrapped in the towel. "What happened?"

"Hit it with the hammer." Getting up, he dumped the melting ice from the dish towel into the sink. He folded the towel and left it on the counter.

"That's not like you."

Shrugging, Ben reached for his coat. "Wasn't paying attention, I guess. Thanks for the ice, Naomi. *Gut nacht.*"

He found Amos in the barn and said good-bye, then hitched up his horse to his buggy. As he pulled out of the drive onto the road, something made him glance back. Rebecca stood at the window, watching him.

Turning back to face the road, Ben rode along, the clip-clop of his horse's hooves on the road a soothing cadence to his thoughts. He passed by the Bontrager property. The old house stood abandoned, paint peeling, windows broken. He'd thought about buying it and fixing it up. The house was in sad shape, but he knew its construction was solid. Windows could easily be replaced, the outside of the house scraped and repainted, the interior cleaned and fixed up. It wouldn't be hard. He was, after all, a carpenter, and many of his friends were tradesmen who could help him with the necessary repairs.

The Bontrager property was only a mile or so away from Rebecca's family home, and he'd thought she'd like that. It would make it handy for him to work with her father as well. He'd wanted to talk to Rebecca about it first, but a man couldn't talk about a future home until he was assured he was talking to his future wife. So he'd waited.

And now everything had changed.

Dragging his gaze away from the lost promise of the house, he stared straight ahead. That was how he'd gotten through the day—doing the first thing on his list, then the next, then the next, without thinking. The first time he'd lost his concentration, he'd hit his thumb. He wouldn't make that mistake again, and not just because his thumb was still throbbing. He was a practical man, and he had his work to keep him busy.

A few days from now, maybe a few weeks, maybe he'd do what some of his friends had urged him to do for some time now: he'd open his eyes and look around at other young women in the community.

* * *

Inventory was a welcome distraction.

As much as Rebecca enjoyed helping customers and ringing up sales and answering the dozens of questions from tourists about her community, doing some mindless counting and tallying was just what she needed.

Ben had been avoiding her. He hadn't stayed for supper since Abram's birthday and was usually gone by the time she got home from work. Her parents eyed her curiously but kept their questions to themselves. Even Marian hadn't said anything, although Rebecca often caught her watching her. Occasionally, one of the *kinner* would ask if Ben was going to stay to eat with them, but the younger ones saw him at midday dinner or after school.

"Hungry?" Anita interrupted her thoughts.

"*Ya.*"

They went into the break room in the back of the store to eat sandwiches Anita had slipped out earlier to buy. As she peeled back the paper from the sandwich, Rebecca hesitated, remembering.

"Did I get the wrong kind?"

Rebecca shook her head. "No, it's fine, thanks. I was just thinking of the last time I went to this restaurant, that's all."

"The day that young man surprised you by coming to take you to lunch?"

Nodding, Rebecca took a bite of her sandwich. She didn't really feel like eating now that she'd remembered, but she didn't want to hurt Anita's feelings. "I remember how you said you have a romantic heart," she said. "Do you think all women have one?"

"I think many do. Most, maybe."

"Do you think any men are romantic?"

Anita smiled and wiped her lips with a paper napkin. She regarded Rebecca sympathetically. "Am I to assume by your question that the young man isn't romantic?"

"Not very." Rebecca drained the last of her lemonade and tossed the paper cup into the trash can. "I'm going to put the rest of this sandwich in the refrigerator for tomorrow's lunch."

"What about other young men in your community? Are they different from—I hate to keep saying 'that young man.' What's his name?"

"Ben. I don't know if he's different from the others. I mean, I think they're more practical than *Englisch* young men because so many of them work in trades or farm or whatever, but I still hear they can be romantic. I see my father being very sweet and romantic with my *mamm* sometimes."

"My Phil was that way. He brought home a dozen roses each week, and he left notes for me when he had to leave the house early and I wasn't up yet." She stood. "Ready to finish up?"

They worked on inventory some more, occasionally exchanging comments about what stock had been popular, what they should order more of, what should be eliminated.

"You've been such an asset," Anita told her as they finished up. "You're good with the customers, you sense what they want before they ask, and you're unflappable."

Rebecca laughed and shook her head. "I assure you, I'm flappable."

Anita handed Rebecca her coat and bonnet. "Your young man really hurt you, didn't he?"

"I don't think he meant to," Rebecca said slowly. "He's been a good friend, gotten me through some bad times since my sister died. But I want . . ."

"You want some romance. You want to believe you're loved."

"Yes," Rebecca said at last. "Yes."

They were silent on the way home and then, just before she pulled into the drive of Rebecca's house, Anita spoke. "You know, I believe that the right young man is out there for you. You're a sweet, religious young woman with a lot to offer. When it's time, God will send along the right man."

Surprised, Rebecca glanced over at Anita. Although the woman was very nice to her, they didn't often talk so personally. Rebecca was glad she'd offered to stay and help Anita with inventory.

"I hope you're right."

Anita smiled and took her hand from the steering wheel to pat Rebecca's. "I am."

The front door opened, and *Mamm* stepped outside and waved.

"Tell your mother I said hello."

"I will." Rebecca started to open the car door, then turned back. "Thank you, Anita."

"You know I'm always happy to give you a lift home."

Rebecca shook her head. "No, that's not what I meant. Thank you for caring."

Anita smiled. "You make it easy. See you in the morning."

CHAPTER 10

Ben was climbing into his buggy when, out of the corner of his eye, he saw Rebecca. He heard her call his name.

"Ben!" She appeared at the driver's side of the buggy, sounding out of breath. "I was calling you!"

"Sorry. Did you need something?" He kept his tone brisk and impersonal.

"Yes, Ben." She tugged at his sleeve. "I need to talk to you."

"There's nothing to say." He picked up the reins, not caring if he was being rude.

To his utter surprise, Rebecca grasped the reins and made him look at her. "I'm sorry, Ben. I'm sorry if I hurt your feelings. But can't we still be friends?"

He stared at her hand over his for a long moment, then shook his head. "I don't think so, Rebecca. I'm sorry, but I have to go."

It felt like something was pressing against his chest; he had to get away.

There was that expression of hurt in her eyes again. But she'd rejected *him*. He steeled himself against it. "I have to go."

When she stepped back, he set the buggy in motion. This time, he didn't look back. He couldn't look back. She'd told him no, and so he had to move on.

He went to a singing the next night, and after he was there for only a few minutes, Mary Anne walked over.

"I don't see Rebecca."

Ben shrugged. "Maybe she'll come with someone else."

Mary Anne's eyebrows arched. "Oh, so that's the way it is."

When the singing began there wasn't another opportunity to talk. But Mary Anne looked over often and smiled at him, and when the food was served, she appeared at his elbow.

"I baked these cookies," she told him. "Try one."

He did and found it delicious. Mary Anne was something to look at, too, with her sparkling green eyes and saucy smile. She had this habit of leaning close to talk to him in a low, intimate tone. She was so diminutive and girlish, he felt tall and very male next to her. She was so different from Rebecca, who was nearly as tall as he was and so independent. Mary Anne made a man feel he needed to take care of her. Rebecca let him know that she could take care of herself.

Rebecca came in with Marian a little while later. Ben was aware that people near him were watching as he and Rebecca carefully ignored each other.

"What's going on?" his brother John came over to ask. "And don't tell me you don't know what I'm talking about."

"Keep your voice down."

"It doesn't matter," John said, but he lowered his voice. "If everyone else didn't know, they wouldn't be watching the two of you and trying to figure out what's going on."

"People need to mind their own business."

John just laughed and slapped his shoulder.

Ben had always considered himself to be an average-looking guy. But suddenly he was getting lots of attention, and not just from Mary Anne. He wondered if the other young women had ignored him because he was always with Rebecca.

So when Mary Anne asked him if he'd give her a ride home, he was happy to oblige. She held his arm to keep from sliding on the ice as they walked to his buggy and gave him an openly flirtatious smile as he helped her inside.

As the buggy rolled away from the singing, he told himself he was glad he'd taken some action and not sat around being miserable. But remembering how he'd seen Rebecca talking with Jacob Stolzfus at the food table made him wonder if he was just kidding himself.

He wasn't a shallow man. Forgetting how Rebecca had been such a big part of his life wasn't going to happen quickly just because someone like Mary Anne—or a half dozen other young women—flirted with him.

* * *

"Well, he certainly didn't let any grass grow beneath his feet," Rebecca muttered as she and Marian rode home later.

"Huh?"

Rebecca realized that she'd talked out loud. "Nothing."

"Who hasn't let any grass grow beneath his feet? Ben?"

Rebecca sighed. "Yes, Ben."

Marian just laughed. "Everyone was watching the two of you."

"Everyone was watching Mary Anne throw herself at him."

"That too," Marian said matter-of-factly. "What did you expect? How long did you think he'd hang around?"

Rebecca blinked. "He wasn't 'hanging around,'" she said, stung. "He was always at the house because he works with *Daed*."

"Right."

"I never said he wasn't a friend. That's hardly 'hanging around.'"

Marian shook her head. "Rebecca, if you want him, I'm sure all you have to do is let him know."

Rebecca laughed until tears ran down her cheeks.

"Whoa, Brownie, whoa," Marian told their horse, and she brought him to a stop. "Are you all right?"

Rebecca nodded, then she shook her head. "It's not true, what you said. I wish life was that simple. The fact is that he let me know he wants me. *Wanted* me," she corrected.

"Oh, how wonderful."

"*Wanted*, Marian." She told her sister what had happened and watched the joy fade from her face.

"I'm so sorry." Reaching over, Marian hugged Rebecca.

"But if you're interested, maybe you can talk to him about it."

"He didn't say he loved me," Rebecca said flatly.

"No, he didn't," Marian said slowly. She called to the horse, and the buggy began rolling again.

"Listen, I haven't told *Mamm* and *Daed* about this," Rebecca said. "I don't want to talk against Ben. They think of him as a son. I wouldn't want anything to get in the way of his relationship with *Daed* about work, either. I'm trying to forgive Ben, and I hope he'll forgive me for not agreeing to what he wanted."

But when she remembered how he'd acted when she tried to apologize, she thought his forgiveness might be a long time coming.

"Sometimes life is a mystery, isn't it?" Marian mused. "We're taught that it's God's will that this or that happened, that God has plans for us. But I still don't understand why Lizzie had to die. And I don't understand why someone like Ben isn't the man God prepared for you."

Rebecca sighed. "Remember Hebrews 11? 'Now faith is the substance of things hoped for . . .'"

"'The evidence of things not seen,'" Marian finished. "I just wish you didn't have to see Mary Anne flirting with Ben. It can't feel very good."

Rebecca bit her lip. "It doesn't. I'm still ashamed of how jealous I was when *you* flirted with Ben."

Marian laughed. "Like I told you before, I was just practicing!"

* * *

Her chatter was driving him nuts.

Comparisons weren't fair, but Ben couldn't help thinking how much he preferred being with Rebecca instead of Mary Anne. Rebecca didn't have to be talking every minute. Sometimes he felt like he couldn't think, his brain was so filled with the sound of Mary Anne's voice.

And what she talked about—well, it was all about Mary Anne. She chattered about every little aspect of her day, and oh, how she loved gossip. She never wanted to talk about something deeper, like faith, the way Rebecca did. He wondered if it was because she hadn't had to deal with something big, something beyond what she'd expected life to deal her, as Rebecca had when Lizzie died. But he was beginning to suspect that Mary Anne didn't ever think about things beyond surface, everyday happenings.

Mary Anne wound down as the buggy turned into the drive to her house. "Thank you so much for giving me a ride home from services," she said, turning to him and smiling flirtatiously.

"You're welcome," he said politely, waiting for her to climb out.

She started to open her mouth to say something else. Clearly, she wasn't ready to leave him yet.

"Let me help you."

"You're such a gentleman," she told him.

Was she batting her eyelashes at him? Yes, she was batting her eyelashes at him. He didn't think a girl had ever done that to him. He didn't think he liked it.

As he rounded the buggy, he saw her bend down to

pick up something from the floorboard. She was holding it in her hand when he stepped to her side.

"What is it?" he asked as she studied whatever it was in her left palm.

"Nothing, just a hairpin I dropped." Her fingers curled around it. She gave him her right hand and he helped her step down from the buggy.

But even after there was no need, she continued to hold his hand as they stood there beside the buggy.

Of course, it was at that exact moment that Rebecca had to drive by with Marian.

"*Wie geht!*" Marian called.

Rebecca's eyes met Ben's, then she looked at him holding hands with Mary Anne.

Great, Ben thought. *Just great.* He tried to pull his hand back and was surprised to feel it held tightly by Mary Anne. Dragging his gaze away from Rebecca, he was startled to see Mary Anne's smile as she looked at Rebecca.

Using more force, he retrieved his hand and backed away. But the damage was done. Rebecca was looking straight ahead as the buggy moved on.

"Well, you'd better get inside. It's cold out here."

"See you later!" she called loudly, as if she wanted the occupants of the other buggy to hear.

Ben climbed into his buggy and continued on home. *What a mess*, he told himself. How he wished he could go back and undo what he'd said that day in town. Then he sighed. No, he'd felt it was time to speak to Rebecca as he had, and now at least he knew he needed to move on.

But he didn't think Mary Anne was the one he wanted to move on with.

* * *

Ben's mother was cooking supper when he walked into the kitchen after work the next day.

"You're home early. Again."

He stopped and stared at her. "*Ya*. Is that a problem?"

She laughed and shook her head. "Of course not. Sit down, I'll get you a cup of coffee."

He sat and watched her reach for two mugs and pour the coffee. She moved a little stiffly—her arthritis acted up sometimes in the winter—but she never complained. Her hair was salt and pepper but her face was smooth, the only lines were those around her eyes when she smiled. *Mamm* was in her sixties. From what she'd told him, he was a surprise gift from God long after she thought she'd borne her last child.

She served him his coffee and surprised him by kissing the top of his head before she joined him at the table with her own cup. "This is the only way I can be on the same level with you, since you've grown so tall."

He smiled at her, then his smile faded as he stared into his cup of coffee. "Guess you never thought you'd have me hanging around the house so long, did you?"

"Now you're being a *bensel*!" she said fondly.

"I'm hardly a silly child," he told her. "I'm twenty-two. Most of my friends have married. Some of them even have *kinner*."

"You're hardly an old man. It just hasn't been your time yet."

He traced the grain of wood on the table with his forefinger and avoided looking at her.

"*Sohn*, do you want to tell me what's troubling you? I think it must have something to do with Rebecca."

His head shot up. "Why do you say that?"

She smiled gently. "You've been home for dinner every night lately."

"Maybe I missed your cooking."

Laughing, Emma shook her head. "I don't think so. But I think you're missing Rebecca."

"I'm seeing someone else. Mary Anne. You know her."

"You're missing Rebecca," she repeated. "Otherwise you would not look so miserable, *mei sohn*."

She put her hand over his. "I do not wish to pry if you've decided to see Mary Anne instead." She paused. "But I think something has happened, something that hurts you so much you would stay away from a young woman you've cared about for years. She was your friend, if she was nothing more."

"She turned me down." Ben looked up. "I asked if she would marry me, and she turned me down."

His *mamm* stared at him, clearly shocked. "Did she say why?"

"She said if I didn't know why, she wasn't going to tell me."

"*Ach!* She didn't!"

"She did."

Leaning back in her chair, she studied Ben. "Tell me what you said to her."

He shrugged. "I just—you know—asked her if she would marry me."

"Exact words, please."

He relayed the conversation as precisely as he could remember. His mother listened without expression or comment until he was finished, but he thought he saw her wince once. Maybe it was his imagination.

His father came in then, stamping his boots on the mat by the door.

"Why, look who's home." Samuel took off his coat and hat and joined them in the kitchen.

"I found out why," Emma said, getting up to pull a meat loaf from the oven and set it on top of the stove to rest.

Samuel took the mug of coffee she poured him and joined Ben at the table. "Figured you would." He turned to Ben. "Good day at work?"

"*Ya*," Ben said, relieved at the change in subject.

"Aren't you going to ask me why?" Emma asked, putting her hands on her hips.

"Emma, you know it's not our way to pry into how our young people court."

Ben's head snapped up. "Court?"

"I didn't tell him," his mother assured him. "How could I? You and I were just talking now."

"I've got eyes. And ears," his father said. "I see things. Hear things. If Ben wants to tell me, he will." He glanced pointedly at the meat loaf.

His mother let out a gusty sigh. Going to the stove, she transferred the meat loaf to a platter and set it on the table. "Well, I don't want to get in between a man and his stomach."

"*Gut*," Samuel said with a grin. "That's why we've been happily married for so many years, *mei fraa*."

If Ben hadn't been watching his mother, he might not have seen the gleam come into her eyes. She finished putting the food on the table, bringing a plate of sliced bread and a crock of *budder*. They bent their heads for the blessing, then it was silent at the table for a few minutes while they filled their plates and ate the savory meat, carrots, potatoes, celery, and parsnips.

Emma cleared the empty plates, brought a *snitz* pie to the table, cut two large slices, and served them to her men. She picked up her mug of coffee. "I think I'll let you two men talk over dessert," she announced.

"You're not feeling well?" Ben asked her.

She shook her head and stroked his hair the way she'd done when he was a boy. "I'll have some later. I think I'll go put my feet up for a few minutes. I was on them quite a bit this afternoon helping a friend with some cleaning."

"You're sure you're feeling okay?" his *daed* asked.

Emma smiled at her husband. "I'm fine." She kissed his cheek. "Maybe you can tell Ben how you asked me to marry you."

Daed tilted his head and studied her. "I could do that, if he wanted to know."

Ben watched his father's eyes follow his *fraa* as she left the kitchen. Then he began eating the pie.

It was quiet in the room, with just the scrape of fork on plate and an occasional slurping of coffee by his father. Ben could hear the ticking of the kitchen clock.

Ben was used to his father's stoic ways, but finally

he could stand it no longer. "Well, are you going to tell me?"

Samuel looked at him. "*Ya*, sure, if you want to know."

More silence filled the room, as Samuel cut another piece of pie and poured himself more coffee.

Ben rolled his eyes. "*Ya*, I want to know."

* * *

He was ready for winter to be over. As he hunched inside his coat, riding to Rebecca's house, he looked for signs of spring.

Each year, when winter came, Ben saw a sadness come over Rebecca. Then, this year, he'd seen a change in her, a moving past the tragedy of Lizzie's death. She was growing, changing, even laughing. Oh, how he loved her laugh!

Perhaps he hadn't waited long enough for her to really look out at the world around her—and at the man looking at her. He'd thought only of his own wants and needs. He'd convinced himself that it was God's will that they should be together. Now.

She'd tried to apologize to him for saying she didn't want to be courted, and he'd been angry and turned her away.

It wasn't one of his shining moments.

He needed to tell her he wasn't angry with her. She had a right to say no. Maybe she'd grown so used to seeing him in her home that she'd begun to think of him as a brother. He shuddered at the thought. He certainly didn't think of her as a sister.

But just because she wasn't interested in him as a future husband, was he really willing to throw away the years of friendship with her, the memories? The answer was no.

But he didn't know what to do with the love he felt for her.

Ben jerked on the reins, and Ike stopped abruptly, then turned to look at him as if to say, "What?"

Glancing around, Ben was grateful there were no cars behind him. He could have caused an accident. Pulling over to the side of the road, he stared at the frozen pond in the distance. What he'd said that day in town came rushing back.

He hadn't said anything about love.

No, he'd been so nervous, rushed at things as if it were a job to be completed quickly instead of a foundation to build a future on. He had talked about how they "suited" each other.

As if they were socks and boots pairing up to stay warm for the winter, he thought, instead of two souls who loved each other and would merge in God's presence to form a loving union.

What a fool he'd been!

Even his father, whom he didn't think of as an articulate or romantic man, had done better than him. The comparison had made him wince.

He needed to talk to her and make things right between them. Even if he wasn't as gifted with words as other young men, surely he could find a way to tell her that he was sorry for his anger, sorry for the way he'd asked to court her.

It was one of her workdays at the shop. Ben decided to drive to her house and meet her there when she arrived, ask to speak to her. Surely she wouldn't refuse him that.

* * *

Rebecca's day had been stressful. Customers had been standing at the door when she arrived. A tourist had pointedly remarked that she was five minutes late opening.

Since one of the reasons people came here to visit was because they wanted to experience a slower, more peaceful way of life, Rebecca had been surprised at the comment. She was going to tell the tourist that Brownie had not been feeling well that morning and she'd had to arrange for a ride to work, but changed her mind when the woman quickly pounced on their most expensive quilt and proclaimed she had to have it.

Anita called in to say she had a plumbing emergency at her condo and would get in as quickly as she could. The whole day was hectic, and Anita finally arrived the last half hour the shop was open, apologizing profusely.

But that wasn't the end of their bad day.

On the way home, they had a flat tire. Grumbling, Anita pulled onto the side of the road. Anita rooted around in the trunk and brought out a spare tire and a jack.

She looked at Rebecca. "I've never changed a tire. You?" Then, realizing what she'd asked, she started laughing.

Rebecca laughed too. What else could they do?

"Wait a minute, what am I thinking?" Anita said suddenly. She pulled out her cell phone. "I have road-side service."

But before she could dial, a buggy stopped beside them. "Rebecca! Do you need help?" a man called.

"Jacob! *Ya*, we have a flat tire. Do you know how to change it?"

"Of course." He pulled his buggy over and joined them beside the car. After touching the brim of his hat and introducing himself to Anita, he set to work. In no time, the tire was changed, and the flat one and the jack were in the trunk.

"Well, I hope your mother isn't worried that you're late getting home," Anita said.

"I just went by there, looking for you," Jacob told Rebecca. "She said she expected you soon."

"Jacob, would you mind taking Rebecca home? I'd like to take this tire by my garage before they close."

"Of course."

"Thanks for everything. See you, Rebecca." Anita winked at her when Jacob started toward his buggy.

Rebecca didn't feel at her best after the long day at work, but she was grateful for the ride home. Her back and feet were aching, and she was afraid her stomach was going to growl at any moment. She'd been too rushed to stop for lunch.

All she wanted to do was eat her supper and put her feet up and relax. But Jacob was being charming and acted so interested in talking to her.

Obviously, Ben had decided to do what she'd heard

the *Englisch* call "moving on"; maybe it was time for her to start looking at someone new too. She'd gone to school with Jacob, and he'd always been nice to her.

When they pulled into the drive, Rebecca saw Ben sitting there in his buggy.

Jacob glanced at Rebecca and raised his eyebrows.

"He's probably here to see my father," Rebecca said. Why else would Ben visit? "They work together."

"*Ya*, I know."

"Thank you for the ride and for changing Anita's tire."

"I was happy to help. Rebecca, I came by because I thought I'd see if you'd like to go for a drive sometime?"

"I'd like that."

They set a day and time. She climbed out of the buggy and waved as he drove off. Then she turned and found Ben alighting from his buggy.

"What was he doing giving you a ride?"

When she stared coolly at him, he shook his head.

"I'm sorry, that was none of my business," he said.

"Did you come to see *Daed*? You could have gone inside. It's cold out here."

"I came to see you. Can we take a drive and talk?"

Rebecca rubbed at her aching forehead. "The other day you didn't want to talk. Now you do?"

"I was wrong," he said simply. "I came to apologize."

The memory of how he'd hurt her was as sharp as the cold winter wind. "Apology accepted." But her lips were stiff as she spoke the words. "I—Thank you for coming by." And she rushed inside.

CHAPTER 11

Sunday was her favorite day of the week.

Rebecca loved gathering with friends and family to attend services and sing God's praises. And every other week, when there were no services in a member's home, she loved gathering with friends and family just to enjoy the day.

Today, services had been in the home of Ben's parents. She had to admit that she was a little apprehensive about seeing them for the first time since she'd turned Ben down. She didn't think Ben's mother would be rude to her—that wasn't her way. But she'd been nervous about how much he might have said to her about what had happened between them two weeks ago.

She told herself that chances were good that he hadn't even told them.

"So good to see you again, Rebecca." Emma's hug was warm and welcoming.

If Emma knew anything, she wasn't going to let it affect how she treated Rebecca. Rebecca felt herself relax.

Other women bustled about them in the kitchen after services, chattering as they prepared the light meal that would be served before everyone departed.

Mary Anne sidled over, holding out a plate of

butterscotch cookies. "Emma, I made Ben's favorite cookies." She gave Rebecca a superior look.

"Very nice. Why don't you put them over there on the counter?" Emma said.

Was it Rebecca's imagination that Emma wasn't as welcoming to Mary Anne as she'd been to her? Then she heard Emma sigh as she watched Mary Anne smile smugly as she showed off the cookies to a friend standing on the other side of the kitchen.

The older woman turned to look at Rebecca. "I haven't seen you for a long time. How is the family? Work?"

"The family's fine. Work is busy like always." Rebecca glanced around. She had arrived right on time and had missed seeing Ben.

"He's out in the barn."

"Who?"

There was a distinct gleam of mischief in Emma's faded blue eyes. "You know who. My youngest son."

"I—wasn't looking for him."

The gleam of mischief faded, and Emma took Rebecca's hand and drew her into the hallway for what privacy they could manage.

"You've known my son for a long time. You know words don't always come easy to him. He's like his father in that respect—he's a good man, but a quiet one. Some women might not recognize that."

Rebecca glanced down at the work-worn hand that held hers, then looked up at the older woman. "I do. But . . ." She struggled for words. "Emma, Ben doesn't feel about me the way you think he does."

"Really?" Emma looked disbelieving.

Mary Anne took that moment to walk slowly past them. Rebecca noticed that she took her time and swept the two of them with an assessing look.

"Ben is . . . looking in another direction." Her gaze followed Mary Anne as she found Ben and stopped him to talk.

"Promise me you won't do anything quickly," Emma said.

Puzzled, Rebecca stared at her. "Like what?"

"Like look elsewhere yourself."

She thought about Jacob. But one drive to have lunch was hardly looking. *Jacob is nice, but he's not . . . Ben.* "I'm not, Emma. I'm busy with my job and helping out at home. And it's not like there are a herd of suitors chasing after me," she admitted ruefully.

To her surprise, Emma touched her chin with her hand, and Rebecca was forced to look up at her. "I know you must have felt you lived in Lizzie's shadow," she told her quietly. "She was so exuberant people couldn't help noticing her. But there's an expression I always thought fit you: 'still waters run deep.' You have a sweet, thoughtful nature, and you look out for others before yourself." She smiled. "Now, I probably shouldn't have spoken at all, but my heart prompted me to. Give it some time, *liebschen.*" She walked slowly back into the kitchen.

Rebecca was relieved to watch her sink into a chair. It was obvious that her arthritis, which was worse in winter, was making movement difficult for her today. Yet Emma hadn't been willing to cancel services or stay in bed while others were guests in her home.

Time. How could time resolve the differences between herself and Ben?

"Why are you frowning?" Sarah Fisher stopped to ask. The rosy-cheeked toddler she balanced on one hip held out her chubby hands.

Rebecca smiled and took Katie Ann and held her high. "I can't have been frowning, not when this sweet *kind* is anywhere near." She held her close and inhaled the special clean baby scent. "Oh, whenever I see this one, I am so very happy for you and David."

Sarah nodded. "I prayed for a long time for God to send me David. And to send me a *boppli*."

"David?" Rebecca stared at Sarah. "He was always yours, from the day he saved you from that stray dog that was chasing you. What were you, twelve?"

Laughing, Sarah grasped Katie Ann's hand as she tried to pull one of the strings on Rebecca's *kapp*.

"Sometimes other people see what we cannot," Sarah murmured obliquely. "He never lacked for the attention of the other girls at singings and such." She stroked her child's cheek. "But he was so worth waiting for. He got me through the pain of my miscarriage and the waiting for Katie Ann here. It was God's will if we had children, if we received this precious gift, he kept telling me, and if we didn't, we would be a family, the two of us."

Rebecca bounced Katie Ann, and she gurgled.

"Could you watch her for a moment for me?" Sarah asked. "I need to use the bathroom. I've had to run to it three times already this morning." She laughed when Rebecca's eyes widened. Glancing around, she leaned in and with her eyes sparkling admitted, "Yes, I'm wondering if I'm pregnant again."

Swaying and bouncing Katie Ann, loving the way the toddler giggled and giggled, Rebecca walked around the room.

When Katie Ann squealed with delight, Rebecca turned to see David approaching and handed her over.

After greeting Rebecca, he looked at his daughter. "So what did you think of the services today, Katie Ann?" He listened with a thoughtful expression as she babbled baby talk. "*Ya*, the singing was my favorite part too."

"She's quite a talker."

David nodded. "Takes after her *mamm*." When Rebecca looked over his shoulder and smiled, he rolled his eyes. "She's standing behind me, isn't she?"

"*Ya*," Rebecca said, and she laughed.

David turned, and his grin faded. "Sarah, are you all right? You look a little pale."

"I'm fine, but do you think we could leave now and eat at home?"

"*Ya*, sure. I'll go get the buggy and meet you out front. Be sure to bundle up."

He put Katie Ann in her arms, then turned to Rebecca. "Sarah and I are feeling a little tired. Katie Ann had a tooth coming in this week and kept us up."

Sarah and Rebecca exchanged glances.

"What?" David looked from one to the other.

"I'll tell you later," Sarah said.

Rebecca helped Sarah put Katie Ann's coat on. It took two of them because Katie Ann was laughing and pinwheeling her arms. Sarah got her own coat on, and then Rebecca hugged her. "I'll be praying for you," she whispered to Sarah.

"I said I'd be happy if God sent me one child," Sarah whispered back. "But now, if He sent another . . ." She stopped, as if she couldn't even envision such happiness.

Rebecca nodded. "I know."

She was standing at the kitchen window, watching the buggy leave, when Amanda joined her.

"Are you coming to the singing tonight?"

"I'm not sure." As if drawn by magnets, her gaze locked with Ben's on the other side of the room.

Amanda's gaze followed hers. "You care for him, don't you?"

"Shh!" Rebecca glanced around to see if anyone had heard.

Ben was opening the oven door for his mother, but she was talking to him, and there was so much chatter and noise with others moving about in the room, she realized no one could have heard.

"Besides, it doesn't matter."

"It *does* matter!" Amanda insisted in a lowered voice. "Go after him if you want him." She gave Rebecca a not-so-gentle push.

"Not now," she told Amanda.

"Then when?" Amanda demanded. "When?"

Don't be afraid!

"What is it?"

Rebecca blinked. "What is what?"

"You just looked funny—kind of startled. What is it?"

Don't be afraid!

Although she realized that Amanda was staring at her, waiting for an answer, Rebecca wasn't about to explain.

* * *

Ben used potholders to pull a heavy casserole from the oven and set it on top of the stove. He closed the oven door and turned to her. "Anything else you need?"

"No, thank you, *Sohn*."

He saw Rebecca standing, looking out the window near the front door with Amanda and wondered what they were talking about. When Rebecca looked over and saw him, then glanced away quickly as Amanda did the same, he suspected they were talking about him.

He wondered if that was a *gut* thing or bad.

Then something Amanda said to Rebecca upset her. Amanda walked away and Rebecca stood staring after her, her forehead creased in thought. Ben started to walk over to her but found his way blocked by women hurrying around in the kitchen. By the time he could move forward, Jacob was standing there talking to Rebecca, and he lost his chance.

Ben knew that women found Jacob attractive. He was fair-haired, with blue eyes and dimples. He was several years older, and his farm was one of the most prosperous in the county.

An unaccustomed jealousy flared up in Ben as he watched the two talking. It was so immediate, so strong, that he felt his steps propelling him toward the door and outside into the chilly day.

It took several minutes for him to become aware that he'd left his jacket and hat inside. Feeling a little foolish, he debated going back inside for them. He heard the door behind him open, then shut.

"Forget something?"

His *daed* held his coat and hat in his hands.

Looking sheepish, Ben took the coat and pulled it on, then accepted the hat, settling it on his head. "*Danki.*"

They stood staring at the fields surrounding the house. "I saw you come out here after Jacob began talking to Rebecca."

Ben gave him a sideways glance but said nothing.

"You know, I'd always been taught to turn to God, to pray to Him as my Father," Samuel said after long moments had passed. "After I had children, I started thinking about what it must be like to be God watching over His children. You know, He sees them happy, and He sees them sad or hurting."

He paused and glanced over at Ben. "The happy part would be easy. But I wondered how He felt watching them when they're having difficult times. It's hard for a father not to jump in and try to fix things, like you fix an engine that's not working or repair a broken fence. I asked myself if our heavenly Father had trouble not jumping in to fix things for His children."

He turned as a couple emerged from the house and said good-bye to them. After they were out of earshot, he turned back to Ben and laid a hand on his shoulder. "It's been a long winter."

Ben nodded. "For years it's been a sad time for

Rebecca. But she's finally more at peace about Lizzie and looking happier."

"And maybe becoming interested in someone?" his father asked quietly.

"Yes, it seems so," he said finally.

"Just like you and Mary Anne."

Ben's head shot up. "Not because I wanted to."

"Don't see any harness on you," Samuel said, and with that, he ambled back inside.

Laughing ruefully, Ben stared after him. No, Mary Anne had no harness on him.

But there was sure something tying him to Rebecca. Always had been.

Amanda came out of the house. She stopped and looked at Ben. "Are you going to stand out here forever?"

"Just getting some air."

"Awfully cold air."

Turning, he looked at her. "Is there something you want to say, Amanda?"

Her hazel eyes sparkled with mischief. "I think you should come to the singing."

"Because?"

"*Ya*, because." With that she fairly danced down the steps.

Ben wondered what was going on. He'd known Amanda all his life. While she was sweet, she was always nosing about in someone's business—not for bad reasons, but because she cared.

He guessed he'd be going to the singing tonight. Then he stopped and laughed at himself. He'd been so upset, he'd forgotten—his family was hosting it because they'd had services here earlier and the benches and hymnals were already present. It was obvious God's hand was at work.

. . .

Rebecca knew the minute Ben walked into the singing.

If she hadn't, Amanda's sharp elbow in her ribs apprised her of the fact. "Go over there and talk to him," Amanda hissed in her ear.

"He just came in."

"Are you going to let Mary Ann fawn all over him? Or are you going to do something before she gets her claws into him?"

The image made her laugh. She saw Ben's head come up, and he stared at her from across the room. And then Mary Ann walked up and put her hand on his arm.

Rebecca took a deep breath and let it out. After the services, she'd returned to her house and gone to her room to read for a while. Instead, she'd lain there and found herself thinking about what had happened earlier, when she'd been talking with Amanda and heard that inner voice urging her not to be afraid.

It was time to be brave, to approach Ben and tell him she was sorry about what had happened between them. Maybe she couldn't get their relationship back to what it had been, but she didn't want this rift, this distance between them.

As much as she fought it, Ben mattered to her. Each day that passed made her miss him more. She missed talking with him, missed him listening to her with that quiet, intense way of his. Missed doing things with him and being with him and seeing the way he showed what a big, generous heart he had every time he was around her family or his.

She hadn't appreciated what she had when she had it, she thought. It was as simple as that.

"You're looking *lieblich* tonight," Jacob said, his voice low and intimate in her ear. "That color is very pretty on you. Brings out the green in your eyes."

Rebecca stared down at her dark green *frack*, then up into his eyes. There was frank interest in them. But while it was flattering to have him tell her she looked lovely, she noticed that he was looking around the room, assessing not just her but other females there as if he were in a candy store.

"Why don't I get us something to drink?"

When she nodded agreement, he sauntered off.

Ben wanted to marry her. She knew what kind of husband he'd be, since they'd spent so much time together. And she knew he had the qualities to make someone a good *mann*. Other young women might not mind that he didn't have the right words, and maybe she wouldn't have minded either. She'd just needed more than to be told they'd "suit."

It wasn't often that Rebecca acted on the spur of the moment, but the last time she had, when she'd asked Ben to a picnic, well, that had turned out well, hadn't it?

She found her steps carrying her across the room to Ben. As if he were attuned to her thoughts, Ben looked up and saw her. He started walking toward her.

"Rebecca? Rebecca?"

Blinking, she stopped. Jacob stood before her, holding out her soft drink.

"Where were you going?" he asked.

And then he saw Ben.

"She's with me," Jacob said bluntly, even a little belligerently.

"Rebecca says who she's with," Ben told him in his quiet voice. "No one owns her."

"*Ya*, you had your chance." Jacob moved possessively, positioning himself to block off Ben.

Rebecca held up her hand. "Jacob, I just need to talk to Ben for a moment."

Jacob glowered at Ben for a long moment, then he nodded and walked off.

The moment he was gone, Rebecca and Ben turned to each other.

"I—"

"I—"

They stopped and laughed.

"Ladies first," said Ben.

"I'm sorry for what happened between us," she began.

"Me too," he said, moving closer. "I've been wanting to talk to you about it. Could we maybe go for a ride?"

Rebecca glanced around. "I should tell Jacob—" She broke off.

Mary Ann was standing with a group of her friends, showing them what looked to Rebecca like a small card in her hand.

"What is it?" Ben asked her.

There was a buzz of conversation, and several people

looked over at Rebecca. Mary Ann was walking toward her, a gleam in her eyes.

"Is this why he hangs around with you?" she asked Rebecca, holding out the card. "Does he feel sorry for you because you've got . . . emotional problems?"

Rebecca stared at it blankly for a moment. It was one of Dr. Prato's business cards. "What's this about?" she asked, lifting her eyes. "Where did you get this?"

"Why don't you ask Ben? I found it in his buggy." With that, Mary Ann strolled back to her friends.

Feeling as if someone had pulled the rug out from under her feet, Rebecca looked at Ben. "I don't understand. Ben? What was this doing in your buggy?"

"I can explain."

She looked around and saw that Mary Ann and her friends were staring at them. "Did you go talk to Dr. Prato about me?"

"I talked to her, but she didn't tell me anything confidential."

Rebecca shook her head. This was like a nightmare. "And you shared it with Mary Anne?"

"No. You heard her. She found the card in my buggy. I guess I dropped it. She must have figured one of us went to visit the doctor and decided it was you."

"Lucky guess." Rebecca crossed her arms over her chest. "And now she's really enjoying herself, isn't she?" she said as she watched the other woman talking with her friends.

"I'll go talk to her."

"No." She put a hand on his arm to stop him. "I will." She marched over to Mary Ann, and all talk stopped.

"I'm not ashamed of going to see Dr. Prato. I don't have 'emotional problems.' But even if I did, I'd be proud of myself for going to someone to help myself. I hope that you never go through what I went through," she said in a steady voice. "I didn't want to live after Lizzie died. Dr. Prato helped me through my grief."

"You should have gone to God about it," Mary Ann told her in a superior tone.

"'Judge not, that ye not be judged,'" Rebecca replied. With that, she turned and walked away.

"Rebecca!" Marian caught up with her. "What's going on?"

"Mary Anne's just trying to cause trouble."

"How? Why?"

People were still staring.

"I don't want to talk about it now."

"Do you want to go home? We can go home."

Rebecca shook her head. "I don't want to spoil your time."

"I can take you home," Ben said quietly from behind her. "Please let me."

"No. I don't want to talk to you now," Rebecca told him without looking at him.

"Fine. Then I'm coming over tomorrow, after I finish work."

Rebecca turned to tell him not to, but he was already striding away.

CHAPTER 12

R ebecca laced up her ice skates and stood.
There was no voice this time urging her not to
be afraid. Maybe that was because she was facing her
fears. At least, facing one of them.

It had taken her five years.

She wobbled, and her arms shot out and flapped as
she fought for balance. Finally, relieved that she wasn't
going to fall on her bottom, she cautiously pushed out
onto the ice. She wobbled again for a moment and then,
to her utter amazement, it came back to her—the balance, then the miracle of skimming along on the ice,
free as a bird.

It was so quiet here, just the scrape of ice beneath
her feet, the cold wind against her cheeks. Freedom,
such freedom. A sense of being outside herself, of
doing what she couldn't do when she was walking on
the ground.

She stayed in the area where everyone skated, mind-
ful of the fact that it was late in the season. There was
no way she would risk what had happened to Lizzie.

She'd gotten home early that afternoon and felt restless. She knew Ben was coming and they'd have to talk.
But she couldn't sit still.

So she'd started out for a walk and then turned back, impulsively running upstairs to get her skates.

Around and around the pond she skated; then, after a time, she experimented with a small twirl, a jump, a backward circle. Oh, it was nothing compared to the way she had skated before, but the joy was there. The joy was there.

She'd seen an ice skating movie once, during her *rumschpringe*, with Lizzie and other girls at a nearby theater. Of course, Rebecca was the first to admit that she was in no way as good as the skaters in the movie, not back then and certainly not now since she was out of practice. But she'd always enjoyed it and spent every free moment on the ice on the pond in the winter, so she became more skilled than the others.

Not that she drew any pride from it. *Hochmut* was sinful. She simply skated because of how calm, how free it made her feel. All else faded away.

A little out of breath, she skated over to the edge of the pond and sat down on a log someone had put there. Maybe she'd take a rest and then skate just a little more before heading home. She'd promised Ben she'd talk to him after work. No doubt he'd come find her if she wasn't there.

"Rebecca!"

Looking up from lacing her skates, she saw that Lizzie was already streaking across the ice. It was just Lizzie's way—it wasn't that there was a competition and she wanted to be first. She simply couldn't wait for anyone else when she was ready to dive into her next adventure.

Lizzie wasn't as good a skater as Rebecca. She was

enthusiastic, but she wasn't willing to practice. If it didn't come easily and wasn't enough fun, Lizzie moved on to something else.

As Rebecca stepped onto the ice, she watched her sister zoom by.

"About time, slowpoke!" Lizzie called, laughing as she executed a sloppy twirl.

There were two other skaters on the pond, boys she and Lizzie had gone to school with. While Rebecca skated by herself, Lizzie and the others played tag and generally whooped it up.

Rebecca felt her skate boot wobble and skated over to the log to retie her laces.

"Hi."

Looking up, Rebecca saw Ben. "Hi. What are you doing here? You don't have any skates."

He shrugged. "I was on my way home. Thought I'd stop and watch for a few minutes." He gazed out at the ice. "Lizzie's sure having fun."

Rebecca felt herself withdraw. Yes, people usually noticed Lizzie with her vibrant personality. Bending, she retied her skate.

"You looked like you were enjoying yourself out there," he said. "I don't think I've ever seen anyone skate as well as you."

"You should have seen the movie Lizzie and I saw. The skaters were amazing." She remembered the costumes the skaters had worn. They were short and colorful and so formfitting, like nothing she'd ever imagined. Looking down at her own long dress, she wondered how it would feel to move without the restriction of a long skirt.

There was loud laughter out on the ice. Rebecca looked up to see that the two boys and Lizzie had joined hands and were doing the whip, with Lizzie at the end. Faster and faster they skated, and Lizzie was laughing, her skirts flowing out behind her.

"Faster!" she shrieked. "Faster, faster!"

Then she lost her grip, and she was hurtling toward the farthest edge of the pond. Her shriek was cut off as her foot must have hit a rough patch and she went sprawling.

And then they heard it—an awful crack! and the splash of water as Lizzie vanished from sight.

Ben was the first to move, running and slipping toward the hole in the ice. Rebecca jumped to her feet and raced over on her skates.

"Get back!" Ben cried as he stopped near the edge of the hole. "It's not safe!"

"Lizzie!" Rebecca screamed. "Lizzie!"

Ben lay down on his stomach and edged toward the hole. Turning his head, he called to the boys to hold his legs as he inched forward, calling Lizzie's name.

Lizzie popped to the surface, gasping, and Ben grasped one arm, then the other, and dragged her toward him. But she slipped from his grasp once, twice, before he was able to grab the neck of her dress and pull her toward him.

Rebecca and the boys inched back and back until Lizzie had been pulled from the water and they were all safely away from the edge of the hole. Then one of the boys ran for help.

Her face was so white, her body so still. Rebecca felt for a pulse. "She's not breathing!"

Ben pushed Rebecca aside and turned Lizzie to her side, pressing on her back. Water flowed from Lizzie's mouth, but her chest didn't move. He began pushing on her chest and then breathing into her mouth. Rebecca had never seen anyone do such.

"Breathe, Lizzie!" she cried hoarsely. "Please, God, make her breathe!"

A siren blared down the road, getting louder and louder as it approached. An ambulance screeched to a halt, and men came running.

Tears ran down Rebecca's cheeks as she remembered that day.

"Oh, Lizzie, I miss you so much."

She wiped her tears away from her cheeks with her hands. Looking upward, she shook her head. "*Mamm* always said you'd get to heaven first if you weren't more careful."

There was a splash of color on the bank of the pond near her, a purple crocus struggling up through the snow. It was a tiny reminder that spring was coming. Reaching over, she plucked it up.

Rising, she skated over to the center of the pond. "'To every thing there is a season, and a time to every purpose under the heaven,'" she recited. "'A time to be born, and a time to die; a time to plant, and a time to pluck up that which is planted' . . . and a time to heal. Good-bye, Lizzie," she whispered, and she threw the flower over to the place where Lizzie had fallen through the ice.

She heard something behind her. Turning, she saw a buggy pull to the side of the road and a man get out, waving his arms frantically. Frowning, she squinted to see better.

It was Ben.

* * *

What was she doing?

Ben couldn't believe his eyes as he drove his buggy down the road to the Millers' house. That was Rebecca, skating out in the middle of the pond.

Didn't she know that no one had skated there since last week, that the pond was showing signs of an early thaw? A sign had been posted, but he didn't see it now.

As soon as he could get his horse to stop, he jumped from the buggy and began yelling and waving his arms. She must have heard him because she turned.

He didn't hear the car coming until he heard the screech of brakes. Turning, he saw the driver fighting for control as the car slid on the thin ice covering the road. Ben threw himself toward the side of the road, but he felt the bumper hit his hip and toss him high in the air. His breath rushed out as he slammed down in the snow and his head hit something hard.

He woke. His head hurt, and someone was screaming his name.

Rebecca came into view and knelt by his side. She was praying as she put her hands on his face.

He reached up his hand and touched her cheek. "I'm okay." To prove it, he tried to sit up, but he fell back and passed out.

* * *

The driver of the car, a middle-aged woman, came running over with a blanket to cover Ben.

"I called 911 on my cell phone. They'll be here any minute." She wrung her hands. "He ran right in front of my car. I tried to stop, but the car slid on the road."

"I know. I saw." Rebecca took the blanket and tucked it around Ben. She didn't know how much good it was going to do. He was lying in the snow.

The woman looked up and down the road. "Why aren't they here yet?" She wrung her hands as she turned to Rebecca. "What else can we do?"

"There's another blanket in the buggy."

The woman ran for it, then glanced at Rebecca's feet. "You're wearing skates," she said. "I'll go get your shoes."

Rebecca put the second blanket on Ben and tried not to think about how the wait for the ambulance for him felt even longer than the one for Lizzie had. She busied herself with unlacing her skates and pulling on her boots.

As she waited, Rebecca wondered why Ben had been making such a commotion, yelling and waving his arms at her instead of walking to the pond to talk to her. It wasn't like him.

She was so absorbed in watching for the faintest movement from him, a flicker of his eyes opening or his hand stirring under hers, that she didn't realize at first that the woman had knelt in the snow beside her. "What is it?"

"I'm so sorry . . ."

Rebecca patted her hand. "I saw what happened. I don't know why Ben didn't watch what he was doing."

"You know him?"

Nodding, Rebecca touched his face with hands that shook. His face was so cold.

The woman gave her an impulsive hug. "This must be so hard for you. Thank you for not blaming me."

Rebecca took a deep breath, lifted her shoulders, then let them fall. "It wasn't your fault. But even if it had been, it's not our way."

The police and paramedics arrived, and within minutes Ben was carefully loaded up into the ambulance and Rebecca was allowed to climb in with him for the ride to the hospital. They seemed to assume she was his wife, and she didn't bother to tell them any different.

After all, if she hadn't been such an idiot, she'd be engaged to him by now.

At the hospital she was separated from him. She filled out the paperwork as best as she could and went to sit in the waiting room.

She felt so guilty. This was what she got for not being afraid and skating, she thought. Ben had been driving to her house to talk to her, and he'd seen her and become upset enough to walk into the path of the car.

The antiseptic smell of the hospital was bringing back awful memories. To distract herself, Rebecca looked at the program on the television. A man was reading some news stories, and then there was a woman standing before an animated map of the state. She talked about spring coming early.

Engulfed in worry and guilt over Ben, Rebecca

realized why Ben might have been creating a commotion—had he worried that the ice wasn't frozen enough to skate on?

Samuel and Emma came rushing in at that moment, looking frantic, and a nurse took them back to Ben. *They are family and I'm not,* Rebecca thought, sinking down into her chair. If things had gone differently, she would have been regarded as family; she would be able to go see him.

All she could do now was sit here and think the worst. No, she told herself. That was *not* all she could do. She could pray. Bending her head, she asked God to please heal Ben, to make him well.

When she opened her eyes, Emma was taking a seat next to her. "He hasn't regained consciousness yet. They're doing some tests." She traced the rose design on the wooden cane in her hands. "Ben made it for me. Rose is my middle name." Tears welled up in her eyes and ran down her cheeks.

Ben had made a thing of beauty out of a simple piece of wood to help ease her steps, Rebecca thought. He didn't always have the words. But it was obvious that he had the heart.

Grabbing some tissues from a box near her, she pressed them into Emma's hands. Then she put her arms around the older woman. "He's going to be okay. He's got to be."

"Rebecca!"

"*Mamm! Daed!*" She threw herself into their arms. "I'm so glad to see you."

Amos turned to Emma. "How is he?"

"They're doing tests. Samuel is back there with him." She paused, her lips trembling. "They don't think he's in a coma, but he hasn't woken up yet."

They all looked up as a nurse came approached. "Would you come back with me?" she asked Emma.

Rebecca was able to wait until Emma had left the room, but then her tears started. "I can't go back. I'm not family."

Naomi urged her down into her chair and sank into the chair that Emma had vacated. "I know, *liebschen*. I know."

"God wouldn't take Ben, would He? It's not fair! I lost Lizzie. I shouldn't have to lose Ben too."

She looked up to see her parents exchange a look.

"I know, I was so foolish. I should have told him how I felt. I was going to, today. He was coming to see me." With tears hitching her breath, she told them what had happened.

"You were skating?" her *daed* asked, his voice sounding funny.

"*Ya.*" She watched the color drain from his face.

"Signs were posted on the pond last week. The ice is melting early. No one's supposed to be skating on it."

"There was no sign," she whispered, staring at them in shock. "Someone must have taken it." A strange feeling swept over her. So that was why Ben had been so upset, why he hadn't watched out for his own safety. He was trying to warn her.

"I decided I didn't want to be afraid anymore." She swallowed hard. If not for Ben, her parents might at this moment be mourning the loss of a second daughter.

"I was saying good-bye to Lizzie," she said. The tears started again. "I can't say good-bye to him too."

Her *mamm* patted her back. "Don't think that way. I'm sure he'll be all right."

The nurse came out again. "Rebecca? Would you come back with me?"

It had to be good news, she thought as she jumped to her feet. She glanced at her parents, and they gave her reassuring smiles.

"We'll pray for him," they promised.

* * *

He saw her skating like a graceful bird on the pond, and for a long moment, he just stood and enjoyed the sight of her gliding across the ice. He didn't know anyone else who could do such twirls and turns and leaps on the ice. She was a beautiful bird that soared.

Then he saw the ice opening and Rebecca—no, it was Lizzie—no, it was Rebecca—screaming and falling into the icy water. He tried running to save her, but his feet were sliding on the snowy road and he couldn't get to her. Something hit him, and he flew into the air, but not like a bird, for he fell hard and hit his head.

Everything was so mixed up. His head and his hip hurt and he was so cold. And there was a funny smell to the air. He told himself he needed to get up and make sure Rebecca was safe. He had to get up before she was lost forever.

"Rebecca!" he called urgently. "Rebecca!"

* * *

"Shh, I'm here. I'm here."

He opened his eyes and saw Rebecca sitting beside his bed.

"I'm here," she whispered. Tears were sliding down her cheeks. "You scared me to death."

"You're okay? I'm not dreaming?"

"I'm okay."

"You scared *me*," he told her. "No one was supposed to be skating on the pond."

"I didn't know." She bit her lip and shook her head. "But you're the one who got hurt." Brushing at her tears, she got up.

"Don't go!"

"I'm not. I promised the nurse and your parents that I'd let them know when you woke up. I'll be right back."

If he woke up had been on the minds of all of them, even though the doctor had assured them that while Ben had a concussion, he didn't think he was in a coma.

Rebecca went just a few steps out of the room and caught the attention of a passing nurse.

"I'll get the doctor," the woman assured her.

"And his parents?"

The nurse nodded and rushed away.

Rebecca returned to Ben's room and stood by the side of his bed. He held out his hand, and she took it. "I want to explain about Dr. Prato," he said.

"Not now," she told him, squeezing his hand. "It's not important. I need to tell you something before everyone comes in." She paused, took a deep breath. "Before I lose my nerve."

Don't be afraid!

"Ask me again, Ben Weaver. Ask me to marry you."

His expression was a little wary. "You're not feeling sorry for me?"

"No. If you don't want me, I imagine that Mary Ann will be around very shortly."

"Don't you dare!" he said, some of the old sparkle showing in his eyes. He tried to sit up, but it felt like his head would fall off. "Come here."

She moved closer.

"I fumbled when I asked if you'd marry me before," he said quietly. "But I know how I feel. I love you, Rebecca. I should have told you that when I asked you to be *mei fraa*."

Those were the best words, she thought, and her eyes filled. "And I love you!"

He pulled her toward him for a kiss.

The door opened. Rebecca jumped back guiltily and spun around to stare into the faces of both sets of parents.

"Uh, Ben's awake," she told them.

"*Ya,*" Samuel said dryly.

"She was attacking me," Ben joked.

"Stop that!" she hissed and felt herself blushing.

"Does this mean what I think it means?" Emma asked, smiling as she walked toward them.

Grinning, Ben nodded. "*Ya,* Rebecca asked me to marry her."

"Ben!"

His grin faded, and he looked at her with such love in his eyes. "I told her what I should have weeks ago. I love her."

Rebecca was so relieved he was all right, so glad they had a life ahead of them, she bent and kissed him in front of all the parents and the doctor who'd come into the room.

"Congratulate us," she said with a smile. "Ben and I are engaged."

Discussion Questions

1. Rebecca has felt for years that she isn't as attractive or interesting as her twin. Do you have siblings to whom you feel you come in second in some way? Why?

2. As the oldest child in the family, Rebecca feels she has to be the caretaker. What role do you think birth order plays in a person's development?

3. How do you personally know when something is God's will for your life? When have you been right about this? When have you been wrong?

4. It takes a long time for Rebecca to make peace with her sister's death. What would you say to someone who is having trouble coming to terms with the death of a loved one? What do you feel God wants us to learn from the death of someone we love?

ACKNOWLEDGMENTS

AMY CLIPSTON

As always, I'm thankful for my loving family. Special thanks to Janet Pecorella for your friendship and encouragement. I'm grateful for my special Amish friend who patiently answers my endless stream of questions. You're a blessing in my life.

Thank you to Jamie Mendoza and the members of my awesome Bakery Bunch.

To my agent, Natasha Kern—I can't thank you enough for your guidance, advice, and friendship. You are a tremendous blessing in my life.

Thank you to my amazing editor, Becky Monds, for your friendship and guidance. I'm grateful to each and every person at HarperCollins Christian Publishing who helped make this book a reality.

Thank you also to editor Julee Schwarzburg for her guidance with the story. I always learn quite a bit about writing and polishing when we work together. Thank you for pushing me to become a better writer. I hope we can work together again in the future!

I'm grateful to editor Jean Bloom, who also helped me polish and refine the story. Jean, you are a master at connecting the dots and filling in the gaps. I'm so thankful that we can continue to work together!

Thank you most of all to God, for giving me the inspiration and the words to glorify You. I'm grateful and humbled You've chosen this path for me.

Barbara Cameron

I'm so grateful for my family and friends for their love and their support of my writing. Thanks to Linda Byler and Dr. Beth Graybill, agent Mary Sue Seymour, Natalie Hanemann, editor at Thomas Nelson, and to LB Norton, who along with Natalie helped make *When Winter Comes* a stronger story. And most of all, thank You, God. You heard the desire in my heart to write when I was a teenager and have blessed me with so many opportunities to write.

ABOUT THE AUTHORS

AMY CLIPSTON

Amy Clipston is the award-winning and best-selling author of more than a dozen novels, including the Kauffman Amish Bakery series and the Hearts of the Lancaster Grand Hotel series. Her novels have hit multiple bestseller lists including CBD, CBA, and ECPA. Amy holds a degree in communication from Virginia Wesleyan College and works full-time for the City of Charlotte, North Carolina. Amy lives in North Carolina with her husband, two sons, and three spoiled rotten cats.

Visit her website: amyclipston.com
Facebook: Amy Clipston
Twitter: @AmyClipston

KELLY IRVIN

Kelly Irvin is the author of the Amish of Bee County series, the Bliss Creek Amish series, and the New Hope Amish series. She has also penned two romantic suspense novels, *A Deadly Wilderness* and *No Child of Mine*. The Kansas native is a graduate of the University of Kansas School of Journalism. She has been writing nonfiction professionally for thirty years, including ten years as a newspaper reporter, mostly in Texas-Mexico border towns. She has worked in public relations for the City of San Antonio for twenty years. Kelly has been married to photographer Tim Irvin for twenty-seven years. They have two young adult children, two cats, and a tank full of fish. In her spare time, she likes to write short stories and read books by her favorite authors.

Follow her on Twitter: @Kelly_S_Irvin
Facebook: Kelly.Irvin.Author

Barbara Cameron

Barbara Cameron is the author of fifteen novels and three nationally televised movies (HBO), as well as a recipient of the first Romance Writers of America Golden Heart. Her Amish stories are inspired by her visits to Lancaster Co., PA.